Land Beyond Maps

by

Maida Tilchen

Savvy Press
Salem, NY

Published by: Savvy Press, 479 Beattie Hollow Rd, Salem, NY 12865
http://www.savvypress.com

ISBN: 978-1-939113-45-0
LCCN: 2008904357
Printed in the United States of America
Second Edition

Cataloging Data:
Tilchen, Maida.
Land beyond maps / by Maida Tilchen.
p. cm.
Summary: Just before the stock market crash of 1929, Laura Gilpin accompanies
her partner, nurse Elizabeth W. Forster, to an isolated Navajo community. There,
Betsy provides medical care while Laura finds her artistic vision photographing
the Navajo people and the southwestern landscape. Based on the true story of
Laura Gilpin (1891-1979), the distinguished American landscape photographer.
ISBN 978-1-939113-45-0
1. Gilpin, Laura – Fiction. 2. Women photographers – Southwestern States
– Fiction. 3. Lesbian artists – Southwestern States – Fiction. 4. Southwestern
States – Fiction.
2008904357

Cover painting by Douglas T. Yazzie. All rights to this work are owned by Maida
Tilchen in its name or otherwise.

Douglas T. Yazzie is originally from Pinon, Arizona, thirty miles southwest
of Chinle. Born in1950, he attended school in Idaho, Utah, and Chinle, and
graduated from Chinle High School in 1970. A self-taught artist who has won
numerous awards, he works in acrylic and gouache. He has coached amateur
boxing for many years and has four sons who are all amateur national champions
in one or numerous weight classes. He lives in Chinle, Arizona with his wife,
Darlene Yazzie, who has been a teacher at Chinle Elementary School for more
than thirty-five years. He can be contacted by writing to Douglas T. Yazzie, Box
1813, Chinle, AZ 86503.

[The tourist]can tell us not only something about what the West was, but much about what it wanted to be and pretended to be, and what he thought it was. —Earl Pomeroy, *In Search of the Golden West*, 1954, xvi–xvii.

Because of these creative writers we see the Southwest differently than we would if they had not written. By the power of their prose, their vision becomes our vision…. We see New Mexico as Calvin, Lawrence, and Luhan, Rhodes and the Fergussons saw it…. How real they are! I close my eyes and there is Zane Grey—I mean Lassiter—straining to roll the rock. There is Miss Cather and her friend, lost in canyons below Mesa Verde…. Across the wide southwest I am ever aware of my historic predecessors…all of whom came this way and left their books on the land as legacies to those who follow…legacies to us their grateful beneficiaries. —Lawrence Clark Powell, *Southwest Classics*, 1974, pp. 10–11.

"Seek essences, enduring things, touchstones, and symbols; try to recreate in prose what makes this country so increasingly meaningful and necessary to one. Altitude, distance, color, configuration, history, and culture – in them dwell the essential things, but they must be extracted. 'Crack the rock if so you list, bring to light the amethyst.' Costs nothing to try. Some have succeeded – Lummis, Lawrence, Long, La Farge, Horgan, Waters, the Fergussons – proving that it is possible. Stand books on the shelf, hang up maps, gaze in the turquoise ball, finger the fragment of red adobe from Pecos, reload the blue Scripto, take a fresh yellow pad, then sit down and see what comes." —Lawrence Clark Powell, *Southwest: Three Definitions*, p. 21.

How shall I defend that I am constant to mine own Judgement in this Design, and that I thrust my Labours into the World? What warrant can I plead, that I build a new Cottage upon the Waste? —John Hackett, quoted in Catherine Drinker Bowen, *Adventures of a Biographer*, p. 231.

Lost Wash, Arizona
Spring, 1929

Morna

"It is in our idleness, and in our dreams, that..." Morna couldn't remember the rest of the quote. Virginia Woolf? She would know if she had any brain left that the sun hadn't burned out or the stink of the lacquer countertop and molding Indian blankets hadn't rotted.

Virginia Woolf and the rest of her literary heroes were in her trunk in the storeroom, untouched since she and Jack had first arrived at the trading post. No doubt the mice were eating holes right through Virginia Woolf's finest words, like they ate through everything. It had made Jack furious to see them scatter out of the crate of cornmeal he had crowbarred open that morning. A dead mouse lay in the bottom of the crate. Back in Manhattan, they'd fought roaches in their apartment near the Art Students League, but never mice. So here she was, crawling around the storeroom floor, knees aching, scraping up the last of the spilled cornmeal and dried mouse.

The cowbell hanging over the door clanged and the door slammed as someone came into the trading post. At least the screen door kept the damn flies and other vermin from the horses and sheep out. One less thing for Jack to yell about, or even worse, to send him on one of his too-cheerily whistling sulks.

"Anyone here?" a woman's voice called out. Well, it wasn't an Indian, for the Navajos never called out a greeting, but just stood there staring at the cans and the flour sacks. They'd sneak glances at the jars of licorice and jawbreakers, but usually only took the staples in trade for their wool, rugs, and occasional furs.

It would be good to see a white face. How long had it been? Since before Easter. Perhaps this was the first of the caravans of tourists that Jack was convinced would save their skins. He insisted they had just bought the trading post a few years too early. Now the roads were coming in, now the tourists in their new Model A cars would be coming, soon they would be doing well enough to sell the place and get out. Meanwhile, no one had come through since Herman Schweizer, the trader from the Harvey Company, who bought Indian silver jewelry and pottery that Jack sometimes accepted in trade or unredeemed pawn from the Indians.

"This stuff's no good," Schweizer had said the last time he visited. "I can't sell this. Tell them squaws to put more color in. That's what sells. The pots are too gray and the blankets are too brown. I'll take some this time to keep you in business, but I can't keep this up. You city folks better learn fast that this is no Manhattan Island. This is no art museum. We sell to tourists. You gotta learn what they want." Schweizer was sneering at a small pot and couldn't see Jack behind him, imitating his grumpy, downcast face. Jack liked to say a man came west so nobody could tell him what to do. But Schweizer sure told them all the time, and he wasn't the only one.

"Hello?" the woman called. She had a sweet voice.

Her knees cracking as she straightened up, Morna brushed back the blanket covering the doorway and headed into the trading room.

The customer was tall and thin with a face more open than anyone who had been in the dust-covered, dingy store for a long time. Unlike the shy faces of the Indian women, her wide smile made Morna shiver right down to her legs. She remembered feeling like that the first time she saw Jack.

"Hi," said the woman. "We're glad to find your place. Have you got anything fresh and cold? Well, sort of fresh?"

Morna noticed another woman looking at the Indian baskets piled on the woodstove, which in the summer was just another shelf. Most tourists were so glad to get to the trading post for food and water they barely noticed the old baskets, but this woman was so intent she didn't look up. She was stouter and shorter than the smiling woman. They both wore city clothes, but not expensive or dainty. The shorter woman wore trousers.

"There's pickled eggs and plain old pickled pickles. Also some salt fish and salt meat. Not much fresh out here. The Indians just keep sheep, no chickens," answered Morna.

"I'd love a pickled egg," said the first woman. "How much?"

So they were counting their pennies. Morna was surprised. On the rare occasions when white women stopped by, they were usually dripping rich with a chauffeured car outside. She didn't remember ever seeing two women alone like this. Maybe they were from the government. With the big tongs, she plucked a pickled egg from the jar and said, "Just a penny.

You have some business with the Navajos?"

"No, just on vacation. We're from Santa Fe."

Maybe Schweizer had been right when he claimed tourists were bound to start coming through soon. Trips to the desert would be all the rage, not just for the rich in their Pullman train cars, but for regular folks in a brand new 1929 Model A, or even an old Model T. Schweizer said they'd be stopping at the trading post to get food and buy the Indian crafts, and that the store would do well if they could just hold out. Jack wanted to believe him, but Morna no longer could, or she didn't want to. She didn't want Jack to have any more reasons for them to stay.

The stout woman came to the counter. She had a soft round face and wore spectacles. She looked younger than the other, but they both looked about ten years younger than Morna. Neither wore a wedding ring. As Morna passed her the pickle, she flicked her finger to flash her little diamond. When she and Jack were young art students, it had been fun to shock others by not marrying, and Jack had said that he respected that she was an independent and progressive New Woman. But by the time she reached her forties, Morna had winced at the pitying glances from the women faculty at the art school, and from some of the young women students who she suspected had an eye for Jack. They were thinking she was kidding herself that he would ever commit.

Proving them wrong had become more important than shocking them, so they had married five years earlier, not long after Jack stopped painting hay mows, dancing peasants, and still lifes of fruit in the European style, and started painting the Western sunsets, desert rock formations, and Indians. He had never seen these sights except in the paintings that had become the rage of the New York art scene. It was called the Taos school, led by his old pals from his year at a Paris art school, Ernest Blumenschein, Bert Phillips, and Joe Sharp. While Jack stayed in their New York studio, his easel right next to Morna's potter's wheel, they'd gone west to paint, and their paintings sold in New York and were exhibited around the country. Dealers told Jack his old work was out of style and his new work couldn't compete, so he finally decided to go west too.

Jack researched the trip as obsessively as he painted every little detail in a bouquet of flowers. Just like the Russian revolutionaries, he devised a five-year plan. They would make their money by running a trading post in the Navajo land, then move on to Taos to paint. The last of the little inheritance Morna's parents had left her for a dowry would pay for the trading post. But after four years and eight months, they still hadn't visited Jack's friends in Taos. There was still time, he said, reminding her that the

Russian revolutionaries had extended their five-year plans.

Morna waved her hand in the air and asked the ladies, "Would you like anything else?"

"I'm Betsy, and this is Laura," said the tall one. "This hits the spot, I was so dry. What's your name?"

"Morna," she said shyly. Then, knowing it was ostentatious, she added "Morna Brewster." But they wouldn't know Brewster was her married name. "Mrs. Jack Brewster."

"So you're not Mrs. Barnstable? Like on the sign outside?" Betsy pointed out the door, over which a faded, weather beaten sign hung by one loose nail.

"Barnstable's the guy we bought—" she paused. She had almost said "this trap from." Barnstable hadn't told them how far from a good road the trading post was, so that tourists almost never came by, only Navajos with bags of dirty wool to trade for small, measured sacks of cornmeal.

"Barnstable was the guy we bought this store from. We've been here five years. My husband Jack and I, that is." She wanted to make sure they'd know she was no spinster like them. There was no one else to impress, because Navajo women all married young and assumed she had also. It had been a long time since she had the chance to impress a white woman with her ring.

But the women hardly noticed. Laura held up her hands to form a box, moving back a few feet while still looking right at Morna.

"Laura, don't be rude," said Betsy. It wasn't said sharply, the way Jack snapped at her.

"I'm sorry. Would you mind if I take your photograph?" Laura asked.

"Laura is a professional photographer," said Betsy. "She mostly photographs wedding and graduation portraits, but on our vacation, she's going to take photos of landscapes of this beautiful country." Betsy leaned toward Morna as she continued. "She's entering a competition. I just know she'll win. In fact—" she leaned forward and lowered her voice. "She's just had a photo accepted by the Library of Congress itself! For their permanent collection."

"Betsy, you don't have to tell everything!"

"No need to keep a secret," said Betsy. "And I'm sure Morna would keep a secret anyway, wouldn't you?"

They must figure Morna for some hick who had never met a professional photographer, let alone dated a few at the Arts Students League back before Jack finally noticed her. She had even considered majoring in photography for a while before discovering the potter's wheel and the kiln. Sure, she could keep a secret. She didn't want to explain to anyone why she was spending her mornings sweeping up dead mice. But Betsy's face was friendlier than any she had seen for a long time. She wished she could just sit down and explain to this warm woman everything that was going wrong with her life.

"But if a wish isn't kept secret, it won't come true," Laura was telling Betsy.

"Your wish is already coming true," said Betsy. "You're going to take pictures no one's ever seen before. And you need her permission. I'm sure Morna wants to know why."

Morna knew exactly why. She could have also told Betsy and Laura exactly which theories of art, argued endlessly by her old friends back in New York, would make anyone want a picture of her as she looked now, in a dusty dress still stained with a spill from the molasses barrel weeks before. She'd clipped her hair back quickly this morning as she rushed to start Jack's breakfast, and her nose was sunburned from helping pull their truck out of the arroyo.

"It's okay," Morna answered. "Tourists love to take photographs. We're thinking of carrying film to sell in the store."

"Tourists!" said Betsy. "Well, I guess we are. But Laura's not taking Kodaks of sunsets."

"Oh, you don't want a picture of me."

"Sure she does, you're a desert flower," Betsy said with a reassuring grin. Morna felt that warm shiver again. She was about to answer back when Jack walked in.

"Why, what are you ladies doing in the desert?" he boomed out in the tone that Morna had once thought of as charming. The two women stared at him.

"Dry throat? Lost your tongues in the sun? I got just the thing for you," he said, and reached into the glass jar of throat lozenges. "Horehound? Honey drops, it'll grease you right up again."

"I'm sorry, we were just startled when you walked in so suddenly. Didn't hear you coming," said Betsy.

Morna thought it interesting the way she said "we," like the two women were one.

"You sisters?" Jack asked, and Morna cringed at his rudeness.

"No," Betsy replied. She was about to say more, but Jack cut her off again.

"What else can I get you then, ladies?" Jack said.

Old maids, Morna thought. Pretending her ring didn't make them jealous. On vacation alone. Well, with each other. But at least they were on vacation. She and Jack hadn't had one since they had bought the trading post.

"What will it be today, girls? Candy, staples for the road? I've even got beads for the Indians. You can trade 'em for their pots and blankets. Just like we got Manhattan from them. They don't know the meaning of the dollar."

Having seen Jack give up way too much for far too few sacks of wool, Morna held back a snort.

Betsy turned away from Jack and spoke directly to her. "We were just getting some pickles. And perhaps a little salt fish, Morna?"

"Oh, so you gals are old friends." Jack looked thoughtful, and then glanced around the counter. "Morna, go out to the storeroom and bring in some more pickles, won't you?" Betsy smiled at Morna as she left.

"You can come with me," Morna called back over her shoulder to Laura, "and take that photograph."

"What photograph?" asked Jack.

"Laura's a photographer. She wants to take a photograph of me."

"Great idea," Jack said. "A photograph to send back to my mother. Can you do that?"

Morna was shocked that he'd said that. He hadn't spoken to his mother since he'd been disowned for going to art school instead of into his father's shipping firm. He wanted to sound like what he thought of as down home, like he was some native prairie dog here. He only put it on for tourists, because the Indians weren't fooled.

Laura looked uncertain.

"Laura takes portrait photographs for work, but this is our vacation. When you are in Santa Fe sometime, Laura can take your photograph in her studio," Betsy said. "We can leave a card." Morna wished she could talk to Jack like that, firm but sweet. They were always snapping at each other lately. The eternal glaring sun wasn't helping one bit, either.

If she and Jack were on vacation, Morna knew she would be sweet, too. These women probably weren't so sweet at home. At home? She pictured them just like a married couple, maybe even more married than she and Jack. She could see them in the evenings, side-by-side in big easy chairs, reading. For a long time now, Jack had spent the evening in the store with the account books while Morna was in the kitchen, cooking and ironing.

Morna had seen inside the Navajo hogans, where they all gathered in one round room with a fire in the middle. The whole family was together all the time, sitting on blankets on the floor. They always looked content with each other, the Navajo husbands and wives. Jack said it was because the Indian women did whatever their men said, with no talking back, but lately she had noticed that the Indian men usually did what the women said. It was the Indian women who came to trade their pottery or rugs for goods or money.

The Navajo women always wore silver jewelry, some of it with silver coins hammered in. Morna couldn't remember the last time she'd had a silver dime of her own in her hand, not that there was any place within hours to spend it. The Navajo men wore some silver in their belt buckles and wristbands, but the women had the most.

"Morna, how 'bout those pickles?" Jack called out. Morna went quickly, thinking that her life had gotten terribly narrow if she didn't want to miss a moment of watching two old maids buy pickles.

Morna hadn't always been a drudge in a lonely outpost. She had done a year of college and then the Art Students League, the most innovative art school in Manhattan. She had worked in an office as a stenographer to support Jack while he painted and taught and waited for a big critic to notice him and give him his big break. They had been part of the set of folks who wrote or illustrated *The Masses* magazine. Some of the painters were called "the Ash Can school." But since the Red Scare laws during the Great War, the old gang had broken up. Some were deported back to Russia, and others went willingly, waving sadly as their ship pulled away because not all their friends were joining them to see the Leninist future.

After the war, the Art Students League focused on art, not politics. But even when Jack grudgingly painted fruit instead of grimy workers, his work didn't sell and his teaching jobs disappeared. When he was young and rich and studying painting in Paris, he and his buddies Ernest Blumenschein and Bert Phillips had dreamed of success, but now they had it and he didn't. He was always saying that if only he'd gone west with them in 1898, instead of returning to New York, he would be as big as them. They had a head start, but he said he would catch up, for great art knew no age. He said the sunsets and scenery in Taos had made Blumie and Philips look like much better painters than they really were. He was going to New Mexico, and Morna could go with him if she wanted.

What she missed most about her home in New York was her vases and other ceramic pieces, which had been too fragile for the trip west. In New York, tired after a day's work, Jack still out drinking with his friends, she had often spent hours arranging and rearranging the beautiful objects she had created, in a trance that took her far from their sixth floor walkup that always smelled of paint and thinners. While they were waiting to leave, she had imagined their home and studio in Taos, Jack painting and she over her potter's wheel. Now, instead of her artwork, she could only rearrange the canned food on the shelves of the trading post, lining them up first by brand, then by the colors on the labels, then by the contents, and then back to the brand again, until Jack caught her and sent her to the dreaded storeroom to replenish the bulk goods, warning her that if she were losing her mind, she might just as well go back to New York. The last time he said that, she had asked him straight out for money for a ticket. He laughed her off.

Morna hurried into the storeroom, worrying that by the time she got back to the store the women would be choosing their last purchases and leaving as soon as they could, embarrassed to face the shame of her submission. But when she ducked back under the low beam of the doorway, Betsy stood alone by the counter. Laura came back in, carrying a big camera on a tripod.

"I asked him to check the oil and the tires," said Betsy. "Because he told us we little ladies really shouldn't be out here alone." They both giggled.

"I'd sure like to take that photograph," Laura smiled at Morna. While Betsy had impish bright eyes that challenged, almost flirting, Laura's eyes darted everywhere, taking in everything, but never locking in with Morna's glance.

"Let me get something nicer. This apron's all splattered," Morna said.

"No, that's fine, I'd like it to show how you really look here in the trading post. A hard-at-work day. Just a regular day like today."

But this wasn't a regular day at all, with these women here. And besides, hadn't Betsy called her "a desert flower?" What desert flower worked?

"When we came in you were in the back room. Is that something you do on a regular day?"

Morna pictured a photo of her crawling on the floor with the dead mouse's tail in her hand.

"Mostly I work in the front. I sell from behind the counter. I also stock the shelves."

"That must be quite a job," said Betsy, and they all laughed, because although there were plenty of shelves, many were empty and others held just a front row of cans, bottles, or piles of cloth. Morna saw the store through their eyes and was embarrassed. She smelled kerosene from the generator humming in the corner and the scent of the Murphy Oil soap with which she had just scrubbed down the big oak counter. High above their heads hung a row of galvanized buckets. A scraggly hide, still vaguely in the shape of a deer, hung from one of the thick log beams holding up the roof. Morna could see bare blotches where the moths had been getting at the hide. She followed Betsy's gaze over the sturdy wood counters, the sawdust-covered planks of the floor, and the roughly hewn logs that held up the ceiling. She hadn't swept the floor recently, and clumps of mud and sticks lay where they had dropped off boots and moccasins.

Betsy looked over to the locked glass cabinet, where silver necklaces and wristbands sat, each banded with a pawn ticket with the name of its Navajo owner and a date. Laura pointed to the bench near the woodstove. It was under the one window through which the bright sun was providing the only light in the room.

"I bet that's cozy in winter," she said. "Should we take the photograph there?"

Morna looked hesitant.

"It doesn't have to be there. It's just that the light's really good. Looks like a nice place to sit and dream a bit, relax from the chores."

"I've never sat there," said Morna. She heard Betsy mutter something about Jack and slave driver.

"That's where the Indians sit, the men I mean. There's usually a few here just talking, especially in the winter. Right now they're getting ready for sheep shearing. I don't sit down with them. Their own women never do."

"I understand," said Laura. "How about just standing by that counter, right in the sun, with the shelves behind you, just showing you and your store? And I'll make sure to get your address so I can send you a copy."

"Oh, it's just Trading Post, Lost Wash," Morna agreed.

Through the window, she could see Jack washing the windshield of their old car. He was talking to Jim Begay, one of the Indians who was usually found leaning on the counter facing the cook stove. That would keep Jack outside while Laura set up her camera. Morna leaned against the counter, just like she had when she'd modeled for painting students. It was a pose she hadn't been asked to do much since she'd gotten older. It was one more reason she'd been grateful to marry Jack.

Laura set up the tripod near the pile of Navajo horse blankets that covered one corner of the room. The Navajo children liked to sit there, looking hopefully at the candy jars while their mothers traded. Morna saw Jim Begay and Jack nod at each other, then Jim walked off. She wished Laura would move faster, but at the same time, she admired how deliberate and careful Laura was. She knew how to handle a camera. Most tourists took pictures without even asking. It would be a quick snap of their Brownie camera, and they left without a thank you, as if Morna were part of the scenery. It did feel good that Laura was making sure the photo would be a good one and was going to send a copy. Like Jack, though, Morna wished it were a dress-up portrait.

Laura lifted the big camera onto the tripod and put her head under the black velvet cloth. Morna smiled.

Jack came in the door. "Hey," he said in his best fake western accent, "that's quite a camera for a lady." The shutter snapped. Morna knew her face had changed in that instant.

Morna wanted to drown Jack and his unbearable cowboy act. When they had first met, he'd been fresh back from Europe and pretending he was a real Parisian painter. She'd thought his acting clever and playful. Now he just seemed phony. Why was she so damned critical of him lately? Why was she so out of love with him? Would she ever be in love with him again? If she wasn't, what was she doing here living like this?

"That's enough," said Laura. "Thank you so much. When we get back to Santa Fe I'll print it out and send it."

"Why thanks, ma'am," said Jack. "A picture of my wife. I'll treasure it always. And I believe she was smiling at me when you took it."

Laura raised her eyebrows. "Hmmm, I guess she was."

Within a few minutes, the two women had finished their purchases and their car chugged off on the bumpy road.

"How 'bout those gals?" Jack said. "Them and those lady archaeologists. Next thing, women will be wearing trousers everywhere. Makes you wonder if suffrage isn't bringing out the wrong kind of thing."

"But Jack, you applauded when I marched for suffrage."

"You know how far to take it. Some women don't."

"You didn't talk like that back east."

"I've been watching those Indians. The men are men and the women are women. The way they dress, the things they do."

"The women own the houses, Jack. They have their own herds."

"Yeah, but they always know who wears the pants. Not like some modern women, like that photographer's friend."

Morna didn't want to hear him say anymore against Betsy and Laura, so she gave up, finding it interesting that Jack had been looking at the Navajo people so differently. To her, the way they dressed didn't mean as much as that the women got a lot more attention and respect and were in charge a lot more than white women. Morna's name wasn't even on the deed of the trading post, even though she had put up most of the money. She hadn't even tried to get on it. But if she had owned it, maybe she would feel like more than a servant taking orders. The Navajo women were quiet, but maybe it was because they knew what they were worth.

Morna replayed the women's visit for the rest of the morning. They had said they weren't sisters, but Jack had interrupted the rest of their answer. She wished she had a friend that close. She wished they were her friends, both of them. She was going to stay out front in the store all week, so she wouldn't miss them if they came back.

But no tourists ever returned.

Jonnie

"We strike the Great Desert, with its wilderness howl, with its cactus and sage, with its serpent and owl" was the song Jonnie and her sister Marla often sang to each other. They had read it in a book about taking the Santa Fe Chief out west. They especially loved the map that was right inside the front and back cover of the book. It showed the Navajo country, with only a few tiny lines of roads, and on the blank space that was the uncharted desert were drawings of cactus, jackrabbits, and Indians. They would be in bed together, all snug up with blankets, a snow squall outside, the wind fixing to blow their creaky wood house right down into the iced-up waters of Gloucester harbor. But they would pretend they were in the desert, imagining that the howling wind blew hot and that the snow was sand.

Under the covers they would have a dolly tea party and sip pretend cactus tea. Jonnie would serve Marla a pretend serpent steak, and she'd say "Jonnie Bell, I don't want any serpent steak, I had flounder today for breakfast, flounder for lunch, flounder for supper, and if you don't mind I'd like some of that fricassee owl." Marla liked the word "fricassee." They weren't sure what it meant, but she read it one day in a cookbook and then she wanted all her pretend food that way.

Once Jonnie had asked their mother to fricassee some flounder, but she had told them to get up on the top floor porch and watch for their daddy's boat. He wouldn't be back for another two months, but she made them look anyway. Jonnie hated it up there, where the cold wind went right through her jacket. Marla would tell her to think about the Great Desert and the hot wind and to forget about the rest of it.

If only Marla was with her now, on the *Santa Fe Chief* going west at last. The train had just passed into New Mexico, and she was finally seeing the desert. The Great Desert. It wasn't a covered wagon, and Jonnie wasn't a pioneer—but she felt like she was. No one she knew in Gloucester had ever gone this far west. She was going to pick cactus and sage to send back east for her cousin Jenny to sprinkle on Marla's grave.

The next stop was Lamy, New Mexico, which was as far as Jonnie's ticket went. Marla's death had made her want to do more with what was left of her life. She wasn't young, but she wasn't too old to finally see the serpent and the owl. All the fish she had packaged in thirty-five years in the cannery wasn't much to show for her time on the earth. Even Marla had left her garden. Folks said it was a miracle garden because flowers grew in all that salt air and harsh wind off the harbor. But it was Marla's garden. Jonnie had just done the weeding. With Easter over and green shoots starting up, Jonnie couldn't face gardening alone. She'd bought her ticket west at last.

It wasn't the flowers that she cared about, anyway. She liked the mosses and lichens that cover the New England rocks. Some summer people said the rocks were bare, but they were city people and couldn't see. The people on the train said the desert looked empty like the sea, as if nothing grew there. But Jonnie saw plenty of little trees and bushes. Was that cactus? Was there a hidden beauty on the bare rocks here, too? When Jonnie looked out to sea, she often pictured the ruins of shipwrecks far under the waves. Was a lost world buried in the desert, too?

Her plan was to be a Harvey Girl. She had read about it at work, in a newspaper that she wrapped fish in. Mr. Harvey opened clean, decent restaurants at railroad stations so the people on the trains wouldn't have to bring their own food or eat in dirty places. He hired girls from the East to be the waitresses. Most were young and pretty, but they didn't have to be. They just had to work hard. Jonnie had always worked hard. Many of the Harvey Girls left to get married, but Jonnie wasn't looking for a husband. She hoped the Harvey people would snap her right up.

Since leaving Chicago, the train had stopped at four Harvey Houses. They were as fancy as the Union Oyster House in Boston, where fish caught by Gloucester boats was served. Jonnie didn't even have the money to eat at the less expensive Harvey House lunch counters, so she ate dried fish on the train. When the train stopped, she wandered in the restaurants as long as she dared. A waitress told her that if she headed further west, where it got hotter and drier and there wasn't much of a city yet, they might hire an old girl like her. They had a harder time getting young girls to stay in the smaller places. Jonnie would have to wear long dresses and keep her apron white and pin her hair back, but it would be worth it. For a long time this had just been a dream, but now it was really happening.

When the train stopped at Lamy, Jonnie was all set to walk right into the Harvey House and claim her job, but there was nothing there but cactus and a few big old cars. The closest Harvey House was in Santa Fe, seventeen miles away. The bus ride there cost the last of her money.

The Santa Fe Harvey House was the biggest and fanciest of them all. It was in the middle of town, on a pretty plaza with a big stone church like the Portuguese Catholics had back in Gloucester. That church was the only building that reminded Jonnie of home. Everything else looked like it belonged in a cowboy movie.

The Harvey House in Santa Fe was called La Fonda. The lobby was all heavy dark wood and pretty painted glass and deep leather with cowboy designs. Jonnie wanted to act like it was her new home. She nodded at the waitresses like the old friends she wanted them to be someday. They smiled back with that Harvey Girl smile, as they had in St. Louis and Kansas City.

When one waitress asked what she wanted, Jonnie said "the manager." She said she'd be right out, and would Jonnie like a menu. "No, I'm here on business," said Jonnie, and was led to a seat by the kitchen and told to wait. As she sat there, the waitresses came in with their order books and went out with their trays so many times she gave them names like "green eyes" and "pert little bottom." None looked as old as she was, but none looked as strong, either. Even loaded down with platters and dishes, their trays looked light compared to the barrels of fish Jonnie had carried at the fish cannery. She told herself that the manager was going to hire her, but she worried because the waitresses, after first smiling at her, were getting a funny look on their faces, like there was something wrong. She sniffed at her arm, wondering if her clothes smelled like the dried fish she had been eating all those days on the train. Some of the folks on the train had backed away. But here, so far from the ocean, things were sure to change.

Ruth

Ruth Weinstock's parents had said they were sending her west for her own good, but she knew it was because her wheezing and coughing embarrassed them. They were afraid their friends would think she had TB. Those few who understood that she had asthma said it was all her mother's fault, according to the latest from Dr. Freud. But everyone agreed that the only cure was to go to the hot, dry West, so this morning she had been stretchered from the big dark bedroom at the back of their Bronx Parkway apartment, carried to an ambulance, and loaded right onto a berth on a train at Pennsylvania station.

Mattie, a nurse, had been hired to make the trip to Santa Fe with her. They had never met before the train left. Ruth had already had to tell Mattie to close the compartment door. She had been standing in the doorway flirting with the salesmen passing through to the club car. She was supposed to be holding Ruth's hand as she suffered, but instead she complained that there were no chairs because the seats made up into a bed. Grudgingly, she climbed the ladder and sat down hard in the upper berth. Ruth could hear the pages of her movie magazine turning.

For lunch, Mattie brought her a tray of food in porcelain dishes and silver platters, but it was Mattie who ate it all. The doctors in New York had told Ruth's mother that the cure for asthma was to eat heartily of steak and eggs and cream. The cream gurgled in her throat and lungs day and night as she bent over coughing, but her mother would sit by the bed watching to make sure she choked down every disgusting bite. Mattie half-heartedly told her that she had been instructed to make sure Ruth ate, but as with everything else she did, Mattie didn't care that much. She was glad to wolf down the food Ruth didn't touch, even steering Ruth away from some of it by wrinkling her nose as she offered it to her. Ruth ate only the oranges, relieved to eat as she wished, and momentarily grateful for Mattie's attitude.

Her Pullman compartment was a tiny room with a tiny bathroom. As she lay in her berth, Ruth looked out the big windows. It had been so long since she had seen anything but the view from her bedroom window at home. The last week of April had been unusually grey and wet and she had rarely been out of the house. As it traveled farther from New York, the train rushed past thick forests of bushy trees with new green leaves. Dust-speckled sun warmed her face. Could it be she was wheezing less, even though the air in the train was as hot and stuffy as their Bronx apartment in winter? Maybe this trip might work. At least she wouldn't die without ever seeing what was beyond New York City.

Laura

The car bumped so much that Betsy and Laura could only laugh at each jerk. The old Buick was holding up, despite the obstacle of the dried ruts that were the road. It had been a long time since they had spotted Shiprock in the distance. Betsy was sure there would be a road sign soon, but Laura thought they might be in trouble. Still, when Betsy got Laura laughing, it didn't matter. This vacation had been a long time coming.

"You didn't have to tell her so much," Laura said.

"I'm proud of you. You're on your way."

"Oh sure," Laura hung her head. "Just ten years behind the rest of my class. I've got one photo in the Library of Congress while they're getting into museums everywhere. And gallery shows."

"You'll win that Guggenheim grant and you'll be all caught up," Betsy said. "You're on your way already. And how many of them had to stop photographing to run a turkey farm so their father didn't go bankrupt?"

"I can just see it," Laura laughed. "I can just see all my rich classmates in their finest clothes, stepping daintily through the slop floor of the barn."

"Yes, and hauling their cameras along, too."

"Maybe I should have taken photos. 'A Study in Turkey Crap,' to be published in *Photo Secession Journal* by Mr. Alfred Steiglitz, subscriptions to be taken now."

"Oh, anyone can photograph turkey crap."

"Stop making me laugh so much, I can't drive."

"No, really. You're going to take photographs like no one else. Look out there—" She pointed to the endless layers of pink rock that spread before them in all directions. "That's why we're here. So that everyone back east can see what we see now."

"Well, it better be out there or back to the turkey farm."

Betsy replied with a gargling turkey gobble.

"Don't, please," said Laura, laughing and tickling Betsy's ribs. "If I have to go back there, you're coming, too. See how you like getting up in the dark, cold dawn, wading through a sea of stinking turkeys pecking at your legs, and all of them screaming for food."

Betsy gobbled again.

"I can't go back there. The turkeys might as well gobble me to death."

"Oh, I'll gobble you up long before that," Betsy said, nibbling her neck so that Laura's arm jumped and the car swerved. Laura swept her eyes slowly over the vista. But when she spoke, she couldn't help exaggerating the bounce of the car with each syllable.

"Betsy," she said, her voice going up and down as her body bounced. "How long would you"—she went way up on the "you"—"say it's been since we left the road?" "Left" came out with a little shriek.

"Huh? This is the road." Betsy took another look. "Isn't it?"

"You're the one navigating. You've got the map."

"But this is a land beyond maps," Betsy said. "That's why we're here."

"It's getting late."

"A few minutes ago you said that you couldn't wait for the sunset."

"Oh my God, do you think the sun's getting lower?"

"Maybe we should check the gasoline level." Betsy reached for her gloves so she could open the cap on the tank.

The car sputtered to a stop, shook, and sank into the dried mud. Without the chug of the motor, it was very quiet. Laura tried the engine but nothing happened. She stared at the only object bigger than a cactus bush in view, a big butte with a promontory at one end that looked like a turkey all roasted and trussed up for Thanksgiving. How much food did they have in the car? How much water?

Betsy ran around the car and pulled Laura's door open. She tugged on her arm.

"Laura, come out, it's so lovely. Look at those strange rocks! Get your camera. Isn't this why you're a photographer? You're out of that studio now."

Usually Laura loved Betsy's touch, but she pulled back against the leather seat, squinting at the empty distances around them.

"Oh, honey, don't be scared. How long has it been since that trading post? With that poor little Morna and that terrible Jack? We can go back there and see them again. It'll give us enough to talk about the rest of the trip," said Betsy.

They had been talking about that sorry place for many of the last slow miles.

"It's at least ten miles. It was noon when we left," answered Laura.

"That's walkable. Two and a half hours? And we've got plenty of water. I'll go. You stay and watch the car." Betsy was always the first to volunteer.

"No, I'll go. Sitting here alone will make me even more scared."

"You could take your camera."

They both laughed at that. The camera weighed fifteen pounds, without the tripod.

"I should have bought you that little Brownie for Christmas."

"You needed new shoes—you can't walk around on cardboard. Anyway, they take tiny lousy pictures not worth my time. Don't you ever listen to me?"

Laura was immediately sorry for snapping. Betsy was always so sweet.

"Okay, Miss Grumpy, you go walk it off. They sold gas, didn't they? How come we didn't get any?" asked Betsy.

"You were so busy flattering poor little Morna."

"Me!" Betsy teased. "I saw you watching her reaching deep into the pickle barrel."

"No I wasn't. Didn't even notice it. Must have been you watching."

"I only have eyes for you watching other girls." She leaned into the car and pecked Laura's cheek. Laura pulled her onto her lap and into her arms.

"Betsy, I'm scared. This isn't like being lost near Santa Fe."

"We'll be okay. I think the desert critters only come out at night. I'll get you some water and food. You get ready to go."

But neither moved out of their hug.

"We're certainly alone out here, you know," Betsy said suggestively.

"Yes, and they'll find our bleached bones, you sitting on my lap, and they'll know all there is to know about us." Laura gently pushed her off and stood up.

Jonnie

From the high window in the kitchen door, a woman peeked out at Jonnie. It didn't look like she wanted to catch Jonnie's eyes, but Jonnie smiled at her and she came out. She was almost as old as Jonnie and wasn't wearing an apron like the waitresses.

"I'm Mrs. Monahan, the manager" she said, "I understand you want to talk to me."

"I'm Jonnie Bell Axtell, and I've come all the way from Gloucester, Massachusetts, to be a Harvey Girl." But it felt like something was missing. It was the way the waitresses always ended their sentences. She'd show Mrs. Monahan how quickly she learned. "Ma'am," Jonnie said, with a tiny curtsy.

"Gloucester?" said Mrs. Monahan with a delighted smile. "I'm from Dorchester myself. Been out here fifteen years. I worked at the Alvarado at Grand Canyon, and before that in Kansas City. Tell me, do you have fresh flounder still on Fridays?"

"If I never have flounder again, I'll die happy," Jonnie said.

"Never again! How can you say that? I miss the ocean, I miss it all. It's a long way from here. You'll soon miss it."

She had said the wrong thing. She wanted to kick herself. The moment was lost.

"So, Miss Jonnie Bell, how can we help you?"

"I'm here to be a Harvey Girl. It's been my dream ever since I read about it in *The Saturday Evening Post*.

Mrs. Monahan looked Jonnie up and down doubtfully.

"I'll miss the ocean, but I know I'll love the—" Jonnie tried to think of something wonderful she had seen, but so far it was all so strange and new that she hadn't picked any favorites yet. Then she had an inspiration, remembering a woman on the train whose terrible cough had woken her many times.

"I'll love the dry air, it will be good for my health," she said.

Mrs. Monahan shrank back. "You have a cough, do you?" she said with concern. "You aren't a lunger, are you? We don't allow any girls with a tubercular condition. You wouldn't want to eat in a place that did, would you?"

"Oh no," Jonnie cried out, "I'm perfectly healthy. Been working the hardest line at the cannery for the last ten years. I can lift seventy pound barrels of fish all day. Those trays full up with food will be nothing to me. I can haul 'em with the best. That's what everyone bragged at the cannery. It's what the fishermen say when they pull in the nets."

"*Ladies* don't *haul* trays around," Mrs. Monahan said, dragging out the words. Anyway, tell me more about your health. How long have you been coughing?"

"Really, I don't. Never coughed in my life. See?" Jonnie pretended to fake cough, but there was a frog in her throat, and the cough had a gurgle to it that sounded like a fish drowning in a barrel. Her face went bright red.

"I'm sorry," the manager said. "I'm sympathetic, you being a Gloucester girl and all, but Mr. Harvey's standards are very particular. Maybe after you spend some time in the—" her voice sank to a whisper, "sanatorium," and then rose up, "you'll be able to get some other job in town. This town's growing fast. Being a Harvey Girl's just one thing. We're flattered you wanted to be so." She patted her pocket as if to protect herself, and turned her eyes across the room where one of the waitresses was having a problem with a very large man who wasn't letting her pass.

"But you've got me wrong. I'm so healthy if I was a man, I'd be the best of the fisherman. My father always says it's a real loss to Gloucester to make me work in the cannery instead of out on the sea. Sea air, you know, it's the best there is for the lungs."

Mrs. Monahan pulled a pad out of her pocket and signed the top piece of paper. Handing it to Jonnie, she said, "Here, have a meal on us. Mr. Harvey would be very pleased to hear how much this means to you, if he were alive I mean."

Women can't wait to get away from me, Jonnie thought. Saying the wrong thing, wearing the wrong clothes, smelling the wrong way. Why had she ever believed this would work? Now she was two thousand miles from home, not a fish cannery in sight, and nothing ahead. Well, she better enjoy this one last meal, because she hadn't a dime for another.

Laura

With canteens strung both ways around her neck and her pockets stuffed with food, Laura set out. She pictured herself as Shackleton the arctic explorer, leaving his men in a cave on Elephant Island while he hurried off for the whaling station and rescue. The Shackleton image helped a great deal as the sun blasted down on her. She forced out of her mind images of Betsy sitting obliviously in the car while off in the distance a ring of feathered tips of headdresses appeared. They had seen that scene in all the cowboy movies they had watched while waiting for the Louise Brooks movies to start.

She tried to focus on the latest Brooks film they had seen, *Beggars of Life*. Louise had disguised herself as a boy to travel as a tramp, and they had speculated on whether either of them could get away with that. Betsy had said that Laura's bosom was too big, and Laura had said that Betsy's voice was too high.

Sucking on the cold metal of the canteen, she watched the rocks turn blazing red as the afternoon sun descended. Should she have taken her camera instead? Which was more important at this moment: water or her chance to take a prize-winning photo? She was so bored with the endless wedding photos of her commercial business. Winning the Guggenheim grant would get her out of the studio and into beauty like this. She had saved up all year for the film and chemicals and paper for this trip, now all she needed was the perfect place and the perfect time. Was she missing her chance right now?

Seeing towering cliffs off in the distance, she thought of the photogravure that had hung in the parlor of her childhood home. It was the

Edward Curtis' photo *Riders in the Canyon*, showing seven Indian horsemen so dwarfed by huge cliffs that they looked like spiny ants at the foot of an elephant. The other photos in her home were grimly posed portraits of long-dead relatives and equally stiff living ones. They always made her think of death, but she been inspired by the Curtis photo. Like a painting, it showed a beautiful land that hid mysteries in its shadows. The Indians who had attacked wagon trains and pioneer farmers had been defeated after years of bloody battles, and Curtis showed them as they were now, compliantly riding toward a future in which they would disappear into the endless landscape. So many times Laura had wondered what was above and beyond the massive cliffs in the photo. When she had received her first Brownie camera for her twelfth birthday, she had tried to take photos like Curtis, but everything farther than a few feet from the camera was tiny and blurred. She tried better cameras and lenses, until the challenge to learn all she could took her to New York City and the Clarence H. White School of Photography.

Trying to keep her mind off the heat and glare would have been easier if her mind hadn't kept returning to the letter she had received just the other day from Brenda Putnam. Her best friend from her days in New York City only meant well to send Laura news of their friends, but hearing that two of the men from her class at Clarence White's were steadily getting commissions and museum purchases made her wish she had never opened it. She thought of their class photograph, in which she had grabbed the center of focus by sitting in the middle with a huge hat. She had stared straight into the camera while the others were asked to look at her. It seemed then that she was sure to be the star and that all the others had conceded. Ten years later, they had all moved ahead. She pictured historians looking at that photo, pointing out all the other famous photographers, and asking "That woman in the ridiculous hat, does anyone know her name?" Betsy had faith, but time was zipping by.

For now, time was stopped. She knew she was walking, but none of the strange rocks in the hazy distance were getting any closer. Her eyes were so dry she kept blinking, and she licked her lips so much her tongue hurt. The sun burned her now, but if she didn't get to the trading post before it went down, her situation would be worse. Although she had gone to boarding school in Connecticut, a conservatory in Boston, and photography school in Manhattan, she had lived in Colorado when her father had moved the family there when she was a girl, so she wasn't any green Easterner. This made her feel all the stupider for running out of gas on the desert. But this Navajo country was new to her. She had always meant to see it and never had the time or a car. Now that Betsy was working at the sanatorium in Santa Fe and her own photography studio was doing well enough, she was finally on her way. Except for forgetting to check the gas, which was worse than forgetting film.

Laura stood beside a hill shaped like a turkey on a platter, grateful for a moment of shade. She leaned back against the rock, but leapt away immediately. The sun had moved but the rock kept the heat. When she turned around, little stick men and lizards glared at her from the rock's surface. Their friend June had told them about these rock pictures the Indians had made. June was working for Dr. Morris, the archaeologist, who thought the pictures were maybe as old as when Jesus walked the earth, but nobody knew for sure. He was excavating an ancient Indian site, the place they were heading for. Would she and Betsy end up as bleached bones that archaeologists would someday discover?

Betsy

Betsy watched Laura walk away until she finally disappeared into the glare. The car was hot but she was shaded by the roof. She felt terrible thinking about how the sun must be burning Laura. She had insisted Laura take almost all the water, and if she herself was going to make it, she would have to stay very still. Even sweating could lead her into kidney failure that much faster.

She imagined she was sitting under the willow tree by the mossy creek on the South Carolina plantation where she had spent her childhood. When that didn't work, she thought of all the grayest, wettest Christmas mornings in the years after her father had moved their family around the South. It had been inspiring to look down into the chill rivers from the bridges her father had designed. She thought of the cold nights in the barely heated dormitory of nursing school at Johns Hopkins in Baltimore. She pictured the ice-cold glasses of milk she held up to the lips of the wretched patients at Sunmount Sanatorium. That helped a little, but finally she had nothing left but a very hot, thirsty body and the stark scenery. She was no Willa Cather to be poetic about it. She was just hot.

Seeing the beauty in the land was Laura's talent. Betsy's was people, and when there weren't any around, she was restless. She pulled out her medical manual to check the information on dehydration and soon moved on to the sections on snake and scorpion bite. She rifled through her first aid kit to make sure it had fresh razor blades.

As she examined the suction cup for drawing out the venom, a shadow fell over her. A man leaned into the window. He'd come up so silently. He was a Navajo man with a bright red silk scarf tied around his forehead so that his hair stuck out behind it. He reached into the car and the silver buttons on the cuffs of his black velvet shirt flashed in the sun. Betsy screamed and he drew his hand back. She jumped to the other seat, but there was a man on that side, too. He had a drooping mustache.

This was it. Every one of those movies they had thought so silly came to her mind: the settlers' wagons burned, the scalped bodies strewn about, and the pet dog sniffing sadly at their remains.

Or was it? The razor blades in their sterile paper coverings had fallen to the floor of the car when she jumped seats. The two men were talking to each other through the windows of the car. They had her trapped, but they seemed to be disagreeing about what to do. Slowly she inched her hand down toward the blades.

She was trying not to look at the men, hoping this wasn't really happening, but Red Silk tapped her on the shoulder and she looked up. There was an open, friendly smile on his face. She looked at Mustache. He was more guarded. Still, they didn't seem anything like the war-paint covered Indians in the movies. Red Silk pointed to a half-eaten Hershey bar melting on the dashboard.

Betsy's first impulse was to hand it right to him, but she wondered what he would think if she gave everything to him right away. Her throat was very dry from heat and fear. She pantomimed thirst. He motioned for her to wait and went to his horse. While he was untying something, Mustache stuck his head through the window and examined the dashboard.

Red Silk handed her a clay jar in a leather harness that allowed it to hang off the saddle. He showed her how the lid opened. Drinking the surprisingly cold water calmed Betsy down, and she smiled at him gratefully. He pointed at the Hershey bar again. She had to scrape it off because it had melted and oozed onto the surface. Mustache came around the car and the two split the candy, even offering Betsy some.

As Red Silk walked around the car, Betsy noticed that he was limping and grimacing with pain. She pointed at his leg and imitated the expression on his face. Mustache laughed and imitated her imitation. They all laughed. She held up a roll of gauze from the First Aid kit, and the injured man reached in and took it. He unrolled it slowly, as if looking for something hidden within. When it was completely unrolled, he nodded as if complementing Betsy on the beauty of the white cotton, and carefully rolled it up again. Then he jerked his chin at the clay pot of water, as if asking if she considered this a fair trade.

Mustache reached into the back seat of the car and came up with a deck of cards. He held it up for Red Silk to see. Red Silk smiled at Betsy invitingly. The men squatted in the tiny shadow of the car and began to deal on the ground. Clearly they knew a lot more about poker than about First Aid. They had left a space for Betsy in the shadow. She tried to squat as they did, but her 43-year old knees weren't about to let her. Sitting on the running board of the car, Betsy was soon engrossed in the game.

Laura

Laura wanted to stay in the shade of the flat rock, but the shadows grew visibly as the sun continued to sink. Picturing the Indian warriors moving in closer to Betsy in the car, their tomahawks raised, she left her little oasis at a run—which quickly slowed in the glare of the sun. But she stumbled on. Trying to keep her mind off their present danger, she thought back over the way they had met.

In 1918, everyone in Colorado Springs felt out of the way of most of the nation's and the world's troubles, but the influenza epidemic had found them nonetheless. Laura's time in New York City studying photography had been ended by what her father tried to call "business reverses" but were better described as yet another in his endless series of too risky business ventures. This time he had traded his interest in a small railroad for a silver mine up in the mountains. There was no sign of silver, so Laura had soon been forced to leave school to help him run a turkey farm on the acreage that came with the claim. He continued his search for silver while she searched for ways to feed the turkeys.

The first wave of the influenza epidemic caught her father and the two hired men. The men had no family nearby, so Laura nursed them in the rough cabin while trying to keep the turkeys alive. One of the hired men died, and the other grew strong enough to leave. Slowly, her father came back to health. He was barely walking again when Laura came down with influenza. She was grateful that the virus had waited long enough to let her save her father.

In a feverish state, Laura had been lifted onto a hay truck to be taken to a boardinghouse in Colorado Springs, while her father sobbed that only a woman could care for a woman, and that he didn't know what would become of the turkeys while she was recovering. Her head pounded and her eyes bulged with pain as he assured her that the silver lode was only days from discovery and then he'd be able to move her to the finest hospital west of the Mississippi. To the extent she could think at all, Laura wondered whether she would prefer to be buried in an already very crowded churchyard in the city or up on the mountain with the hired man. The view of snow-capped peaks and pine forests was one she had always wished to photograph.

Looking back on her recovery, Laura was glad the silver lode never came in. She was barely aware of Betsy, the visiting nurse who cared for her during the month in which she had gone from sleeping to feverish tremors to delirious chattering to moments of lucidity and strength, then back to sleep as the cycle started again. But there had finally come a day when they both realized that she was going to make it. For a few days she slept more peacefully and woke more lucid.

One morning, she saw Betsy holding a red cotton cowboy bandanna, about to place it in a pot of boiling water to make a poultice. There wasn't much else a nurse could do for influenza. Laura had done the same for her father and the hired men. But before the edge of the bandanna touched the hot water, she grabbed it. Betsy leaned over the bed, softly asking, "Are you thinking okay? Say something so I will know you're not delirious."

Without knowing why, thinking maybe she was delirious, thinking that's my permission to do this, Laura looped the bandanna around Betsy's neck and pulled her closer holding a corner in each hand. She began to tie the ends in a loose knot like the cowboys wore.

"Here, have a gift," Laura said, "a pretty scarf for you." As she tied, their faces came close together. Suddenly Betsy's mouth was all Laura could see. Their lips brushed, then touched, then stayed. She was lost in a soft, wet world until a wagon clattered down the street outside, and Laura suddenly realized what she had done. She jerked back, but Betsy threw her arms around Laura's neck, and drew her close again.

"I am delirious," Laura murmured.

"You are delirious," Betsy said softly. "And I am, too."

A gasping, cranking sound interrupted Laura's memories. She searched the horizon and saw a big black car crawling along the ruts. It had turned onto the road and was heading away. She broke into a run, screaming and waving her arms, running as fast as she ever had in her life. The car didn't stop, and her side hurt terribly, but she thought of Betsy alone except for the Indians and grabbed her side and staggered on.

The car disappeared over a rise on the horizon and she felt her eyes bulge as she desperately tried to see. There was something there—was the car backing up? It was so far, and she was too faint to tell. Then the car grew larger. It had turned and headed toward her. Laura collapsed onto the ground, panting heavily. The car stopped, the doors flung open, and people poured out like from a clown car at the circus. They all slapped wide-brimmed hats on. Most were dressed in heavy brown pants with suspenders and long-sleeved white shirts. The few women wore long skirts and smaller hats.

"Are you all right?"

"What are you doing here?"

"What's happened?"

"Laura! Oh my!" came a scream from one woman. Everyone stared at her instead of Laura.

"Laura," the woman screamed again, coming towards her. "What's happened? Where's Betsy? Are you all right?"

It was June, the archaeologist friend they were going to visit, with what must be her colleagues from the field camp. Still gasping, Laura explained about the car breaking down and Betsy being alone. June and a man helped her up and they all piled back into the car. It stumbled along, slowly retracing her path. Gratefully, Laura sucked at a canteen.

"Sounds like you broke down pretty close to our field camp," said one of the men.

"Looks like we came along just in time," said another. The sun was visibly low now.

"It's getting really dark. She's all alone," Laura couldn't stop mumbling, her fears all tumbling out. "I shouldn't have left her like that. Our car isn't worth it. How could I have left her like that?"

"I'm sure she's fine," said June. "We're out here all the time. Nothing scary but the Ancient Ones. Can't wait to show you our site. This is the friend I told you fellows about," she announced to the rest of the passengers. "Well, one of them anyway."

That was just like June, thought Laura. She was all work and don't let feelings interfere. She and Betsy had been around when June had broken the heart of a sweet girl who had thought being in love would settle June down. The next time a new girl met June, they had been tempted to warn her. They had argued about June, because Betsy wanted to stay away from June, but Laura didn't want to lose one of the few friends who were like them. Betsy, the sweet nurse, always ended up being the comforter.

"That must be the car!" shouted the driver. "Look at that!"

The car was ringed with horses, and several more Indians stood near it.

"Oh Betsy, all those men, oh no! Do you have any weapons?" Laura shouted at the archaeologists. "No, they've already seen us. How could I have left her here alone?" Laura wailed.

The car stopped and the two groups stared at each other.

"Betsy, Betsy" Laura screamed, struggling to climb over June and push open the door. From the middle of the circle of men, Betsy's head emerged. She smiled and waved, holding up something small in her right hand that Laura couldn't make out. They all piled out of the car and ran to her.

"I'm fine. We're playing rummy. What's wrong?" Betsy showed her a handful of playing cards.

When she saw how upset Laura was, Betsy threw the cards down and held her while she sobbed.

"I was so scared. I thought the worst had happened."

"No, they're nice fellows. They don't speak English, but we've been kind of talking anyway, with our hands."

Laura grew calmer as June stood by, babbling on to Betsy about field sites and archaeology and Dr. Morris. Betsy listened, but had something else on her mind.

"I think they want us to visit their homes," Betsy said.

"It's just fly-covered babies and stinky sheep," said June. "We hire the men to dig for us, but we don't go there."

"I'd like to see for myself," said Betsy.

"Come see the real Indians," said June. "The ones we're digging up."

June's friends siphoned gasoline into the car. After Betsy reluctantly left the Indians behind with a deck of cards, some cans of food, and vigorous hand signals meant to indicate that she would come again someday, Betsy and Laura followed the archaeologist's car to the field camp. Both were soon asleep. But the next morning they were up bright with the sunrise and the taps and rattles of the archaeologists at work. June brought them tin cups of coffee as they stumbled out of their tent.

"I'll show you around," June said. "There's Dr. Morris' tent, and there's the cook tent, and there's where we label the specimens. Climb up and I'll show you why we're here." She led them to the bottom of the steep wall that wrapped around the flat plain they were on like a horseshoe. Above them, in the overhang of a cave, were ancient cliff houses. June pointed to a stairway of shallow, smooth, foot-sized depressions in the cliff face.

"That's a stairway made by the feet of the Indians a thousand years ago. You go first. Have I told you how we know how old it is? It's a whole new theory. Everyone's talking about it."

She babbled away about counting tree rings and ancient charcoal while

Betsy headed up the stairs with Laura following. At first Laura wished June had gone first, but then she was glad, because they were moving faster than June and her voice faded away. Laura wobbled on the rounded surfaces, but then gained her balance and kept moving, soon learning not to grab the dry cactus for support. On the warm steps in the rising sun's path, she pictured women climbing there a thousand years before, their babies slung to their breasts. She wished she could take their photograph. Then Betsy screamed.

She had turned a corner above Laura, going out of sight behind a boulder. Laura scrambled up, wondering why she heard June laughing beneath her.

Betsy was frozen in place, staring in shock at the doorway of one of the ancient rooms.

"Oh Laura," she choked out. "Oh Laura, it's terrible." Her body blocked Laura's view, so Laura leaned in beside her while throwing an arm around her. In the doorway was a seated Indian, all stiff and dry like straw, with torn remnants of blanket stuck to leathery bare arms. Empty eye sockets, big broken teeth, and the hole of a nose stared back. Laura screamed and the sound echoed and magnified against the rock walls. Loud laughter came echoing back from all sides. Cold fingers grabbed Laura's shoulders as June, laughing uproariously, hoisted herself alongside them.

"So you've met Grandmummy," she said. Betsy and Laura gaped open-mouthed back and forth from June to the body.

"That's a real mummy," June said. "We like to give our visitors a formal introduction." She waved to two laughing co-workers who leaned down from a room above, watching.

"This is called Mummy Cave, in the Canyon del Muerto, the canyon of death. That's why so much archaeology is done here. The dry air preserves everything like dried fruit. This cave has that big overhang which kept the rain out, so there are more mummies here than in most sites. When we find 'em, we like to leave 'em sitting like that. It scares away the Indians from stealing from the site. And it's a good laugh when we have visitors." June rubbed her hands and said proudly, "That's why I urged you two to visit. Wanted to see your faces." She threw back her head and laughed.

"How old is she?" asked Betsy, pointing to the mummy, but Laura knew she was really commenting about June.

"Well, I just explained about the tree rings. It's probably from about the time of the Magna Carta. Thousand years or so."

"But why isn't she buried?" asked Betsy. "How can you leave a body sitting out like this? That's ghoulish." It wasn't like Betsy to make judgments.

Laura knew she was ripping mad.

"Should we give her a Christian burial?" said June. "It's just a dead Indian."

"But she was a living person," said Betsy, "She—"

June cut her off. "You have to understand our work. We're uncovering the history of humanity, right here. The pots, the tools, and we've even found a knapsack for holding a baby. The mummies are part of our research, too. Can't you get a joke?"

"I don't care why you do it," said Betsy. "You can't treat a body like this."

Laura had rarely seen Betsy so angry, except when she had thought the poorer patients were being overlooked at Sunmount. Laura wanted to look around more, but Betsy pulled her off to the side to talk in angry whispers.

"I can't believe we were ever friends. She didn't get this way lately, did she? She had to have been this way before. How did I never notice it?"

"Mmph," Laura replied. Now that the full sun was up, she was seeing so much to photograph that she couldn't let her eyes close long enough to blink. The patterns of light, the contrasts of the stone walls against the natural cliffs, the water stains that added even more texture: it was everything she had studied in photography school in New York City. After all the control and flatness of studio photography, it was like moving from charcoal to a full palette of oil paints.

It wasn't just the shadows and lights and sunbeams, but also the glow the old ruins gave off that was somewhere between red and gold. She wasn't going to use color film, so she knew the challenge would be to keep that glow in black and white.

"Oh, Betsy, it's just like when Tom Outland first sees the Cliff Palace in *The Professor's House*. Do you remember how he first sees the stone city high above him, through the falling snow?"

"Remember how she treated that Melissa she got involved with? I should have seen it then."

"Remember when we read the book together, out loud? Remember that moment when he first sees the cliff city? How we both practically screamed with surprise?"

"She'd treat a live person as bad as a dead one, don't you think?"

"Don't think about it. We came all the way here, and the car broke down and everything to see this, and you're not even looking. Look!" Laura pointed across the whole panorama of cliff dwellings bounded by walls of piled rocks, going on until the cliff turned a bend and disappeared into the huge blue sky.

"It's something," Betsy agreed. "Do you want to take pictures? I can help you with the camera." She started to head down for the car. "I don't want to run into June, I'm so mad."

"I'm not ready," Laura said. "I have to think it out. This isn't like the studio. The light is always the same there. Here I have so many choices."

Betsy sat on a boulder, still upset.

"It's not so easy, you see. I've got to decide what I want the viewers to feel when they see the photos."

"I thought you wanted them to feel like Tom Outland in the snow."

So she had been listening. Laura wanted to kiss her, thinking that once again, in her magical nurse way, Betsy had put her finger right on the pulse.

"That's exactly it. I want the photos to look like Willa's words." They always called their favorite author Willa, because they thought of Willa Cather as their friend. They had spent many cozy nights reading her books aloud. "I want them to feel how old it all is, and how different it must have been to live this way. Hard to get up there." They stared at the narrow, barely visible trails up the cliff.

"I don't know how the ancient Indians did it," Betsy said. "What happened when someone was injured up here?"

"Maybe June and her gang will find some ancient stretchers," Laura's words broke the spell.

"June's going out on one, if you ask me," Betsy snapped. "How long do we have to stay here?"

"But this is where we're going. This is our vacation." Laura was almost blubbering. An image of her father, who never let her have a free moment, ran through her mind. He was grabbing the camera right out of her hands. "There's so much to photograph here."

"Hey, I'm sorry," Betsy said. "It's okay, you can take pictures." She rubbed Laura's shoulder, but Laura glanced around to make sure no one was watching. It was an argument they had had many times. Betsy would say that no one thinks twice when women touch comfortingly like that, but Laura would say that they know it's more than that and things could end up terribly for just a little hug. Laura thought she saw a shadow move on the cliff above, so she moved away.

"Do you know what I'm thinking?" Betsy said. "It's those Indians we met. Do you think they need a nurse? Do you think they'd let me help them if they were sick or hurt, or do you think they'll only go with their own people?"

"Didn't June say something about that? Some of her friends study that stuff."

"The way she talks about the dead Indians, I don't want to talk to her about the living ones."

"I'm sure we can find out. But if you were their nurse, you'd have to live out here. When would I see you?" It had taken a long time to get just this week together. Dr. Mera's sanatorium hardly ever gave Betsy two days off in a row. "It already seems like I never get to see you, Betsy. You wouldn't really think of moving all the way out here, would you?"

"Laura, don't worry about us, we'll be all right. But there's something here, well not here, but out where the car broke down. Something happened to me there."

"What happened? What didn't you tell me? I should never have left you alone like that!"

"Nothing bad. Something happened inside. It's like what you said about always taking the studio photos and then having something this beautiful to photograph. I like working at the sanatorium, but I've been there a long time. I'm tired of so many patients dying. If I was out here with the Indians, there would be births and children and seeing more of the sick people get well. Laura, I've got to find out. I have to do it, somehow."

"But what about me?" Laura wailed. "What about us?"

Betsy reached out but Laura jerked away. "The good light won't last long. I have to get going. That's why we came here, after all."

Soon she had her camera. Betsy stayed near the cook tent, talking to some Navajo workers. Laura walked far enough to get all the trucks and tents and signs of the archaeologists out of sight, and framed photos with her hands. In every direction was the beauty she had planned to photograph, but everywhere she looked, the photo by Edward Curtis that had inspired her hung over it like a scrim. It was possible she was looking at the actual place where the row of Indians on horseback was dwarfed by the massive cliff.

Turning in other directions, she imagined other Curtis photos: their backs to her, Indians rode past a huge tumbleweed. From a point high above, a hazy Indian surveyed the scene below. Curtis had taken all the photos that could be taken here. There was no way to improve on his perfection.

But she hadn't come here to photograph Indians. It was the light and the landscape she wanted to grasp. She pushed the images of Curtis aside and took some pictures, but it just didn't feel right. Her mind was on Betsy, the light was different from the studio, the heat was unbearable, and it was all different than she had imagined in the months she had been looking forward to this trip.

Off to the west was a pile of rocks that could almost be the ruins of an ancient dwelling. Laura had seen places like this before and knew it was just detritus dropped by an ancient sea, leaked by a volcano, and carved by the winds. It had a courageous beauty, a landmark in the sandy canyon floor. She sat down with her head in the shade of an overhang and her legs in the sun, leaning back against the warm rocks. Was it only yesterday she had desperately gone for gasoline and thought she would die in the desert?

This should be the moment when she would have clarity, like Thea in *Song of the Lark,* her favorite of Willa Cather's books. Exhausted and frustrated from the failure of her operatic career, the singer had stayed at a remote Arizona ranch and spent her days resting in a sunny cliff dwelling once inhabited by the Old Ones. There Thea picked up a broken piece of a pot, admired the artistry of the delicate black, brown, and red design painted on it, and wondered at the woman potter so long ago who had made the effort to beautify an everyday object. It gave her the sudden revelation that had renewed her and given back her voice and her art.

Laura's toe rested against a hard knob of something darker in the sandy pink earth. She reached down to scratch it out, and when it resisted, she pulled hard with both hands until it broke off. But it was only a clod of rock that crumbled apart as she wrenched it out. Not a bone or a potsherd, just another piece of the endless earth. Nothing to inspire her as the beautiful broken pot had thrilled Thea, seeing in it a revelation about art as a beautiful vessel in which humans try to capture and hold life flowing by. Laura wished she could remember the exact words, something about a sheath and a river and an instant of time. It was Thea's—no it was Willa Cather's—revelation, but she could feel it herself now.

No she could not. She could remember the book and the page and even where the paragraph was, but she could not feel even the emotion of that moment when she and Betsy had thrilled over it as they read it aloud together, over and over, not long after they had gotten together and shared their favorite books. It still meant something, a memory of how she had felt, but she didn't feel it now. Of course she couldn't feel it. She must have her own revelation, not Willa Cather's. A bird flew over, blanking out the glaring sun for an instant. It was so quiet she heard its wings flap. This had to be the moment.

But all she felt was a need to get out of the draining heat. Laura looked for the bird, but there was nothing but flat blue sky. Her legs were burning and the rocks under her thigh were hard and uncomfortable. She wanted to get back to the site and have lunch. She shouldn't go, she should wait for that revelation, but all she could think about was how much more comfortable the soft leather seat of the car would be. She was thirsty. She should have brought her canteen with her if she was going to sit in the sun. Leaning hard on one hand to push up from the ground, Laura stood and headed back.

Jonnie

"There you go, Boston, straighten them trousers, put on the cap, and let's see how it looks. This here's the kind them ship captains wear back home, don't it make you feel like you're right home again?" said Grates, her possible new boss, as he spit right across the room and into a horse trough.

The building had once been a stable, but now it was a garage for the gleaming new 1928 Model A parked in what had been a stall. Jonnie wanted to tell him that a real ship's captain back home wore a business suit and fedora, just like gangsters in the movies, and that only in the movies did sea captains wear funny peaked caps with shiny visors like this one, but she kept her mouth shut. If she got this job, at least she wouldn't have to wear the long dress and apron of a Harvey girl. Those clothes would have made her feel like she was still in the cannery.

"Fits you just right. I wouldn't even guess you got a bosom. That little fellow had the job last had the smallest coffin I ever seen. We had it special-made for him. You must be just his same size. Looks like you got the job."

"When did you say payday was?" Jonnie asked as casually as she could.

"Slow down, filly, you ain't even driven across the street yet. You's more like an old gray mare than a filly, though," he laughed.

Jonnie didn't get angry. The guys around the cannery were meaner than him, and she had taken their insults with a fish knife in her hand. But if she knew when payday was, her fantasies of eating again would be much happier.

That morning, after a night spent trying to sleep in a shed near the big cathedral, she had chewed hardtack for breakfast. She had found the box hidden between the shirts in her trunk. When she'd left home, her father had told her not to expect much but that he'd do what he could for her. She hoped that hiding the hardtack in her suitcase wasn't all he would ever do, but she was glad to find it. The hardtack and the shed had been a godsend during a hungry week of looking for work.

If she got this job, she would have a bed and food in a room over the garage. Compared to the cannery, it would be glamorous work. She would wear handsome clothes that were meant to be kept clean, not covered in fish blood and guts, and she would drive a fancy new car with soft leather seats. All she had to do was keep the car gleaming and drive rich people from the train depot in Lamy to the Sunmount Sanatorium in Santa Fe, or bring them from the Sunmount back to the depot. Most of the patients had tuberculosis, but she wanted the job too much to worry about that.

Even though the past week had been hard, she had felt bright and shiny every day, because she was here where the bright sun burned everything. There was never any grime or slush like back east. The funny brown mud houses they called adobe, and the dried-out dark green bushes scattered in the pink earth, were clean as a good-swept floor all the time. Even the earth itself looked like it had been worked over by a persistent housewife. Maybe her next meal was just a dream now, but meanwhile she felt just right in her little outfit, captain of that big car, ready to sail out over the mesa land.

Ruth

If it wouldn't have made her cough even harder, Ruth would have screamed at the woman driving the limousine. If it was a woman. She looked like a man and wore a tuxedo. Whatever she was, she didn't know how to handle an invalid. She had bumped Ruth so hard getting her into the ugly limousine that she had coughed the whole bumpy way from the train to Santa Fe. The car lurched all over the twisting roads. Ruth wished she hadn't fired Matty the nurse for neglecting her on the train. She should have waited to see if the accommodations at Sunmount were all the brochures had promised.

Laying low on the seat, Ruth couldn't see out the window, and she felt that her life couldn't get much more out of her control. It was worse than even a sweaty horrible night at home, curled up in a ball wheezing, expecting to die at any moment. Now she was sick and also far from home, sweating and wheezing and choking dust, in this car that smelled of leather seats and closed up her throat even worse.

But she didn't think she would survive this car trip to the sanatorium. If her lungs didn't close up forever, she was sure they would crash right into one of those funny looking little brown clay houses she had seen from the train. They looked like sandcastles at Coney Island, but with bright turquoise wooden doors. Had she seen something like them in a book of photos about strange lands and savage peoples?

Nothing out here looked real, but nothing in her life had felt real since the day she started to wheeze and cough and cough and wheeze. Ten years had passed in a haze of doctors and beds and dark rooms for the pain in her eyes. Her hands had trembled. She had to stop reading. Nothing the doctors advised worked. They said going to the desert was her last chance.

No one in our family has ever gone west of the Hudson to where the cowboys and Indians live, said her mother. She said the cowboys were American Cossacks, and the Indians were their Jews to terrorize. She made Ruth promise never to leave the sanatorium grounds—not that she could walk more than a few steps anyway. Ruth would certainly never get in this car with this mad woman driver again. The blare of the horn made her head feel like a Purim grogger, like a rattling noisemaker. When would this terrible bumpy ride end?

And where would she be then? She didn't want to be among the wretched, wracked people dying of TB in a western sanatorium. If there had been any place just for asthma, she would have gone, but there wasn't. Her mother had asked a lot of people until she heard about Sunmount. She was told it was the finest sanatorium in the Southwest. Her mother had gotten Ruth's brother into Harvard, despite the university's dislike of Jews, and every friend of theirs knew it. If Ruth was to die in a sanatorium, at least her mother could brag that it was the finest one; that it was only Ruth who was inadequate, the sickly daughter who couldn't find a man. Well, at least since she had been sick they had stopped trying to pair her up with the sons and cousins of her friends. There was a certain protection in having a scary cough.

Jonnie

"How are you doing back there?" Jonnie asked. She wished the woman hadn't dismissed her private nurse at the station. She felt she ought to keep an eye on her coughing passenger, but the roads were so twisty and narrow, with the adobe garden walls of the houses almost scraping the sides of the big wide limousine, she had to keep her eyes straight forward Her neck was so stiff she could feel the muscles freezing into a position that would hurt all night.

"Just drive," said a weak voice from the back.

"Are you sure you're all right?" Jonnie asked.

"The doctors will take care of me. You do your job."

Her passenger reminded Jonnie of the captains' wives in Gloucester. Even if they had been girls at high school together, once they married and went off to live in their big houses, they never had a nice word to say to the old chums who ended up working in the cod-liver-oil plant or the liquid fish glue factory, even though those stinking barrels of fermenting livers were making the captain's families richer and richer. Well, she wasn't standing around covered in fish slop and blood today; she was driving a fancy car and wearing a crisp uniform. She loved the little tie, which she was relieved to discover clipped on, since she had no idea how to tie it.

The limo hit a particularly deep rut that bounced it up and down. The passenger yelped with each jerk.

"Get out to the edge of the road," the sick woman said. "Get where it's flat."

"It's not flat anywhere, this is New Mexico. These roads aren't like in the East. These are just mud that's hardened. Like the houses. They're called adobe." Jonnie felt like an old-timer compared to her passenger. It already felt like she had been here forever, not just the hard days it had taken to find this job.

While Jonnie had looked for work she had learned all she could—it helped to keep her from thinking about her hunger. One morning she watched Indian women put a mud paste over the bricks of an adobe house. She asked for a job, but they just giggled, and Jonnie looked back in confusion. Finally one woman held her mud-covered light brown hand next to Jonnie's white one, as if to say that a white hand couldn't get muddy. Jonnie had pointed to the calluses on her fingers that had been there since she went into the cannery at fifteen. The Indian woman rubbed her own hand softly against them, as if to rub them away. Jonnie felt warm and they smiled at each other. The woman reached into a pretty clay pot covered by a folded flour sack and drew something out which she carefully laid in Jonnie's hand. It was warm and soft and smelled spicy. She gestured with her hand for Jonnie to eat. It was her best meal since the one at La Fonda. Jonnie promised herself that when she had money and a kitchen, she would learn to cook like that. Maybe a nice Indian woman would teach her, like back in Gloucester when the women shared recipes as they stirred the fish liver barrels.

The car bounced across a hole and the woman in back moaned. "It's not much farther," Jonnie said. She wouldn't try to be friendly again. Twisting and turning along the narrow streets, the car finally reached the edge of the city and she turned onto the Camino Del Monte Sol, a curving steep road that would take them to the sanatorium at its peak. The passenger was so quiet now Jonnie couldn't even hear her raspy breath.

She had been told not to bring stretcher patients to the tall carved front doors of the main building, where they might be seen by the healthier patients relaxing on big slatted wooden chairs. She swung around to the rear and with great relief finally pulled the car up to the stretcher entrance.

When Jonnie opened the door, the lady lifted herself up on an elbow, struggling to sit up. Her breath came in big loud whistles, and her face was greenish. Her elbow crumpled and she reached out desperately. When Jonnie caught her, she lifted the passenger right off the seat, because she weighed almost nothing, her body hollow as pieces of horseshoe crab shell. She screamed in shock and then retched all over Jonnie's tuxedo suit.

The attendants arrived, pushing Jonnie aside as they took over. One of them grimaced at Jonnie, whose tuxedo was as covered with vomit as her apron had been doused with fish guts at the cannery. She felt as if she hadn't moved up in the world at all.

A magpie flew overhead, flapping its white wings and tail slowly. Jonnie had never seen one back home, and she loved to watch their slow flight. Not too far in the distance was Monte Sol, from which Sunmount took its name, a gumdrop-shaped little mountain looking more like the green hills of home than the bare peaks of the Sangre de Cristos behind it. Jonnie was learning those beautiful Spanish names. Back home, names were as sharp as the waves smacking the rocks at Halibut Point: Gloucester, Essex County, Commonwealth of Massachusetts. Here, names were as soft and curving as the adobe buildings and the sturdy women who built them.

Ruth

On her first night at Sunmount, Ruth was too worn from the journey to sleep. She lay in her room wheezing and dazed, barely aware of the furniture or decor. Coughing from the adjoining room went on and on until she almost screamed for silence. Then suddenly it stopped. The windows were open and a wave of cold clean air blew in. She could hear a tiny tinkling sound, almost like leaves in the wind, but not quite. She had never heard anything like this before.

In a few minutes the breeze stopped, the tinkling ended, and it was unbearably quiet. She missed the familiar sounds of her city apartment, of the elevated trains and the horse-drawn trucks and the trolley bells. The silence from the room next to hers was chilling. Had her unseen companion coughed her last? In the distance an animal howled, then several animals, like a pack of dogs. There was a shriek and the howling crescendoed. Her own breath stopped—not from the asthma, but from terror. Should she check on her neighbor? Shouldn't someone be with her?

Ruth struggled to sit up but could barely rise on her elbows. Even in the cold air, sweat poured off her body. She would be next to die alone here. She gasped for breath. She fell back on the pillow, trying to relax. Pray, she told herself, at least die with the "Sh'ma" on your lips. She said aloud, "Hear O Israel, The Lord our God, the Lord is One." In this strange place, the words comforted her in a way they never had before. In this strange place with wild animals and dead bodies, she didn't feel alone. She was with all of Israel in the desert.

She had been such a tiny girl when her mother first took her to the synagogue. In the deep velvet cushions of the pews, her legs were too short to reach the floor. They sat in the first row of the women's balcony, where Ruth stood on tiptoes, leaning over the railing, to see the men below with their heads wrapped in their white linen tallit, swaying and mumbling. As in a slow dance, some would stand by the Ark and the Torah, and then glide back to their seats while others took their places.

"Mother," Ruth whispered, "when can we leave?"

"Shhh. It's the most beautiful part. Now we say the Sh'ma. Remember how we practiced? Now you can say it, too."

The men droned something vaguely familiar, but they were in their own world. There was no place for her little voice.

"Ma, please," she whined. Her mother stared into the distance, mumbling along with the men. Ruth's foot had fallen asleep and she rubbed it. Her wriggling made a scratchy noise from her crinoline skirts.

"Ruth, you must behave." Her mother grabbed her hand and held it. Below them, a man sang a long sad song, his voice rising loud and falling away into whispers, over and over.

"Mother," she whispered, "you're right, there's that song we learned."

"Shhh."

"Are they going to sing "Bicycle Built for Two?" Ruth whispered. "Because I know that one better." She had learned it from a player piano roll.

"This time I really mean it," her mother whispered harshly. Ruth went back to trying to see her reflection in her shiny Mary Jane shoes.

Ruth must have fallen asleep to this memory, because she was startled awake by a crashing sound in her room. In the dim light she could make out a very small man picking something off the floor just a few feet from her bed. Did he have a knife? Should she scream? But no one had come for the cougher. Perhaps no one would help her.

"Please," she rasped, her throat dry and nose stuffed. "I'm only a sick woman. Please don't hurt me."

Morna

The truck carrying the order for canned goods rumbled across the wash and up to the trading post. The Navajos in the store smiled happily when they saw the crates marked "Heinz" being unloaded, because they knew these had their favorite food, canned tomatoes. Morna never wanted to eat another canned tomato in her life, and she wished they could be more varied in the goods they offered, but she and Jack had learned the hard way. Their biggest mistake had been canned sardines. When they found out what was in the greasy, paper-wrapped little tins, their customers had walked out of the store en masse. Navajos considered the eating of fish to be barbaric. Jack had lured them back with a free smorgasbord of their favorite canned tomatoes and crackers.

As she tried to think of a more creative way to stack cans, the truck driver pushed a small pile of mail into her hand. There was a stiff envelope postmarked "Santa Fe." Morna didn't recognize the return name or address, but when she opened it, she was startled by a photo of her face with a strained look on it. It took a moment for her to remember the woman photographer who had passed through. She had clicked this one quickly just as Jack came in. Morna stared at it, fascinated, seeing her face as she had never seen it before. It was her face, but she didn't want it to be. It was the face of a woman who had forgotten love and hope and joy.

Before moving west, Morna had read all the books she could find about the West. She and Jack had both been working long hours to earn the money for the move, and a trip to the library or the bookstores was their big treat. She remembered one early spring day, when on their walk to the library they had watched the few purple crocuses struggle against the city cement and talked about how wonderful it would be to go to a place without cement and the skyscraper canyons that had begun to rise in Manhattan.

In books about the pioneers, Jack was taken with the pictures of cowboys in their leather pants and big hats. He'd joked about how their old friends Bert and Blumie must dress this way now as they painted their landscapes of Taos. Jack pretended he was wearing the leather pants and shook his groin suggestively. But Morna had noticed something else. All the women in the photos had pinched, dour faces. Sad women stood by covered wagons. She felt as if they were trying to tell her something. Now, as she saw this photo of her face, she recognized that same look. She felt as if she had ignored their warnings. She remembered how she had been about to show the pictures to Jack, but he had grabbed the book and found some pictures of an Indian dance, and they had gone home chattering about all the sights they would see and paint. Morna had forgotten about the pioneer women's faces.

She thought back to the day the two women visited the trading post. What were their names? One was Betsy, but she wasn't the photographer. There it was on the back of the photo, stamped "Photographic Studio of Laura Gilpin, Santa Fe, New Mexico. Finest Portraits in the Southwest. Experienced Photog. Graduate Clarence White School of Photography, New York City."

Clarence White School. The name jumped out at her. Laura may have been going there at the same time she herself had been at the Art Students League. But Laura looked so natural here, so much a Southwesterner, not a New York transplant who stuck out as Morna did. Laura had trained in New York and come to the Southwest, too. But how was it she had her own studio now and was doing the work she had trained to do?

But hadn't Morna said that she needed the vacation to the Navajo country to do what she loved? Still, at least she was doing photography and had her own studio. The only thing artistic Morna did these days was try new ways to stack cans. She wished she could ask Laura how she'd gotten so far. You'd think a woman without a man, or even two women without men, which Morna was pretty sure the two of them were, would have a harder time of it than a married woman with a strong husband. But at the thought of Jack as a successful wage-earner and provider, Morna choked on a laugh and ended up in a snort that made the Indians in the store stare.

Morna looked at the picture some more, thinking of the smiling picture she had hoped it would be. Back in art school, there was a lot of talk about truth in art. This wretched face was true. Would a smile have been true? Maybe Laura wasn't happy doing portraits, but she was true to her art. Morna had to credit her for that.

"Miss," said a Navajo man who had come right up to the counter. He started to lean over to see the photo, but Morna snatched it away. Then she wanted to kick herself, because it was a rude thing to do, and they were working so hard to build friendships here. The Navajo man said nothing, just turned and started to walk out.

"Come back," she said contritely. "You can be the first to try our new shipment of canned tomatoes." But he didn't turn, and she saw Jack glaring at her.

She didn't want Jack to see the photo and see how she had looked at him, so she hid it, but she couldn't stop moping about it. Whenever she smiled ingratiatingly at a customer, she was aware of the insincerity she was selling along with the canned tomatoes. She had never warmed up to the Navajos nor they to her, but they were honest and she knew she wasn't. She was pretending with Jack, too, just to keep up enough of an illusion to make her trapped life bearable.

Some white people idolized the Indians and tried to copy their ways. Jack tried that, although it never went past the way he held his body or the accent he tried to put on. It made him even phonier. The old trader who'd sold them the trading post had done better. It had been his sincere demeanor that had convinced them to buy the place. She and Jack had once laughed about the New York art scene and how their fellow students had groveled to the rich and powerful in their scramble for patronage and exhibition space. By going west, they were going to escape all that. But wasn't she in worse shape now, forcing out phony smiles for people who could barely scrape out a nickel for a box of crackers? She was selling herself for nothing. No, not nothing. She was doing it to get to stay here for more of this hopeless, endless life they had built for themselves.

They had gone west to live with beauty and art in Taos, and instead they were living with mud and horseshit thirty miles from some big rock, and not even a rock beautiful enough that an artist would want to paint it. Meanwhile, Jack's old friends in Taos were now a "school" of artistry, and their paintings were turning up on calendars and advertising and museums all over the country. Jack's brushes were dried out and useless from his last impatient attempt to get going again. She remembered the night when she had sat on the roof of their Greenwich Village walkup, picturing herself gathering clay from the same rich beds the Indians potters did, yet she had never tried to do that in all these years here.

Tomorrow, she would tell Jack she was taking some time off. She would get clay to work with. She could set up a work space in the storeroom. She would take a little time off every day, and do a little at a time, and soon she would be a potter again. It wouldn't matter what else she did all day, because she would be thinking and dreaming about art again. It would soon be her fiftieth birthday, but it wasn't too late. Georgia O'Keeffe, who she remembered vaguely as just one more woman painter at the Art Students League, was the toast of New York now, and she was past forty.

Jimmy Klah, wearing a plaid wool red and black lumberman's shirt tucked into red, white, and blue striped pants that must have come from an Uncle Sam costume, came in for his weekly purchase of chewing tobacco. Morna usually dreaded looking at his stained teeth, but as she looked out the open doorway in the direction of a wash that she thought might have a clay deposit she smiled at him. It was a real smile, full of promise and promises to herself.

Ruth

"Buenos Dias," said a high, child's voice. The small man who had scared her was just a dark-skinned boy with a very round face and a friendly smile. "I make you fire," he said, and held up the bucket of coals that had scared Ruth when he dropped it. "I am very sorry for you wake up. I will be quiet." He proceeded to build and light a little stove in the corner of the room.

Despite the scary night in this unfamiliar place, Ruth was relieved to find herself warm and rested. Her head felt clearer and her breathing so much easier than usual that she felt good enough to sit up and look around the now sun-lit room. Her traveling trunk, with "Ruth Weinstock, 145 Utopia Parkway, Bronx, New York City" stenciled on it, was near the open door. A dresser with a rocking chair stood beside it. At the foot of the bed was a colorful striped blanket that she wished she had the strength to reach out and touch. The windows were covered with white lace curtains. If they were pushed aside, perhaps she could see the mountains as she had from the train.

The whitewashed walls were bare, except for a framed set of "Rules of the Establishment," which hung on the door. Ruth smiled as she read them. She certainly had no intention of lighting the fire. The Mexican boy was perfectly adequate. And in her weak state, she would certainly not be making noise or cooking in the room.

Over the fireplace hung a picture of a Madonna with waves radiating from her head, like the Statue of Liberty.

"The Virgin of Guadalupe," said the boy, who had just finished with the fire. "She protects us. Do you know Mary? She is like Mary for my people." He made the sign of the cross on his heart.

"I don't know Mary," Ruth answered. "I'm a Jewess."

He started at Ruth blankly.

"Jewess, I am Antonito," he said.

"Oh that's not my name," Ruth said. "I am Jewish."

He squeezed his lips tightly together as he thought, then he broke into his bright smile again.

"I am Tewa," he said. "I am from San Ildefonso pueblo. Where is your pueblo?"

"The Bronx," Ruth said. "New York." They smiled at each other. The heat from the stove was reaching her, and she liked the cheery dance of the flames. Suddenly a terrible coughing sound came from the next room. Ruth was glad to hear this sign of life from her neighbor.

Holding up his matchbox, the boy said, "I have many fires to light." Smiling, he pulled back the curtains and left. Immediately a man came in. He didn't say anything, and Ruth grasped the blankets high to cover her nightgown. He gave her a funny smile, the meaning of which became clear when he replaced her bed pan with a clean one. She closed her eyes with embarrassment and didn't see if he smiled at her again.

Now someone else entered the room. It was another boy, taller but so identical to the first that he looked as if he had somehow expanded. He was struggling with a heavy tray. He wore a gleaming white jacket. Ruth slid over as he placed the tray beside her in bed. He snatched the covers off the dishes and left.

Ruth felt so lazy, staring at the food with everyone rushing around her. Eggs, toast, hot cereal, cream, and orange slices were stacked high on heavy white china with blue rims. She sucked a bit on an orange slice. Everything else looked beautifully prepared, but too rich for the crisp air that delicately blew in. The curtains were now open. In the distance, the bright glare of the sky formed a corona on the soft contour of the distant mountain range. The mountains formed the profile of a sleeping woman, as if she could see herself lying in this bed.

Soon a nurse came in. She was tall and thin with sparkling eyes.

"No appetite?" she said. "Or just not a breakfast eater?"

Ruth shrugged. She had been in many hospitals and dealt with many nurses, from the condescending baby talkers to the ones who acted like commanding generals. She had learned to get the feel of a nurse before letting on what kind of patient she was. She was also so caught up in the new environment that she resented finding herself in that same old role of the invalid in the bed. She was in a new place but still the same old person, still the sick one to be served by the healthy.

"That's okay. There'll be plenty of food all day. Just eat what you can, and if you want something else later, just ask. My name is Betsy Forster and I'm a nurse."

Ruth was pleased that she gave her last name. She hated that most nurses said only their first, some as if it meant they were instant friends, others as if it meant they were to stay passing strangers, despite the intimacy of bedpans and scrub baths they were to share.

"All you need to do is rest," Betsy said. "Many staff people will stop by to make beds and so on. When you feel better, please feel free to sit out in the sun. There's no need to dress."

Ruth stared at her.

"I mean, a bathrobe will be fine. Have you been to New Mexico before?"

"Never been west of Manhattan."

"Can you smell the sage in the air?" She breathed in deeply and Ruth followed, although her breath was always so shallow. There was an unfamiliar scent.

"When you're feeling stronger, you can walk around the grounds. It's so lovely out there. I'm just back from vacation myself, out where the Navajo people live. There's so much to see!"

Betsy left and Ruth basked in the warm sun, surprised by Betsy's warmth and suggestions. Most nurses treated her as if they expected to find her body cold the next time they saw her. Betsy had said she would become strong and go on walks.

"Maybe I will," she said out loud. Already her voice sounded stronger.

All that morning, people went in and out of Ruth's room. A boy swept the floor, then a maid changed the sheets after helping Ruth over to the rocker. A large black and white bird flew slowly across the sky. Ruth wanted to take a closer look.

A boy in a white jacket brought a clean glass of cold water and a sheet of paper with a menu on it. She had him move the rocker so she could sit with her face practically in the window. She could see how the land dropped off just a few feet beyond her room. She was on top of a hill. The land below was a dusty brown and there were no houses.

When the boy came back to take her order for lunch, she wasn't ready. She stared at the list of foods, delighted to have a choice. Although the doctors in New York had always urged her to eat all the roasts and heavy soups she could, and her mother had stood by to make sure she ate it all, the heavy food had always repulsed her. At home and in the Jewish hospitals where she had stayed there was only kosher food. Before sending her to New Mexico, her parents had held long discussions with the rabbi about the non-kosher food she would be served. The rabbi had decided that to save her life, the rules were allowed to be bent, just as a nursing mother is allowed to eat on the fast of Yom Kippur. She had promised not to eat pork and not to mix milk with meat.

Ruth checked off the fruits and vegetables. There were also foods she had never heard of. She could choose red or green chile, so she took both. She wanted to know everything about this strange place, even if she couldn't yet walk in those beautiful strange lands out the window.

When the food came, she wasn't sure what was what, but she ate it all. Some was so spicy her throat burned, but after a few minutes her nose felt unusually clear and she was breathing in the sage air deeply.

After lunch, Nurse Betsy returned and took Ruth's pulse and temperature.

"How was the food? Is there anything else you would like?"

"The fruit is so fresh."

"The orange groves in California are not that far. You look like you're feeling better."

"It's so beautiful here. I wish I could take a walk."

"I'll bet it won't be long," Betsy said. Ruth was too shy to look at her. She looked far out the window.

Later that morning, with a boy holding each arm, Ruth climbed into a wheelchair. It was rolled onto the sunny porch and a colorful blanket wrapped around her legs. The porch was built flat on the ground, and faced a courtyard of porches all around, except for one side which opened to a view of the mountains. In wheelchairs and rockers, many other patients sat facing the sun. Some read, others rested with eyes closed or covered with washrags. There were blissful, relaxed smiles on most faces.

In her lap was the latest book by Willa Cather. Pain in her eyes and head let her read only in short spurts, so she used every chance she had. But her attention was soon caught by a soft tapping sound. A large black bird with white wings and a prominent tail slowly flapped its way across the courtyard.

She must have looked very startled, because a woman nearby spoke up.

"It's a magpie," she said. "Have you never seen one before?"

"No."

"You must be from back east. The birds are different here. See that blue bird?" She pointed to a blue jay that had just landed on a funny, gnarled tree nearby.

"It's a blue jay," Ruth said.

"Look closely," she said.

She saw that although it was a blue jay, there was something rougher about it.

"Looks like it just tumbled out of bed without combing its hair."

"Just like people. Refined in the east! Scruffy in the West!"

Ruth pulled up the blanket to cover her bedclothes, feeling anything but refined.

"We call that a piñon jay." Ruth liked how she rolled the n in "piñon."

"Do you know a lot about the birds?" Ruth asked.

"Just from sitting here. You get a lot of time to watch them. Better get used to it."

The magpie took off again. It flew so slowly Ruth could see how its wings, tail, and feet all worked together. When it disappeared over the rooftop, she wanted to call it back so she could study it more.

It was hot under the blanket so she pulled it down. She felt warm and cozy from the sun, and something about watching the bird made her feel excited in a way she hadn't felt in a long time. She could see another bird far off, flying in from the mountain. There was something about the light that made her feel that her eyes had sprouted telescopes. She wanted to know everything about these birds, and about the strange gnarly tree the piñon jay sat on. Was it like anything back east?

Something was happening. She was discovering a new world. Was it the liberation of finding her breath again? Or was it this combination of light and warmth and sights to see? Maybe this trip was not a last resort, but a new beginning.

Jonnie

Jonnie knew that the only reason Sunmount Sanatorium gave her the job was because she fit the uniform. She was the only woman driver they had ever had, and she overheard the guests complain, especially the really rich ones who were used to a piss-elegant Brit or something to drive their cars. "I thought this was five-star, I didn't feel safe with that weird one driving" she heard one say. Jonnie wished she could explain that there was nothing wrong with her driving. Those city folks just weren't used to bumpy unpaved roads.

She preferred the few poor patients, who were thrilled to find themselves in a fancy car with a chauffeur. One of them even said, "I can die happy now, I been treated like a queen."

She hadn't seen much of Dr. Mera, who ran the place. When she wasn't driving, she was supposed to stay in the garage. She had to go in the back door of the kitchen for lunch. The Spanish help lived with their families in little adobe houses, and some Indians lived at the pueblo, but the white help bunked together in a fixed-up chicken coop on the edge of the grounds. It was crowded, and she had only a bunk and a little shelf, just like a sailor. It made her feel that they were all on a crew. Maybe it was more like working on a luxury liner than on a fishing schooner, but there was the good feeling of being part of a gang. All day she heard "Howdy, Chonnie," and "Buenos Dias, Chonnie." She was already learning a few of the Spanish and Indian words. She didn't miss home at all, because it was as if she had moved to another little town.

But there were a lot of deaths for such a small town. It was probably a good thing Jonnie didn't get to know the patients well, because some didn't stay long. Back in Gloucester men were lost at sea and never seen again. Here they sent the bodies off to the funeral home in town quietly and quickly. She drove for that also, in what the staff called the death car. That was creepy.

Just like back in Gloucester, the rich people, which most of the guests were, wouldn't talk to the working folks, even if a few minutes before they had held them while they coughed what sounded to be their last. The nurses weren't really friends with the kitchen help, and the kitchen help looked down on the maids and house boys, and they all looked down on the cleaners who took care of a room after a guest died.

The nurses were all white, the kitchen help Spanish, and the cleaners were Indians. And then there was Jonnie, who didn't fit anywhere, even though she was white, because most of the nurses looked down at her for being the driver. A few tried to be nice, especially Betsy, a happy woman who seemed to follow her own rules with the patients also. It got so Jonnie would go out of her way to run into Betsy just to get a friendly smile from someone. But Betsy had mentioned that she was leaving soon to work on the Navajo reservation.

Jonnie could see that Sunmount was just right for the sick guests. Those who could sit up spent all day in the sun. They could ring a bell for a house boy to bring chocolate milk on a silver tray. They slept in lovely whitewashed rooms scented by the fresh sagebrush breeze. The service made most of them perk up like a fish thrown back in the water. It was good to see, except that as they got to feeling better, they would get back to being more of whatever they were like before they got so sick. The arrogant ones would boss everyone around, and the kindly ones would take care of the scared newcomers. With all the leisure time, gossiping tongues wagged like a deck awash with fresh catch.

What bothered Jonnie was how they would change toward her. Many passengers cried during the car ride from the train, telling her their every misery and fear as if she was their only friend so far from home. But once they got well enough to bicker over who got which rocker on the portal, they would look right through her. The same woman who had sobbed to her that she feared she would never see her dear son again, she would now hear muttering that Jonnie must be a very strange woman to wear trousers and a tie.

Jonnie wondered when Dr. Mera would insist she switch to a new uniform with a skirt, but he didn't seem to notice. She liked wearing trousers, which were easier to get around in than in long skirts. She hardly ever saw other women wearing trousers. It was like back home. You weren't supposed to look different. Gloucester folks didn't mind a girl hauling heavy barrels of cod livers, because cannery work is girl's work, but after the time her father took her out on the boat because her brother Joe had gone off drinking, he got ragged on by all the other guys, and she got looked at funny by all the women. Jonnie had loved it on the boat. The wind hit hard in her face and everything happened so fast, especially pulling in the nets and seeing the catch, but her father never took her out again.

She really liked this driving job, especially standing proud next to a big shiny car in her fancy uniform when she met the train, but folks wouldn't let her be. Movies and books about the cowboy life had made her think there was a place out west where people could do what they wanted, even women, but now she wondered how much farther west she would have to go to find that. But she didn't want to leave Santa Fe. She liked it here even with the problems.

On her half-day off, Jonnie wanted to explore her new neighborhood. She needed a change, because she couldn't get her mind off a patient whose body she had driven to a funeral home that morning. She'd asked the Spanish cook how she dealt with all the dying patients, and was told to go to the church, so she decided to take a look.

She didn't see any white shingled Unitarian Universalist churches like in Gloucester, with just a simple cross and altar. The Spanish church reminded her of the Portuguese church back home, Our Lady of Good Harbor, which had a bright blue dome instead of a steeple and lots of fancy decorations. Inside the Spanish church in Santa Fe she marveled at the big dolls dressed up like Jesus and the saints and Mary and another lady with lights coming out of her head who they called the Virgin of Guadalupe. Her picture was everywhere, even in the restaurants.

The altar was a fancy wood carved one. The winding staircase to it was carved from tree roots. Colorful carvings and paintings and tin crosses covered the wall in front. It was a brown adobe building with thick walls, but it didn't have any stained glass windows, because in the days when the Indians might attack, it was the place the Spanish went to hide. The walls inside were all whitewashed, but there were painted sunflowers on tall thin stalks right up the side of the wall. She had never seen anything like it, and she was so busy looking at everything she forgot to think about why people get sick and are in such misery and finally die. She decided that maybe that was how it worked for the Spanish, too.

Ruth

Sunmount Sanatorium had a better class of people than Ruth had expected—fancy enough to satisfy her mother. If only they would stop coughing and start looking pink and ruddy, her mother would probably be finding out who was Jewish so she could try to marry her off to a lawyer or businessman. When they talked on the portal, you would have thought they were sophisticated and charming folks on a relaxing vacation. It reminded her of how they "took the waters" in *Anna Karenina*.

"What's it worth to you, Sharon?" a man a few rockers down the portal called to the woman to her left. They had been flirting all day, between his racking coughs and her gasps for breath. At first, scenes like this had looked as tragic to Ruth as watching Mimi in *La Boheme*. But after a few days, she had settled into the sanatorium way of life, in which sickness and dying and even death alternated with a sun-warmed face, a glass of chocolate milk delivered on a silver platter by a smiling boy, and the ongoing entertainment provided by the charm of some of the guests. All around her strangers met, commiserated over their symptoms, shared their stories of cross-continental travel and their wonder at the western landscape, and gradually settled into daily routines of sunshine and rocking chairs.

What they didn't do was whine or speak in the hushed, pitying tones she had heard from her family for so long. There was a lighthearted way of being at Sunmount. She wasn't sure if it was a way of coping with all the sickness, or the joy that came from sitting peacefully in the sun. In any case, it made her happy, too.

Ruth's mother had mailed her a package of evening clothes. Since she spent the whole day happily wrapped in a brightly striped Indian blanket over normal clothes, she gave the gowns to the ever-friendly chore boys to give to their mothers and sisters. She asked her mother to send a fine pair of binoculars, with which she watched the birds every day. When she saw a bird, she wrote down the time, and soon learned that their routines were as regular as that of Sunmount's staff. At first she wrote on the vellum "Sunmount" stationery, but one day she glanced at the methodically organized medical records clipped to the end of her bed and saw a better way to log the lives of the birds. Soon her notebook filled with detailed notes of the times and places of their movements.

Ruth was disappointed when Nurse Betsy told her she was leaving to work in a Navajo community, because Betsy was the only person who always asked to look over Ruth's notebooks.

"I've been wondering," Betsy said. "Would you like to try painting the birds? We have handicraft classes here if you'd like to learn how."

"I have better ways to spend my time," Ruth snapped, the words tumbling out before she thought. For a moment they stared at each other, Betsy surprised at Ruth's anger, Ruth embarrassed at her rudeness and angry that Betsy was leaving. Betsy had been a gift, and Ruth was more comfortable with her than anyone else. She looked forward to the daily sponge baths, when Betsy would patiently listen to Ruth's chatter about the lives of the magpies and jays.

"I'm sorry, I was sharp," Ruth said. "It's just I don't like painting."

"No harm done. And you don't have to do anything. You're here to heal," Betsy said soothingly.

Ruth didn't know what to say as Betsy finished up her work and left the room. She had seen Betsy as a friend, not like the hired help at home. But her thoughtless tongue had pushed her back over that line. She had been on a pink cloud in this happy place and now she had ruined it for herself. Betsy would remember her with pity instead of friendship. Ruth was miserable for the rest of the day, half-heartedly watching the birds, whole-heartedly beating herself up.

The next day, Betsy was friendly as ever, but in her misery Ruth could only feel the stiffness between them as they went through her morning medical routine.

"You're not saying much about the birds, today," Betsy finally said.

Ruth waited for her to ask condescendingly, "what have you seen lately?" like some of the other patients did, but she didn't. She fell silent again. It was why Betsy had become special to Ruth. She couldn't lose her. Suddenly, her thoughtless tongue knew what to say.

"It's just I had to go to art school," Ruth sputtered. "It didn't seem I was going to marry young, and I wanted to go to the Massachusetts Institute of Technology and study science like Ellen Richards, but my parents said that was no place for a girl. They said I should go to art school 'like a young lady' or no school at all. So I went, and I did the classes and the exercises and spent so much time on how to hold a paintbrush. They wouldn't let me go to the live model class, where I could have learned about muscles and how bones move. That was the only part I might have enjoyed, but they said a respectable girl shouldn't be in a room with a naked man or even a naked woman. So that's why I don't like to paint."

"Oh," said Betsy. She looked thoughtful, not pitying. She was always touching Ruth, with a sponge, or to help her into bed, or to give her medicine, but right now Ruth's hand reached out wanting to touch Betsy.

"Art school is where I first got sick, too," Ruth said. "The doctor thought maybe it was something about the closed hot rooms with all the paints and thinners. I'd always been healthy, but suddenly I was gasping for breath every night. At least it got me out of going to that school. I was glad about that, but I just ended up back at home with mother, sick in bed. My brother would come home from Cambridge on school vacations and tell about football games and drinking clubs and going sleighing with girls, but nothing about his classes or his laboratories at Harvard College. He had all I wanted and threw it away.

"I had hoped to get a job and live on my own and do what I wanted, but soon I was too sick. That's how it's been for all these years. I did everything the best doctors said. I ate steak and heavy cream even though it made me throw up. I kept the bedroom windows open at night, even when the howling winds of January blew right through, and I had snow on my bedcovers right in our apartment. It was like living in a log cabin on the prairie. But my asthma only got worse. That's why I'm here. It's a last resort."

"Are you feeling better here?" Betsy asked.

When was the last time she had woken up in a twisted sweaty ball? When had her eyes stopped hurting so badly she covered them with a wet cloth? How long had it been since she had worried that her next breath would be her last?

"I think I am," the words struggled out of Ruth's mouth. "I am getting better." A jay screamed outside the window.

"She wants you to join her," Betsy said, pointing toward the sound. "I know you will."

Laura

"Do you know where my green hat is?" Betsy asked, poking her head into the room in their home that was Laura's studio. Laura twisted the knobs on her view camera up and down, trying to remember how it had been set for an unusually good portrait she had taken the week before.

"That wool one I got last Christmas?" Betsy continued.

"Christmas! We almost dried into mummies out in that desert only a few weeks ago. You don't need a wool hat."

"It won't be summer forever. I can't run home every time I need something."

Laura stopped fiddling with the camera and looked up just as Betsy went back into their bedroom, which was the room that had the door to the studio. At the moment, the bed was covered with suitcases and clothing. "How often will you come home?" Laura called out.

"I don't know. If I'm there to help sick people, I need to be there all the time. Besides, who will pay for gasoline? I'm hardly getting enough to live on."

"But when will I see you?"

"You'll visit every few weeks. We'll save our money for that. You'll take photos." Betsy had come back to the doorway and they stared at each other.

"I've got to get back to work," Laura said. "I have a model coming in. That Guggenheim application is due—"

"We haven't thought this out much, have we?" Betsy said. She was always the one to keep them talking.

"What difference does it make, you're going." Laura turned back to the camera.

"But the Navajo people—" Betsy started as the bell jangled and in walked a white man almost bent over from the heavy camera case he carried. He stumbled and almost dropped the tripod. His clothes were rumpled, his wispy white hair stuck out all different ways, and tufts of whiskers came from his ears. Just as the door was about to slam behind him, in glided an Indian, graceful and erect, his mahogany skin dark against the white sheet he was wrapped in.

Betsy discreetly went back into their bedroom and closed the door.

"Hello, hello," said the white man to Laura. "This is Martin, our model. His cousin is the governor of Taos pueblo. Have you ever seen cheekbones so sharp? They create shadows on their own." His gaze invited Laura to join him in staring at the man.

Martin stared back and Laura dropped her eyes. He looked like he had walked out of an Edward Curtis photo. It wasn't that long ago that Curtis had taken the photos; perhaps this man had been in them. How old was he? It was hard to tell when it was so hard to look at him. She had to pull herself together and get the argument with Betsy off her mind.

"Where do you want to set up, Irving?" she asked the other photographer.

"It's smaller here than I thought," he said, Laura winced. "Maybe we should do this one at a time."

Laura pointed Martin toward the thick adobe bench under the window. "You might as well have a seat. This could take a while."

"Ladies first," Irving said.

"I'd like to watch you. I've never had a model to myself before. Just in classes."

"Okay." Laura moved her camera out of the way and Irving set his up, facing the studio wall that had a bland background that she used for the wedding and graduation photos that were her bread and butter.

"So, uh, how, uh…." Laura tried to speak to Martin, but realized she had no idea what to say. She wished Betsy would come back. Betsy had made friends with the Navajo men so fast the day they got lost. When she visited Betsy, would she ever know what to talk about with the Navajo patients?

Martin sat erect on the bench, not even leaning against the wall. There was something angry about him, but that was good. That was the quality in the most famous portraits of Indians. Having a model cost plenty, and she was losing an afternoon of work. She had been taking studio portraits of white people for years. How different could it be to take a portrait of an Indian in her studio?

If only the pictures from Mummy Cave had come out better—but they hadn't. She just wasn't good enough yet at photographing the huge open landscapes. When she visited Betsy, there would be so many beautiful vistas, but it would take time to learn and so much money for film and chemicals. She had to get the Guggenheim this year, if she was ever going to photograph anything more than wedding and graduations and funeral portraits.

"Okay, chief, do you know how to put these on?" Irving asked. Out of his suitcase he brought a fur jacket and a tangle of rattling jewelry. Laura saw Martin scowl. Carefully placing the jewelry on the bench, Martin held the jacket out in front of him. It was a bearskin, the head hanging limply backwards.

"Genuine Comanche," Irving said. Martin sighed as he draped it over his shoulders. Irving pulled on the clump of jewelry until he had freed a necklace of bones and bells which he put over Martin's head. He slipped an armband of sharp animal teeth around each arm. All the while Martin's face grew fiercer than the clothing.

"Now, stand that way," said Irving, pointing Martin so he was in silhouette to the camera. "Just like the penny."

Laura envied how confidently he turned the knobs to set the height and angle of the camera. Then he adjusted her studio lights so much she was embarrassed. Oh well, Irving Couse was a painter more than a photographer. Working with color, he had a different set of values about light. But even when color film became affordable, she would never choose it over black and white. She would use the shadows and glare on Martin's face while Irving held Martin's chin and turned the Indian's head.

"That's it, don't move," Irving said, running back under his black cloth. Martin was already so expressionless and unmoving that it seemed unnecessary to say it. For the next few minutes Irving clicked the shutter, changed the lights, adjusted the model, and put in more film than Laura used in a month.

She could hear Betsy in the next room. How often would they see each other? They had lived together for twelve years now, except for the miserable year she had gone back to Colorado Springs to help her useless father bring his turkey farm back from near bankruptcy. What would it be like to sleep alone, night after night? She hadn't told Betsy everything. Betsy had been so happy since the day she got the letter from Oliver LaFarge at the Indian Association saying that she had the job at Red Rock, that Laura hadn't told her about the calls from the printer who had done her Pike's Peak brochure, demanding the rest of his payment and threatening to go to court.

When Laura had studied at Clarence White School of Photography in New York City, one of her most unforgettable afternoons had been spent at the New York Public Library looking at reproductions of the books that the poet William Blake wrote and illustrated. There wasn't a dot on a page that he hadn't planned. The words and the pictures more than went together. They were exactly as Mr. White taught, that the design of a page should be as composed as any other design.

From the day she first saw them, Blake's books had been Laura's inspiration, although it wasn't until she returned to the West that she was able to make her own brochure. With all the tourists staring at Pike's Peak, she was sure it would sell.

It hadn't been easy to find a printer in Colorado Springs who didn't mind Laura hanging around and being bossy. Most printers would have just thrown the photos on the page any which way, snipping that "we aren't used to letting the photographers tell us how to do our job." But this one had done exactly what Laura asked, putting some photos across the page and others vertical, and placing her words telling about the photo just where she wanted them. Blake's drawings and handwritten poems were swirled every which way, but photographs had to be squared off and captions placed in the most effective position.

When the brochure was finally done, Betsy had turned the sixteen pages as if she was looking at the most beautiful object in the world. Laura had beamed with pride. But only a handful of the brochures had sold. Laura had lost her nest egg and still owed the printer. Betsy's job on the Navajo reservation meant there would be even less money for repaying the debt. Well, she wasn't going to get perfect photos today by worrying. She watched Couse fiddling with the knobs.

"I'm just not getting it," said Irving. "Just don't feel it. Oh well, I'll just fix it in the painting." Laura thought he said it to put a spark in Martin, but Martin's expression did not change. It wasn't proud anger so much as resentment. Even if all the settings and shadows worked out, it would never be what she needed. A sulky Indian was not the story her photo must tell.

Irving moved to the side as Laura set up her camera. She adjusted the knobs self-consciously, wishing things were different. Maybe if she had the model to herself. Maybe Martin just didn't like Irving. Maybe Betsy would stay a day at the Navajo reservation and come right back.

She wasn't sure how to set everything for the man's dark face. Had she only photographed white people? She had never thought of it that way.

She didn't have the supply of film to waste that Irving did, which meant she didn't have the time to get Martin in the mood. Then she had an idea. She would take the first several photos with empty film holders. It was a trick she had used before with anxious sitters.

The first pictures went so badly she was glad she hadn't used film. Although the fur fit snugly on his wide shoulders and the armbands made his muscles bulge, somehow Martin looked like a man whose clothes didn't fit. Were they too large or too small? But it wasn't the clothing. It was his attitude. How could she tell him not to be so resentful? He was being paid well. Irving hadn't needed to give much direction about Martin's facial expression since he could paint whatever he wanted. But with a photo, it was there or it wasn't. Right now, it wasn't.

Maybe if she put film in. Maybe he sensed she was faking it. She reloaded for real while Irving rustled through his suitcase.

"Ah, I did bring this. It's a New England Indian war club. Genuine." He handed it to Martin and directed him to hold it like a scepter.

But Irving looked bored and Martin sullen. It wouldn't even be worth the chemicals to develop these photos. This whole session was an expensive mistake. What else could she do in time for the Guggenheim deadline? She should cut her losses now.

"Thank you, that's all for today, you can get dressed." Martin moved more quickly removing the costume than he had all afternoon. Laura went to get her wallet. When she turned back he stood with the white sheet wrapped around his head, his forehead and chin almost covered, his eyes slightly wet. She couldn't identify the emotion in his face, but this was it. She reached to the camera and snapped the shutter. Martin jumped back, startled. The moment was lost but she knew that she had it. She had it forever, if her lights and camera had been right.

"Man in a sheet," said Irving. "Looks more like an A-rab than an American Indian. Wasted your film on that one."

"We'll see," said Laura. The man who had not been there all day had been there for that instant, as if he had just walked in. Who had worn the bearskin? If the Indians believed that some other spirit took over when you wore the skin, it had not been a spirit she could use in a photograph.

Later, when she came out of the darkroom, the wet print dangling from tongs, she almost pulled the doorknob off going into the bedroom.

"Betsy, I've got it, they might as well give me the Guggenheim."

Betsy's hair was wrapped in a towel and she was looking critically at a dress with a huge stain on the bodice.

"You always say that," Betsy said. "And I'm never drinking wine again."

"Look at this. I'm sure this will do it." Laura held up the print.

Betsy took her time looking at it. It was one of the reasons Laura loved her so much.

"I think you're right. This is gorgeous. It glows like there's a light right in him. And there's something about it, hmmm."

Laura thought so too, as she had thought when she snapped the photo, but she waited to see if Betsy could say what it was, because she couldn't put it in words.

"I thought Irving Couse brought a lot of Indian stuff for him to dress in."

Laura's heart sank. "He did, but it didn't look right. I don't think he's the right kind of Indian for those props. I took that when he put his own clothes back on." She paused, afraid to ask more. "You think he needed the props?"

"No, I don't. That's what's so beautiful about this. I see a man, not a costume. With Irving's paintings, I get so distracted by the jewelry and feathers. That must be why I've never liked them. I see a person here."

Laura breathed out, relieved.

"You know," Betsy continued, "I just don't look at the Indians the same since that trip. I don't think I would have seen this before I played cards with them. And meeting the Navajo workers at Mummy Cave. Don't you feel that?"

Laura didn't, but maybe that was why she had been so frustrated with the model. A model—what did that mean? In his own clothes, it was a photo of a person, like those she took so often.

"Well, since you're sure to get that Guggenheim, we won't have to worry about you visiting. There will be time and money" Betsy said as she hugged her. "It will all work out. This is our time for doing what we dreamed of!"

Morna

Jack griped so much about being left alone in the store without the truck that Morna reminded him of the lofty ideals he'd held about the modern woman's potential when he was tossing back a few with their friends in New York. She felt low thinking how far they had slipped from their dreams. It wasn't just Jack. What had happened to the white dress she had trotted out for so many suffrage marches? In those days, women stuck together. Now she was the only white woman for forty miles and the only woman likely to march for the vote. She pictured her customer Mrs. Manyskirts in a white Victorian sundress. She'd wear it over her black velvet tunic, coils of silver necklaces, and many long brown skirts. Morna giggled, picturing herself leading a parade of Navajo women so dressed.

She was actually giggling! It was a gorgeous day, and she was happy to bounce along the ruts in the truck that Jack almost never let her drive.

The pink earth and piñon-covered hills made her want to bury her hands in and dig out rich, lovely clay for potting. Off in the distance were red, blue-black, and black flat-topped swatches of land, which the Indians had been turning into colored pottery for centuries. She imagined having an exhibit at the Metropolitan Museum of Art. For the opening, she would invite all the old gang from the Art Students League, even that teacher who had given her a pitying look every time he checked her work.

Perhaps, like Georgia O'Keeffe, who only wore black, she should always dress in a particular style. Georgia's success had something to do with the way Steiglitz presented her to the American public so that she stood out as much as her art. Maybe she should have nude pictures taken, as Steiglitz had taken of Georgia. Perhaps that woman photographer from Santa Fe could take them. But picturing herself naked in a studio before another woman, especially that somewhat masculine one, gave her a chill.

Better still, she would make lovely, unique pottery, carefully ship it and herself back to Manhattan, find a new lover with a new camera, and present herself in authentic Navajo finery to the museum curators. She could dress just like a Navajo, only without all the dust and dung on the bottom of her skirts, and New York would take notice. Georgia O'Keeffe would be yesterday's news.

She was headed to where the Indians got their clay. By paying far more attention to them lately and starting conversations about pottery making, she had finally hit pay dirt. The week before, a truckload of Indians had stopped by late in the day. They looked hot and tired, but happy, as if they'd come from a picnic in the sun. The children's faces, hands, and clothes were streaked with a reddish green mud. The woman who purchased some canned food had a clump of mud in her hair. With her few words of Navajo and gesturing with her hands, Morna found out which direction they had come from and how far they had driven. Now she was driving that way herself, at last. Everything was very dry and although there wasn't really a road, she soon picked up a rutted track, which made her hopeful.

Grinding slowly along in the ruts, she watched the colors of the earth. There was a reddish cast like the streaks of mud on the Indians in the store. The ruts ended in tire tracks, as if they'd parked the truck, so Morna stopped, too. Not too far away was a cave-like hole in the red mud, with many footsteps leading to it. It looked like a heavy bucket had been dragged along the ground.

The hole itself wasn't very big. She would have to get down on her knees and reach in. What if it was an animal's home? She needed a stick to prod first. What if an angry animal jumped out? But all the noise of the truck hadn't caused that. She didn't see any paw prints.

How would she dig the clay out? She had only thought to bring empty cans to carry it in. There weren't any strong branches in this barren place, just the reddish soil and brittle shrubs. She checked the truck, hoping Jack had some tools there. Of course! Jack kept shovels and crowbars for digging the truck out.

Gingerly, Morna poked the longest shovel into the hole, almost doubling over to do it. Her shadow made everything dark. The shovel scraped against a rocky surface. She pushed harder. The shovel clanged against rock, but then sank into something soft. She dug in to loosen a clump, then pulled the shovel out and set it on the ground. The dirt was pebbly like gravel, dark, reddish brown with green spots, and felt noticeably moist in this otherwise totally dry world. She wanted to dig and dig until some hidden spring burst forth, with a waterfall of cold, crystal water she could sit under. But if that had been possible, the Indians would not need to visit their trading post for water.

She plunged the shovel back into the hole, eager to pile up the clay, picturing the filled cans. Soon sweat poured into her eyes and her shoulders ached. It was hard to push the shovel in from her low bent-over position. When she pulled it out, the clay dropped back into the hole. Her skirt was soon streaked with clay like the Indians had been. She would lie to Jack that she had fallen pulling the truck out of a ditch.

Morna could see why the Indians made a party of work this hard. She hadn't expected it to be like this. She wasn't sure how much clay she needed, but since she might not get another chance, she wanted to fill all the cans. But her back twinged with every move, and she just wanted to get done and leave. She was also beginning to wonder where she would hide the cans near the trading post.

A strong hand clamped her shoulder.

Morna didn't want to turn around. She just wanted to crawl right into that hole of cold, silent clay. Jack had followed her, and now she had to explain. Maybe it was just as well. Maybe they would finally talk about what had gone wrong with their lives and dreams and marriage.

But when she turned around, it wasn't Jack at all. It was Mrs. Manyskirts, and she didn't have that concentrated look of slow deliberation she had when she was choosing how to spend her pennies on the goods in the store. In the trading post, Morna always stood behind a counter which was constructed so that the storekeeper would always be taller than the customers. Here this very short Navajo woman was looking down at Morna.

Mrs. Manyskirts loosened her grip enough so that Morna could squirm out of her grasp and straighten up. They stared at each other. Morna was never sure how much English any Indian understood. As children, many had been sent to boarding schools for years, but they didn't like to let on they could speak English. Mrs. Manyskirts had never said much.

"I want to get some clay. I want to make some pretty pottery," said Morna, forcing out a friendly smile and holding out her hands as if displaying a bowl.

"No," said Mrs. Manyskirts, emphatically shaking her head.

"I'm sorry," Morna said. "I just thought, it's just dirt, there's plenty of it."

"No," she said again.

"Do you make pots?" Morna asked.

"Dine land," Mrs. Manyskirts said, pointing at the hole and the ground. Dine was what the Navajo people called themselves.

"I know it is," Morna said. "I'm sorry, I should have asked your permission first. Do you think I could have some clay? I just want to make some pretty pots."

"No," Mrs. Manyskirts said. Morna inched toward the truck, hoping that if she could get her into a conversation, it might help.

"Do you have some pots I could sell in the store? We sell so many rugs, but I hardly ever get a pot to sell."

"I don't know."

Morna had learned that "I don't know" almost always meant "maybe."

"You might? That would be wonderful. What do you have?" Mrs. Manyskirts just glared at her. Morna continued on to the truck.

As she was about to climb in, Mrs. Manyskirts said so softly she almost didn't hear, "You come."

She led Morna not very far from the hole. Hidden beyond a rise was a hogan. Morna had thought she was alone and unseen, but now she saw how easily her truck had been spotted.

In the hogan a little girl was playing with a toddler. Both dressed in long skirts and blouses, they were miniature versions of their mother. The older girl smiled when she saw Morna, perhaps thinking of the candy jars at the store. Morna pulled out some mint drops she had stuffed into her pocket that morning. She held them out to the children, who silently plucked them from her hand.

On the floor of the hogan were a few pots. They were more tall than wide, with a crude line of decoration near the flared rim. The color was a dull red. Mrs. Manyskirts indicated for her to pick one up. It was nothing like the delicate bowl with the rabbit design that had so inspired Morna. Even if she had been able to get clay and learn to make pottery without a wheel as the Navajo potters did, it would take a long time to do something even this rough. The impossibility of her latest dream lay in her hands.

Mrs. Manyskirts placed her thumbs at either side of her neck and ran her hands down to join below her breasts. This was how Indians communicated when they pawned their jewelry. She was saying she would trade the bowl to Morna in return for her silver squash blossom necklace, which had been locked in the trading post pawn safe all summer. Normally, when her sheep were shorn and their wool sold, she'd be able to redeem the necklace. That was the credit system on which the trading post worked.

This rough pot wasn't worth the necklace, but if Morna didn't do it, she knew she would be in a lot of trouble. This little trip to take clay from the hole was as much a theft to Mrs. Manyskirts and her people as if they had come into the trading post and taken a necklace out of the display case. Morna didn't know what she would tell Jack. She could only hope he wouldn't notice. She smiled at Mrs. Manyskirts as gracefully as she could.

Betsy

Seated on a hospital cot in the bare bedroom of Betsy's new workplace and home, Laura's face was grim. None of Betsy's arguments were working.

"You could be happy for me. You could try," said Betsy, but Laura just glared.

"We'll see each other," Betsy tried again. "You'll be able to get here every few weeks." Laura shrugged.

"Look at these rooms. All ours. For once we'll have some privacy."

That last argument got a slight nod from Laura, who was often concerned that their neighbors in Santa Fe were learning too much about their relationship. The hospital building was a long adobe. A series of small rooms were connected by low doors—just right for Laura, but Betsy had to stoop. The rooms opened onto the portal. At one end of the building were some rooms for overnight patients, then the dispensary in the middle, and at the other far end, two little rooms all for Betsy. Nothing and no one but coyotes and prairie dogs went near those two little rooms.

"Laura, think of it. No nosy neighbors." They had been living with other people in earshot all their years together. In whispers they had giggled and laughed and tried to muffle their joy with each other. Laura made a sound somewhere between a grunt and saying "mmm" as if tasting delicious food.

"Stop trying so hard to be miserable. Do you want things to be the same forever? Years will go by and you won't know one from the next? This isn't like you. You've always been the one wanting adventures, wanting to take the photos and all."

"It's all happening so fast," Laura sniffled.

"That's how much they need me here. They've been waiting so long for a nurse."

Laura gave Betsy a sulky stare.

"Wait a minute, I think I understand. The adventures were supposed to be all yours. I was just always supposed to be the little wifey at home to kiss your bruises. You can't stand that I want more too."

Laura said nothing, so Betsy continued. "Why would you think that? Do you think we're like a husband and wife? If I wanted that, I'd be married. When we read Elsie Clews Parsons' books about the modern woman, and how she needs more than just the vote, I thought you saw what I saw. Well I guess you didn't."

"Maybe I just better leave," Laura said in a tiny voice.

"That's it? You're just going to leave like that? I thought we had something together all these years. I know I did." Betsy was almost crying.

Laura burst out "Well, which is it? Do we have something or not? You just said we weren't married."

"We're not married."

"I thought we were," Laura said.

"You did?"

"In my heart I did. I don't need a man with a Bible to say so."

"You thought that? That's so pretty of you. I didn't know that."

"Well I did."

Betsy could never stand how they both got when they fought, all closed up and cold. She was always the first to give in, this time reaching over and poking Laura's thigh. She was afraid Laura would shove her hands away, but she didn't.

Someone came to the door. They jumped apart just as arms carrying a steaming pot of food held in a small hand-woven blanket appeared in the doorway, and a voice said "Hello Mrs. Nurse, praise Jesus Lord."

"But I'm unfaithful to you with my profession," Betsy whispered to Laura and went to take the food.

She had met the tiny woman that morning. Her name was Mrs. Ben

Kellywood, and she lived in a hogan not far from the little hospital. They had struggled to communicate with their hands and smiles. The only English words Mrs. Kellywood knew were phrases from the Bible, thanks to the work of the missionary and his wife, who were the only other permanent white occupants of this little community.

The mission was a boxy plain wooden house that looked derelict next to the lovely sprawling adobe clinic. Betsy's new home looked as much a part of this country as the buttes off in the distance. But the mission building was an intruder. Over its doorway was a sign with fading Navajo words. Betsy hadn't met the missionary yet, but when she had stared at the sign, Mrs. Kellywood had said "God Bless Us. God Bless Us. God Bless Us" until Betsy finally realized it was what the sign said.

Betsy had been assured she would have plenty of patients from the homes spread out across the miles of desert all around her. When she had first arrived, she had spotted only Mrs. Kellywood's squat log hogan, but now, by looking where she saw a few horses tied or cattle grazing on the bare land, she could make out more homes. She hoped Mrs. Kellywood would invite her into her home, so she would know what to expect when she went from hogan to hogan to find out the general state of the community's health and to deal with immediate cases. Betsy was so ready to start that she almost wished sulky Laura would leave. But then she was mad at herself for thinking that. There would be plenty of lonely nights ahead, especially until she learned to speak Navajo.

In the meantime, she was worried that she and the missionary would also not have much to say to each other. When she'd been hired by the New Mexico Association of Indian Affairs, she'd been told that the missionary had tried to block the reopening of the hospital and the return of a public health nurse to Red Rock. Having seen the statistics on the health of her new patients—including the high infant mortality, the short life span, the prevalence of diabetes, the rising rate of alcoholism, and the preventable deaths caused by delay in getting care—Betsy was already angry at anyone who would object to having a nurse on site. The best she could think about the missionary was that at least he apparently wasn't hoping for a nurse to provide his own health care.

"I have to get going," Laura said. She rose to get ready for the long drive home.

Mrs. Kellywood wanted to tell Betsy something. She made a cross with her fingers and held her hands in prayer, then pointed way out in the distance. She held the middle and index finger of one hand over the index finger of the other, like someone riding a horse. Betsy understood that she was trying to explain why the missionary wasn't there. Betsy sensed that Mrs. Kellywood thought highly of the missionary and was eager to introduce them. If she wanted him to change his mind about her, she would have to let go of her anger at him. They would have to work together. Back at the sanatorium, she had gotten even the most depressed patients to smile with her charming bedside manner. She could win him over, too.

Laura would loosen up once she gave it a chance. Maybe the Navajos would let her take pictures of them. Betsy liked Laura's landscape and sunset photos, but when she looked at Mrs. Kellywood's face, so dark and different from her own, and the layers of skirts and strings of silver jewelry she wore, she wanted a photo. She also wanted a photo of Mrs. Kellywood's hogan blended in with the land, and her children playing outside.

There was so much for both of them to see and do here. Betsy didn't want to let anything stop her, not even Laura's moodiness. In her last week at the sanatorium, when they brought her a cake to celebrate her forty-fourth birthday, some of the other nurses joked about her age, but she felt born again, and not in the way a missionary would mean it. There was so much life here after working with dying people for so long. This was her new sunrise in a beautiful land.

Jonnie

Jonnie had noticed that Ruth had been doing well since that first grouchy car ride to Sunmount, but she was still surprised when Ruth asked her to meet her at dusk behind the building and not tell anyone. Ruth didn't outright order Jonnie to help her sneak out, but it felt that way.

"Can you ask Dr. Mera if it's all right?" Jonnie said.

"No," she yelped like a cat that's been stepped on. "If you don't want to do it, don't. Just please don't tell anyone."

"I won't," Jonnie said as she turned away, walking as fast as she dared.

"Wait," Ruth called out. "Have you ever walked out there?" She pointed over the fields that surrounded Sunmount and the mountains in the distance.

"In the mountains?"

"No, just that flat part nearby. You're from the east, too, aren't you?"

"Yes, ma'am, Gloucester, Mass."

"Do you like it here? The way it's different from the east?"

"Sure do."

"But you haven't done much exploring?"

"I've been working pretty much all the time."

"Do you want to?"

"Sure, I don't mind working."

"Not that! Don't you want to see what's out there in this strange place? The birds and the insects and the plants?"

Jonnie thought for a moment. "I saw a big spider the other day. Manny the houseboy had it in a pitcher. It was the ugliest thing I ever saw."

"He did! Oh I wish I'd seen it. Now tell me, why exactly did you find it ugly? Did it have little whiskers on its legs?"

"It was all hairy but I didn't look that closely. It was sort of like a little lobster with mangy fur."

"Do you think he still has it?"

"Mrs. Mera told him to make sure it was dead."

"Oh," said Ruth, as if grief-stricken. "This place is so full of wonders, and I'm not getting to see anything. That's why I need to get out there." She stared into the distance, and then right at Jonnie.

"I can't go alone. I need someone to walk with me. We'll see things you've never seen before, Jonnie. Isn't that why you came out west?"

"Guess so. And to get to do what I wanted."

"There you have it. I want to do what I want to, but no one's letting me. How'd you like to sit in a rocker all day and drink chocolate milk?"

Jonnie had often wondered this while she hustled around Sunmount working and getting orders barked at her, and she had sometimes been envious. But now that Ruth was putting her to the test, she had no doubts.

"It might be fun for a day, but I'd want to get up and get moving."

"That's how I feel staring out there at it all. I have to go see it. I'll go alone if I have to, but I'd really like someone with me. And you want to see it all, don't you?"

"I do. But why can't you tell Dr. Mera?"

"He's like my parents. They made up their minds I would die in bed, and they've spent the last ten years making sure of it. The best thing that ever happened to me was coming out here. I feel good, but no one seems to believe me. They want me to stay sick in bed. You'd think a doctor would want me to get well. Doesn't anyone ever get well here?"

Jonnie didn't want to answer, finally saying, "I haven't been here very long myself. I think maybe some do, but I haven't seen it." For a moment, they looked into each other's eyes. They were about the same age, fifty or so, but Ruth's face was sallow and pale. Jonnie's face was ruddy and pink.

"All right," Jonnie said. "I guess I'd like to see what's out there, too. I'll meet you, if nothing sudden comes up for me to do and all."

"Perhaps we'll see some snakes," Ruth said, looking hopefully at the ground.

Betsy

It was only hours after Laura had left, the two of them hardly speaking, that a steady stream of Navajos sitting tall on horses or bouncing along on wagons passed Betsy's new home. She tried to clean, but finally put down the mop and stood in the doorway watching.

Lilly, a Navajo woman of about sixteen years old who had asked to be her interpreter in return for room and board, had been helping clean, but she too stared wistfully outside.

"Where are they all going?" Betsy asked.

"It's a special day," Lilly said. She waved at a woman passing by with a child on her lap. Betsy thought the woman's smile faded as she saw her unfamiliar face.

"Oh," said Betsy. She had been so focused on getting here that she hadn't had time to think about how she was going to have to make friends and a place for herself here.

"It's a chant. When someone is sick, their family will hold one. There's lots of food, and the medicine men do ceremonies. Everybody comes. Maybe you would like to see?" Lilly asked.

"Are you sure?"

"You can come with me. We can bring guests, and you're more than a guest here."

With a determined smile, Lilly took Betsy's hand and led her over to the line of wagons, where she negotiated a ride for them. Soon Betsy sat on a very hard bare wooden bench, bumping along through a cloud of dust, and peering out through the white canopy arch that covered the bed of the little wagon. She soon lost all sense of time and distance.

As they bobbed along the rutted desert floor, Lilly talked about her life. "I was taken from my parents when I was six, and sent away to the boarding school to learn English and to be a Christian. At first I didn't want to go, and I was very scared. But I like reading and writing. They gave us the Bible and silly books about animals that talk that I didn't enjoy, but I had a wonderful teacher, Miss Rea. She gave me better books to read. Have you read George Eliot?"

When Betsy nodded, Lilly smiled and grabbed her hand.

"No one around here has but me! I loved the part when that rich lady realizes what a mistake she made marrying the old man. It made me see I had to be careful who I married too. Around here, that's not easy. Everyone expects you to marry young, and they have a lot of opinions who it should be. Soon I'll be old to not be married, for a Dine. That's why it's so important to me to work for you. My family won't have to feed me, so they'll be more patient. If I were at home now, I'd have to sit on the floor weaving all day. I hate weaving!"

"You hate weaving! I never realized that could happen," Betsy said.

"Many women like it. It brings in money. But I hate sitting on the floor, doing the same motions over and over. My mother and my grandmother, and my sisters and my aunts, are all very good weavers. I'm sure they will make a rug for you to thank you for employing me. They had just started teaching me on my own little loom when I was taken off to go to school. When I came back from school last year, they started teaching me again. But you have to sit on the floor from when you are a little girl. It hurts so much to start now."

Betsy didn't know what to say. So far she had only seen the Navajo people from a distance, where they always looked so sure of themselves, so rooted in their land and families. Up close, this was a picture she hadn't expected. She decided to say what she might say to any girl this age.

"What would you like to do?" Betsy asked.

Lilly smiled and pressed her hand.

"No one ever asked me that! Maybe it's silly. What I'd really like to be is a teacher. I would teach the Dine girls about George Eliot. Oh, I would teach them about the ceremonies and the land and all the beauty of our lives here," she said with a slow sweep of her hand to take in the pink sands and the clear blue sky. "But I'd also teach them to love books. To know that there is more to do than to weave. I love my mother's rugs and blankets, I love their beauty, but I don't want to spend my life like that. You can't read and weave at the same time."

Then she turned her face away. Betsy wondered if Lilly was afraid that Betsy wouldn't want her to be the way she was, that she would want her to be more like the other Indian women. She had to admit to herself that she was thinking that way. She wondered if most of the Indians would surprise her like this. But why shouldn't they?

"When I was a girl," Betsy said, "my brother was a doctor, and I wanted to do what he did. Everyone said that I was so pretty that I would soon be married. But I didn't want that, so I went to nursing school. Then they wanted me to work for my brother. He runs a little hospital near Denver. But I wanted to be on my own. That's a reason I came here. At my own clinic, I can run things my own way."

Lilly's response surprised Betsy again.

"I hope you won't be like Dorothea in *Middlemarch*. She wanted to help the poor people, but then she forgot about them when she fell in love with the minister. White people come out here to help us, but they don't always help us. But I like what you are saying to me. Nobody ever asks me what I want to do. Can you help me become a teacher?"

"I could try to find out."

"Reverend Luck said he could send me to a Bible teacher's college. But I don't want to learn any more about Jesus. I like our own stories about our sacred mountains and Spider Woman. I don't believe in Jesus, but I would have to say I did to go to that college. Do you think I should?"

They stopped at a great circle of wagons. Horses rested while people in blankets and skirts ran about. Lilly helped her jump off the back of the wagon.

Betsy saw several small gatherings, something like a three-ring circus. She wasn't sure she was supposed to be here, so she hung tightly to Lilly's hand as if it were an engraved invitation. Lilly stopped outside a huge circle. In the center of the ring were a few young men in breechcloths and leaning over them were two men in masks and costumes performing a ceremony. At first Betsy thought it was only for the young men, but then she saw some girls waiting to enter. Their shiny black braids hung low over their shoulders. There was plenty of noise and children running around, but this group was solemn as a church. Clearly, it was some kind of ritual, and she wished she knew more of the language.

Lilly pulled her away. They walked past a line of tables of food. There were greasy puffs of bread, tiny peaches, and cans of tomatoes. It reminded Betsy of a church bazaar, but she had never been at a church bazaar while a religious service was also going on. Lilly led her into a large hogan made of carefully cut, handsome logs. Sunlight through a smoke hole in the center of the ceiling illuminated the floor, which was almost completely covered by a brightly colored painting. The colors were bright red, black, blue, yellow, and white. There were designs on it in black. She recognized an arrow and a stalk of corn in each corner. A man squatted in one corner and slowly trickled a red powder through his fingers. It went right through, as if his fingers were a sieve. He finished off the last corner and straightened up. The sand painting covered the whole floor except for a border just wide enough for a ring of men to sit around it.

Betsy leaned forward to see more of the picture, but Lilly took her arm firmly and pulled her into a line of people who were slowly circling the edge of the hogan, tiptoeing carefully behind the men's backs. Betsy was afraid she would fall on a seated man in the solemn tent, and she was relieved when Lilly led her back out again.

The sky was turning pink from the setting sun. There were many small cooking fires and soon wisps of smoke drifted everywhere. Two long lines had formed, one of men and one of women. They ended at the hogan where she had seen the sand painting. Lilly led her to join the line of women. Two men were carried up to the hogan and seated against the wall. They passed closely enough for Betsy to see their pale, almost yellow faces. Betsy wanted to go help them, but Lilly sensed her straining and gripped her hand tightly.

At the far end of the long lines, a group of male dancers appeared with a loud clattering burst of energy. They shook gourd rattles with one hand and evergreen branches with the other. Fox skins hung from their loin cloths. Feather bracelets circled their wrists and calves. They wore raccoon masks with black circles around their eyes. Their high headdresses made them very tall. Where their skin was bare, it was painted in gray and black striped mud. A low pulsing chant and drumbeats throbbed from all around Betsy.

The most ornately dressed man led the chant, and the two sick men answered his song. In the darkening light, eyes would occasionally flash in the firelight. Betsy felt the throbbing rhythm vibrate in her chest and imagined the power that the two sick men must be feeling as the force of the crowd's energy directed to them. She thought of the times when she had held the hand or hugged the shoulders of a sick patient and tried to will her health into their body. Sometimes she had felt the patient take in the surge of energy and swell with new vigor, so she could understand how this healing ceremony was meant to work. She felt stronger herself, as if this day was also initiating her new life here.

There was a sudden pinch at her shoulder, and Lilly dropped her hand. Betsy's heart sank as she realized she wasn't supposed to be here. She looked at the Navajos around her, expecting fury and distrust in their faces. She pictured the clinic unused because of this terrible mistake she had made on her first day. But it was a tall white man in a preacher's collar and hat who put his face, red from both smoke and anger, right in front of Betsy.

Jonnie

All day, Jonnie worried about Miss Ruth's request to walk outside the grounds of Sunmount with her. Jonnie had broken rules in her life, most recently by coming out west instead of spending her life in a cod liver factory, but she was still scared. No staff member had ever said, "Jonnie, don't take a guest for a walk," but she had never seen anybody, guest or staff, walking in the strange no man's land beyond the buildings. She thought that it might belong to the Indians. Maybe they had their burial grounds there. She hoped she would be called on to pick up some new TB guest at the station at the time she was supposed to meet Ruth, but it was a quiet afternoon.

Miss Ruth was already waiting behind the building. She wore big field glasses around her scrawny neck and carried a notebook.

"Come on, it's getting dark. We won't have much time. Next we shall do this at earliest dawn, so there's more light. But dusk is when the birds are out."

Jonnie followed her. Her walk was shaky and Jonnie asked hopefully if she would rather do this when she felt stronger.

"I'm just weak from being stuck in that rocker. I have to get my legs back working." She pulled up her shoulders and walked straighter. Jonnie was still a little angry for being pulled into this, but at the same time she had to admire Ruth. She was a brave woman to do this while all the others were happy to just sit and rock. Since she had been wearing the tuxedo and driving the limo, Jonnie had been watching for women who weren't behaving in the usual ways, like Nurse Betsy, who took time to talk with her like a friend instead of a more lowly staff member.

Ruth must have planned out the route with her field glasses, because she quickly walked down a slope and out of the view from the sanatorium. From a distance, Jonnie hadn't thought there was much to hide behind, but she headed for a place where the scrubby little trees and cactuses were about as tall as they were. Suddenly she stopped dead in her tracks and Jonnie stumbled right into her. Ruth gasped in pain but said nothing but a tiny "shhh." She was staring at a bird that pecked at the ground. It's just an old blue jay, Jonnie wanted to say, but she watched it solemnly, as if she had never seen one before.

Ruth stood silently as the jay pecked at the ground. Even fishing, Jonnie had never been this still. After a while, she forgot about trying to keep her breathing quiet and watched the bird, too. It wasn't exactly like a blue jay back home. It was blue and big for a bird, but the colors softer and the points not as sharp. It made her think about living in the West, how you didn't have to dress so neat or act so perfect. This blue jay looked like it was on vacation, relaxing on a camping trip. She liked how it poked in the ground, looking for food. It reminded her of her own hard days without money.

It was fun to watch up so close. Jonnie could feel how happy Miss Ruth was, as she very quietly slid a pad out of her skirt pocket and began to sketch. The blue jay didn't notice them. Jonnie thought that if she had been alone it would have flown off, but Miss Ruth seemed to want it there so much it stayed for her. Maybe she convinced it somehow, as she had persuaded Jonnie to help her take this walk. But now Jonnie was glad she had given in. One of the big black and white birds slowly flapped over a twisty little cactus. Miss Ruth balanced her pad on her knee and her pencil dashed over the page.

As the sun came down, the reddening sky colored everything. There was a little breeze, the chatter of birds, and the scratchy sound of Ruth's pencil. Jonnie felt calm, remembering times when she had sneaked out of the hectic cod liver oil factory to sit on the quiet wharf listening to little waves lapping.

You're doing great, Jonnie Bell, she told herself. You're out west, you have a good job, people like you and ask for your help, and you're seeing things you never saw. She let out a sigh of relief so loud that Miss Ruth looked around to see if some new animal had just poked out of the brush.

There were sudden loud snaps and cracks, and Dr. Mera stamped towards them. He was a big, clumsy man who broke through the quiet scenery like a steaming locomotive. All the birds immediately flew off. Miss Ruth straightened up and waved her arms behind her as if she were trying to hide Jonnie.

"Why Miss Weinstock," said Dr. Mera, slowing to a gentler pace, "It's a lovely day for a walk, isn't it?"

"I've been wanting to take a closer look at the birds and plants," Ruth said, in a sweeter voice than Jonnie had ever heard her use.

"How nice," he said. He didn't acknowledge Jonnie. "Why don't you tell me what you've seen?" He moved closer to Ruth. Excited by his interest, she told him about the jay. He took her arm and steered her in the direction of the sanatorium. They walked slowly, Jonnie trailing behind. They missed what she saw then, a hawk flying across the sunset. It was beautiful but she knew that somewhere out there it was going to swoop down and snatch up something soft and gentle and unprotected.

Back at the big building, Dr. Mera and Miss Ruth disappeared inside. Jonnie headed to the garage, took out a can of wax, and started shining furiously. She hoped he would see and remember what a hard worker she was. He wouldn't want to lose her. Maybe he hadn't even noticed her; maybe she had somehow been invisible out there. She was willing to stay up all night polishing the cars, but when hers was the only light still on, she turned it out. There was no need to remind him.

The next morning, Mrs. Mera came into the garage. She had never been there before. She held out a small envelope.

"Dr. Mera won't have employees who encourage the guests to be rebellious and endanger their fragile health," she said. "We've given you a lot of leeway, but we suspected a woman who'd dress like you would go too far."

"But Miss Ruth wouldn't take no for an answer," Jonnie said as the envelope was shoved into her hand.

"Be sure to leave the tuxedo with the laundress," Mrs. Mera said as she walked off.

Betsy

By the side of the angry preacher stood an equally tall, bony, and angry woman. For a moment they all stared. Finally the woman gestured with her chin at the man and he spoke as if she had just wound him up.

"Sister, we mustn't encourage them," he said. Still holding Betsy's shoulder, he tried to pull her away from the crowds of Indians. She looked around for help, but Lilly was gone. The Navajos hadn't made her feel like the only white person in the crowd, but this white man did.

"What do you think you're doing?" Betsy said, moving out of his grasp.

"Sister, I am Reverend Luck. I have been saving the souls of these heathen for many years," he said in a rehearsed manner. Betsy immediately pictured herself mimicking him for Laura's delight.

"Sister, the Association of Indian Affairs has charged me to look out for your safety. I shall be glad to accompany you back to the field hospital."

"And I am Mrs. Luck," said the woman, moving a little closer to him while he inched away.

When he hired her, Oliver LaFarge had warned Betsy that the local missionary might be a problem. He certainly hadn't said they had asked

Luck to look out for her, in fact, he had steered her to look out for Luck, because the last nurse had left in frustration from the missionary's interference. "All your references say how calming and charming you are with your patients," LaFarge had said, as Betsy blushed. "Just stay your sweet self with him and everyone else. Many Navajo people are sincerely drawn to what Christianity offers. Others see it as a way up from poverty and go along with him. Many will resent the threat to their traditional ways. They're just like people everywhere, every one with their own needs and beliefs. You're going to have to pick your way through it all carefully. Just don't let the Reverend get to you. We need you to stay long enough to help."

It had seemed easy then, but now Luck had already "gotten to her." She wanted to stay as long as the chant lasted and learn as much as she could about her new community. But through the smoky haze she could see some of the Indians watching. The Lucks had already been so rude in making a scene, and she didn't want to make it worse. When the missionaries turned and walked away, she followed, feeling the eyes of the Indians watching their backs.

"Mrs. Luck and I would like you to join us for prayer service each morning at eight sharp," Luck said as she got into their car. As they bumped back along the road, Mrs. Luck mumbled lines from the Bible, sometimes under her breath, sometimes loudly. Betsy felt very tired from the long, extraordinary day. She wished Laura was with her, but then she was mad at Laura for not being there. It was this man who suddenly had taken a lot of power over her who she should be angry at, but it was easier to be mad at Laura.

"Sister, would you tell me what church you have attended? You will find that our services are open to all Christians. And heathens, too, of course, who come to accept Jesus Our Lord," said Mrs. Luck.

Betsy didn't want to answer. When she was a child, a neighbor lady had antagonized the churchgoers by reading fortunes from strange playing cards. She considered making up a story in which her parents shared in that religion, but she worried it would make them even more rabid to control her soul. The drive would take a while and she didn't want them stopping the car out in the desert to pray over her. She needed a strategy, but she was tired and her skin felt encrusted in smoke. She wanted a bath and a clear brain, and time to think about the healing ceremony and whether all that smoke and noise could possibly help the men with the yellowed skin.

"Sister," Mrs. Luck said more loudly. "Are you awake?"

Taking that as an escape, she pretended to be asleep. It gained her a few seconds. But must she let this woman make her act like a child? Without any pretense that she was suddenly waking up, she said, "Reverend Luck, I was not aware that the Indian Association had any connection with a missionary group."

"We are all one in the Lord," he said. "And we are all charged to bear witness to these unfortunate people. I myself have saved the souls of many. Mrs. Kellywood and the others who will be working with you are all Christians. It is the reward our Lord gives them for their faith."

Betsy wondered just how saved Lilly must be to have wanted so much to go to the chant that she had brought Betsy along.

"You have been rewarded for your faith," Mrs. Luck said. "Without the faith of your forefathers, you too would be living in dirt and painting yourself with mud like these savages. Can you deny that faith has lifted you up?"

When Betsy didn't answer, she went on.

"These women die in childbirth. These men die of little scratches that fester. These children are covered with flies and blind with trachoma from the sandstorms. Is this how you would want to live? Jesus took us out of these hovels."

"But I'm a nurse. Don't you think I will be helpful here? But first I need to learn about my patients."

"Our mission is hoping to send us a Christian nurse to join us here. But perhaps you are a Christian woman. You haven't said."

Of course she had been raised Christian. But no one had ever put her on the spot like this. Betsy couldn't help but think about the lions and the Romans. If she defended herself, she would again be in that childish position of doing what the Lucks wanted. If she threw the question back in Mrs. Luck's face, she knew she would feel like the angry adolescent she had once been, sassing her mother whenever she could. Was there no way to just be an adult here? Reverend Luck and his wife looked not far past thirty years old. He could be Betsy's son, but she could not picture this horrible woman as her daughter. A daughter of Betsy's would be loving and happy. This woman's mother must have been like one of the grotesque masked creatures at the Indian chant.

"I'm here to serve the health needs of this community. I have thirty years of experience as a nurse. I shall be glad to serve the health needs of your family, also, if you wish. The Indian Association is satisfied with my qualifications, I am sure."

"The Indian Association! Do you know who pays their bills? Freethinkers and artists! Alienists and seditionists! Rich nonbelievers! I've heard of their parties and their wild houses in Santa Fe and Taos! They admire the heathens and they collect their idols. I believe they even worship them. You should look to where your money is coming from, Sister. They don't care about the Indians. Do you know why they want them to stay healthy?"

"Why wouldn't they want them to stay healthy?"

"They just want them to continue living in their hovels, making their pots and weaving their rugs, so they can all make money off the Indians. They are the ones who exploit them, who don't want them to change and grow into good Christians living Christian lives, rising above the dirt. They come here in their big cars, they wrap themselves in Indian blankets, they take part in the heathen ceremonies. They keep them down! They don't let the Lord let them rise up!" By this last part, she was shouting and he was pressing so hard on the gas pedal that the car bounced along the rutted road, and the ride was as bumpy as the hard seat of the Navajo wagon had been.

"Is that what you want for them, Sister? Because I don't, and I don't just visit them to stare at their strange ways. I've lived here for years, I know their souls. Do you think in one day you know more than me? More than us?" she added with a glance at her husband.

Betsy didn't have an answer, but she was glad that they were talking on the level of adults. This is only the first battle, she thought. What a day this had been! She had started it with hope and joy and plans. She had spent hours in the mystery and wonder and something of chaos of the Indian gathering, and was ending it now, as his car drew up to the clinic, with her skin and hair covered with a layer of smoke and grease and the realities of their presence and arguments. Right now Laura would be cozy and warm and clean and soft in their bed, but she was here in the very cold light of dawn trying to leave his car with as much dignity as she could.

"Eight sharp, Sister," Mrs. Luck said. "We shall expect you for morning prayers."

Inside her new home, Betsy was preparing to heat the kettle for a bath to clean off all the smoke and grime of the fires at the Indian ceremony when someone pounded on the door of the clinic. An agitated young man stood on the doorstep, gesturing desperately with his fingers. He hadn't had time to put on a shirt, and his hair streamed loosely down his back instead of pulled up in the tight complex knot the men usually wore. He held his arm and screamed with pain, then pointed off in the distance. She threw some clothes on and grabbed her medical bag. She headed for her car, but he shook his head, mimicked having to push it through deep sand,

and helped her onto his horse. Then he climbed on the saddle ahead of her, and they were off across the desert.

Betsy had never been much for riding, but realized that she had better get used to it. She bounced and bounced until finally he stopped and helped her off.

All that was in sight was a steep dune-like hill. He signaled for her to follow him up the slope. By the time she finally saw the hogan, Betsy was breathing hard. He lifted the blanket that covered the little doorway and she climbed through and down into a round windowless room.

A little girl lay on a pile of blankets, her mother wailing as she stroked her head. The child's right arm was blackened and swollen. They had cut the sleeve off her pretty blouse, and her long skirt was half charred. She was breathing shallowly and appeared to be in shock. Betsy bent down and examined the wound. She was relieved to see that it looked much worse than it probably was. If they could keep it clean, it would heal all right. As she worked, the parents calmed down and the mother offered her some bread still warm from the stove that the girl had stumbled against. The mother kicked at the stove to show that she was angry at it for burning her child.

As the sun rose higher in the sky, the room grew light enough for Betsy to see more. The walls were thick logs interwoven to form almost an octagon. The floor was just the desert sand, with piles of rugs here and there to sit on. There was no furniture. A big black hat with a tall crown and wide brim hung on the wall. One area was the kitchen, with the few pots and baskets and cans of food neatly stacked against the wall in what would be the corner of a square room. A stovepipe ran from the small cast iron stove up to the very peak of the roof.

As she came out of shock, the little girl began to cry. Betsy could see she was as scared of Betsy's presence as she was in pain, so she smiled and patted her. She was demonstrating to the mother how to change the dressings when there was a commotion outside, followed by the entry of Reverend Luck holding a Bible before his chest like a shield.

"We missed you at morning prayers, Sister," he said to Betsy. "So I've brought them to you."

Behind him stood the Navajo father. His face was blank, but when Betsy shot him a look as if to say "What is this jerk doing here?" he shrugged his shoulders helplessly. Reverend Luck pulled out a prayer book and leaned over the little girl. The parents glared at him. The father tried to motion him out, but he brushed past and fell to the ground by the child.

"We call on Jesus to help this child. Jesus helped the little children," he muttered over the child. The mother ignored him and gestured for Betsy to go on showing her how to do the dressing. Reverend Luck was caught up in his fervor and didn't notice. A few minutes later another Navajo man came in.

"I'm Mathew," he said, "I help the Reverend to bring the gospel to my people."

"I am the Rock and the Redeemer," shouted Reverend Luck, his words booming through the increasingly crowded little room. Matthew said something in Navajo to the parents, and Betsy realized he was interpreting Luck's words into Navajo. Luck smiled and began telling a story about someone named "Eye-ti-zack" and his son, and Mathew would repeat each line enthusiastically. The parents were watching their daughter and paying little attention.

Luck was so dramatic in his storytelling that it was a few minutes before Betsy realized it was the story of Isaac and the sacrifice of his son, with God and Jesus and the sacrifice of His son mixed in. If she could barely recognize it, she wondered how close Matthew's interpretation would be. She looked forward to when she understood enough Navajo to find out what Matthew was actually telling Luck's flock.

"And so, the Lord Jehovah said," roared out Reverend Luck, "you must give up your child unto the fire, so that you can be born again, in Jesus name." When Matthew told that to the parents, both gasped and glared at Luck. The mother shook her finger at the stove and then at the Reverend. He put his hand on the big cross he wore on his chest, and smiled benevolently upwards.

"What's going on?" Betsy asked Matthew.

"They have only had the stove a week. Reverend Luck's home church in Pennsylvania raised the money to put modern stoves into five hogans. But the little girl didn't understand that the fire is inside the stove, so she got too close. Two Sheeps"—apparently the father's name—"and his wife are angry at the stove and at the Reverend for hurting their child."

"They'll learn that the stove will help them," said the Reverend to Betsy. "They are Christians now and they cannot live like savages in a cave with an open fire. Matthew, I need your help." He turned back to his Bible, and Matthew went back to his task.

Soon the child was sleeping peacefully. The mother was content, and seemed to understand Betsy's instructions. As soon as Reverend Luck left the hogan, Two Sheeps said something to Matthew, who nodded reluctantly. Betsy looked at Matthew inquiringly.

"He has asked me to send one of our own healers for the girl, and I said I would."

"But what about Reverend Luck?"

"Two Sheeps is my cousin, so I have to help him. Reverend Luck won't know. Are you going to tell him?"

"Of course not."

Mathew smiled appreciatively, so Betsy felt comfortable to ask, "How did he know I was here? And he found me at the ceremony yesterday."

"He always knows what's going on. His most devoted followers tell him. But they don't tell him everything." He smiled at Betsy conspiratorially. "We live across miles and miles, but many people are on the move with their sheep and horses. There isn't much to talk about, and someone new is big news. Already everyone has heard about the new nurse. Soon everyone will come to take a look at you."

Matthew explained the conversation to Two Sheeps and his wife, and they smiled at Betsy. Mrs. Two Sheeps took a can of tomatoes from her tiny open-air pantry and handed it to her gratefully.

Jonnie

Getting away from home, being in a new land, seeing new faces, knowing she wouldn't die keeled over a reeking barrel of cod liver in the factory on Gloucester wharf, Jonnie told herself that she had enough. She hated to lose the Sunmount job, but there would be another job. She had saved a little money.

But she had lost a place to eat and sleep at the sanatorium. She also missed wearing the dapper chauffeur's outfit. Fortunately, she soon found some work at La Fonda. Mrs. Monahan, the manager, had taken a liking to her, even if she wouldn't let Jonnie wait tables. She gave Jonnie driving jobs for the restaurant, because the men would get drunk or into a card game and forget to bring the deliveries, but she knew a Gloucester girl would come through. She let Jonnie eat in the kitchen sometimes.

She found a place to live in an abandoned adobe. There were quite a few around the outskirts of the city. Folks didn't tear down houses when they got old. They just let them slowly sink and rot and go back to the mud they were made out of. Neighbors noticed she was living there, but no one said to get out.

Her new home was halfway falling down. At one end most of the roof had fallen into what must have once been the bedroom, and at the other end, well, there wasn't another end. The wall had fallen over into what must have been the garden, because squash and corn were growing there all on their own. Jonnie slept in the middle room, which had once been the kitchen. The walls and roof were soft and flaking off chunks, but they were standing. The first night she was so scared that it would all fall on her that she laid her bedroll half out the doorway, but once she got through that night she stopped worrying. In a crack in the crumbling wall was an old newspaper about the Rough Riders, so Jonnie figured if it had been falling for 30 years it wasn't going to go while she was there. It didn't rain much at night, and there were none of the screaming mosquitoes they had back home, so most nights she slept out in front of the house.

Best of all, she had found a pile of old Indian blankets. She hosed them down and let them dry in the sun, and soon she had the most beautiful bedroll a cowboy ever saw. One was red, black, grey, and white, with diamonds and lightning bolts woven into it. Another had a picture of a little train with smoke coming out of the smokestack. She guessed that the Indian weavers had woven in the news of the day, back when the train was big news. She made a bed of hay and cleaned up some old horse blankets to cover it. With a few flowers in a Mason jar by the foot of the bed, she had a cozy home.

Sometimes at La Fonda, she watched the waitresses, trying to figure out what they had that she didn't. She thought maybe she could learn and finally be a Harvey girl. Then one day she watched one come out to polish the sign. Her long white apron kept blowing up in her face, and she almost tripped on the porch in her tight narrow shoes. It finally hit Jonnie that she would much rather be outside and wear pants than doing anything a Harvey Girl did. If Mrs. Monahan had let her have a waitress job, she would have to live in their crowded convent dormitory attic instead of wrapped tight in her bedroll, watching the stars. Jonnie thought about her hay bed and decided she was doing pretty well.

The Harvey girls were friendly, stopping by to chat while she ate in the kitchen. She was invited to little parties up in their living quarters. They liked to talk about how to find a rich businessman to marry, or which customer might be a rich landowner. They were always pumping Jonnie for what she found out as she drove around town picking up the supplies. Jonnie was learning who owned what around town, so they said she was in the best position to pick out a good husband for herself, but she told them that if she had wanted to get married, she would have done it back home and been some fisherman's wife. They asked why she didn't, and she said she wanted to see the world.

She had to be careful what she said, and what she did and how she dressed and everything. One reason she had left Gloucester was because everybody knew everybody's business going back to their grandparents and beyond. Here everybody was new, and nobody knew any one else's family, but they soon knew all about you. At La Fonda, Jonnie felt people watching her as much as they had at Sunmount.

She wished she could drive out of town and into that wild-looking scrubby country where Miss Ruth had tried to walk. Maybe out there, Jonnie could do what she wanted. There it was more like the Wild West of the magazine articles and movies. It was too late to homestead like the pioneers, but she wanted to save her money and buy some land of her own. But she didn't know what she would do on the land, because there was as little water around Santa Fe as there was too much of it back home.

One morning, she was outside of La Fonda when a big black tourist autobus pulled up. In front it looked like a car, but it went back and back and back with lots of seats. A dozen or so people piled out of it. They were all badly sun burnt, but they were smiling and chatting.

"I'll never forget how you looked climbing up that footpath," laughed a lady, clapping a man on the shoulder good-naturedly.

"How 'bout how you looked when you backed into that cactus?" said the man.

"I feel like I'll never get this out of my mind," said another woman. "And I never want to. It's the most beautiful place I've ever seen."

"I just hope my photos come out," said the first man. "Hey, let's get some food before the train comes." They all headed into La Fonda, leaving only a tall woman unloading suitcases from the back of the car. Now that the crowd had moved off, Jonnie saw a sign on the car that read *"Indian Detours."*

She loved how the tall woman was dressed. It wasn't like the Harvey Girls, whose black Mother Hubbards reminded her of how she had been made to dress when she first started at the fish canning factory back in 1895. When she looked at their clean white aprons, she pictured them covered with the slime and blood of fish guts.

This woman was dressed how Jonnie thought a woman should dress in the West. She had a velvet jumper blouse and a plain kind of skirt, but it was the jewelry that made her so pretty. Her belt was like the ones some of the Indian men wore, a string of silver disks big as saucers. Her necklace was turquoise beads and silver pieces. Around her wrists she had bracelets like silver cuffs, hammered into a pretty design. Her hat was like those the men wore who went to fight in the Great War, a fedora with the brim turned down all around. Jonnie wanted to get one of those to keep off the sun and the wild, sudden rainstorms. She really wanted a genuine cowboy hat, but women didn't wear those. This woman's hat was the next closest thing. She wanted bracelets and a belt like that. If this woman could wear them, Jonnie could too.

Trying to see, Jonnie moved towards her without meaning to. They bumped right into each other.

"Sorry," both said at the same time, only she said it fancy like her clothes, while Jonnie said it like the fisherman's daughter she felt like next to this elegant woman.

"Do you want to see?" the woman asked and held up her arm. The designs were lovely, mountains, birds, suns, and moons, all done in simple lines pounded into the silver, but Jonnie could tell what each was.

"The Indians can tell a whole story from it," the woman said. "Have you been out to see the Indian lands?"

"No ma'am."

"You should come on our tour," she said. "Koshare Indian Detours. We can take you to see the pueblos where the Indians live now, and the ancient ruins of the Anasazi, even Grand Canyon."

"I could go?" Jonnie said. "I'd sure like to. But I'm not going anywhere. Don't I have to be riding on the train?"

"Most folks are traveling by train, but you don't have to. I'm Erna Fergusson. Koshare Indian Detours is my company. My idea, too." She held out her hand, and Jonnie got a good look at her ring.

"Or, maybe you'd just like to see my jewelry."

"Sure, but I want to see where the Indians live."

"How about this? We've got a tour going out next week to the Navajo country. They do all this silverwork. You can see where they live and buy what you'd like at the trading post. We'll stop there, and there's plenty of time to look it over and decide. I know I spent a lot of time to choose this."

She held out her necklace. "See how it's like a squash blossom? That's what they call it, too."

Jonnie ran her hand along her own thin money belt.

"So how much will it set me back?"

Erna told her, and Jonnie tried to look as if she spent that kind of money every day for first class dinner at La Fonda. Then she got an idea.

"Say," Jonnie asked, "I bet you'd like having that car all shiny and clean?"

Morna

The next time Mr. Schweizer stopped by the trading post, Morna waited until Jack had gone outside to talk with a customer. She slipped into the bedroom and took out the laundry basket in which she had hidden the pot from Mrs. Manyskirts. So far Jack hadn't noticed that Mrs. Manyskirts' squash blossom necklace was missing from the case of pawned jewelry.

"Mr. Schweizer," she said quietly, "I've got something to show you." She put the basket up on the counter and lifted the towels that hid the pot.

"Hmmm," he said, lifting the pot and holding it in the light. "So you've become a collector?"

"Not exactly. I'm hoping to be a dealer. I know the people here. I can get more of these to sell."

"Oh," he said, straightening up and putting the pot back in the basket. "Well, that can be a lucrative trade. Mr. Harvey has done well."

"Because of you," she said. "Everyone says you've got the best eye in the Southwest for value. Everyone talks about the great pots and rugs and baskets you've put on sale at La Fonda and Alvarado and the rest of the Harvey Houses."

"Well, thank you, that's very flattering." He turned away to check the tobacco shelf, and Morna could see Jack heading back in.

"So what do you think? Can you use this? If you bought what I have here, I'd be very flattered."

"Well," he said, "this is very nice but I'm afraid it's not what we're looking for right now."

Jack was coming in the door, so she folded the towel and slipped it back on the basket. Schweizer watched with a knowing smirk. While he and Jack talked, Morna listened, hoping he wouldn't mention her offer. Finally Schweizer had his tobacco and headed out to his car. Jack stumbled over the laundry basket and shot Morna an annoyed look, but nothing fell out.

"I've got to hang a few things outside," Morna said, grabbing the basket. She caught up to Schweizer smoking by his car. "Can you tell me what you are looking for? Because I'll find it for you."

"This is contemporary Navajo. They're weavers, you know. Not potters like the famous Maria at San Ildefonso. Sometimes the Navajos find the old Anasazi stuff when they're out with their sheep. That's what I can sell. Just go to La Fonda and look at our store there. You'll see what's selling for hundreds and thousands of dollars. But that's not so easy to find. The supply has pretty much dried up. So many collectors and museums! But you might have a chance, being out here and all, to stumble over something the archaeologists miss. You let me know. Here's my card." He slipped it to Morna while giving her a lugubrious handshake, making it clear he had seen her hiding her actions from Jack.

She stood there with the laundry basket, thinking about how easy he made it seem. "Just go to La Fonda." She and Jack hadn't been to Santa Fe since they'd bought this forsaken place. Santa Fe, where he'd expected to be known as a great artist. Well, at least now she knew her next step. The trick would be getting up that step, and doing it before Jack noticed the necklace was missing.

Ruth

Dr. Mera truly surprised Ruth. When he'd found her in the brush, he couldn't have been more gracious and apologetic, and she had to remind herself that her parents were far away and that she could stop being afraid that other people would try to control her. Of course, she wished he would let her stay outside, but he'd taken her arm and headed back to the sanatorium, asking her what she had seen and listening with great attention. Maybe it went with being a doctor that he appreciated science, because few of the patients had more than a polite interest. She had tried to point out the unusual birds or talk about why hummingbirds are brave while titmice shy away, but most would soon go off to their endless card games or just sit dazed in the sun.

Perhaps because they were so much sicker, the TB patients needed the time to think about where their lives might too soon be headed, but she didn't see why they wouldn't want to understand the intricacies of life at a time like that. When she had an asthma attack—and she hardly had them anymore—she often wondered why it was happening, not on some metaphysical level, but in the basest way. What combination of air and liquid and pressures and gravity and temperature all added up to her trying so desperately, yet not being able, to breathe? Was there some answer there that could stop her spasms and congestion and turn her lungs as clean and crisp as the night air at Sunmount?

Lately Ruth had been walking outside in the middle of the night. A second door in her room opened onto the flat roof of the bedroom below, creating a private deck where she could stand under the endless stars. She especially watched for owls, whose sounds she heard. Sometimes she thought she saw their silhouettes in the boundless black sky.

She kept an illustrated log of everything she saw. Much as she had hated those drawing lessons at the Art Students League, the training was coming in handy. She no longer resented the tedious hours spent learning how to do shading, perspective, and geometric forms. It was just the knowledge she needed to draw the living bodies of the birds. She was amazed how lively her bird drawings were, because in school, even in live sketching classes in Central Park, her animal drawings had been particularly dull. Perhaps she had found a spark here in the West.

When Dr. Mera could spare two strong boys to go with her, Ruth was able to go out in the brush again. Apparently, that strange Jonnie had quit her job rather suddenly. It was too bad, because Ruth would rather have had Jonnie go with her. The boys were impatient. With all that Indian blood she thought they would enjoy the land and the birds, but they wiggled all the time, crunched twigs under their heavy steps, and scared away the wildlife. She could see that they were eager to get back to whatever they loved the way she loved to see the birds. She had only asked Jonnie to go with her because she couldn't risk going alone, but now she saw that Jonnie had also been a rare person who could enjoy the hike. She had to find someone else to go along, although her health was getting so much better that she was beginning to believe she might go out alone sometime. *I am fifty years old and I want to go out without a chaperone!* She told that to her lungs, her bronchial tubes, and her sinuses.

Jonnie

Miss Erna drove a hard bargain, but Jonnie was happy to be out in the sun, sloshing soapy water onto her autobuses. The big white tires were the hardest. She scrubbed and scrubbed. The work wasn't all that different from keeping the limos clean at Sunmount, but knowing that these cars would take happy tourists out on exciting trips and that these tourists would return sunburnt and broke but satisfied helped to take her mind off all the death and gore she had been dealing with. She hadn't realized how much it had been getting to her. In Gloucester every time a schooner sailed out she had a lump in her throat that she might not see an old school friend or a friend's brother, or even her own father again. She had thought she would leave it all behind by taking the train so far away, but at the sanatorium she had only found a new way to stare death in the eyes. This new job was more fun, and it would pay for her vacation trip.

Erna had said if Jonnie washed cars for a week, it would cover her ticket on the grand deluxe tour. Erna's company, Koshare Indian Detours, had four long autobus cars. Each had seven rows of seats and seven windows to a side, with a long hood in front for the big motor. Spare tires were mounted on the sides and the back. Jonnie would send a car out gleaming and polished, and it would return from even a one-day trip through the desert looking dustier than a collapsed adobe. There would be new dents from kicked-up rocks and new scratches from driving through cactus and brush. But she found a lot of satisfaction in shining the visor over the windshield until it beamed like a mirror and polishing the broad running boards like a dance floor.

With every scrubbing stroke, Jonnie counted the minutes until the next Saturday, when she would join a tour that would start when the 9 o'clock tourists arrived from Lamy train station. When she wasn't working, she was getting her clothes ready. She didn't want to look like she had been washing cars. This would be her chance to go first class for the first time ever!

Saturday morning she was at the garage before Erna got there, sitting on a bench. Erna and the driver usually came to the garage about half an hour before the tourists arrived. But the time drew nearer, and there was no sign of her. Jonnie was fit to be tied. She wanted this to be perfect.

Whenever tourists arrived, the energy of the plaza picked right up, so Jonnie knew they were coming before she could see them. Soon the big cars drew up, and not just the children but the grown men and women dressed in their fancy traveling clothes were hanging out the windows, smiling, waving, and gaping at La Fonda.

In front of the hotel was Erna's sign, which marked where the tourists who had signed up for the Indian Detours should go. On it was painted a woman dressed just like Erna, pointing at one of her autobuses, with desert and adobe buildings in the background. That's where you're going today, Jonnie grinned to herself. The cars stopped and people poured out, but there was no autobus and no smiling Erna standing by the sign to greet them. Jonnie went over to the sign and tried to do her best, but she knew she looked nothing like the lady on the sign. A man came over to her.

"Is this where to go for the tours?" he asked. "The ones out to the Indian country?"

"Sure," Jonnie said, "it's a once in a lifetime experience." She had heard Erna say that every morning that week. Why wasn't Erna here?

"But where's the car?" he asked.

"Oh, it will be right along," Jonnie said. "Why don't you get some breakfast at La Fonda and we'll be ready to go."

He smiled happily and went back to his wife and gang of small children. Other folks headed her way. Every time a scowling tourist looked at the sign, she directed them into La Fonda with the friendliest smile she could manage, trying to hide her own disappointment. Where was Erna? This did not feel like she was going first class. But she was so used to working that it felt natural to wait on others.

It was so far past the time they were supposed to meet the autobus that no newcomers arrived. Jonnie wished she had money for a meal. She scanned the street both ways for Erna, but only saw some Indians packing up the pottery and blankets they had hoped to sell to the tourists, ready to head back to whatever else they did. Some returned to an adobe wall they were plastering.

The door of the restaurant opened and Jonnie recognized the first family that she had sent there to eat. Mother, father, and their string of children headed right towards her in a determined little parade. It had been easy to act as if Erna would be along soon, but now they would expect her to come through with their delayed ride. They were distracted for a moment looking at the buildings, but then the door opened and the next couple she had sent to eat came out. They headed her way, also.

"Lady, what's going on here?" The man with the string of small children demanded. "Where's our autobus? I thought you were the driver."

"I'm sure they'll be right along," Jonnie croaked, glancing desperately around. But it was nice that he thought she worked for Erna.

"We'll be going very soon," called a voice from the rear of the crowd. The angry customers parted to let Erna stride through, the big silver concha disks on her belt clinking. She put her arm on Jonnie's shoulder. Jonnie liked the heat from her hand.

"I hope you've all had a lovely meal," she said, "and are all ready to go visit all the exciting and spectacular sites you've been dreaming of. Now who's from the farthest away? Is anyone here from Kansas?"

A few eager hands went up.

"Hey, I've got an idea," she said. "Why don't we see where we all come from? Is there anyone here from New England? Why don't you stand over there on the left, and any one from New York, you stand next to them, and let's make a line from east to west just like the United States of America."

The crowd was so caught up in this task they forgot to be angry. While they stumbled into each other trying to line up, Erna squeezed Jonnie's shoulder tighter and whispered.

"Didn't you say you drove the limo for Sunmount? Can you drive the autobus? The driver's dead drunk. I had to get another man to punch him so we could get the keys back. I can't believe how this morning's going. Thank you for holding these lions back. Can you drive?"

Her words came in such a rush all Jonnie could do was bob her head.

"Here's the keys." She handed them over. "Bring it right in front here and we'll load up.

The Indian Detour autobus, fully loaded with screaming kids and bug-eyed adults, was hard to control over the bumpy roads. Jonnie steered the bus away from the familiar parts of town. She was torn between keeping her eyes on the rutted road and wanting to watch the scenery, but she was thrilled to be driving.

"That flat-topped hill is called a mesa," Erna explained. "If you look really carefully, way up high, do you see the caves? Do you see the holes? Indians lived there. We're going to go see where they lived."

As they drove along, Erna explained all about the Indians and how they had lived. Jonnie had learned some, but much was new. She explained how only the Indian women fixed the adobe walls, how almost every time it rained it had to be done, and how little it rained. Jonnie wanted to remember everything. She wanted to understand this wonderful place so it would be her home even more. She wanted to know about all the other people who also had called it home.

Erna directed her to drive off the main road and go down a long, very bumpy, dry set of tire tracks. If the car broke down, it would take everyone to get out and push, so Jonnie drove as slowly and carefully as she could, while the children screamed at her to go faster. They went through an adobe archway and right onto a flat, open courtyard ringed by adobe buildings, crumbling walls, and a few spreading, gnarled trees with leaves that shimmered in the sun. Jonnie thought it was a deserted, lost city with no signs of life, when suddenly Indians wearing colorful blankets streamed toward them, holding out arms full of objects.

Jonnie thought she recognized the woman who had given her food that day when she was so hungry. She had always wanted to see her again and thank her. She flung open the door and went over to the woman. When they came face to face, she saw a tiny flash of recognition, but then it was gone. Her face was friendly, but at the same time empty. She was holding out a basket filled with shiny red and black pots.

"Do you remember me?" Jonnie asked. "You gave me some food a few days ago. It was so nice of you."

She smiled and nodded uncertainly. All around them, the tourists were pulling out their wallets and bills were starting to flash. Shaking her head suddenly, she nodded at Jonnie once more and strode off toward the best dressed of the tourists. She had to make her money, too.

Erna explained to the few who were listening that the courtyard was called a plaza and the few big trees were cottonwood. Jonnie remembered Miss Ruth pointing one out on their short hike. She wondered how Miss Ruth was doing, or if she was even still alive. Even though she had ended up having to be the driver on what was supposed to be her own first class excursion, Jonnie was happy. No one here was likely to die soon. She was coming up in the world, even if her clothes weren't. If she had her little tuxedo on, would the Indian woman have thought she was rich?

Some people just wanted to see what was for sale, but Erna led the rest around, explaining that even though there was a pretty little church, there was also a kiva, a kind of basement where the Indians had their religious ceremonies. Jonnie wished they were allowed to go in. You had to go up a few adobe stairs, then climb down a hole. It was like going down the hatch on a fishing boat. She imagined that down the hole was a big hold full of fish, but Erna said it was a round meeting room where the Indian men sat against the wall in a circle and had secret ceremonies. Jonnie asked where the women went to practice the religion, but Erna didn't know. She thought maybe they went to the pretty little church.

"You mean the Indian men and the Indian women are different religions?" Jonnie asked. "Back in Gloucester, if a Portugee Catholic married a Scotch Unitarian, that would start everyone in their families fighting and they had to pick one religion or the other, or they had to leave town."

Erna looked a bit upset that Jonnie had asked a question she couldn't answer, so Jonnie turned her gaze away and let it drop. Erna led them through one of the low doorways into a small room where a very short Indian woman showed how she made the pots by rolling snaky coils of clay one on the other. She said she dug the clay herself from a special riverbed that had been her family's secret for generations.

Even at no cost for the clay, the Indians didn't look like they were making much money. This room was a little store, with pots to sell on the tables, but it was otherwise bare. There was nothing that wasn't for sale. They couldn't be making much of a living, and if they sold anything it would mean losing what they'd worked so hard on and all the beauty they'd created. This wasn't like selling fish for a living. Their work made Jonnie think of Mr. Atthorp back at home, an old ship's carpenter who had retired from the sea to carve figureheads. When a new ship was launched at Essex boatyard, everyone in town was excited to see his latest work. Canning fish or driving a car was work too, but it wasn't making anything beautiful.

A beautiful bird slowly loped across the horizon. The sky was almost the color of the turquoise jewelry Erna was wearing, and for a moment even the children were quiet. Everything was so clean, sparse, and lovely. The Indians and their buildings lived on the earth as naturally as seals sunning off Bass Rocks back home. Most of Jonnie's life she had been stuck with whatever the day's catch brought in. But something here made it all fall into place and she felt her life now to be like a properly stowed line, coiled and smooth and ready for use. She wanted more than getting enough to eat and a place to sleep. She wanted to know all about what she saw, like Erna, and to be part of something larger and timeless, like the Indian village.

Too soon Erna herded everyone back in the autobus. She pointed toward some towering canyon walls and directed Jonnie to drive that way. The tourists chattered happily, showing off their purchases. The road was a sea of flat dry sand over which the car slowly labored, the occasional rock towers that they passed providing the only sense that they were progressing. As the heat and monotony quieted the chatter, the tourists dozed off, with an occasional dreamy yelp from a child. Even Erna nodded off, her body slowly leaning over until her head was resting on Jonnie's shoulder. Jonnie remembered Erna's frantic face that morning. She had to be very tired from all the worry.

Jonnie drove with her left arm so as not to wake Erna, which wasn't hard to do on such flat ground. She thought that it must be like this during the midnight watch on a fishing boat. The sailors asleep, the sea calm, the course set, the destination far and unseen. The occasional flash of a jackrabbit would be like the quick pass of a dolphin. But this was no dark Atlantic night sky. Bright blue and hot sun glared down on her. It was hard to stay awake, and she sucked at her canteen constantly. Her lips were chapping as if it were January in Gloucester.

At last she could see the canyon walls, and as she drove parallel to them, Jonnie began to panic. Had Erna pointed wrong, or had she gone off course? There was no break in this monolith. Just as she was about to wake her, Erna snorted in her sleep and her hand brushed Jonnie's thigh. She felt a rush of warmth in her face that made her smile and keep driving.

Suddenly they turned a corner, and the car went through an opening into a shadowy tunnel created by red walls towering hundreds of feet above. They were inside the canyon on a narrow, twisting strip. In the mirror, Jonnie saw nothing but wall behind, and ahead was the shortest vista she had seen since moving to this wide open land, because the walls and road twisted and turned, cutting off her view. She was in a crooked maze of rock and sand. Somewhere above, first shining, then hidden, was the sun. This didn't feel right and she wanted to go back, but could she turn the long car in this narrow space? Now she was afraid to wake Erna. She didn't want her to wake up to one more disaster today.

But the children were fidgeting, the adults waking up yawning, and finally Erna sat bolt upright.

"Oh, isn't that shade wonderful after all the sun?" she murmured, still dreamy. "Of all the sites we visit, this is my favorite." She swung around and spoke loudly to the tourists.

"Everyone, this is Mummy Cave. We will visit the archaeological dig site of Dr. Earl Morris of the University of Colorado. Please remember to watch your step, because history will crackle beneath your feet. And look up!"

They all craned their necks out the windows. The kids were screaming and pointing. Jonnie tried to drive and look at the same time. Just ahead and high above, almost hidden in the folds of the rock cliff, she could make out little stone walls.

"Those are Cliff Dwellings," said Erna. "Built by the Indians long ago. Dr. Morris and his crew are exploring them. And here is Dr. Morris."

A hat and a head suddenly popped up in front of the autobus, and Jonnie hit the brakes hard. Shoulders, arms and the rest appeared as a man in a khaki shirt, jodhpurs, and high leather boots climbed out of a hole and waved at them to wait. While they watched, he poured a trowel of sand into a box beside his hole, then sifted expectantly through the dirt with his fingers. Looking a bit disappointed, he stood up and came toward the autobus.

"Erna, good to see you again." He was a handsome, ruddy fellow with a full beard, looking glamorous as Charles Lindbergh. Dr. Morris and Erna spoke about the canyon and the archaeological dig as they led the passengers away from the car, around a bend in the wall, and up to a jumble of small canvas tents. Tables, crates, pots and pans, buckets, notebooks, picks, shovels, rakes, ropes and broken pottery lay every which way. These adults were living like children with their toys all thrown about. After all the order and cleanliness of Sunmount, Jonnie sighed and relaxed from the freedom of it. Several archaeologists walked up to the tents. They were dressed much like Dr. Morris. Under the tall hat one had long hair, caked with dust, and soft pink cheeks framed by her cowboy bandanna. Could this be a woman? Jonnie had never seen any woman dressed like this.

"Erna," the woman archaeologist said, in a strong, sure voice that so few women have. "I'm so glad to see you again." She smiled at the tourists who were all gaping at her. Jonnie must have been the most openmouthed, because she looked Jonnie up and down, ending with a look as if they shared a secret.

"And who are your friends, Erna?" she said, still looking at Jonnie and not at any of the bug-eyed children.

"June, this is Jonnie," said Erna. "She's filling in for my driver today and doing a great job." Erna smiled at Jonnie.

"You mean Charlie's on a bender again?" June said, and Erna looked flustered and tried to stutter out a response. June looked around, saw that Dr. Morris had walked away, and continued more quietly. "Morris says we're not to help pull your bus out again. I hope you've found someone sober enough to stay out of quicksand."

"He said that?" Erna looked anxiously at Morris who was showing the children something that looked like a skull.

"So what about Miss Jonnie here?" asked June. "Do you drink much?"

"Drink?" Jonnie gulped. "Never!" Then she was embarrassed at how loudly she had spoken.

"There's your new man!" said June. "Haven't you had enough of those useless cowboys, Erna?"

"You might be right, I'll think about it." Erna wriggled uncomfortably out of June's gaze and headed into the shade of one of the tents. June leaned closer to Jonnie.

"If you get the job, you can buy me a drink."

"I never!" Jonnie yelped.

"Can't you take a tease? Would you like to see the dig?" She headed up a chalky slope, and Jonnie scrambled to follow. When June stopped suddenly, Jonnie almost crashed into her. June grinned proudly at what Jonnie thought was just mud-caked rubbish, but June squatted at the edge, picked up a trowel, and pointed to a pile that looked like the dried out rope that collected on the beach at low tide back home.

"That's a rabbit fur blanket. Basket Maker Three. See the basket?" She pointed her trowel at what looked like a straw hat that had been dragged through mud and then dried in the sun. "What do you think of that?"

Jonnie mumbled uncertainly. She was eager to look up at the little rock castles high above in the cliff, not down into the ground.

"You probably think this is just garbage, but it's 1500 years old, much older than those." She shrugged her shoulder up toward the cliffs. "The people who made this blanket didn't even know how to make pottery. Touch it," she pointed with the trowel at the part she'd said was a blanket.

Thinking of the rotted and sometimes sharp fish parts usually embedded in objects like this on the beach, Jonnie poked it lightly with just the tip of her finger.

"Go ahead, you won't hurt it any worse than sitting underground for 1500 years has," said June. Jonnie poked it again, just as lightly. June placed her hand on Jonnie's and guided it, rubbing over the blanket and the baskets. June's hand felt hot, soft and moist, especially compared to the dry blanket. She let go of Jonnie's hand and plucked out the rabbit fur blanket, slowly unrolling it.

"Darn," she said. "Sometimes these blankets hold baby mummies." Jonnie gasped and jumped away.

"It's not scary," June said. "The babies are wrapped in rabbit fur blankets and buried with baskets of food."

"It's a grave," Jonnie said.

"But this is science," said June, straightening up so that she looked down on Jonnie, the sun glaring behind her shoulder. "This is history. We're discovering the secrets of our past here. Without us, these people would be forgotten. Nobody would know how they lived or how they died. I bet you'd guess that they raised their babies up in the cliff house."

"I guess."

"A baby wrapped in a blanket like this would have been dead for hundreds of years before that house was built. Wouldn't you like to know where the baby lived? What food was in those baskets? How they made that blanket?" Not waiting for an answer, she laid the blanket beside the hole and squatted a few feet away from it.

"You try it," she said. She held the trowel out for me. "Dig. This bumpy place here is a good bet. You never know what you'll find. That's what makes it so much fun."

Jonnie stared at the hump of earth. There was something unnatural about it, as if it had been shoveled or blown over an object. She remembered the day she and her sister spent a day digging holes in their garden, searching for pirate treasure, until their father had seen and stopped them with angry words and punishments. They had talked of trying again, but were only allowed to dig on the beach, where water soon filled the holes. Not letting herself look at the blanket, Jonnie jabbed the trowel in.

"Gently," June said. "You don't want to break anything." She watched as Jonnie pulled out a few scoops of sand. Jonnie could feel the sun burning the back of her neck. Her knees hurt. She wondered how long she would have to do this. The trowel clinked on something hard.

"There you go," June said. She leaned over, pursed up her lips, and blew some sand away. Some wisps of hair had stuck to her cheek, and Jonnie wanted to brush them away. Her cheek was an apricot color from the sun.

"Now you pull." June pointed to a curved hard object sticking out of the sand. Jonnie gripped it and it wobbled like a loose tooth. She pulled harder and it came out into her hand, a jagged piece of broken dish.

"You're the first to touch that since an Indian woman probably broke it one day while cooking, a thousand years ago."

Jonnie turned it over in her hand. It was white on one side, red on the other with a wavy black line. She couldn't decide which side to look at. She held it up to catch the right angle of the sun to see fingerprints.

"Did you ever touch anything a thousand years old before?"

"Well, there's these old graves back home."

"How old?"

"I guess 1640s maybe. From when they first settled my town."

"1640s. That's five hundred years after this bowl was holding rabbit soup over the fire." June started to take it back, but stopped so that they were both holding it. Jonnie wasn't sure how she felt about the pottery or the ungraspable thought of a thousand years passing, but she wanted June to stay close. Nobody had talked so closely to her since she had come west.

June straightened up suddenly and moved back. Her shadow fell on Jonnie and the glaring sun stopped for a moment.

"Well, it's something I love, but maybe you don't," June said.

"I do!" Jonnie said, surprised at how strongly she said it. "This is really something. I've never seen anything like this." She held out the piece, hoping June would grab hold of it again.

Erna called out. "Jonnie, we've got to get going. Can you help me find everyone?"

"This is really something," Jonnie said again, desperately searching for more to say. "You have a really exciting job. I'm new here. This is all new to me." June leaned back in her direction.

"Maybe I can show you more," June suggested.

"I'd like that."

"If Erna gives you that job as driver, you'll be back here a lot."

"I better go do a good job, then." June took her hand and pressed it between her own.

As she helped Erna gather everyone back into the autobus, Jonnie could feel her heart pounding. As she drove off, she caught a glimpse of June in the mirror, carrying a big pottery jar. She wanted to jump out of the car and help her.

"Can I keep this job?" The words came out without thinking, because all she was thinking about was June.

"I have to give it some thought," said Erna. "It was a bit indiscreet of June. I feel put on the spot."

"Please don't blame June. I was thinking the same myself. You've seen what a good job I can do." Jonnie surprised herself, being so forward.

"Well, I can't discuss it here." Erna turned toward the tourists in back of her and began to explain the geologic history of the area. Before meeting June, Jonnie had been fascinated by Erna's talk, but now all she could think about was June and the baby blanket and the pottery and all that she had seen and touched.

The sky was a deep, dark blue when Jonnie parked the autobus in front of La Fonda. Erna and the tourists had slept through most of the ride. June had caused an awkward situation, but Jonnie was glad she had. She would never have boldly asked about the job, but would have waited too long, hoping and wishing, until Erna found another loafing cowboy to do it.

She knew she couldn't be a courier, as Erna called herself. It was a fancy word for tourist guide. A courier had to look great in those long skirts, Navajo blouses, and strings of turquoise and silver necklaces. Erna already knew that Jonnie was no elegant dresser, especially after seeing her wash the cars in a stable stall all the last week. It was too late to impress her that way. But she liked Jonnie's driving and said so when the tourists were gone.

"Jonnie, thanks so much for helping me out today. Here's some pay for your work. I'm sorry if you didn't get enough chance to see the sites. Would you like to go out with us next week as a passenger?"

"I'd much rather go as a driver."

Erna wouldn't look at her.

"Don't you think I'm good at it? And I'm very reliable, you know that."

She blew a little air out of her lips, pausing to think. "It's just people feel more secure with a big strong man. What if we get stuck? It happens all the time. We have to pull the car out. You and I, we're just two little girls and that's a big car and you saw how deep that sand and mud can be."

"Do you know what a barrel of cod liver oil weighs when it's curing? I've been lifting them for years back home. Besides, before the car gets stuck someone has to drive it into the wrong place. I'll see that doesn't happen. Because I'll be paying attention at the wheel. I've seen how those cowboys drive. When they show up." It was a low blow, but Jonnie was feeling more and more desperate. If Erna didn't hire her, she wouldn't be able to visit June's site until she had earned the money for her own car. That could take years.

"I'll think about it," Erna said finally.

Laura

Laura sat at Betsy's kitchen table and watched the first patients gather quietly in the rising sunlight. Betsy put down the coffee pot and hugged Laura from behind. Her warm arms formed a pillow for Laura to rest her head back on, but Laura sat stiffly. Betsy massaged her shoulders.

"It just wasn't your year to win. You can apply again. They'll be sorry they didn't find you sooner! It's their loss. They won't be able to brag about what a great photographer they discovered."

"But we need the money now. You're here and you love what you're doing. I needed that Guggenheim grant to do what I love doing. And now I can barely afford to visit. I'll never see you!"

"It's not the only way to make money. What about that idea for a lantern slide show of photos of Indians? The one you would go around showing at churches and schools?"

"Everyone's doing that now."

"Not with photos of Navajos, I bet. You could set up a trip east, stopping on the way to give the show. At least it would get you to New York for the reunion of the Clarence White School."

"Don't remind me. Everyone else is moving along but me."

Her coffee cooling, Betsy rushed to clear the dishes so she could start work.

"Well, it's an idea," Laura said. Outside the clinic, they heard some children squabbling. Laura went to the window. "There's already a line out there to see you! Can I take pictures while they're waiting?"

"How'd you like it if you were waiting in pain to see the doctor and a Navajo man wanted to take your picture?"

"Oh," was all Laura could say. Betsy was right. Laura was used to eager subjects coming to her studio to have their portraits done, or taking pictures of landscapes. She had never photographed people who were neither paying customers nor part of the scenery.

It was well past lunch time when Betsy's morning clinic ended. Laura helped her as much as she could, although holding onto a bleeding, whimpering patient while Betsy treated her brought back far too many memories of treating her father when he had the influenza. But Betsy leaned over and whispered, "Remember how I held you when you were sick?" and Laura remembered those days when she feverishly wavered between grim thoughts that her own influenza death was near and a warm and soothing hallucination that an angelic woman softly rubbed her back and held a cold, wet cloth to her hot forehead.

Grabbing bread, cheese, and canteens, Betsy hurried them into her car. "We've got a lot of stops to make before the sun goes down," she said. They headed for some hogans to the west, where Betsy needed to check on a pregnant woman and some coughing children.

Outside the pregnant woman's hogan, a girl squatted on the ground surrounded by a flock of sheep.

"Her oldest daughter is staying nearby in case she's needed," Betsy said. Laura held up her hands to frame the picture she wanted to take, then looked up at Betsy hopefully.

"I think it will be okay," she said. "If her mother is all right, we can stay a few minutes longer. Why don't you go talk to her, get to know her a bit?"

"Talk?" Laura said as Betsy disappeared through the little door of the hogan. From those first men she had met when their car had broken down, Betsy had been able to communicate somehow with the Navajos, but when Laura tried, she always found herself waving her hands in the air and looking desperately for Lilly. She knew she didn't have Betsy's sensitivity for people. She just wanted to take pictures. Right now, she just wanted to take out her camera and hide behind it. But she had better do as Betsy suggested. With a friendly smile, she walked toward the girl. Immediately, the sheep bounded away and the girl stood up, giggling. Laura froze. The girl, the sheep, and Laura stared at each other. The ground was hot, and Laura wished she had grabbed her hat from the car. The sheep walked slowly back towards the girl, as one bold ram headed toward Laura, his moist nose sniffing at her.

A little lamb leaped into the girl's arms. She hugged it, with the furry chin resting on her knee. She stood perfectly balanced, a perfect composition for a still-life, with a range of textures from the woolly back of the sheep to the smooth tight weave of the girl's dress to the glint of sun off her silver necklace and earrings. As the lamb stared dumbly out at the horizon, the girl looked at Laura, not boldly and directly, but not shyly, either. Laura slowly bent down to squat facing her. It seemed right not to say anything. The lamb jumped to the ground to try to grab a teat on her restless mother, only to be flung off while the mother searched for the bits of hay scattered into the dirt. Laura and the girl both laughed.

"I see you've learned how to talk." Betsy's voice startled Laura, so intently caught up in the silent conversation and watching the sheep.

"This is great. The lambs are so funny. Sit down and watch."

"I wish I could, but we've got to get going. They just told me about a hogan over that way where the baby hasn't been gaining weight. But there's time for you to take a picture, if you still want to."

Laura was so content in this sun-warmed circle of life that she had forgotten about her camera. She didn't want to leave. But these moments could be saved forever, if she could take the picture just right. She didn't want it to be stiff like a commercial portrait or most postcard pictures of Indians. It shouldn't look like an oil painting of the Old West, as she'd been taught at Clarence White's School. This girl and her sheep and the ground she sat on, the way they were at this hour when she had learned to laugh with a Navajo girl, were what she wanted to look at again and again.

Laura smiled at the girl and pantomimed taking her picture. The girl recognized the motions and nodded slightly, which made the lamb jump back into her lap, where she petted its floppy ears and it settled down again.

Laura went back to the car for her camera. It was a big box that took 8"x10" photos with fine focus and grain that would show all the details. Her commercial portrait work was almost always done indoors with lights, so this was a technical challenge. She thought back to the problem-solving assignments at school, remembering a photo she'd done of old people sitting in Washington Square Park. Mr. White had insisted it look like a painting done in hazy light, using a soft focus. But Laura wanted the sun shining just right on the Navajo girl's face and the face of the lamb, with the shadows trailing behind them, and every detail crisp. Could she figure out how to do it? Each sheet of film was expensive. Betsy stood back, watching admiringly, but Laura knew her mind was on the sick baby they still had to visit and the infection she might find.

Setting up the tripod, Laura couldn't help but fantasize projecting the photo in front of an awed audience, although somehow every face in the audience looked like Betsy as she watched now. She saw herself being handed a tidy pile of cash receipts, and thought of all the film it would buy. As she tightened the screw that held the camera on the tripod, threw the black velvet over her head, and looked through it at the dim cross-hatched image of the girl, she wondered where that girl would be on the days her picture would be projected on a wall for the entertainment of people looking for something new and exotic to stare at. The sun popped out of a tiny cloud, and Laura snapped the shutter. She could take more pictures, but that had been the right moment.

She came out from under the camera's veil and walked to the girl, pulling her purse from her pocket. She had some small bills and coins. How much would be enough? How much could she afford? She held out her hand, which the lamb immediately tried to lick, and they both laughed. The girl stared at the money for a moment, then gestured at the camera with her chin.

"You want a copy of the photograph?" Laura asked. She gestured at the camera again, pretending to pull the photograph out of the camera and hand it to her. She nodded. Laura was trying to mimic the truck coming with the mail, when Betsy said something in Navajo to her and pointed at the camera. The girl smiled agreeably.

"I told her I would come again with the picture. I think she understood."

As Laura packed up the camera, Betsy said, "Maybe someday, I'll go into a hogan and there will be a photo you took, tacked to the wall. I'll feel like you are there with me."

"And back in Santa Fe, I'll have this photo on our wall, and I'll think maybe that's who Betsy is visiting today."

Ruth

There wasn't a boy who worked at Sunmount who could stand still outdoors. They fidgeted away what would have been the most wondrous moments out on the desert. It was clear to Ruth that the only way she would be able to go where she wanted and do what she dreamed of would be by getting out of the sanatorium and away from Dr. Mera's, her parents', and everyone else's power. But it all depended on her health.

One morning she thought about their grocer's daughter, Gertrude Ederle. When she had been the first woman to swim the English Channel in 1926, she was the toast of New York City, ticker tape parade and all. Her parents, who had bought food from Ederle's for years, laughed when they read about it.

"Did you hear what Mayor Walker said?" As usual, Mother was reading *The Times* at breakfast. "He said Gertrude Ederle's heroic swim was like Moses' crossing of the Red Sea."

"What's that Irishman know of Moses?" stormed Papa.

"That Gertrude," said her mother. "She must be that queer girl who delivered the food sometimes. The one with shoulders like a man. Remember, Ruth, how one day I said 'thank you sir' and she said 'I'm not a sir,' and I still thought she was a man, and I said 'well okay, thank you son' and she snapped 'I'm not your son, either.' But her voice was higher when she said that and I finally understood. Then she apologized because she was afraid I'd tell her father how rude his delivery boy was."

Ruth remembered the incident and that her parents had talked about it for days. She had never seen Gertrude again, but she had never forgotten Gertrude's body, which was so strong at a time when her own was so weak. Before she realized Gertrude was a girl, she had already noticed the glowing health of this delivery boy. From the rocking chair on her bedroom terrace, she had watched him bicycle up to their house. It was because she had wanted a closer look at him that she had been in the kitchen that memorable day. It was four years later that Gertrude became so famous.

Papa had scanned his own copy of *The Times*. "Covered her body up with grease to swim fourteen hours," he said, with some admiration.

"*Treyf* from her father's store," said mama. "Covered with garbage! What a thing for a girl to do. No man will marry her now." She looked Ruth over in that way she very rarely did, as if she was actually taking some pride in her dowdy daughter. Had she thought that even at forty-five years old and near death every night with asthma attacks, Ruth was more marriageable than ruddy Gertrude from Amsterdam Avenue?

A mockingbird flew across the courtyard just as the man closest to Ruth on the sun porch went into a horrible fit of coughing. Attendants rushed to his side and wheeled him back to his room.

Ruth remembered how her father held up the newspaper to show her the photo of Gertrude. Water streamed off her everywhere as she took a big stride up to her thick calves in the surf, her arms outstretched from her huge shoulders and a sure, confident smile on her face. Ruth had never seen a woman looking like that.

"Just look, she's in her underwear on the front page of *The New York Times*," said mama.

"That's just her bathing suit," said papa.

"It's just panties and brassiere" said mama. "What kind of girl dresses like that in public?"

While they quibbled, Ruth admired the photo. There was no mistaking her for a boy there. Her hips were big and curved. Ruth had always been thin, and since she had been sick she was so frail that sometimes she felt that she barely took up space on this earth. Gertrude looked like she seized every molecule around her. You could almost feel the heat radiating from her body as she stepped out of the cold ocean tide and into the admiring eyes of the world. She'd had a goal and she'd made it. She'd had plenty of reason for that smile.

Mama had looked at the ads from Loehman's and Bergdoff's. "Ruth, look at this darling chemise. Isn't that sash just right? It's only a month until Rosh Hashana, shall we have this sent over for you to try?"

Ruth looked at the face of the model in the sketch. Her little hat hid her eyes, and her mouth was a tiny spot. She could still see the photo of Gertrude. Her eyes were covered by her black swimming goggles, but her mouth was wide open and her teeth showed. The model's body was one straight line, as if she had no hips.

"Look, mama. It's the model who looks like a boy now."

"What are you talking about? She's just what a woman should be, and that frock is just right. I'd like to see that Gertrude in that dress," she laughed. "Why she'd burst right through it with those big muscles. She's unnatural. I'm not so sure she is a woman."

Ruth wondered if Gertrude had been thinking about her goal of swimming the channel on the day that she had delivered the food. Perhaps she had just done an exercise workout. Did she train at a pool or in the river? Maybe she did grease herself up with chicken *schmaltz*. The thought was disgusting, but on the other hand, she did what it took and she accomplished something no woman, had ever done, and she had done it faster than the two men who preceded her. On the power of her own strong shoulders and legs, she had crossed the English Channel in fourteen hours and thirty-one minutes, despite the almost freezing water, the waves, and the sharks. In the length of a day in August, she'd gone from England to France in fourteen hours of constant strength and determination.

If a woman could do that, what could Ruth do? Was she going to spend the rest of her life quibbling with Dr. Mera to let her take a little walk to watch the birds? This was it. She saw it clearly now. Like Gertrude, Ruth was going to train and train and build up her strength and do whatever it took so that she could swim her own English Channel to her own freedom here in this beautiful place full of wonderful animals and plants. She was also a girl from the Bronx and she was going to be as powerful as Gertrude. Just the thought had Ruth leave her rocker. Patients were encouraged to promenade around the courtyard for exercise. She would go round and round until the patients and staff grew so dizzy they would beg her to walk out onto the desert.

Betsy

There were so many times in the day Betsy wished she could talk with all of her patients. She was trying to learn Navajo, but she made one mistake after another. She might have told someone else that making mistakes was a good way to learn, but she couldn't afford to make them. If she didn't gain her patients' trust quickly, she would be seen as just another white person who failed them, like so many before her. Her clinic building had started as a small field hospital run by the government, but after a few years it had been closed without warning, leaving nothing but an empty building and more distrust. Oliver La Farge's Indian Association was trying to restore the Indians' confidence in their work.

Every morning but Sunday she held open hours at the clinic for drop-in patients. There was always a line in the yard outside. Bah Tauglechee was her first patient today, and the oldest Betsy had treated so far. She suspected that the oldest people, who were rare to begin with, didn't have much use for white doctors. They could call in their own medicine men and probably themselves knew many herbs and roots for self-healing.

Mrs. Tauglechee's cheekbones stuck out like buttes on a face that was dry and rutted as the desert. A bandanna of trading-post fabric was tied under her chin, the ends almost hiding her exquisite silver necklace. Its silver beads were shaped like insects with three humps to their bodies plus antennae. Or were they the shapes of the kachina costumes Betsy had seen at the dance, with the antennae being short legs? She hadn't seen any other jewelry in this design. It must have been a very old style that wasn't being produced for commercial trade. She wondered if it had a sacred meaning that the Indians didn't want to reproduce for sale.

Lilly nervously led Mrs. Tauglechee to the examining chair.

"Now, what seems to be the problem?" Betsy asked in her cheeriest nurse voice. The patient stared back through eyes fogged with cataracts.

Betsy motioned to Lilly to translate. Lilly reluctantly asked something, but there was no answer. Through the door, waiting patients watched. Betsy would have loved more privacy, but it was too hot to close the door.

"Why did you come to see me?" Betsy asked, but again Mrs. Tauglechee ignored Lilly's translation and stared at her. There was a pointedness to her disregard of Lilly that would have been terribly rude back in South Carolina.

"Lilly, why won't she look at you? Why won't she answer?"

Lilly didn't answer right away. She walked a few steps away, and said softly, almost murmuring, with her back to Betsy, "She thinks I'm too young.

She won't answer a question from a young person. It's not our way."

"Oh, is that all? Why didn't you tell me? Lilly, it's okay. I understand. When I was your age, if I had gone right up to my grandmother's best friend and asked her a question, not even one this personal, my grandmother would have glared at me and silently ordered me out of the room."

When Lilly turned to face Betsy, she looked as scared as when she had asked for the job.

"Lilly, you're a wonderful interpreter. I need your help." At that, Lilly smiled more confidently.

"Let's try this. Tell me how to say 'Do your eyes hurt?'" Lilly translated. Betsy thought Mrs. Tauglechee showed a flicker of interest as she continued to look only at Betsy.

Betsy repeated what Lilly had said as closely as she could. Everyone who could hear snickered; she must have said something with another meaning entirely. The Navajo language required correct pitch to get meaning, something that is rarely true in English. But Mrs. Tauglechee sat up and brushed her hand toward her eyes.

Betsy wanted to ask Lilly for more words, but she could see that Mrs. Tauglechee was quickly losing respect, perhaps because Betsy relied so much on such a young person. She decided to try something else. With the Navajo people she had already made friends with, a connection had come out of a kind of silent communication. Laura had been amazed when Betsy had made friends with the two men who found her in the car in the desert. How had she done that? It hadn't been with words.

"Lilly," Betsy said, "I'm going to try something different. I don't want you to feel that I don't need you. But let's see what happens."

Betsy pulled up a stool and sat near Mrs. Tauglechee, but didn't smile at her. Listening to the impatient coughs and sneezes of the line waiting outside, it was hard but she sat calmly and silently. Mrs. Tauglechee's breath was short and slightly wheezy, and soon Betsy was breathing in her rhythm. Finally, in a very soft voice, Mrs. Tauglechee spoke, startling Betsy, who had never heard her voice. She gestured toward her throat. So it wasn't her eyes she was here for. Perhaps Betsy could get to that later. She looked at Lilly.

"She says it's hard to swallow. Her throat hurts her all the time. Her own medicine isn't working like it used to."

Betsy soon had her tongue depressor out and was busy treating her symptoms. Silence, she told herself, is the way some people talk. It's not to make me feel ignored. It's to give me a chance to come closer, really. She thought back on some of the attempts she had made lately to make friends, and when they had worked and when they hadn't. The best had been when she had sat by a Navajo woman as she suckled a baby. She wouldn't have talked to a woman while she nursed her baby in South Carolina, and she didn't here, either. But by the time she put the baby down to sleep, the mother was ready to talk. Betsy had thought it was cooing over the baby that won her, but it must have been her silence and patience until the time was right.

Laura

Back from visiting Betsy, Laura soon developed the film and tacked the photo of the shepherd girl with her lamb to the wall of her studio. She stepped back until she was against the opposite wall, then stepped from side to side. From every point the little girl looked trustingly at her. She was especially pleased with the detail in the print. Unlike her teacher, Clarence White, she no longer wanted to see blurry, dreamlike effects achieved by putting Vaseline on the lens or holding gauze in front of it. That would make them like Curtis' Indians, out of focus, disappearing, dream-like, unreal. This girl was as real as every other human in America. She was as real as the immigrant portraits by Lewis Hine, and the now-popular portraits of the rich done in Fifth Avenue studios by celebrity photographers. She was not disappearing, she was not mythic. Why did Curtis photograph that way? Maybe that was how the government and missionaries like the Lucks wanted to see the Indians disappearing into the modern world, but the Indians were still here. They had endured. At least this was true for the Navajo people. In her photo, she saw a future for the little shepherd girl whose sheep would grow into large herds. The girl would become a woman, wearing her wealth in silver and turquoise, with a husband and children. She was a real person with a home and work and dreams, as Laura saw her through Betsy's eyes. Edward Curtis had told his story of a vanishing Indian. Laura saw in the photo how she would tell the story of the enduring Navajo people.

The bell rang as a customer entered. It was Mrs. Chalmers, a rich architect's wife, arriving for her second session. She had been so bossy at the first sitting, posing herself and telling Laura how she must be portrayed, that the photos had come out too honest for her vanity, showing a controlling woman insisting on what her image must be. Laura had been surprised she had wanted to try again, and she wasn't hopeful about the results.

"I'm ready to try again," said Mrs. Chalmers, starting to remove her white gloves, than putting them on again. "This time I thought perhaps more from the side. Everyone has always admired my profile, you know." Before Laura could answer, Mrs. Chalmers headed for the stool. Laura knew it would make her look even more stiff and had already decided to pose her in the soft armchair.

Mrs. Chalmers halted before the photo of the shepherd girl momentarily. She shook her head as she turned away.

"Those people!" she said. "Do you know, when we first moved here, and we've been here since we were first married, twenty-five years you know, everyone told us about the lovely Indian dance, so we went to that pueblo to see for ourselves. It was the special dance day, they said, the one you just have to go to. Well, when we got there, the gate was locked. Not even a sign! How rude. How like them! Well, we've never bothered ourselves again."

"That's a Navajo girl," Laura said. "They don't live at the pueblo."

"Oh, what's the difference? If they can't conduct themselves with simple courtesy! And even after we've paid to send them to boarding schools! Boarding schools! I can barely afford that for my own children."

"I've heard that if there's a death in their community, the Pueblo Indians have several days of ceremonies. They don't want other people staring at them. Perhaps there had been a death." Should she be making excuses for the Indians? But this woman had been here twenty-five years and never gone to see what the Indians were like? Resentful as she was about Betsy being away, Laura was treasuring the adventures they were having and all that they were seeing of another way of life. She felt sorry for Mrs. Chalmers who had chosen to miss all these opportunities. But good for the Indians that there was one less person staring at them condescendingly!

"There's no excuse for rude behavior. They should have carried on." She took another glance at the photograph, shook herself, and sat smartly on the stool. She tapped her foot impatiently as Laura went to load the camera.

Ruth

Ruth had built herself up so that now she could walk a figure eight route around the whole sanatorium and its various outbuildings and woodpiles. It took her through the unnatural-looking gardens, into which were poured endless amounts of water in an effort to create a flowery, eastern-looking space. She supposed this was expected to comfort the guests from wetter places. There was a lacy wrought-iron bench in the middle of the garden where she rested and watched the hummingbirds as they buzzed at each other at a little red feeding station. If their endless energy hadn't inspired her to walk more, she would have spent all her time there. But she would watch them, think of Gertrude Ederle, and march on.

Her stamina was growing, and soon she didn't have to stop at the hummingbirds. She hadn't had an attack since that first scary, lonely night. Every night she checked it all off on a calendar.

"Dr. Mera," she said, following him on his springy morning walk around the portal where he would say hello to all the guests. "I was wondering how I can tell when I'm cured?"

"Cured?" He looked at Ruth pityingly.

"Yes, I haven't had an asthma attack since I arrived. I would like to start making plans to leave."

"But you were sick until you came here. Now you feel healthy. Doesn't it seem to you that staying here is what you need?"

She stared back, her mouth biting air. It was the kind of overly logical argument that her mother often used.

"But I thought I came here for the Cure. What is the Cure?"

"Lots of rest and sunshine and good food. Now, if you leave, how will you get those? You're from New York City, aren't you? How sunny is it there?"

Ruth pictured her dark apartment, and how she had languished on the velvet covered heavy furniture. The thought of the wood polish almost made her wheeze, but she swallowed the sound so he wouldn't hear.

"I don't think I'll go back to New York. You are right, I need the sun here. But although Sunmount is lovely, I don't want to stay here forever." Sunmount was lovely, but it was the confinement that she couldn't bear another day of. She felt so free of her parents now and only needed to be free of their surrogate, Dr. Mera.

"Some of our patients who have healed have found homes here in Santa Fe. Perhaps you could do so. Let me know what you decide so we can inform another worthy patient that a bed will be opening up." That last sentence was a threat for her ungrateful desire to leave, but it didn't matter. He wasn't offering any help, but he'd given her the hint she needed.

She wished she could find that strange lady chauffeur, Jonnie. She could hire her and a car to take her around to find a place to live. Ruth had always lived with her parents in their brownstone. Where could a woman without a family live in Santa Fe? The next morning, when the maid came to sweep her room, she tried to find out.

"Carmencita, where do you live?"

"With my Alberto," she said. "His father left him a ranch that his grandfather left to him. Far, far back, Alberto's abuelos came here with Coronado to seek the gold, and they stayed to be ranchers. We have goats and sheep. Alberto made a new bedroom for our daughters. We can see all the mountains from our home."

Ruth had thought Carmencita was just a maid, but now she saw her as the lady of a manor. She had thought of herself as rich compared to Carmencita, but it was the other way around.

"Where would you live if you weren't married?"

"At the pueblo. I have a room there until I die, and then it will go to my daughter. Right now it is empty. I go there every season to burn the piñon and sage so it will be dry and smell good."

"Would you rent it to me?"

She giggled. "Oh Miss Ruth, only the Indians can live at the pueblo. I wish I could though. I would like more money."

"Do you know anywhere I could live? I want to leave here."

"You are cured, Miss Ruth! It is a miracle. I will light a candle for you at the church. You know," she said, her voice dropping to a whisper, "most of the people here don't get cured. They are carried off to Jesus. But first they had a happy life here."

"You think so?"

"Yes, they spent their last months sitting in the chairs in the sun, drinking the chocolate milk, thinking about their lives. Even if they are young, they get to do this before they die. When I am dying, I think I will still be worrying about how the horse got out, or where Alberto has gone with the money, or if the influenza will come back and take my mother too. Do you really want to leave here?" Before she could answer, a nurse came in, glared at Carmencita for working so slowly, and she hustled out with her broom.

Ruth asked around some more. Everyone had an opinion about her future, but no one had useful advice. Patients were allowed to hire a Sunmount limo to go into town for shopping and sightseeing, so Ruth decided she was ready to do some exploring.

Betsy

Betsy's life at Red Rock was never slow, even if the pace of the soft-spoken little shepherd boys and girls and the calm adults sometimes moved as if they were all wrapped in medicinal gauze. She was almost always on the move. The morning clinic would bring Mrs. One Shoe needing drops in her eyes for trachoma, Mr. Killed A Cow with an ear to be irrigated to remove a louse, Gilda Lee's girl Dneziba with impetigo scabs, and, too often, an infant with pneumonia. Pneumonia was rampant, and even if the patient survived the bumpy sixty mile trip to the hospital, sometimes it was too late. At least so far there had been no more outbreaks of the smallpox or influenza that had wiped out large parts of the group in the past. Emergencies could take her out to the hogans at any time, and on these regular rounds she saw patients too sick to travel to the clinic. Their high fevers, abscess gums, or hardness in the abdomen had her rushing them to the hospital. At least she had a car, an old one that had been donated to the Indian Association. The car seats were getting covered with stains of blood and pus and worse, so she scrubbed them with carbolic until the car smelled more clinical than the clinic.

She was furnishing her new home piece by piece. Most of the furniture had been sent to the Lucks by their supporters back east, and they passed their rejects on to her. Fortunately, the Lucks tended to like the ascetic hard-backed, stiff-seated chairs, so Betsy got those with suggestive and cozy curves. She painted the walls cream, the ceilings white, and where there was a wood floor, she varnished and waxed it. The well was finally supplying the sinks. She couldn't have kept the clinic going for long without running water.

Laura's letters were brief and rare. She was sulking because Betsy was so far away. Her next visit was weeks off, and Betsy couldn't go to Santa Fe and leave her patients without a nurse. In their twelve years together, she and Laura were always switching between what Betsy thought of as their "close-nesses" and their "far-nesses," because sometimes they were so sweet on each other they practically read each other's minds, but other times they were so cold with each other it was awkward to ask for a hug. She didn't know how long she would stay away, but she had to find ways to make it work for both of them. Laura was hurt, but Betsy couldn't imagine the whole trajectory of her life without this adventure. She was hoping that if Laura did more with photographing the Navajo people it would become her experience, too.

Things were going well, except for the inescapable Reverend Luck. As Mathew had explained, he always knew where she was. He turned up at the most remote hogan or shepherd's camp and even the brush-awning structures up in the hills the Indians called their summer houses, always taking the opportunity to turn her visits into what he called "hogan prayer meetings." She suspected it was the only way he could feel "invited" into many homes where he normally was not welcome.

"Where you go today Miss?" asked Mrs. John Billy as Betsy put drops in her baby's eyes at morning clinic. She had always communicated by signs before, so Betsy was startled that she could speak some English. She was even more delighted that Mrs. John Billy trusted Betsy enough to use it.

"I go to...." Betsy stopped. Would the woman run to Reverend Luck to tell him where to follow her? The baby wailed, so Betsy pretended he needed more attention and didn't finish the sentence. By the time the baby quieted down with a few last gasping cries, Mrs. John Billy was staring at the floor again and didn't seem to be waiting for an answer. She took the baby and left with just a shrug of a good-bye. If that had been Betsy's chance to make a new friend, she had ruined it. If Mrs. John Billy thought that Betsy had found her English incomprehensible, she would never try again.

She wished she could drop the Lucks in quicksand. But then she recalled some words from the sermon at the last Sunday service Reverend Luck had forced her to sit through. She had struggled to sit up straight on the backless bench. To keep her mind off the discomfort, she listened to Luck's voice as it reverberated like a radio preacher.

"If you live in fear, it isn't because of Jesus. You must blame yourself, because if you believe in Jesus, you don't have to live in fear."

The words came back as she watched Mrs. John Billy round up the rest of her children and some lambs she'd brought in for the trader. Betsy was the one living in fear and letting it rule her. Why blame Luck for her own shortcomings? All she could do was blame him for turning up everywhere she went. She didn't know if the Indians were spying for him, but she was letting her suspicions ruin her new and potential friendships. If she didn't trust her patients, what could she accomplish? If she kept on like this, she would soon see the Indians as Luck and his wife seemed to, only as added names to the baptism registry. Would Betsy number them as cured cases of chicken pox or pinkeye or bronchitis, and would she gloat when they came to her and not their medicine men?

Jonnie

Jonnie knew she wasn't her first choice, but Erna hired her as driver. She warned that if Jonnie couldn't dig the autobus out every time it got stuck in the sand, she'd have to let her go. Jonnie promised herself never to get stuck. She knew that was unlikely, but she tied all the shovels and spades she could onto the back of the autobus and hoped for the best.

She was saving every penny by living in the crumbling adobe, but one dark evening when she returned from a long day of driving, she found the door of the house nailed shut and a "No Trespassing" sign tacked to it. When she tried to climb through a window to retrieve her blankets, a huge dog growled and barked frantically trying to get at her. She fell back to the ground.

She walked back into town, tired and dirty. There was an alley of boardinghouses, but only one had a sign that said "Respectable Women Welcome." El Ristra was not much different from the fishermen's boardinghouses back in Gloucester. It was in a run down building above a printing shop. The whole place smelled like ink. There was still a light on, so Jonnie headed up the narrow tall stairway. Right on the door was a sign saying "We trust in God—all others pay cash" just like they had at the Crow's Nest bar back in Gloucester. But the lady who came to the door had a nice smile.

"Oh," she said, "I thought you were one of my guests. We're closed for the night. I was just up knitting."

"I need a place to stay," Jonnie said, and showed her the cash. "There aren't a lot of places will take a single woman."

She looked at Jonnie's clothes, covered with the day of dust and desert. Jonnie wished she had stopped first to wash her grimy face.

"Oh, dear," she said, "you're not a young woman. I do make a safe place here for respectable women. But how did you get so dusty?"

"I drive the autobus for the Koshare Indian Detours," Jonnie said proudly.

"You can drive the big car! How did you ever learn to do that?"

"I used to drive the limos for Sunmount."

"Of course! I've heard some of my ladies speak of you! I get many of Dr. Mera's amazing cured cases. The man is a miracle healer."

Jonnie tried not to laugh at that, knowing that his miracle cure was an almost empty wallet.

"Yes, I've heard about you. Everyone remembers the woman who—" Here she broke off for a moment. Jonnie was sure she was about to say they gossiped about the man's suit she wore. "The woman who can drive a car like a man," the landlady rescued herself. "But you don't work for Dr. Mera any more? Why not?"

Jonnie was still standing in the doorway. Across the room was a big cozy couch, covered in a flowery fabric with an Indian blanket draped across the back. She wanted to collapse on it after this long day. If she couldn't stay here, she could sneak back into the stable with the autobus, but what if Erna caught her there? For the first time since she had left Gloucester, she felt like she had fallen into water too deep. She pictured her little attic bedroom in her father's house and wanted her own pillow and comforter. She didn't want to explain that Dr. Mera had fired her for disobeying his rules. This landlady wouldn't understand that a patient wouldn't let her say no.

"Oh, he wanted to hire a man to drive," she mumbled out the lie.

"No one seems to understand that a woman can do just as well. You'd think with the Vote and all, they'd let us," a new but somehow familiar voice interrupted. There, behind the landlady, stood Miss Ruth. Or Jonnie thought it might be. This Miss Ruth had pink cheeks, not sallow, and her face was round and happy, not drawn and sick. Jonnie couldn't help but stare.

"Miss Ruth, you look wonderful!"

"I told you Dr. Mera performs miracles," said the landlady.

"I've been feeling better," said Ruth. "Since I left Sunmount, I've been going out for lots of walks. It's very healthy for me. And Mrs. Landauer's wonderful food has helped me, too," she said, nodding at the landlady.

"That's true," said Mrs. Landauer. "So you know this woman?" she asked Ruth.

"Yes, Jonnie was very kind to me at Sunmount."

"I'm looking for a place to stay," Jonnie explained. Mrs. Landauer smiled at Ruth in a way that made Jonnie suspect that Miss Ruth hadn't come here with an empty wallet.

"Well I'm full up right now, but would you want to stay on the couch for tonight?"

Betsy

Three men who looked tough and gnarled as the wind bitten trees walked into Betsy's clinic. Lilly gave the nurse an uneasy glance.

"Aze" said the one with the stiffest face. "Aze" was the Navajo word for Betsy's kind of medicine, which they knew often had alcohol in it.

"First I have to find out what's wrong with you," Betsy said, and Lilly translated. The man scowled. Betsy picked up her clipboard and started a new record for him.

"Your name is?" she said. She already knew this was shaky ground because the Navajo people wouldn't tell non-Navajos their real name. Most had a different name they told white people.

"Tom Killed-a-White-Man" he said. Startled and wondering if he was trying to intimidate her, Betsy wrote it down.

"Your symptom? What hurts?" After a slow, lingering cough, he spat out the word "Aze" again. Behind him, the other two men coughed slightly and fidgeted.

"Now let me check," Betsy said. She held her stethoscope up to his chest, pantomiming opening the buttons of his shirt. He moved back, angrily closing his open top button. Betsy held the stethoscope up and pointed at his shirt. They glared at each other stubbornly. "Tom Killed-a-White-Man" sounded in Betsy's head like a rhythm. One of the other men took a step in the direction of the medicine cabinet.

"I have to hear," she said, pointing again at his shirt. 'That's a very bad cough, don't you want me to examine you? Can I take your temperature, then?" She held up a thermometer. Flinching his head away, he undid the buttons and pulled his shirt open. She poked and listened and finally straightened up.

"You can button up," Betsy said. 'You have a cold, nothing serious. Can you try to stay warm and get some rest for a few days? Can you get some hot stew to eat?" Lilly, who had backed away, translated.

"Aze!" he demanded, ignoring Lilly.

"No, I don't think it's that serious. It's just a cold. Just stay warm and dry." Lilly's voice trembled as she repeated the words in Navajo.

Tom said something loudly enough for the line of people outside to hear. Lilly translated: "What kind of a nurse is this? Where are the things a nurse should have?" While Lilly spoke, Tom watched Betsy as if expecting her to crumble from his words.

Meanwhile, his friends inched closer to the cabinet of drugs. The lock hung open. If they wanted to raid it, there was nothing Betsy could do. As they all stared at each other, she calculated what would happen if the men emptied it. People who didn't get medicines they needed could become far more seriously ill. There was already a pinkeye outbreak going on. It could be weeks until most of the drugs were replaced, and by then there could be an epidemic. The Indian Association would be furious about the cost. They would lose confidence in her.

Should she keep up this charade, or just give him what he wanted and hope that he'd go? There was a big bottle of *George Halleck's ITSPEP Potion*, 85% alcohol that she could give him. But how soon would he be back for more? What if word got around to the others? How could she protect the clinic from this?

The three men watched her intently. Like gunslingers in a cowboy movie, they waited to see who would reach for their weapon first. Suddenly Betsy had an idea. She threw her hands high in surrender and pretended to cry.

Her voice shaking, she asked "Huh, huh, Tom Killed-a-White-Man. Huh-huh, have you ever killed a white woman?" They stayed locked in their stares, so she increased her playacting, trembling so melodramatically that even the worst theater actress would have been embarrassed. Catching on, Lilly put her arm protectively around Betsy's shoulder as she translated.

Tom's tightly set lips broke into a smile, and his two buddies immediately joined him. Soon they were all laughing. Betsy was afraid that their laughter might suddenly turn sour again, but for the moment she seemed to have charmed or at least disarmed them. Tom Killed-a-White-Man stood up, nodded, and walked out with his friends following. She hoped the little wave he gave to the people waiting outside was a sign of approval.

She wanted to ask Lilly about Tom's name, but the next patient came in immediately. She was an older lady, and now Betsy knew not to ask her a direct question. Fortunately, the patient spoke first.

"You are a good healer to make Tom Killed-a-White-Man happy."

"That's an interesting name," Betsy said.

She didn't say anything, but held out her wrist, wrapped in a canvas chicken feed bag. As Betsy cleaned the infected burn, the old woman said, perhaps more to distract herself from the pain than anything else, "Oh we all know that story. He was traveling in the winter, and it was very hard, and he ran out of food. He was very hungry. There was a white man with a fire and he had beans cooking, but he didn't offer any to Tom. It was a long time ago, but we still tell the story."

Betsy wondered if now they had a new story to tell about her bon mot. In any case, she felt great relief as she snapped the lock back on the drug cabinet and closed the clinic later that day.

Ruth

Although at first she reminded Ruth too much of her mother's bossiness, it was an incredible gift to find Mrs. Landauer. A Jewish landlady in Santa Fe! It was so good to be with someone who could cook kugel and bake challah, which the rest of the boarders called "that twisty sweet bread." On the other hand, it made her feel she hadn't traveled far enough. But it did help with her parents. They had talked with Mrs. Landauer on the long distance telephone, and she had assured them that her place was respectable and that she would hear if Ruth had an attack during the night.

Ruth's parents still couldn't believe the attacks had stopped. Ruth couldn't believe it herself and still faced a night's sleep with a certain dread, but she would wake up happy and energetic and ready to go on her new regimen. Every day she headed out with a little pack of food and water, a straw hat as big as the four-gallon ones the Indians wore, and wearing the new men's boots she had bought at the Santa Fe Trading Post. The Trading Post was owned by Mrs. Landauer's good friend Mr. Goodman. He was Jewish, too. At first he said he didn't have any heavy boots small enough for a woman's feet, but when she said she would like to try the boys' sizes, he conceded.

When Jonnie had showed up so late that night, Ruth had been glad to see her again. At first she thought that now she would have someone to hike with, but she had been fine going out alone all these weeks. She had wished Jonnie was still around, so she could ask her how a single woman could live and get along in this city, but now perhaps she had gone further then Jonnie had, since Jonnie was the one looking for a place to live. Ruth knew that if Mrs. Landauer liked Jonnie, she'd find her some little space in her rambling old building.

If she could get a car, maybe Jonnie could drive them to the remote places she wanted to explore. Or even better—she'd get Jonnie to teach her to drive. She was already saving some of the money her parents were sending. Someday she would buy her own car and drive herself.

As usual Ruth headed out at sunrise. All week she had been working toward exploring a trail along Big Tesuque Creek. A fellow from the Geologic Survey who was mapping the whole state had given her maps and instructions. First she had to walk to the trail that led to the creek. Every day this week she had gone farther, feeling stronger each time. Jews don't believe in reincarnation, but sometimes she felt as if she had once been one of those quick lithe lizards that would go shooting across her path, perfectly suited for this place, perfectly happy to be here.

Beyond the dry rutted tracks that went for roads here, she was on a rising trail through a deep forest of juniper and ponderosa. Goodman had given her his daughter's *Scouting for Girls Handbook*, and she was learning the names of all the plants and scurrying animals. With the money her parents sent "for new dresses now that you can go out more," she had bought the latest guidebook to Southwest nature. As she climbed higher, the trail narrowed and the forest turned to white pine and fir. It was harder to keep a footing in this sandier soil. In dainty lady's shoes, she would have slid back with every step. But in boots, she walked confidently. A thrush zoomed by, perhaps surprised to find a human up here. She tried to step quietly, which was hard to do because she loved stomping happily along, feeling strong, breathing deeply.

Even before the asthma got so bad, Ruth had never felt so free to swing her arms and plant her feet. Was it possible that this old lady of fifty felt better now than she had at fifteen? She grinned at the thought as she came to a little clearing with some tiny flowers she hadn't seen before. She squatted, then lay down to look even more closely with a magnifying glass.

This little family of flowers was so peaceful, living together off the side of the trail, happy to be together, unlike her own family. She couldn't find the lovely flowers in her field books. She looked again, thinking she must be mistaken. But there was nothing like them. Was it possible she had discovered something the naturalists didn't know about? She sat for a long time with her notebook in her lap, sketching. When finished, she delicately lifted just one plant out and pressed it in her book, mumbling apologies to the flower family. She would send the drawing and cutting to the Museum of Natural History. Maybe someone there would want to know what she had found.

At Sunmount, Ruth had grudgingly agreed with nurse Betsy's encouragement to try drawing again, never imagining how different it would be compared to those awful years in art school. Now she used a magnifying glass to see the tiniest little grasses and bugs, and binoculars for searching the ground when the shadows of hawks and vultures swooped over. From sketch pad and pencil she had progressed to easel, paints, pens, and inks. She had a special basket made to hold her art supplies while she scrambled across the arroyos and washes.

At first Mrs. Landauer had worried over her. "Your parents, they don't know how you go out alone like this. They trust me that I'm taking care of you."

"I'll be fine. There's nothing out there that can hurt me."

"Thirty years I lived in this place, do you think I ever walk out there with the snakes and bugs? And the quicksand?"

"You sound like my mother. "

"God forbid. I came west to get away, too. I'll stop right now," the landlady said, and she did. Now every day she placed a lunch deep into

Ruth's basket with a large canteen of water.

"You don't need to do that. There are plants I can eat out there. It's all in here," Ruth protested, holding up her *Scouting for Girls Handbook*.

"I don't want you coming back with cactus spears through your parched lips. It's bad enough the way you scrape yourself up out there." Ruth pulled her sleeve down to hide the latest scab on her elbow, but it was too late.

"I've seen the blood stains on your stockings and sleeves." Ruth was embarrassed that she had noticed that. But since Mrs. Landauer washed her clothes, there was no way to hide it.

"Drink plenty of water," she finished her harangue, pushing another canteen into the basket. When she got on her nerves, Ruth would think of Dr. Mera. Why did everyone want to take care of her? Every day she grew stronger. Couldn't they all just leave her alone? She had so much to do.

Mrs. Landauer helped put the heavy basket on her back, taking this as an opportunity to inspect Ruth's neck.

"My God," she said, "what scorpion has bitten you?"

"Just a mosquito," Ruth said, heading out the door as fast as she could under the heavy, sloshing pack.

Jonnie

Even if it meant barely getting back to her bed at Mrs. Landauer's before it was time to get going again, Jonnie cleaned and polished the autobus after every trip. As soon as she could, she bought two identical sets of clothes, so there would always be a clean one to wear. The cowboy drivers never did these things, but she knew she would have to work so much harder to hold a man's job.

Best was that she got to Dr. Morris' site every few days. If none of the tourists fell into a hole or fainted from the sun, she had an hour while Erna took them around. June was glad to let her help. She had noticed that the Navajo workers would dig and carry dirt, but as soon as evidence of a gravesite was discovered, they moved away and the archaeologists took over. June explained that Navajos believed that touching a dead person, even long after they died, would cause them to get sick or have an accident.

"They're just so superstitious," June said. "But it's just as well. They don't have the training we have. I'll show you when to step back and let an expert take over, too." Jonnie was relieved to hear that. It didn't feel right to disturb graves. Back in Gloucester, everyone had stories of ghosts in the graveyards, and no one liked to picnic on the rocks at Eastern Point, where so many ships had wrecked before there was a lighthouse and a breakwater.

"Aren't you scared of ghosts near graves?" Jonnie asked.

"I'm a scientist. There's nothing there. The Navajos who went to the boarding schools and had some education know that, sort of. They're the ones that want to work for us. The missionaries teach them about this, too. They teach them about Christian burials and all. Look, if you don't want to do this—"

"I do," said Jonnie. "I was just wondering."

So far Jonnie had mostly worked moving buckets of dirt that June would hand her. June dug a hole into the floor and worked sprawled out on the ground with her head down the hole. Her face was always red. When she let Jonnie poke her head in, she had to wear a mask over her nose and mouth because the dust was so thick. It was dark and cool in the hole, despite the glaring sun cooking her legs right through her trousers. She ran her hand in the dirt until she felt a hard knob poking through.

"I found something hard. Should I pull on it?"

"No. Never force anything. Try this." June handed her a little brush. "Go very slowly." The hard bristles scraped away and suddenly the thing came free. It was tiny, like a thick little twig.

"It's in my hand. Oh, I hope I didn't break it."

"Let's see." She grabbed it as Jonnie stood up, her knees cracking.

June held the little grayish bit in the bright sunlight. "What do you think?" she asked.

"Just looks like a piece of stick. Is it really something?"

"Toe bone," she held it right up in Jonnie's face, but it still looked like a dried out stick. "Human."

Jonnie jerked her head back. "You mean someone had their toe cut off, right here?" There wasn't any smell but dust, but she wanted to retch.

"No, the rest of the mummy is down there, too," June explained. The packrats carry off the little bones. It's a little treat for them." When she shook it again, Jonnie couldn't help but wiggle her own toes.

"You sure you have the stomach for this?" June laughed. One of the Indian workers handed her a palm-size piece of pottery with red designs on it.

"There you go," June said, barely giving the shard a glance. "Pueblo II." Jonnie reached out for it. It looked like all the other bits scattered around, but June and Morris and the others could pick one up and know in a glance whether it was from a thousand years ago, or a thousand years before that. Jonnie wanted to do that too.

The autobus horn blared, Erna's signal for the tourists to gather again. June waved and ducked back into her hole. As she scrambled down the tufa cliff, Jonnie grabbed what she hoped were shards and not little rocks. If she got back early enough, she could study them at Mrs. Landauer's dining table, while Miss Ruth examined her books about flowers and birds. Maybe Miss Ruth had found some of the old pottery, too. She knew how to find things out. Maybe she could help Jonnie learn.

Monday was Jonnie's day off. Monday mornings she caught a ride out to the dig with the archaeologists who had spent Sunday night in town. They were usually hung over and let her drive. Jonnie spent the day helping with the dig. When the sun went down, she pulled out her bedroll and slept under the stars, watching the fading campfire throw long shadows on the cliffs above. At first light on Tuesday, the dig cook always went into town for supplies, so Jonnie got back just in time to change into her driving clothes, warm up the autobus, and meet the morning train with Erna. Soon she would be back at the dig with a carload of tourists.

All her life few strangers had known what to make of Jonnie, and it was the same at the dig. Only June talked to her. She was studying at Columbia University. A lot of the other archaeologists were from there or from Harvard. Jonnie stayed away from the Harvard ones, remembering how, back home, they had laughed at her from the decks of their yachts. She was afraid they could see she was just a fish gutter from Gloucester who didn't belong here with them.

She and June were working in the same little area, bent over with little shovels that were almost spoons, slowly making progress almost grain by grain. Her back ached, and the sun went right through Jonnie's hat and shirt.

"It's time's like this," said June, "when I barely remember why I'm doing this."

"I heard Dr. Morris say that anthropologists study how people are different." Lately Jonnie had been thinking that she was the only one who was different. Some of the women archaeologists wore Jodhpur pants and men's shirts, but even wearing almost the same clothes, Jonnie still didn't fit in somehow. She hadn't had the nerve to ask Morris what he meant.

"That's a pretty good way to describe anthropology. Anthropology is the study of man," June said with a grand sweep over the empty vista before them. Jonnie guessed she meant that the whole earth was filled with people for June to study.

"How is that the study of how people are different?" Jonnie asked.

"Well of course they are. Why do you think the Navajo don't like to go near the graves or handle the mummies or bones?"

"They respect the dead," Jonnie suggested.

June thought a moment.

"No, it's not that. We Christians respect the dead. They don't respect them at all. They're afraid of them. They think they have ghosts or evil spirits that will harm them if they disturb the bones."

"Back where I grew up, people thought there were ghosts in the old cemeteries. Especially on Halloween."

"Anthropologists would like to study that! But that was just folklore back in your town. The Navajos are sure the ghosts are real. It's because they don't believe in science like we do."

Jonnie couldn't see the difference, but she had noticed the anthropologists were a bit touchy about their right to mess around in graves, so she wasn't about to argue.

"What's that got to do with people who are different?"

"That's how the Navajo culture is different from Christian culture."

"How about when a Navajo person becomes Christian?" One of the workers, John Billy, had been baptized recently by a Reverend named Luck, and he'd been telling everyone that it had been done in a cleaned up horse trough filled with water, because the washes were all dry this time of year.

"They're still Navajo. They still know the old ways. You wouldn't change your ways that easily, would you?"

She had a point there. One reason Jonnie hadn't let those missionaries get near her was she knew they would want her in a dress first off. It was the missionaries who made the women wear long dresses and long-sleeved blouses from mail order fabric like white women, instead of the beautiful blanket dresses they had once woven.

"The missionaries don't understand. That's why we anthropologists have to talk to the Indians fast, especially the old folks. Because the parents who become Christians will teach their children new ways and they'll forget the old ways."

"That will take a while. You'll have plenty to do here."

"Not really, it's already getting hard to find subjects here. I'm going to New Guinea this winter with my advisor, Dr. Margaret Mead. The people there have hardly been touched by civilization. It's a hot wet place, but the people there still live by hunting and gathering, something like the people who once lived here did."

June was leaving!

"Is everybody going?" Jonnie asked.

Betsy

Betsy went back several times to check on the little girl whose arm had been burned by the stove. Her mother quickly learned how to change the dressings and keep it clean, but in the dusty environment Betsy was always scared to look at the wound. Gradually the black drape of skin turned to scab and finally one day there was new skin so fresh that even on this little child it looked newborn. The mother, the girl, and Betsy all admired it. She packed up her little black nurse bag, and they looked at her sadly, probably thinking she wouldn't be back unless something else bad happened.

"I'd like to visit you again. You don't have to be sick or hurt." She wasn't sure they understood. As she was about to go to her car, the mother put her hand on Betsy's arm, indicating she should wait. She strode among the animals grazing near the hogan, and came back pulling a little goat kid who struggled all the way. Before Betsy understood, the goat was dead.

Unable to watch as she cut up the carcass to wrap and put in the car, Betsy leaned against the fender and looked out at the horizon, trying not to look at the sheep and goats that dotted the view. Patients had brought her gifts of meat before, but not like this. She thought of a particularly difficult patient at Sunmount. Mr. Evans had treated her like a servant, and on the day that he was fortunate enough to leave, he regally pressed some bills into her hand, as if she had been there to carry his valise, not to hold him through feverish nights and stumbling days. "Good-bye," he'd said, squeezing his eyes shut for a moment as if to shut out the sight of Betsy. She wanted to throw his bills back in his face, but Dr. Mera would have fired her if he'd ever found out.

As she placed a bloody flour sack of goat steaks into the car, the mother smiled gratefully, and they both looked over at the little girl, who was keeping an eye on a sheep starting to stray. Betsy smiled at the mother and licked her lips, pointing at the gift.

Laura

"I missed you," Laura said, wrapping her arms around Betsy as she stood at the sink.

"Oh, I'll bet back home you were thinking more of what photographs you want to take than of me."

"Well, I was developing the ones from the last trip and thinking how to do it better the next time. Hey, I never showed you the ones I brought."

She ran for her bag and took out the photos. Betsy took a long time with each one, saying "Oh that's Mrs. Francis. Look at how you've got her mouth, that's just right, she never seems to smile. She's so shy, I can't believe she let you take this. But she's hiding her face, wrapped in her blanket, that's just how she is."

Laura smiled shyly at that.

"The boy with the sheep! Makes me want to run my hands through that wooly coat. And the girl with the wobbly little lamb. Just as skinny and new as she is. Laura, you've got it just right. You know what I like about your photos?"

"Everything?"

"Of course, but I especially like that the people seem just like they are, right now. Not like those Indians in the books we have, the Edward Curtis' ones, where they look like they got lost here from some other time, like they don't belong here anymore so they are disappearing into the landscape. In your pictures, they are so right, as much a part of today as city people are in photographs of Manhattan. This is their place, and they are here now. That's what I see here."

Betsy tapped her finger on a picture of a grandmother whose hands rested calmly on her flowery skirt, the gravity of age tugging her breasts down as much as it pulled at the silver bracelets and necklaces she wore. She had a sly, satisfied little smile and her eyes seemed to be looking upon a world she had under control.

"See how firmly she stands on the earth, no matter how the years have hollowed her bones," said Betsy. "When I'm as old as she, I want to stand as sure, my eyes looking around and ahead at life as hers do." They stood side by side contemplating the picture, Betsy pressing her warm hand against Laura's arm, Laura's arm around her waist. No matter how much Laura looked at her photos, Betsy always saw something more.

While they talked, Betsy continued to boil and iron a pile of big white collars for her nurse dresses, a task she seemed always to be doing when Laura visited.

"Laura," Betsy said, "Remember that brochure you did about Pike's Peak? You could do a book on the Navajo people like that! On pretty blue paper? With a woodcut for the cover again? It could be a Navajo design."

"I didn't tell you," Laura said. "This awful woman came to the studio and looked at my picture of the girl with the lamb. She's the kind of woman you would think would buy my book, but instead she was awful. She said terrible things about the Indians. If a lot of people feel that way, I'll lose money again." She didn't want to say anything about the bills from the printer.

Both stared at the floor, thinking of the disappointment of those days.

"That's just one person," Betsy said. "Not everyone feels that way. Besides, these days the whole country's feeling rich. You're sure to do better. Most people like to look at pictures of people. Especially interesting people like the Navajo." This was an old discussion. Laura found so much to look at in a landscape, but Betsy was always more delighted when Laura photographed a person.

"That is the great thing about taking pictures of the Navajos," Laura perked up. "There's both landscape and people. More people are taking auto vacations now than when I did Pike's Peak. I could make this book smaller so they can bring it home from their trip. I've got to think about what will sell. That's what I didn't do with the brochures. You know what I wish, though?"

Betsy put down the iron and looked right at Laura, in the way that made her feel so wonderful and so sure that all her funny ideas would come true.

"I wish I could hold off taking the photographs of Navajo people until I have the money to do their book perfectly. I wish I didn't always have to think about money first."

"You could do both," Betsy said. "Think about it both ways. Do the moneymaker now and you'll get the money to make that perfect book someday."

Jonnie

The weather out West always surprised Jonnie, who had only Gloucester to compare it to. When August came, there were sudden and violent rainstorms that left as soon as they came, and everything dried up so fast she would wonder if she had imagined them.

Something that wouldn't dry up and disappear fast, no matter how much she wanted him to, was Roy, Erna's new driver. When Jonnie came to work one morning, there he stood next to Erna, who was up on her tiptoes so he wouldn't tower over her quite so much.

The first thing Jonnie had noticed about Roy was his long legs. He wouldn't have to sit all the way forward on the seat to reach the pedals. Roy could just sit back all sprawled out with one sunburned arm on the windowsill and the other around the back of Erna's seat. Roy had a big white Stetson, and a turquoise, black and white shirt that was embroidered with curlicues of spurs and saddles in red and gold thread. Roy was never drunk and always on time. His big white teeth gleamed as he smiled at the lady tourists, and the little boys watched his every move breathlessly. He knew as much about getting cars out of quicksand and flash floods as Jonnie did, but he also had strong arms to lever the car out. Somehow if the car got stuck when Jonnie drove, there was always whispering about "That queer woman driver took us right into the mud. She's damn lucky it drove itself right out." As if all her shoveling and prying did nothing. But when Roy had a stuck car, the tourists would be recounting the tale of how strong he was and how smart to solve the problem.

Worse yet, more autobuses were on their way, and Roy had arranged for his brother and his cousin to be driving. "You can trust these fellows" he said. "You'll have yourself a little army of drivers, Erna." He never called her Miss Erna. Didn't know his place, like Jonnie did. The tourists asked him more questions than they asked Erna, because they all wanted his attention. They all wanted their pictures taken with him. Nobody had ever asked Jonnie for that.

Erna was planning to have her own posse of drivers dressed in cowboy clothes, but she made Jonnie dress as a schoolmarm in a white blouse and skirt. She pinned a cameo to the collar. Jonnie thought it made her look like she was going to church, not doing the same job as the team of fake cowboys. "It's an idea I have of how the Koshare Tours should present itself, and you've got to fit into it," Erna told Jonnie, "Business is booming, times are good and this is my chance to corner the market. I've been the pioneer here, and now I've got to stay ahead of the competition. You go talk to anyone that's been here a while, they'll point around the plaza and down San Francisco Street, and they'll tell you which stores have come and gone, and which ones have stayed, and the ones that have stayed didn't get lazy for a minute."

"I'm not lazy," Jonnie muttered.

"Jonnie, I'd never say that. But you've got to understand how business works. Or I have to, anyway. Back east a woman would hardly get the chance to have her own business. Here, it's been wide open and I've had a chance good as any man. I was born in Albuquerque, I've lived here all my life, and I've seen businessmen strike it rich then lose it all, over and over. It's as bad as the prospectors who gamble away their nuggets. You just can't assume that if it's working now, you'll be rich forever. You have to change with the times. You're a good and dependable driver, but tourists want to see cowboys. They want to see their fantasies about the West."

Meanwhile, the real cowboys in town were laughing at Roy. They called him "movie star" and dared him to get cowshit on the cuffs of his pressed pants like a real cowboy. They called him "sissy boy" the same way she had heard them mutter about her queer clothes, but Roy just never seemed to hear or care. It was one more thing Jonnie was stewing about.

Betsy

Laura pulled out of Betsy's arms, sat on the edge of the bed, and then stood and tiptoed across the floor.

"Come on back to bed, honey," Betsy whispered.

"No, I'm awake. I'm still thinking about what we were talking about last night." Slowly waking up, Betsy remembered how late they had stayed up talking about all the ways the Reverend Luck and his wife had been interfering with her work.

"But it's my problem. You just need to listen to me."

"It's my problem, too. I won't let anyone treat you this way."

"It's hard, but I don't want to leave. I can sit through their boring church services."

"You shouldn't have to do that."

"Helping the patients comes first. They really need me. It feels so good to be needed." Laura came back to Betsy and curled her warm, soft arms around her.

"I need you. I know it's hard for you. Don't you think I feel everything you feel?"

Betsy shrugged.

"All right, maybe not all, but I feel a lot. I want to feel a lot. I love you."

Betsy wrapped her arms around Laura. "I couldn't do this without you. Even though it means being away so much."

They were silent for a long time. Then Betsy spoke up. "You know what we haven't done? Come up to the summer camp with me. Some of the families have summer camps up in the mountains where the sheep can graze. Lilly said I should go up there a few times this summer to check on their medical problems."

Laura looked doubtful.

"We'll have a great time. We can camp out in the forest and sleep under the stars. It will be like our vacation at Mummy Cave."

"I guess that means that after this vacation you'll want to move up there and be a Mountain Man," Laura said, but her joke showed she was loosening up. She shook out her muscles from the grip she'd been holding Betsy in. "Let's go. I'm sure to get good pictures."

They packed the car with camping equipment and set off together. After weeks of hot, dry, weather and many hours driving on parched land, the mountains felt like an oasis they had read about in the Bible. As the car struggled to climb, the air became cooler and the vegetation greener. Soon they were driving through groves of pine trees. They decided to camp at a cool stream near the edge of a deep ravine. Across the ravine was a hill covered with aspen. The sun was just going down, and they sat against a tree enjoying the novelty of the dancing shadows of the leaves.

Soon a Navajo man and his two small boys appeared, bringing a leg of mutton. It was Tom Begay, who Betsy remembered from a frantic journey she had made to his hogan to treat the older boy for bronchitis. The boy smiled and pretended to cough, to show that his lungs were still clear.

"I'm very glad you're here, I will do all I can to help you," Tom said. "But there aren't many people here." He pointed over the hill of aspen. "That's where they are, but the car can't go there. I'll go back and get some horses for you."

"First stay and have some dinner with my friend Laura and me," Betsy said. Soon, a fire was going with Tom's leg of mutton roasting over it, the waves of heat and smoke bringing a warm center to the cooling forest. While it cooked, Tom told news of the summer camp.

"It's been dry," he said. "The sheep aren't finding so much grass. We have to take them farther and farther from our camp, and that's making it harder on the people. Cecilia Nez fell on the rocks and her knee is still all big. Her sister Mary has something in her eye, and she keeps it closed like this," he said, squinting one eye and bobbing his chin trying to make them laugh.

"Everyone will be very happy to see you," he said.

Betsy pointed toward the car. "I've got all my bandages and medicines. I'm sure I can help Cecilia and Mary."

The sky was totally dark and it was getting cold. The firelight gleamed on Tom and his sons, wrapped in their brightly colored woven blankets. When a log fell, sparks danced over the high crowns of their wide-brimmed hats.

When the mutton was gone, Tom cut up a watermelon.

"I'm the biggest watermelon eater there is," said his younger son, and the contest was on. They all crammed the big melon slices into their mouths, spit out seeds like threshers, licked the juice from their chins, and then dove into another piece. When there was nothing left but a pile of rinds, every one looked up proudly, but the piles were about equal.

"I love watermelon!" said the older boy. By then the fire was down to glowing coals, and it was time to crawl into bedrolls. Tom and his sons set off over the hill.

Rain woke Betsy up in the middle of the night. They hadn't expected it so they had slept under just a little tarpaulin tied to the car. She wrapped the canvas groundsheet tighter around them and snuggled up closer to Laura. The rain was soft against the tarp, like the tinkling of cottonwood leaves in the breeze. They weren't getting wet, but she felt it could happen at any moment. Laura's hot, soft body warmed Betsy's left side while on her right side she could feel the cold ground through the canvas. Laura rolled closer and soon their hands were everywhere in the warm comfort of the blankets. The arguments and tension that had run between them since Betsy had decided to come to Red Rock all dissolved in the heat between them as the cool rain fell softly beside them.

Sometime and somehow during the night Betsy fell asleep, waking as the sun was just rising. Laura's hand still rested on her thigh, and she pressed her own hand over it. Laura sighed and rolled over. Betsy wanted to wake her to celebrate the sunrise, but knew she would have only grunted at the early hour, so she enjoyed it alone, looking through the breaks in the trees at the rosy sky and at the white spires of the aspen trees. Something crackled out in the brush and soon she saw a quail bobbing through the grass. She could almost see the white tip of his crest, when something almost lost in the darkness of distant trees caught her eye: the shadow of a man walking toward them.

The man came closer, not trying to hide himself at all. He must have seen the car, which anyone local would have recognized as Betsy's. Would anyone not from around here be up in these woods? Perhaps some hermit. Were there still mountain men?

As the man drew near, the sun finally popped out with a burst of glare through the trees, and Betsy saw that it was Jim Ferryboat, who she had met at a sheep shearing. When he came closer, he smiled and held up his finger, which was wrapped in a bandanna. Betsy pulled the blankets up to hide Laura and cover her own nightgown, but he looked unconcerned. Did Indian women sleep cuddled together? Meanwhile, he'd reached into the car and pulled out her medical bag.

"What are you doing up here, Jim?" Betsy asked softly, hoping Laura wouldn't wake suddenly and throw off the blankets.

"I'm looking for my horse," he replied.

"A horse! Was it a big one?" He was tall for a Navajo. Laura nudged her to let her know she was awake.

"My big horse is in this forest," he said, in the way that the Navajo people didn't quite answer questions.

"I think I saw it heading that way," Betsy said as she pointed toward the trees. "You go look for it while I take out my medicine." He handed her the bag and walked off. Quickly, she and Laura tumbled out of the blankets and rushed into their clothes. By the time Jim came back, they had started a fire for coffee. Laura made pancakes and bacon while Betsy treated Jim's hand. If he had any thoughts about Laura, he didn't show it. Jim spoke about as much English as Betsy did Navajo, but she soon understood that they were lucky that a bear hadn't found them. He'd seen it many nights lately in this peaceful clearing.

Tom returned with a burro and an ancient Navajo horse for them. He had several other men with him, and Laura was hard-pressed to put pancakes on the big cast iron griddle as fast as the men took them off, while each man showed Betsy a wound or sickness to treat. When breakfast was done and the morning clinic "au naturel" completed, they left the car in the clearing and set off on their mounts with Tom in the lead.

As Tom said, the summer camps were all on the other side of the aspen-covered hill. These were hogans built for the warm weather, made of a simple frame of strong upright logs with green branches laid across for a roof. On one side, a blanket hung to form a wall, but the shelter was mostly open. The delicate aspen leaves gave a tender peal in the breeze, like whispering little bells in a fairy church. The sunbeams sent dancing spray across the dirt floor.

With Tom showing the way, they went from hogan to hogan. Betsy had treated some of these people before. One held up an arm to show her the barely visible scar while another pointed to an eye to show how well it had healed. She tried to let them know that she remembered them by their faces, not by their wounds. It made her feel good to meet them again and see that she had friends on this mountain where she had never been before.

There were no serious problems, but at almost every hogan someone had a cut or a sniffle. While Betsy worked, Laura wandered around taking pictures. She took photos of the herds of sheep grazing not far away, their little shepherdesses dressed in long skirts and blouses. Each young girl had a necklace with some silver on it, or a silver button or two. The sheep they protected would bring them much more silver in the future, so that someday their necklaces would look like the many strands of silver and turquoise worn by Tom's wife, Daisy.

Laura photographed Daisy at her loom, which was in the open air, close by the hogan. Her two youngest daughters sat on the ground at her sides rolling yarn, and the baby cooed and burbled in his cradle board, which leaned against one of the sturdy log posts of the loom. A slightly older daughter sat nearby, scraping at a lump of mud-encrusted fleece with carding brushes. A little ways off, the oldest daughter was watching the sheep lazily eat the sparse grass.

Daisy sat on a pile of the canvas feed bags stenciled "Cortez. Colo." while she wove. Her rug was the colors of a calico cat: yellow, white, and black. She was weaving a sawtooth pattern of black against a yellow field. Her hands moved fast as she repeatedly reversed the position of the wooden comb she used to press the new line of weaving hard against what had already been done. Betsy stood behind Daisy looking through the strings of the loom, which framed part of the landscape of forest and mountain and flock.

"Let's quit our jobs and become weavers," said Laura, stepping up beside her as she rolled film into her camera. "Maybe they should bring the TB patients from Sunmount up here. What could be more serene and healthy?"

"If that were true, they wouldn't need me here."

"Well, today is like a dream. I wish I could bring my darkroom up here in a wagon, like the photographers who first photographed the frontier did. I'd travel slowly through the mountains, meeting the people and taking their photos. But I do have my big chance today. I should get moving." Giving Betsy's arm a hot squeeze, she went off.

Tom was standing nearby with the horse to take Betsy to see more patients, but she wanted to stay and watch Daisy. Her movements were intricate yet fluid. Betsy could see the patterns and colors changing as the rug grew. She was glad to be there to keep Daisy and her daughters healthy as they learned to weave and to care for the sheep.

When the sun began to drop, Tom took them back to their camp by the car. He needed to get back to his family, but promised to return at sunrise. It was still light enough for a hike, and they found a lovely little meadow.

They were gathering mushrooms for their stew when Laura came up to Betsy with some purpose in her stride. She gestured with her chin between the trees, where a man stood watching. He didn't seem threatening, just looked as if he was trying to make up his mind. For a while they all looked back and forth, but never quite staring. Finally, he walked toward them in a slow and friendly way. As he came closer, Betsy saw his bashful smile. They soon found he spoke no English, but she motioned to him to join them for dinner. He said his name was Setah.

They sat quietly by the fire as the steak roasted, with shy smiles all around. Setah wore black pants with a tightly buckled belt. His stiffly clean long-sleeved white shirt was buttoned right up to his chin, with a leather thong tied tight around the sleeve over his left biceps. He wore a necklace of many strings of squash beads with little bone and turquoise charms. Silver rings pierced both his ears and circled several of his fingers. A bandanna wound around his head was tied over his right ear. Everything about him was tightly wrapped, like Navajo babies in their cradle boards.

When he had sat down with them, he had taken off a loosely packed sack slung over his shoulders, but he didn't take off a smaller buckskin pouch on his belt which Betsy suspected and hoped was his own medicine bag. About one in ten of the Navajo men were medicine men.

He didn't show Betsy any injuries, but pointed to her black leather medical bag. On the picnic blanket, Betsy opened the bag and spread out all the bandages, scissors, and bottles of eye drops and pills. He looked at each object for a long time, then, looking at Betsy for permission first, he touched each one, rubbing his thumb across the silver of the scissors and weighing in his hand the weight of the little hammer for testing reflexes. Betsy stopped him only when he began to unwrap the sterile covering of a bandage.

Although she had seen the medicine men's work during the ceremonies and dances, Betsy had never had a close-up view of their tools. When he finished looking at Betsy's equipment, she tucked everything back into her bag, then gestured toward his pouch, trying to put the same expression on her face that he had used to get her to open her bag. He hesitated, then removed it from his belt and slowly unrolled the old worn leather slowly onto the blanket. Betsy and Laura gasped at the strange collection of objects revealed.

"I can't believe he's showing this to us," Betsy said. "The anthropologists told me this never happens."

"Maybe it's like a professional courtesy. He's recognizing that you're both in the same line of work," Laura said. "Probably he thinks the anthropologists are just nosy."

Most prominent were two tiny, perfect skulls, attached to sticks.

"They might be heron or crane," Laura said. She reached out, but Betsy grabbed her hand as Setah jerked with alarm.

"Don't touch! I'll bet he feels the same way about it as I did about the sterile bandages. His tools will lose their power if you touch them." Betsy clasped her hands together in her lap. Setah nodded approvingly as Laura did the same. They both leaned as close as they could to look at the two tiny skulls.

"I think those are eagle feathers wrapped around the stick," she said. "Look how long and strong they are. Imagine an eagle in flight, a bird that large, how substantial the feathers would need to be."

Tiny shells and arrowheads were tied to the stick with colored strings.

"I wonder how he got the little shells. Navajos must have traded with coastal Indians. Maybe California Indians?"

"Oh my," said Laura, "look at those!" There was a stick strung with many exquisitely delicate cloven bones. "They've got to be deer hooves. I remember them from when my father would hunt, but he'd just throw them out."

The Medicine Man picked up the stick with the deer hooves and shook it.

"Of course. A rattle!" Betsy remembered hearing the sound at the ceremony she had attended on that first night, when the Lucks had made her leave. Just thinking of them made her think of a rattlesnake rattle instead.

The first bag held many smaller buckskin bags, closed with buckskin thongs pulled tight. The Medicine Man opened each and held it up so they could sniff the mostly powdery contents. Betsy recognized cornmeal in one and corn pollen in another. The Indians used these for healing as she did with her own colored powders, pills, and liquid medicines, and who was to say that the scent from the bags, the sound of the rattle, the sight of the skulls, and the touch of the arrowheads were no less healing? At Sunmount, a few patients had told Betsy that hearing her shoes clicking on the floor as she approached their room was the most welcome sound of their day. She had been flattered that they looked forward to seeing her. Looking at this rattle, she wondered if it signaled the approach of the healer as her shoes did. But other nurses wore the same shoes. Perhaps her steps had some special rhythm? She laughed at how she was flattering herself.

Setah turned a larger object over and held it up to show them how he used it as a cup.

"A turtle shell," Laura said. "I've seen big black turtles like that sunning on the rivers back East." He held it up to his lips, and with his fingers he showed a liquid dribbling down. She could see the crack in the very dry and crumbling edge.

"I wonder if I could get him another," Betsy said to Laura. "I've never seen any turtles in the rivers around here."

"I'll try to find one when I'm back in Santa Fe," Laura responded, adding, "But I don't want to kill a turtle!"

"You could bring back a live one."

"Betsy, for gosh sakes! How would I keep it alive?"

"Maybe a store will have a shell."

"That sounds better. I'll look."

As he wrapped his tools back into their pouch, neither Laura nor Betsy could resist running her fingers along the soft, worn surface of the buckskin. One of the few phrases Betsy knew in Navajo, because she often had to ask the age of children, was "how old?" so she asked him that now. Speaking with his hands, they understood him to say that when he was a boy, he had bought it from a very old, old medicine man. Using his fingers as numbers, he said it had cost thirty sheep and thirty blankets.

"I wouldn't have thought they bought their medicine bag," said Laura.

"Reverend Luck has told me it's just a business to them, that one out of ten of the men is 'running this heathen racket' as he puts it. But if Luck wanted to meet a doctor with real dollar signs, he should meet Dr. Mera and those other folks feeding off the dying TB patients."

Meanwhile, the smell of roasted meat was filling the little clearing.

"Can't we serve the meat?" Laura asked. "I'm hungry and it's more than roasted." Betsy looked at it.

"Not quite yet. The Indians only like it very well done."

"I don't."

"We can't be rude. Pretty soon, Laura. How are the mushrooms coming along?"

When they finally ate, the only light was the campfire. Laura kept muttering about how chewy the steak was, but Betsy could tell their guest didn't think it was cooked enough. Setah wouldn't touch the mushrooms.

"Do you think he knows something we don't?" Laura wondered.

"I don't know if they never eat mushrooms, or he just doesn't want these. I think I'm not going to eat any more," Betsy said.

"Me either," said Laura.

After dinner they sat by the dying fire, Betsy surreptitiously trying to pry sinewy bits of meat out from between her teeth. In the soft light of the glowing logs, the Medicine Man leaned closer and began to tell a story with his hands. There was a clap of thunder, and he stopped, indicating that the story could not be told when the thunder was awake. He looked regretful, as if he had failed to repay them for the dinner. Tying his medicine bag and other bundles back on, he waved and disappeared through the woods.

The next morning they headed towards home, their only stop a hogan at the foot of the mountain, where a baby was in need of some help for a rash. The rest of the family was glowingly healthy. They were harvesting their wheat in the Navajo way, the many sons walking their horses over and over a pile of straw to separate the parts. The women and smallest children, all in their colorful clothes, stood nearby shaping the rising mound of winnowed wheat. The sun and the sky surrounded them all, as perfect as a painted backdrop in an idyllic theater. While Laura quietly set up her camera, Betsy basked in the beauty of it all. Finally Laura finished photographing and joined Betsy.

"It's so beautiful," Laura said. "I didn't want you to leave me to come here, but right now I'm glad you did. I don't think anyone has ever photographed this, but more than that I'm glad you're here to help keep it going. This should—" she paused to think of the right words, "this should just be. Just be."

They stood with their shoulders pressed together, watching the horses in their proud gait, the boys in their tall hats, and the silver jewelry and buttons of the women and girls flashing in the sun.

Laura

As autumn progressed, Betsy sent letters describing the Indian chants and dances and all her adventures. Laura felt like a stuffy stay-at-home. The stock market crashed in October, and business was the worst since she had opened her studio. She wanted the work to pick up fast, so she could take a weekend off to visit Betsy. Meanwhile, she made money every way she could think of, handing out advertising cards at La Fonda and spending money she barely had to advertise in the *Santa Fe New Mexican* newspaper. She even asked all the barbers to give her cards to their customers. "*Come get your photo taken while you look your best,*" the card said. It brought in men with fancy moustaches curled up in Wild Bill Hickok style.

It was a good thing she had rigged a bell so she could be in the darkroom and still know when a customer opened the door of the studio, although it always seemed to ring just when the film needed another minute in its chemical bath. She just hoped the caller saw the sign "*Have a Seat While I Give Another Customer's Work the Quality You Will Expect.*"

One day the bell rang, and when she finally came out, it wasn't a man waiting but a lady. Her face was tanned from the sun, and her hair gray. She wore an old-fashioned eastern kind of dress and walked uncomfortably in fancy shoes that looked new. There was something warm about her, like she glowed from the sun itself. Laura thought this must be a ranch wife come to get her picture taken, for she had seen a few before. They hardly ever came to town and they weren't used to speaking to any one but cowboys and cows and their equally shy husbands. But they always came with their husbands. This woman was alone and not even wearing a ring. Laura tried not to look at her too curiously.

"I'd like my photograph taken, please," said a voice that was no shy ranch wife. "I see you have the Graflex." She indicated the camera on its stand. "That's quite impressive."

"You're a photographer!" Laura exclaimed.

"Perhaps I should be," she said, and nodded her head determinedly.

"Pardon?" Laura asked.

"I'm sorry, I was just thinking out loud. I spend a lot of time alone." So she was a ranch wife.

"Where I'm from in New York City, I often had my portrait taken."

"Oh," Laura said, thinking that not only had she guessed wrong about the woman, but fearing she was going to be comparing Laura's work to that of other photographers.

"Those were family portraits. Which is why I'm here. I mean, I don't have a family here, I'm alone here, but I want to send a portrait photograph back to my parents, so they know I'm doing well here, looking healthy."

"Fine," Laura said, showing her where to sit. "I'll do my best. I studied photography in New York at the Clarence White School."

"I know that one," she said. "I studied at the Arts Students League."

"You did! And are you an artist?"

She hesitated. "I don't think of myself as an artist. But I've been going out in the desert and drawing what I see. Do you think that makes me an artist?"

"You are of a certain school," Laura said. "Scientific photos of nature are the latest trend these days. I've been reading about it in *Camera Craft* magazine. But it's not what I want to do with my own art. In photography school we talked about Alfred Steiglitz's theories and how he said you should never phony up your photos. My teacher, Clarence White, didn't agree. He taught us to use gauze to make an old woman's face lose its lines."

"That would be just the thing," she said. "My mother's got to think

I'm in perfect health."

"You look very healthy."

"She won't understand about all this sun on my face. She sent me here to get color, but not this much!" Laura laughed but her customer was too anxious to join in.

"I'm Laura, I'll be glad to do my best for you."

"I'm Ruth," the customer said. "Fire away!"

Betsy

Betsy had thought Red Rock remote in the summer, but as winter set in she felt truly isolated. Snow and cold winds meant fewer Indians came to the clinic except for the worst emergencies. To make matters worse, the Lucks had fewer souls to save, so they were working on hers.

Whenever anyone stopped by, they brought news of big trouble everywhere. It was said that when President Harding died, the traders in remote posts heard about it from their Navajo customers in two days, which was two weeks before the newspapers and mail arrived to confirm the rumors. They heard about the problems with the stock market soon enough. Something had gone terribly wrong. At first Betsy couldn't help but feel smug, picturing rich people pawning their treasures far from her squat clinic in the beautiful desert, but as she heard more about all the people out of work, and some even losing their homes, she realized that like a cancer working its way through a body, the money problems would eventually come their way. The Indians were already so poor that they would be more susceptible than most folks. Her last check from the Indian Association had been late and she had laughed it off to the complicated system of supply trucks that eventually brought the mail to Red Rock, but her current check still hadn't arrived and she was starting to wonder.

Betsy hoped that Laura could explain what was happening on her next visit. She had said she was coming that weekend to see an Indian dance. If Laura came she could tell the Lucks they had to go to the dance so that Laura could photograph it. If Laura didn't come, the Lucks would hound Betsy until she agreed to go to their prayer meeting instead.

In her last letter to Laura, Betsy had let it all out about how much she hated Reverend and Mrs. Luck with their hard benches and endless sermons. When they weren't making her pray in it, they were pressuring her to help find rocks for the walls of their new chapel. "We don't want to use adobe like for the heathens' houses," Mrs. Luck would say. "Our church will be of stone like the great cathedrals of Europe. It will inspire them to want more from life."

Betsy was tired of piling rocks, praying, and having to worry about what Mrs. Luck would think if she talked to a medicine man, stayed too long at a hogan, or told Mrs. Lazyfoot that her child didn't need white man's medicine because the herbs she was using would do fine. Writing her complaints to Laura was all Betsy could do.

When Joe Yazzie, who drove bales of wool to Shiprock, stopped by and told her that the trader had told the wool buyer to tell Joe to tell Betsy that Laura had sent a message saying she couldn't come this weekend, Betsy remembered her recent letters. Had she said anything but complaints? Had she told Laura that she missed her? Had she asked how Laura's photographs were going?

What could Laura have thought but that Betsy only wanted her here as a shield against the Lucks? How could she have been so thoughtless? Why would Laura want to drive so many hours and probably have to deal with a stuck car, just so Betsy would be happy doing something she hadn't wanted her to do?

She wished she could visit Laura, but had no money for gasoline, even if she had the time. Her patients needed her. Little Mamie Yak had pneumonia, and the Redsheep twins were probably spreading their pinkeye to the other kids. She couldn't go anywhere. If Laura didn't want to come to Red Rock, didn't see how important it was for Betsy to be here, well, some people had problems more important than theirs.

Although Laura had been more accepting after their visit to the summer camp, once she was home again she soon went back to saying how hard it was for her that Betsy lived so far away, having adventures while Laura had little to do on many lonely nights. But lately, Laura had been writing about her new friend Ruth, and how she was helping Ruth photograph plants and birds so she could draw and catalog them. Betsy had been glad that Laura didn't seem to be sulking about missing Betsy so much, but now Betsy suspected that Laura felt that seeing her was not as important as taking pictures of pine cones in Santa Fe. Betsy could hardly believe that miserable woman she had known at Sunmount had healed enough to hire Laura to take photos of her hikes. It almost sounded like Laura would have gone even if she wasn't being paid.

Over the years, Betsy and Laura had watched a few couples in their circle of friends split—twice with June as the instigator. They had felt sure of each other, but for the first time Betsy wasn't feeling so self-righteous. Were they growing apart? Betsy had made sacrifices to be here, to accept the heat and sun of summer and now the bitter isolation of winter for the endless line of poor, sick Indians. If Laura had to be sacrificed too, maybe Reverend Luck had a point about how a real sacrifice is the one that really hurts. Maybe this was her real sacrifice.

Didn't the Indians have some ideas about sacrifice? Their healing ceremonies were expensive, paid off in sheep and silver. Apparently the cost was part of the ritual, a sacrifice the patient's family was willing to make to bring back health. The Indians knew about sacrifice. Betsy could do it, too.

She knew that Luck and his wife had suspicions. Mrs. Luck had brought over her Sears catalog, saying they were going to send in a big furniture order and get a truck to bring it out from Farmington, and wouldn't Betsy like to order a second bed for her visitor? Betsy wondered how Mrs. Luck knew that they slept in the one bed. The suggestion was so blatant that she hoped it was innocent.

Mrs. Luck had mentioned the way Laura dressed, which she thought was a bad example for the Indians. Laura wore men's khaki trousers, work shirts, and a Stetson hat so battered even Betsy called it "disreputable." Mostly she used it to shade her camera lens. She didn't dress like that in Santa Fe. No Navajo person had commented about it, probably because they thought whites were pretty strange in how they dressed anyway.

The Navajo women never wore anything but layers of long skirts and silver-buttoned blouses. Betsy had a few nurse dresses, but there was no point in trying to wear white in a place where red dust constantly swirled in the air. The dress she wore most often had turned a light rust color. Every night she boiled the broad collar, trying to keep at least that much of what she wore a hospital white. She also ironed its two sharp points, futile as that was. Her sunhat was almost as tall in the crown as the Navajo men's hats, but the brim wasn't much. She would have liked a wider brim, but then they might think she was wearing a man's hat. She didn't own any jewelry, although she envied how the Navajo women's necklaces and buttons gave them a glow even on the dustiest days.

When Mrs. Luck heard that Laura wouldn't be coming this weekend, she said "Oh, you must be so disappointed. If I saw Mr. Luck so little, I'd be so sad to miss a weekend." She wanted Betsy to confide in her. That would have been nice if she wasn't just baiting her trap, so that she could turn around and add Betsy and Laura's relationship to her list of proof why Betsy wasn't fit to be around Christians or the heathen Navajo, as she called them. With no other women to talk to it was so tempting to Betsy to share more, not just about how much she missed Laura's visit, but even about how tired she was of reading Laura's letters about Ruth, Ruth, Ruth. Instead she just had to keep her head and say, "Oh, Laura can come another time to take her photos," as casually as if that was all Laura came for.

Betsy wished she wasn't always watching out for Mrs. Luck. She wanted to know the real reason Laura wasn't coming. Would she be going on another of those picnic hikes she'd wrote about, involving Ruth and a basket of vegetables and fruits fresh off the train from California, not canned peaches and tomatoes like she'd have to do with at Red Rock? Betsy tried to think of something more to offer her love, but after all, she was the one who had left. Who was there to blame but herself?

One frosty morning before the clinic opened, Setah Begay, the medicine man they had met on the mountain on the lovely summer day so long ago, knocked at the door. He didn't appear to be sick, just very curious to look at her tools and medicines. Betsy went to the storage cabinet where she had put the things that Laura had brought for him from Santa Fe.

When Setah was satisfied that he had seen everything, she invited him for tea, but instead of pouring the drink, Betsy presented his gift. He carefully unwrapped the excelsior in which it was packed and lifted out the turtle shell cup. Betsy couldn't wait to tell Laura how delighted he looked. He immediately filled it with tea as they both watched anxiously to see if it would hold water. When it did, he smiled shyly.

Mrs. Luck came to the door. She recoiled at the sight of the medicine man and Betsy looking so domestic at the kitchen table together. It was early in the morning, and for a moment Betsy felt compromised.

"What's he doing here?" Then she spotted his cup.

"My goodness, what is he drinking out of? Have you no decent dinnerware? I'm sure I can lend you some."

"He's just visiting my clinic. He wanted to see how I practice medicine."

"He's not sick? He's just hanging around here? Where's Lilly? You shouldn't be alone with him."

"Oh but he, he—" There was something she could say, and suddenly the words leaped into her mouth. "Oh but he has symptoms that brought him here. He has symptoms of friendliness."

"Hmmpph," she said. Betsy pictured the imitation of Mrs. Luck she would do when she retold the whole incident to Laura. That "hmmpph" sound would have her in tears of laughter.

After Mrs. Luck stalked out, Setah and Betsy had to stifle their laughter. Lilly showed up next. She spoke to Setah for a moment, then explained that the last time he had tried to hold a sing, which is what they called their healing ceremony, the Lucks had tried to break it up. Asking that they not tell the Reverend and his wife, Setah invited Lilly and Betsy to a sing a few days later at a remote hogan.

On the night of the sing, after a long and bumpy drive through the dark, they entered a very big hogan. They brought gifts of coffee, cigarettes, and sugar, which Lilly said would be expected. The ceiling logs were cut from sizeable trees and the ceiling was high. The tallest men stood easily inside. As she entered, Betsy felt the men looking at her hostilely. Someone said something and they all laughed nervously. She could tell it was something about her. She nudged Lilly who whispered, "Setah said that it's okay, you are one of their own, you heal people." Betsy smiled at the men but they didn't smile back.

Opposite the door, on the other side of the fire, sat Setah. Navajo Jim, who she had met a few times, sat to his left. He was an old man who was always surrounded by many wives, children, and grandchildren. He was very traditional in his dress. He had always looked vigorous, but now he looked frail. He hunched over limply, and she hoped that he was the patient. He lifted his head for a moment, looking a little scared and a little hopeful. It was the look on so many patients' faces while they waited to see a doctor.

Jim's wife sat to his left and many more women relatives nearby. She recognized many of them. Setah's assistants, all men, sat to his right. All were wrapped in blankets and sat on sheepskins. Slowly, more and more people entered and sat, until there must have been more than thirty. It was crowded, but somehow everyone knew their place and all fit. The fire in the center provided the only light.

Setah and his assistants shook their rattles and began to sing. Jim stripped off his clothes. He cringed wretchedly, wearing only a thong. Setah waved his hand, and Jim stood up, towering over everyone. He circled the hogan, casting huge shadows. When he moved close to the fire Betsy could see he was no longer the firm young warrior the shadows had made him.

Jim stopped circling and stood by Setah. The singing continued, a repetitive chant that throbbed with energy and then ebbed solemnly. It came from deep within their throats, with no melody or words, just a chain of energy from sound. Setah rubbed Jim's body with bunches of yucca leaves and other weeds Betsy didn't recognize.

Then two young men stripped and rubbed their bodies with ash, giving their skin a soft color in the firelight. Setah draped their necks and wrists with arrowhead necklaces and bracelets. Their heads were crowned with huge feathers that had to be eagle. With eagle feather brushes they brushed Jim all over, as if sweeping the illness out of his body.

The chanting swelled loudly and intensely. The room was a dark growling cave. Nothing looked familiar. Betsy wanted to run outside. She gripped Lilly's hand.

Yelping like animals in pursuit, the young men chased Jim out of the hogan with their brushes. Their footsteps pounded the dirt around the hogan as they chased him. Betsy was glad she wasn't outside. The fire and smoke died down, and through the fire hole she could see the night sky and a few bright stars. The sight calmed her down as if a soft comforting blanket had been lovingly wrapped around her. She looked across the circle at Setah. Straggly hair poked out of the red scarf wrapped around his head. He smiled at her, and she wasn't scared any more. She just wanted to watch and learn.

The young men and Jim came back in. Setah gave them an oil which they rubbed all over their bodies, and then they put their clothes back on. Everyone filed out of the hogan and most walked away. Setah and a few other medicine men stood together, talking. They kept glancing at her. Finally, Setah waved her over. Rubbing his hand on his throat, he made the gesture he had used before to indicate her medicine bag.

Could it be they wanted Betsy to treat their throats? She was delighted and got her bag. The patients lined up and she doled out cough syrup. Each made a face like a child as they gulped it down but then smiled gratefully at her. Clearing his throat to show how well the medicine worked, Setah spoke and Lilly translated. "He's glad to have you see our good medicine practiced." As she said his words, Setah's eyes twinkled with just a touch of teasing. Holding up his hands, pointing at Betsy and then at himself, he placed his two forefingers together. She knew it meant they could work side by side. In all her time among the Navajo people, Betsy had never felt so accepted.

Jonnie

When the weather cooled down and the tourists thinned out, Erna's business slowed. Roy and the other men quit, so Jonnie was driving again—when the tour went out at all. They couldn't drive to the Navajo land or the field site anymore, because of the deep snow and temperatures that went well below zero. Back in Gloucester people always talked about New England as if it had the coldest, snowiest winters and talked about the Southwest as if it were a hot, dry desert all the time, but Jonnie was learning that the Navajo land could get colder than Gloucester ever did and that the snow was even a worse problem, because there were so few roads and certainly no traffic or plows to keep them cleared. There was more that she had been taught in school back east that she learned was wrong. She was shocked to learn that the Pilgrims hadn't been the first white people to settle in what became the United States; the Spanish had lived in New Mexico long before the Mayflower left England.

Because of harsh driving conditions, they were only taking tourists to places near Santa Fe and Taos. Jonnie liked the Pueblo Indians they visited there, but was eager to learn more of the Navajo language so she could be more helpful at the dig. When she had time off, she talked with Navajo people selling rugs and jewelry on the plaza.

Miss Erna said that it wasn't just the winter that was slowing business, because she'd had many customers the year before. She said it was the stock market falling back in October. Not everyone understood what that meant. Jonnie explained it to Mrs. Landauer.

"It's like the fish market back in Gloucester," she told her. "Nobody knows how good the catch will be, but they have to put their money up to send the fishing boats out. They have to buy the nets and hooks and lines and repairs. If the boats come back soon, loaded with fish, they all get their money back. If they don't do well, and maybe lose a mast to a storm in the Grand Banks, nobody makes money. Least of all the poor fellows who went out in the boat for months. They don't even get their little share of the profits, because there isn't any to cut up. For the few fish caught, the price is high, so the fisherman who walked those slimy decks in high winds doesn't even have the money to buy fish to feed his own family. That's what the stock market crash is. It's like the whole fleet coming back late and empty, and the whole town suffers."

With business so slow for Erna, Jonnie was free to pick up odd jobs at La Fonda and other businesses. She kept busy, always dreaming of getting back to the field site.

Erna was all smiles for the tourists, but dropped it immediately once they were gone. She had a lot on her mind. In the little time they spent alone, she didn't say much, but Jonnie had seen her at the telegraph office looking nervous. She would catch Erna looking at her, then looking away, like it felt when you know it's about you, but no one's talking. Meanwhile, Jonnie did the best work she could.

One day, the autobus got stuck in the sand. Erna had told her to take a shortcut, although Jonnie warned that it wasn't a good idea. Erna said she had to get back earlier and to do it anyway. It took three hours to get unstuck, the few tourists hungry, bored, and angry. Anytime the autobus got stuck, they all blamed Jonnie. They glared at her and she turned her face away, wishing and dreaming she was at the dig, far away.

Jonnie missed June, too. When the dig closed at the end of the summer, she'd gone back to Columbia University, expecting to go to New Guinea with her teacher, Margaret Mead. But the Hard Times had kept her in New York City, working as a secretary for the school. She was saving her money to come back in the summer, but Morris wasn't sure if he could continue the field camp. From Manhattan to Santa Fe plaza, there was nothing to do but hope things would get better soon.

Miss Ruth was always happy, out walking all day, studying her finds at night. Lately, she'd been bringing home bugs and putting them in jars. Mrs. Landauer didn't like it one bit, but Miss Ruth talked her into it, agreeing to keep only one good strong container at a time on the cleared dining room table. She couldn't leave the bottles alone for a minute, so she needed Jonnie to be there, even though she didn't like company.

One night Miss Ruth filled a wooden cigar box with dirt from the mesa. She was studying how the bugs walked. Jonnie wanted to look too, but Miss Ruth was all quiet into herself and her bugs. It was fun just watching her delight as she examined the bugs, taking notes and making drawings in her little leather bound notebook.

"You know, Miss Ruth," Jonnie said, hoping she would be invited to come closer, "your notebook is just like a ship's log."

Miss Ruth stared back with a dazed look, and Jonnie knew she had only annoyed her. Oh well, she thought, and picked up her map to study. She had been collecting maps of the places she drove the autobus. She did everything she could to be better at her job, hoping Erna would notice. But her employer rarely said anything nice. Jonnie liked how it was at the dig, where if someone found something interesting, everyone would run to come see and sometimes cheer.

One day at the dig, one of the men had fallen into a disgusting hole in what must have been the turkey pen of the Old Ones. He had screamed and grabbed his knee, but when he pulled his foot out, he saw the tip of an object that turned out to be a carefully sealed wooden cask. The field camp had a bell of sorts, made from a tire rim hanging from a tent pole. He clanged on it with a pick and everybody came running to see the cask opened. It was jam-packed with hundreds of parrot feathers, which beamed iridescent rainbows of color against the endless dull pink rock and sand. Dr. Morris explained that back a thousand years or more, someone had decided the old turkey pen was probably a good place to hide their treasures. The fellow who had fallen beamed with pride, although he must have been in pain.

Jonnie daydreamed about finding something that would make them ring the bell for her. The archaeologists didn't seem to mind her being at the dig, but she didn't feel she fit in. She wasn't from a fancy college, and she wasn't a Navajo laborer. It was like she wasn't really there, but when they rang that bell for her, they would all know she was there. It was her next goal to accomplish. She had made it West, she had found a great job, and she liked living with Mrs. Landauer and Miss Ruth. Best of all, she had found something she loved to do—when she could get out to the dig.

But it wasn't enough. She thought back to those days at the cod liver packing plant, back on the wharf in Gloucester, watching the boats pass Ten Pound Island and glide up to unload. All the women hated the hot, stinking job, but they hated it together. She wondered how Madge was doing now, or Tinker, or the other women she had stood side by side with to gut fish while they talked and joked. It may have been a life that headed nowhere and had no fresh day's excitements and discoveries like she had here, but there was something she had left back there when she was one of those women that she hadn't found in New Mexico.

It wasn't that the women archaeologists at the dig weren't friendly to her. They just weren't friendly to each other. With all those men around, they stayed apart in a way women never did at the cannery. There wasn't women's work or men's work here, so there never was a group of only women or only men. Some of the women played up to the men, and others paired off with them. Jonnie was glad to do interesting work, but she felt that something had been left behind.

The doorbell rang, and Mrs. Landauer, who was sitting in the corner reading but always keeping one eye on the bug box, let in Laura, Miss Ruth's photographer friend. Laura was always finding reasons to stop by. First she was forever improving her photos of Miss Ruth, making her look healthier and healthier, but after Miss Ruth sent the pictures to her family, she asked Laura to take photos of bugs and plants for her. They spent many evenings planning their trips, and Jonnie felt even more pushed aside.

Laura

Laura had never seen the two women who walked shyly into her studio, but she knew everything about them. They were a few years younger than she and Betsy had been in the year of the flu epidemic. Everyone else thought of it as that horrible year, but she remembered it primarily for bringing Betsy to her feverish body. Sometimes they still joked that she still got feverish for Betsy. These girls were clearly burning with that same ailment.

"We'd like photos taken," said the shorter of the two young women. She was a Spanish girl with black curls and a creamy skin.

"I'll go first," said the other. Her straight hair and chiseled cheekbones made her green eyes dance. "Graciela's never had her portrait taken, so I said I'd go with her. Oh, and I'm Helen."

"Sure," said Laura, but they weren't fooling her. She admired the way they were handling the situation. She and Betsy would have done the same.

Once the single portraits were taken, with each girl hovering over the other's hair and pose, Helen spoke with her back to Laura. "Um, let's have one together, that will be fun. Is that okay?"

"Sure," said Laura, congratulating herself for a good guess. Girls who were just friends came in all the time for a portrait together, giggling all the way and never bothering for the single portraits. Girls with something to hide would do it just like these girls, their love presented as an afterthought. She wanted to hug these girls. She wondered who the Reverend Luck was in their lives.

"Just a minute," Laura said. "I have a really good example I can show you." There were several wedding photos on the walls of her studio that she could have pointed to, but she had another idea. As she stepped toward the door from the studio into the bedroom, she saw Helen glance at Graciela with fear. Her heart sank for them. "It's a picture of two women to show you what I can do," Laura said, trying to smile reassuringly but also feeling their self-consciousness. She wished there was an easy way to tell them they were safe, that she would love to be their friend, even. How had she met other women, like June? It took a June to be outspoken enough. But Laura could speak with her camera.

When she showed them the photo of herself and Betsy, their arms around each other, their faces turned to each other, Graciela and Helen both stepped back, open-mouthed, like two sparrows that had been startled.

"That's you?" said Graciela.

"Yes, with my friend Betsy." She could see the question in their eyes.

"She usually lives here, but right now she's in Red Rock, where the Navajo people live." Their puzzled looks made her go on. She always wanted to brag about Betsy, but rarely had the chance. There was too much that would have to be held back, as these two girls were doing. "She's a nurse and she wanted to help with their health care."

"That's nice," said Helen.

"But she usually lives here?" said Graciela. "You aren't married?" Helen blushed and gestured toward Graciela to stop talking. Graciela was looking at Laura's ring finger.

Now Laura felt on the spot. What if she had misjudged?

"No, we live together. Ten years now." She knew she was bragging, but she had never had the chance before.

"Oh," said Graciela. "That's nice. If I didn't get married, I'd like to live with Helen."

Helen's smile dropped, but Graciela didn't notice it as Laura had.

"You're getting married?" Laura asked.

"Of course," said Graciela. "Everyone gets married—oh, I'm sorry. Everyone in my family does, anyway. Maybe yours is different. I don't have a fiancée yet, but it won't be long." Helen was hanging on her every word. Laura wished she knew what to say.

"Yes, my family is different." She wished she could say that not every woman wanted to be married. "So you want a photo together?"

Laura stared at the primped and posed young women as she focused on them through the frosty glass of the camera. She felt sad for the photograph that would have been of the happy friends. If only she hadn't talked about Betsy, Laura berated herself. But it had felt so good to be able to speak about it.

It was Helen who returned alone for the photographs a week later. There had been nothing Laura could do for it in the darkroom. Graciela's hand barely touched Helen's shoulder, and Helen looked away from Graciela and the camera, her lower jaw tight and her eyes sad. Helen never looked right at Laura as she paid and left, only taking one copy. Laura picked up the proof print, intending to discard it. She looked into Helen's hurt eyes. She looked at the sample wedding photos on the wall of her studio, the self-satisfied smiles of the brides, then back to the photo of the young women. She looked at Graciela's hand, afraid to touch. She went to the darkroom to make a better print for herself. It wouldn't be one she displayed in this studio, in this town where the two women lived, but she could picture it on the wall of a gallery. Next to it she could put the photo of the Navajo shepherd girl. The photos were honest and the people were real. What more could she ask of her art? She had captured an instant of truth in the lives of Helen and Graciela, that would be there perhaps when Graciela's many great-grandchildren were old. Maybe Helen would show it someday to another woman, a woman who was not waiting to marry a man.

Laura thought of Thea in *Song of the Lark,* who saw the broken pottery vessel as the way that art could capture an instant of time. Wasn't a photograph also like this, perhaps more than any other form of art? Laura had wanted a moment like Thea's, and now she had it, looking at the uncertain women whose lives she had unwillingly changed with not just words, but a photo. A photograph had such power. She felt terrible that it had hurt them, although Graciela's plans would inevitably have hurt Helen. But could a photograph change other lives? What about her photos of the Navajo people, the shepherd girl, the medicine man, the men by the firelight, the family in their wagon? Could a photo change Reverend Luck or his wife? Could they see at last the real people before them, not the vanishing ghosts of Edward Curtis? There was a lie about marriage in the wedding photos on the walls of Laura's studio, and there was a lie about Indians in the Edward Curtis photo that had hung on the wall of her parents house, the photo of the Indian horseman passing like ghosts under a cliff palace, their faces with their hopes and loves and pain unseen, their backs almost to the camera. There was more to know about the Navajo people in the face of the shepherd girl and Mrs. Francis and the boy with the sheep than in all these ephemeral men of Edward Curtis and his imitators. Laura was capturing these moments in the sheath of her camera.

Had Betsy's choice, which had caused her so much loneliness and resentment, also brought Laura what she had hoped so long to find?

Betsy

When the fierce cold and snow of winter slowed, the winds came, with roars, shrieks, and whistles almost as if a train was rumbling by. At first the sounds had scared her that it might be a tornado, and there was so much red dust in the air that often it looked like there had been one. She could barely see the Luck's little house. Her windows were pushed down as tight as they went, but in the morning there was always an inch of sand on the sills. When she got out of bed, her feet would raise a cloud of red dust. She scooped up the piles with a dustpan without even sweeping first.

To avoid going face to face with the winds carrying water from the spring at the foot of the hill nearby, Betsy melted snow to drink. Reverend Luck sometimes got the generator going to run the water pump, but mostly he just tinkered with it and cursed under his breath, then coughed to cover up whatever he muttered. Without the generator, there wasn't electricity for lights either, so Betsy used the harsh kerosene lanterns. With her own water and light, she felt a bit like the Navajos in their remote hogans, living independently of civilization, or at least until the kerosene can was empty.

Sunday morning was her only morning without clinic hours. She woke up not ready to face the red desert inside the house and the gusty one outside. If only Reverend and Mrs. Luck would leave her in peace, she could sleep in. Their pounding on their church bell ended her serenity, but she stayed put beneath the covers.

She was thinking of making breakfast when there was a knock at the door. She wanted to pretend she wasn't there, sure it was the Lucks or some embarrassed messenger they would send. She was relieved to see Ned, a young Navajo man who had won her heart earlier in the winter by showing her how the stove worked and re-supplying her woodpile. As he walked in, he slowly unwrapped a buckskin package, all the time smiling almost flirtatiously. Betsy thought of all the unusual objects she had already seen—kachina dolls, feathered prayer sticks, perhaps a silver necklace he hoped to sell to raise some fast cash. But when, with a flourish, he finally revealed his treasure, it was a very familiar object.

"Checkers! You want to play checkers?" Betsy gasped. But maybe he had some other use in mind. It was a red and black checkerboard to Betsy, but perhaps something totally other in his culture. He pulled the thong drawstrings of a little leather pouch and spilled a pile of wooden checkers next to the board. He smiled eagerly and there was nothing to do but to sit down and play. They were evenly matched, and before she knew it the morning was sailing away in game after game.

They didn't need words, which was a relief after weeks of straining so hard to communicate. She had wanted a day off, and this was becoming one. By ten o'clock Betsy was very hungry, so she cleared the board off the table, shooed him out the door with a friendly wave that she hoped said "come back and I'll beat the pants off of you" and finally made breakfast.

She was just washing up when Timothy, Ethel, and their three small children stopped in. They had just sat down when Cecilia and her daughter arrived. They all crowded around the table when Nacahale's second wife and little boy showed up at the door. The children played quietly. They were always so well behaved. Cecilia's baby's smiling face beamed at them, the rest of her head and body completely masked by the wraps of her cradle board. Everyone wanted to know about the boy Betsy had taken to the hospital in Shiprock on Saturday. The nurse tried to explain about a ruptured appendix, holding her side and moaning and pantomiming a doctor cutting something out. They looked horrified until she smiled to show it was a success.

Jenny, who she had treated for strep throat, came by with her friend Mary. Those two were always giggling together as Betsy had done with her schoolmates when she was fifteen. They ran off near the woodpile to whisper together, then came back with Mary all blushing.

"Go on, Mary, tell her," Jenny said. Mary hid her face in her hands.

"I'm listening," Betsy said. But she had to wait while Mary giggled and blushed and tried to catch her breath She keep pointing at Jenny to talk, but Jenny said "Tell it yourself."

Blushing furiously and giggling, Mary finally caught her breath.

"You know Yellow Mexican?" she asked. Betsy nodded. He was a sullen fellow with two wives who bickered so much he had to have a hogan for each of them. She had been out there in the late summer. The older wife had died in childbirth before she arrived. Although their three toddlers looked lost, Yellow Mexican nonchalantly mumbled something about bringing the children to the hogan of his other wife. Was Mary going to tell Betsy that she was going to marry him? She tried to think what to say. Would he be setting this giggling girl up in a hogan with the motherless children? When she saw her next, which might not be until summer, would this happy girl be gone, with only an overworked, neglected, and probably pregnant woman to be seen? Perhaps Reverend Luck was right when he warned the girls to have only a Christian marriage. At least then she would be the only wife.

"My husband will be Yellow Mexican's first son," she said. "Do you know him? He is known as Yellow Mexican's Son?"

"I do," Betsy said. "He looks like a very strong man." Mary giggled and blushed.

Betsy let out a relieved breath. The son was only a year or two older than Mary, a quiet, handsome youth. She could understand the young woman's blushing and excitement to wed a young man. But would her fiancée turn into his sullen, impassive father?

Meanwhile, Mary looked at Betsy expectantly. She was obligated to offer a wedding gift, so she promised her a coffee pot and cups. Mary and Jenny giggled some more.

Ruth

"Won't you look at this pretty thing?" asked Mrs. Landauer as she handed Ruth a large creamy envelope of the heaviest paper. She was pointing to the embossed crest of the return address. It read "American Museum of Natural History, New York City."

"What's that animal, do you think?" she asked. They stared at the strange little picture under the words. It was a something like a lizard, with powerful thighs and a tiny head.

"Whatever it is, if I meet one out on the mesa," Ruth said, "I promise I won't bring it home." Mrs. Landauer let go of the letter but stood by, waiting for Ruth to open it. Ruth wasn't as cruel as to take it to her room, so sat down in the big Morris reading chair in the corner of the parlor and slowly peeled open the flap.

"My dear Miss Weinstock," it read, "Thank you so much for sending the specimen from the hills near Santa Fe, New Mexico. As you surmised, it is not recorded in the standard field guide, and I am so pleased to tell you it has not been observed previously. We should like to do further study, and ask you to send us more specimens. In order that they are most carefully preserved we suggest the following procedures...."

There followed a few paragraphs concerning bottles, fluids, and presses, and a request for photographs and sketches. Then the letter concluded: "It is our hope, Miss Weinstock, that we shall hear from you soon, not only with this specimen but with others. Clearly you are a naturalist of unusual acumen. May I inquire into your training, as it stands you well? Most sincerely, Dr. Clarence Nutall, Ph.D."

Mrs. Landauer slowly wiped off the table and watched Ruth through the corner of an eye.

"Oh, Mrs. Landauer," Ruth said, "the Museum of Natural History believes I've found something!"

"Out there?" she exclaimed. She persisted in the idea there was nothing "out there" but snakes, scorpions and sunburn.

"Yes, that plant I showed you with the serrated leaves."

"Oh, certainly," Mrs. Landauer said politely, since Ruth had shoved dozens in her face that must have all looked alike to her.

Laura was surprised when Ruth showed up at the photography studio, waving the letter and trying to explain its importance. She couldn't get a word in until Ruth finally stopped talking and looked at her.

"What are you smiling at?" Ruth asked.

"You. You're always in your own world of the birds and flowers. It's funny to see you excited about something going on among people."

Ruth felt her face growing hot and red.

"Have you got the right camera lenses? Dr. Nutall is very specific."

Laura read the letter carefully.

"I'm afraid I don't. I don't usually do close-up photography. For this you need a lens like a microscope has."

"How can we get them?" Ruth asked.

"Probably have to order from New York. These are unusual. It might take a while. And cost quite a bit."

Ruth didn't want to wait for anything, having spent so many years in bed waiting for nothing but death.

"We've got to get them sooner, Laura."

"Why, what will happen?"

"The plant will go out of bloom! There's no time to waste with living things. They go on their own schedule, you know. It's already been a few weeks since I sent it to the museum. It was an unusually early blooming plant, and there's no time to waste."

Ruth stared at a print clipped to an easel to dry, its edges curling. It showed a man lying on the dirt floor inside a Navajo house. Some women kneeled nearby, and an Indian in strange clothing threw powder on him.

"Isn't it great?" Laura asked. "I took it out near Betsy's place. I'm getting great photographs out there. Not at all like what the tourists get, with the Indians smiling stiffly for them. This picture shows what it's like when Betsy treats patients in their hogans. No light but the smoky little cook fire, and the patient lying on blankets on the dirt floor. There's the family watching everything she does and the medicine man is burning herbs and throwing the sacred cornmeal. It's nothing like a modern hospital."

The photo reminded Ruth of her bedroom in New York, with her parents hovering nearby as the doctor thumped her chest. Whether in an apartment with oak trim and gilded mirrors or in a hogan of logs and mud, she was glad she didn't need that care any more. She pictured herself in Dr. Mera's sanatorium, in the whitewashed sunny room with its starched iron sheets, alone in her misery with no comfort but the grin of the Spanish boy as he came in to freshen the water jar. But she wouldn't mind having Betsy care for her, remembering how the nurse leaned over to sponge her back. She had been delighted to learn that Betsy was Laura's friend and hoped to see her again.

"I've got an idea," Laura said. "I'll bet the archaeologists have those lenses. They have to take photos of small objects. Maybe I could ask my friend June. She works out at the field site."

"Can you do it today?" Ruth blurted out. Laura had a slow way about her, as if she was always checking out what she saw for what would make the best picture. No doubt it was good for watching sunsets and storm clouds and picking the perfect moment for an exposure, but Ruth had waited all her life to find what she needed to do, and now she couldn't wait any more.

"We'd have to go out to the site, and you have to know the roads well to get out there. Betsy and I got lost when we went. That's when we first met the Navajos."

"Is that the archaeological site that Jonnie goes out to with the tourists? She's always talking about the mummies and the graves. I don't know why anyone would care for all those dead things with all the life around."

Laura nodded.

"I'll see if Jonnie will take us there" Ruth said as she ran out the door. Her mother would have been appalled at her rudeness, but all she could think was that she had to find that plant quickly before it lost its bloom.

Jonnie

Evening thunderstorms had replaced the morning snow, signaling that spring had come to Santa Fe. Everyone was hoping the warm weather would mean the end of the terrible winter of Hard Times, as if money would start to fall from the sky as it heated up. Jonnie had heard from June that she was back with Morris at the field site, although he had barely scraped up the money to continue. He was hoping to do as much as he could this summer, in case it was the last chance for a while. Erna had gone to Kansas City on business, and Jonnie waited for her to get back so she could decide when to start taking tours out to the field site again.

She was polishing the autobus when Erna walked up to her, staring at Jonnie as if seeing her for the first time. While Erna had been away, Jonnie had bought a fancy white blouse with pearl buttons and had her hair fresh cut. She knew Erna's meeting had to do with making the tour service more successful, and she figured this was what she could do to help. Her driving was the best around. The car rarely got stuck, and she pried it out fast when it did. It was always shiny and clean down to the tiniest bit of chrome. All that was left to be improved was the driver, and since she couldn't get any younger, Jonnie was working on her outfit. She wished she had the tuxedo from the sanatorium, but it felt even sharper to wear her new tie with a squash blossom silver bolo—not a thunderbird, because that was the symbol of the Harvey Houses. Miss Erna was always careful no one confused Koshare Tours with them, other than that they met the tourists in front of their hotel.

"Miss Erna, what do you think?" Jonnie finally said, because Erna's stare was making her nervous. "I thought I'd spiff up my costume a bit."

"Jonnie, that's—" she stuttered. "Where'd you get that bolo?"

"Guzman's on the plaza. It's real Navajo pawn. He thinks it might be quite old. In any case, it's pretty, don't you think?"

"Pretty? More like handsome, perhaps," she said, looking away nervously. "It's very nice."

"Don't you like my new duds?"

Miss Erna was holding her clipboard and a pile of envelopes and papers. She dropped her pen, and when she picked it up, the papers started to drop. She stared as everything fell. Jonnie rushed over to help. Erna took them back absently, but let them slip again.

"How was your meeting in Kansas City?" Jonnie asked, trying to start off brightly again. Maybe she didn't like the new clothes and didn't want to lie. Was it the bolo? What did she mean by handsome, not pretty? They had spent so many days together side by side, but Jonnie never felt relaxed with Erna, because she was the boss. Back at the cannery, some women tried to move up to line supervisor. Jonnie did it herself a few times when she needed more money. But when she was a line supervisor, the other workers drew back, even if they had worked side by side for years. She could never stand losing her friends, even for the money, and would soon ask for her old job back. Here, Miss Erna owned the company, she was the boss, and she would always be Miss Erna to Jonnie.

What else could she wear? Where would she get the money for more new clothes? Jonnie had saved for weeks for the bolo and blouse.

Erna started to chatter nervously. Something was definitely wrong.

"Kansas City? It's quite a place. Mr. Harvey's original restaurant is there, you know. They have their corporate headquarters there. I met Mr. Harvey. The original Mr. Harvey's son I mean." She clasped the sliding papers tighter and suddenly looked away, as if searching for some dirt or scratch on the autobus, but they both knew there wouldn't be any.

"You met with Mr. Harvey? But why? I didn't even know you knew him."

"Well I didn't until now. He's very nice. Yes, we had a little meeting. I didn't want to say anything until it was for sure."

They couldn't look at each other. A long moment passed, during which both watched a tourist across the street whose conversation with an

Indian was getting heated. Their words were getting louder.

"What do you mean it's not here? I asked you to watch my camera while I went to get some food," said the man.

The Indian shrugged.

"You're lying. You have it. Don't tell me it was stolen."

Again, a shrug from the Indian. The two stared at each other, then the man swung around to survey the whole street and caught the women watching him. Jonnie and Miss Erna turned back to each other.

"Mr. Harvey has offered me a fine compensation for selling him my business," Miss Erna said.

"But you've always said how proud you are to own a business. And to build a business up from nothing, like Mr. Carnegie and Mr. Edison."

Miss Erna said nothing, just sucked in her cheeks as if holding a lot back.

"You were so proud that a woman could do this, and that you thought of it first. And having me drive instead of a drunken cowboy."

"I was offered a lot of money," she said.

"But look how well you did last summer. Things will get better. You've added Roy," Jonnie was embarrassed to be using this argument, which went against all her others.

"It's my business, Jonnie. I can sell it if I want."

Jonnie thought of the moments they had felt close, shoulder to shoulder under a chassis trying to free a tire from mud. It hadn't felt like a business then. It had never felt like business to Jonnie, because she wouldn't be able to just walk away from this.

Across the street, the tourist screamed at the Indian.

"You know you have my camera! You give it right back. I'm calling the police right now." He turned and yelled to them, "Ladies, would you call me a policeman, right away." They turned away from him and back to each other.

Jonnie knew what was coming, and her usual careful thinking just stopped. Maybe it was listening to that man's rage that made her blood boil.

"All my life employers have hired and fired me and I took it as my lot, but this time I feel there should be more. You're a woman. You own the business. I've done well for you. Haven't I always come through? Haven't I always?"

"If it was up to me I'd keep you, but—"

So she was getting canned. Jonnie spun on her heel and threw the cleaning chamois at the autobus.

"Wait," Miss Erna said, but Jonnie walked away. Miss Erna ran to catch up, her concha belt and bracelets jingling.

"You've got to understand, Jonnie" she said. "I didn't want to do it. I didn't have any choice."

"It's a free country," Jonnie said. "Isn't that why you started the business, to be free?"

"I don't want to lose it either. I don't want to lose you either."

"Sure," Jonnie murmured as she started walking again.

Miss Erna grabbed Jonnie's arm. Putting on a very bass man's voice, she said "Here's what they told me: 'If you don't want to accept our offer, perhaps you'd like to hear about our latest enterprise, the Harveytour.' And then he went to his briefcase and pulled out a portfolio. With a picture of the latest model of limousine bus, and standing by it the handsomest cowboy in a big hat. And do you know what was worse?" She shook her fist and looked down at the ground, and Jonnie saw her hiding a tear. "They told me if I didn't sell, they'd be starting their own operation in three months. 'If you can't lick 'em, join 'em,' ever heard that?' That's what he said. Oh not Mr. Harvey. Mr. Harvey couldn't be nicer. He has Mr. Krause to do his dirty work. By the time Krause finished with me, Mr. Harvey just had me sign right up. So that's it. I didn't have a choice." She bent to pick up the papers that had fallen, her eyes on the ground.

"Erna's Koshare Indian Detours is no more. Now it's Harvey Indian Detours. That's the Harveycar," she waved a finger at the autobus. "They're going to give coupons at the Harvey Houses for a little price cut. They're going to offer lunches catered by Harvey's. And we'll be stopping at Harvey's Indian crafts gift shops. Long stops." She snorted out the last words. "He showed me a photo of very pretty girls at a college having tea, and he said that these girls would be his guides, because these 'young ladies' had all gone to the finest colleges in the East and they knew how to be ladies to impress our tourists with their 'education and erudition.' And that if I sold them my business, he would get me a job training them, since I knew the territory well. Krause laid out the whole plan. I didn't dare tell him where I went to college. Left it to start my own business, anyway. My own business I don't have anymore."

"What about me? What job will he get for me?"

"I told Krause why I'd hired a woman driver, that the boys were always drunk or sleeping it off, but he said he knew how to hire quality, and he'd send his best man out and that man would be developing a fleet of drivers. Because they're going to expand the whole thing. They're sending out four new autobuses by June."

"So I don't have a job."

"It's just a job for you. This is my dream, my business, my—my freedom! My freedom from a boss. But they got me anyway. I'm as trapped as you are, Jonnie. I was only a circus lion that got away for a few minutes, and now the net's around me again. If you feel bad, you can't imagine how I feel."

She walked away, rubbing at her eyes. Across the street, a crowd had gathered around the tourist and the Indian, so no one noticed the scene they had been making.

"Can I take the car for the day?" Jonnie yelled to her. Miss Erna shrugged her back, which Jonnie took for a yes and jumped into the autobus, slamming the door, letting the tires scream on the sandy road as she drove off, and forcing the crowd around the tourist to jump out of her way. The Indian broke away, running desperately. As Jonnie slowed a bit, he jumped onto the running board, grabbing onto the post of the side window, and she sped off as he neatly slid through the window and into the car.

Morna

Morna would usually be jumping out of her skin at how slowly Candelaria made her decision. She could almost see into the Navajo woman's head as she looked back and forth to decide between a can of peaches or a can of tomatoes, or two cans of peaches, no tomatoes, but a penny of candy for the children. Morna forced herself to stand calmly while the slow deliberations proceeded and the three children toddled dangerously close to the sharp iron tools of the woodstove.

It didn't matter. Her restlessness wasn't in the trading post, but out there in the washes and low hills and brush land. Candelaria was not her problem. Her problem was Jack. No, it was money. With money, there would be no Jack, no trading post, no Candelaria. To get the money, she had to get pots like the one Candelaria had sold to Jack. Perhaps the Indian woman had more. The whole winter had passed and Jack still hadn't noticed the missing necklace.

Jack had stepped out with Joe Yez to talk about some sheep.

"Candelaria," Morna said, leaning over the counter and speaking softly. As always there were three men sitting by the wood stove, sharing crackers and arguing about a horse trade that went sour. It had been the talk of the community for so many weeks she wanted to unbridle every horse around, smack it on the rump, and set it free. But not today. Today she had a plan.

"Candelaria, have you—?" That would never work. You had to be very, very indirect with these people. "I'll bet you have some pretty things in your house. You have such lovely jewelry."

Candelaria gave her an annoyed glance and put an arm around the nearest child.

"Two can peaches," she said. "One penny candy for them children."

At least Morna had found out how to get a Navajo woman to make up her mind quickly. That could come in handy. But it wouldn't help her reach her goal.

Candelaria unknotted the handkerchief where she kept her money and plucked some coins out one by one, being careful to hide the rest of the contents in her palm while looking suspiciously at Morna. Morna put the cans in a paper bag, taking the opportunity to look right in the woman's face, as if somehow the secret of how to get what she wanted from the Indians would be written there. Candelaria took the bag and stomped out, with the children clinging to her skirts lurching along in her wake.

As Candelaria headed out the door, three white women waited to come in. Morna hadn't even heard their car drive up. It was Jonnie, the queer woman who drove the tourist car that stopped by very rarely, since the trading post was off its route except for emergencies. With her was a thin, older woman Morna had never seen before. There also was a friendly open-faced woman who looked familiar. Of course! The photographer who had sent the photo. The one who had been with the other woman, on vacation.

"Are you out of gas again?" Morna asked the photographer.

"We're going to the field site to find my friend June and ask a favor," Laura said. If only the Indians would talk so directly, thought Morna.

"We need some cold water, please, and then we're off again," said Ruth, the thin one. But Morna didn't want them to rush right off without even a few minutes of conversation.

"The well's out there and there's a ladle for the canteens," she told Jonnie, hoping that she'd go alone, leaving the other two to visit a few minutes. Ruth was intently reading the labels on the cans and bottles on the shelves.

"How's your friend?" Morna asked Laura.

"Didn't you know? She's the New Mexico Indian Association nurse at Red Rock."

"You're kidding! I hear the Navajos talking about her all the time. They

like her a lot. I hear she isn't getting along well with the bible-thumpers."
Morna immediately regretted saying that. Maybe she had misjudged the
couple. Maybe they were from some religious order, and not what she had
thought.

"The Indians talk about them, too? I'll have to tell Betsy. She wants to
think no one notices. By the way, how did you like the photos?" Laura said
just as Jack came in.

"The photographer!" he said. "Say, whatever happened to those
photos of my pretty wife?"

"Oh, but didn't you get them?" said Laura. "I mailed them right off
when I got back home."

"I didn't see any," said Jack.

"Must have been lost in the mail," Morna interjected. "Happens all
the time. Thank you for trying, anyway." She was hoping Laura didn't
remember her thank you note.

"But you sent the nicest—" Laura started to say, then she caught the
look on Morna's face and stopped. "Well, I'm sorry," Laura said. She looked
thoughtful. Perhaps she was remembering the strange photo snapped as
Jack entered the room unexpectedly, which showed just how Morna felt
about Jack. Perhaps she'd guess why Morna hadn't wanted him to see it.

"Oh yes," said Laura. "I remember now, I was all excited to send it,
and had the envelope all prepared, which is why I thought I'd sent it, but
then when I developed it, something had gone wrong with the film. A bad
batch. Ruined some nice sunsets I took, too. It happens. I wouldn't want
you to think that was typical of my work, of course."

"Of course not," Morna said gratefully.

"That big camera was too much for you, eh?" said Jack.

Laura looked ready to fire back at him, but Morna shot her a desperate
glance to drop it and let him forget the whole subject.

"We really do need to get going," said Ruth, who hadn't followed the
conversation at all, but was examining some unusual rocks in the display
counter. She went to the door to see if Jonnie was done filling the canteens.
Laura looked at Morna thoughtfully.

"Would you like to come with us to the site?" asked Laura. "We'll be
there for a few hours and then drop you back here. Have to get home by
dark."

Of course, that was it! If she got to the field site, maybe she could
find some pots Schweizer would buy. She could sneak them out under her
long skirt. Long dead Indians didn't have to be bribed or traded for their
pots.

"I'd love to," Morna said.

"She can't leave," said Jack. "She's working."

"Yes, I can," snapped Morna. "You've gone off to Shiprock and Farmington, and I haven't gone anywhere for months."

"But—" Jack started as her new friends glared at him.

"All right," he said, "Girls night out, eh? But don't get stuck in any quicksand. I don't figure that one"—he grimaced toward Jonnie outside—"has got what it takes to pull you ladies out." Jonnie appeared at the door, gave a wave to say she was ready, and headed for the car.

"Don't she ever wear dresses?" Jack asked Ruth, as Morna ran into the living quarters to get a hat. The big camera! Don't she wear dresses! His words embarrassed Morna, but she wasn't going to say anything now. For an afternoon, she would be free.

Jonnie

Pulling the autobus away from the trading post, with everyone shouting at her to watch out for this hole or that pile of wood or that dog, Jonnie could see Jack in the rear view mirror. He had acted agreeably when Morna said she was going, and he had waved and smiled as they piled into the autobus, but he didn't look that way now. He was rubbing one hand on his chin and crumpling his hat with the other. She thought of saying something, but Morna was chattering happily to Ruth and Laura. Poor woman must never get a day off. Jonnie found it hard to have only one free day a week. Well, this was why she had decided she wasn't going to be any fisherman's wife.

It was nice to drive friends instead of tourists. Already she felt calmer about losing her job. She had always found another one and she would this time, too. Hadn't it worked out well already that on this day that she had the car, Miss Ruth wanted to go to the field site and would pay for the gasoline? Jonnie had been dreaming of getting a job at the dig. She was getting a lucky chance today to do all she could to get one.

"All these years out here, and all those archaeologists stopping by your store, and you've never been to the field site?" Laura was asking Morna.

"You can't just leave the store. The Indians get in and steal their pawn back."

"Oh," said Laura.

"Yes," Morna said, her voice rising with confidence. "That's why Jack and I can't ever go off for a holiday together. They'd rob us blind."

Jonnie hadn't thought Ruth was listening, but as usual, she was quick to try to think out a problem.

"Why don't you take the valuables with you?"

"Because…because," Morna sputtered. "Well, there's far too much. And we could get robbed on the road and lose everything."

Ruth had spotted a hawk and barely heard her. The car rumbled on.

"How does Betsy like Red Rock?" Morna asked Laura. "She's so far away out in the sticks. Not even a trading post nearby!"

"She likes the Navajo people a lot," said Laura. "She's been learning the language and all about how they live."

"So what's the story with the Reverend and his wife?"

Laura didn't answer right away. "Do you know them well?"

"I don't think I'd want to. The first time they came into the store, I had my wedding ring off because I'd been kneading bread. She stared and stared and I didn't know why. Finally she said, 'The Reverend would be more than happy to perform a marriage service." Jack and I laughed so hard. Whenever we see them coming, I grab my ring off, and we can hardly hide our giggles."

They all laughed, although Laura looked thoughtful, then she said, "I wish Betsy could laugh at them that way. They give her such a hard time."

"What have they been up to?" asked Morna.

"Oh, nothing, I probably shouldn't say anything. The Lucks just have different ideas about the Indians and all. It's hard being so isolated and thrown in together with whoever else just happens to be there. I wish she could see more of you. You being from New York City and all."

They rolled along watching the scenery, which was growing more desolate, with occasional oddly-shaped rock towers and buttes. It was hot enough that soon they all settled back sleepily in the leather seats of the autobus.

"Look there," Jonnie said suddenly. They passed close to a Navajo summer home, empty but waiting for the return of its owners. A structure of crooked thin logs barely held up its roof, where a few sprigs of drying sage flapped in the wind. From a rickety fence hung a string of red peppers.

"Must be nice," said Laura, "to live in a different house in summer than in winter."

"We did that," said Ruth, "I loved it."

"You lived in a stick house like that?" asked Morna.

"Oh, no, I mean in New York. In the summer, we'd go to our bungalow in the Catskill Mountains. Not that far from the Bronx, really, but a different world. There was a waterfall I used to love to sit by, just watching the bees and the butterflies and sometimes a salamander. Not so much different from what I'm doing here now. But my family stopped going there."

"Why?" Jonnie asked.

"I don't know." She thought a moment. "Yes, I do. It must have been my asthma. Those stupid doctors! They told my parents all the wrong things. They must have told them all the pollen in the air there was making me worse. So instead we spent summers in our hot apartment in the city where I could hardly breathe. Coming here has been a rebirth."

"Not for me," said Morna suddenly. "Coming here was the worst mistake I've ever made. I had a good life in Manhattan. I'm an artist, you know."

"You are!" Jonnie said. "You've all led exciting lives. But why'd you come here, Morna?"

"Our friends had moved out here and were doing really well, painting calendars for the railroads and illustrations for magazines. They said it was like a gold rush here for painters. But I guess we waited too long. All the jackpot gold mines were already claimed, Jack said. So he thought if we bought a trading post we'd make enough money to paint. But nothing has gone right. I've got a plan, though."

"You do? A way to make money? What is it?" Jonnie asked.

"Oh, I have some ideas. Nothing for sure yet," Morna's voice faded away. "So you're friends with the folks at the dig?" she suddenly asked.

"Until cold weather came and they all left, I went there on my day off. They let me help them dig. I was learning about what they do. Now that it's spring, I'm hoping to get back to it again," Jonnie explained.

"How much do they pay you?"

"Pay! No, I don't have any training like they do or anything. I'm just glad they let me help and teach me what to do. They feed me, too."

"They should pay you," said Morna. "They pay the Navajos. The Navajos don't do it for fun."

"They couldn't do that. They couldn't have a white woman doing Indian men's work, I don't think. I'm not doing what the Navajos do, because they won't work on the gravesites. And they can't pay me like one of the white people, because I'm not an archaeologist or a student. I'm sort of nothing to them. I guess I'm sort of invisible."

"That's awful," said Laura.

"June's been really nice to me, though. She's the reason I get to go there."

"June! Really," Laura murmured.

"You sound surprised. She's the nicest person. Last fall she taught me how to recognize the different kinds of pottery. She can look at the tiniest piece and say right away how old it is. That's what I want to do."

"Found any whole pots?" asked Morna.

"That hardly ever happens. Just in the story books. All I've found so far is just little pieces. Still, I'm hoping I'll find one someday."

"What would happen to it if you did?" asked Morna.

"If it's really good, it will go to a museum. In Boston or St. Louis or New York."

"And they'd pay you if they put it in the museum?"

"No, whatever I find belongs to the archaeologists. It's their hole, I guess," Jonnie giggled.

"Don't you want to get paid for your work?" asked Morna.

"Of course. But there's other pay besides money. I'm from near Boston myself, and sometimes I think, wouldn't it be great to write to the folks back home and tell them to go to that museum at Harvard and see that old, old beautiful pot I found, that laid there in the desert buried for a thousand years, until little Jonnie the fisherman's daughter dug it up? Wouldn't that be fine?"

"I guess," said Morna. "But do all the finds go to museums? Are they all that good? What if you find one that no museum wants?"

"I never asked."

"Maybe they end up in those Harvey House stores. For the tourists to buy," said Laura.

"I'll bet they do," responded Morna. "Don't you think they should pay you for those?"

"I do okay," Jonnie snapped. "You seem awfully worried about my money." She didn't want to tell them any more about her situation. In Gloucester, if your father or husband's boat came back high in the water and their share of a month's catch wasn't enough to last the family a week, you kept it to yourself and ate beans, if you could afford them.

"I'm sorry," said Morna. "But I couldn't help but think it wasn't very fair. Back in New York, Jack and I used to go to parties with the folks at *The Masses* magazine. They even published a cartoon I did. It was all about how the rich would take from the poor. You don't look very rich to me, and it sounds like they're taking from you."

"Never heard of that magazine," Jonnie said. "Back home we got the *Saturday Evening Post*, though. I like those drawings by that Norman Rockwell. Looks like my own little town. I'm just happy learning about archaeology at the dig. At home, all I learned was how to can fish."

"What have you learned?" asked Laura. "Because Morna's raising an interesting point."

Jonnie nodded over to the west. "We're almost there. Let's see. I've learned how to find something that's beautiful and valuable that's been lost and buried. It might stay broken and forgotten forever, if I hadn't learned how to rescue it. Now everyone can learn about how the Indians lived and see how beautiful it is, if it goes to a museum."

"Isn't all that pottery made by women?" asked Laura. "So you're showing what women can do, also."

"I hadn't thought of that," Jonnie said. "You're right. When I go out with Miss Erna to take the tourists, it's the Indian women making the pottery. And June says that's how they've been doing it for a thousand years, even more. Back home, at the Gloucester Lyceum, they have things the fishermen make when they're out on the boats for months, like scrimshaw and the prettiest fans made of baleen. That's from the whale's mouth. Even saw a chess set once made all of pieces of whales. But I can't think of anything made by women, except maybe dresses and bonnets that the captain's wives owned. They're pretty sure women made the really old pottery, the Mimbres."

"You've found some Mimbres?" asked Morna.

"I've found shards. Nothing whole. It's beautiful, all delicate patterns. Back home I saw the thin porcelain dishes the ships brought back from the China trade. They said it was the finest in the world, but when I held one of those Mimbres shards, it was more beautiful to me. Maybe because I love this country out here, and it felt like I was holding the land itself in my hand. Maybe because it's American. 'See America First,' isn't that what they say?"

"I know what you mean," said Laura. "When I was in photography school, they wanted us to take pictures of flowers and fruit. It just sat there and looked small and dead to me. But out here, there's so much and it's so big and so much happens. The clouds change, and the sun moves, and the shadows, and then there's the rivers. The Rio Grande—I'd like to photograph it from where it starts somewhere up in Colorado, all the way down to where it meets the sea in Mexico. Every time I look at the sky, I see a photograph. If I only had enough money for all the film and chemicals and paper, and enough time!"

"I'll drive you on that trip," Jonnie said. "Wouldn't that be something? We'd see every bit of this country, just about. We'd see how people have lived all along the river. There wouldn't have been anyone out here if there hadn't been water. Why even the road we're on now—June says it was once part of the Indian's irrigation system. It was a canal. She says that airplanes are going to take photographs of everything, and we'll see how it was all laid out. Maybe you can photograph from an airplane, Laura." She glanced back and smiled at the photographer.

"I went to art school in New York when I was a young woman," said Ruth. "They wanted us to paint like they do in Europe. If you couldn't do a portrait of some stuffy old man sitting in his parlor, they said you weren't a painter. I hated it. I thought I hated painting. But now, when I draw the plants and the insects, I love what I'm doing. If they had any beautiful birds in Europe, you'd never know it. Took Audubon to show us what they looked like! You know what I wish?" she added in a whisper.

"To come along with Laura and me to follow the Rio Grande?" asked Jonnie.

"Not exactly. I wish I'd been born a hundred years ago, and a man, so I could be one of those naturalists who were the first white people to see this country. They went out in expeditions led by explorers like Lewis and Clark and John Wesley Powell, and they were there to paint and draw what they saw, from the tiniest insect to the mountain ranges. They would be out for years at a time and all they had to do was paint and draw and make sure their work stayed dry and safe until they could get it back east. They were the first to draw so many places. That's what I'd want to do. But I'm getting to do something like it. I got a letter from a professor back at the museum back east who says he's never seen a plant like the specimen I sent him. So I'm as close as you can get to that in country that's already populated and tramped on by people and cows and horses as this is."

She waved her hand out at the open country all around. There wasn't a person, a cow, or a horse in sight, but they were surely on a road, or at least a pair of muddy tire tracks. She pointed towards a rock tower far off in the distance, looming remote and untouched over a vast plain of dry crusted earth.

Betsy

The eyes of the grandson of Ben Yaz were running. A quoit necklace with silver quarters was tied around the toddler's head. Lifting one quarter, Betsy saw it was covering a flaming boil on his left temple. She gasped and his mother, Gilda Sewscrooked, jerked her head up from patting her infant daughter's back and stared at Betsy, her eyes wide. She said something in

Navajo that probably meant "Is he going to die?" Betsy pulled a lollipop out of a jar and gave it to the little boy. The young mother still stared. Betsy looked to her side, expecting to see Lilly and hear her calm reassurances and then to see her questioning face waiting to be told what to say. But the money troubles of the Indian Association had meant that her interpreter and friend had been forced to go home. Betsy hated to think of Lilly struggling to tie the tiny knots of weaving with her clumsy fingers, her back sore from sitting on the ground at the loom.

The nurse squeezed Gilda's arm reassuringly and made comforting sounds, wishing she had learned more of the language. Since Lilly had left, she had depended on volunteers, but the few people capable of translating couldn't leave their sheep, crops, or weaving for long. She knew the words for the drugs she needed for this boy's boil, but not the words to explain that the shipment of medical supplies was three weeks late and that she had none to give this child.

Only one last lollipop was left in the candy jar, stuck to the bottom. She gave it to the mother with the best smile she could force her face into, but there was nothing to smile about. Ever since November, not long after she had first heard about the hard times that had hit the rest of the country in October, the support she had depended on had ended, often without warning, like the supply shipment. A letter early in December from the Indian Association said that their donations had slowed, but they were hoping to do well with their Christmas fund drive. In January there had been a letter saying Christmas hadn't brought in enough to keep their office in Denver open, and that they were moving into the mansion of a rich donor to keep expenses down and still have money to support their field nurses. In February came a letter saying the rich donor was selling her home, and that the future of Betsy's clinic was uncertain. With each letter came a smaller salary check. She no longer had enough money to feed the Navajo friends who had often joined her for meals. Now they invited her to eat with them in their hogans, but she knew they couldn't spare the food so she found reasons to decline. She missed the crowd around the kitchen table. Sitting alone in the clinic, she tried not to wish someone would get sick or hurt so she would have some company.

There was a knock on the door and the Lucks pushed their way in. The Reverend looked ruddy, almost happy.

"Sister Betsy, good day, praise the Lord," he said. "Two more joined our congregation on Sunday. We're becoming quite the merry group. You should join us."

"Just seems there's always someone getting sick on Sunday," Betsy said. At least they were both lying. Any Navajo person going to pray with him wasn't merry, only desperate enough to try the white man's God, especially when He provided a meal after the service.

"So, what do you think about the plans for the building?" Luck asked.

"What plans?"

"Oh my, La Farge hasn't written you yet? We've known about it a week, but I waited until the mail came yesterday to make sure you knew your position."

"What are you talking about?"

"The Indian Association has sold this building to the Mission Service. And at a very affordable price, praise the Lord. Now we will be able to have our school."

"The building?" she said, so shocked she didn't even think how rude it was when she asked him "With everyone so hit by hard times, how could the Mission Service afford to buy it?"

"The Lord helps us. I'm afraid he hasn't done as well for Mr. Oliver La Farge and his artist friends. I hear there's quite a few fine houses going up for sale in Denver and Santa Fe."

"But what about the clinic?"

"For now you can have this room. But we'll be remodeling the rest. We've been donated lumber from a shed that's coming down in Farmington, and we're building desks and benches. We'll have a regular schoolroom where these children can learn like in our fine Indian Bible schools back east. Just learning to sit still in chairs, that's the first thing they need."

"But my kitchen, and my—" she hesitated to say anything so personal to him. "And my bedroom?"

"We'll certainly need the kitchen for the school, and we're planning to put our chapel in the bedroom. Having a real solid stone building, that's been my dream all these years. No longer having to hold our services out in the dust and rain."

"Reverend Luck, how can I continue the clinic if there's no place for me to live?"

"Perhaps you can move into one of the Indian shacks. You seem to enjoy their way of life."

She hated the gloating look he had.

"Thou shalt not covet thy neighbor's goods," she mumbled.

"What?" Mrs. Luck said. "I'm surprised to hear you quoting Bible. But that's right, Sister Betsy. I can understand you envy our good fortune."

Amazing how she could turn anything around. But now Betsy understood some of the hostility coming from them. They'd wanted the clinic building all along.

"What am I supposed to do?"

"We can't answer your questions," said Reverend Luck. Betsy shot him as hostile a glare as she dared. He dipped his chin and stared at his hands.

"Because only Our Lord can," spat out Mrs. Luck. She straightened up and looked right at Betsy. "Our Lord sent us here to do His work, and He makes sure we can continue." When the nurse didn't respond, she continued. "Obviously your support has deserted you. If you care about these...." She almost said heathens, but deferred to Betsy's sensibilities. "...people the way you claim to, you should be happy that at least the Lord is here for them, even if the Indian Association is not."

They all stood frozen and silent, until finally Betsy got an idea.

"How do you know the Lord doesn't want you to share? I could still have the clinic and you could still have your church."

"The Lord wants us to have a school," said Mrs. Luck. "Someday these children will become nurses and even doctors. They will take care of their own. Are you saying you don't want that? You'd rather have them need you? The Lord helps those who help themselves."

"I want all that, I do. But right now, half the kids have conjunctivitis from so much sand in their eyes. You've seen how many go blind. Many will get bronchitis or pneumonia. How many will live to make it to high school even?"

"I don't disagree," said Mrs. Luck. "But the Lord has decided that we should have a school. The Lord will take care of their medical problems. We will drive them to the hospital at Farmington. You are not the Lord's vehicle. And I'm sure you know why."

That was the most direct attack Mrs. Luck had ever made about Laura's visits. Betsy was so surprised she didn't know what to say.

Luck started backing out the door, pulling his wife along. They were looking at her strangely, but she knew it was the look on her own face that was strangest.

"Take the time you need to absorb the news, Sister Betsy. We'll be coming by tomorrow to start measuring the schoolroom."

When they left, the room was silent again. There was no line of sick and injured people with their children, lambs, and dogs. There was no Lilly sitting on the stool off to the side. No Mrs. Lamehorse in the kitchen waiting for Betsy to take a break and share coffee and biscuits. No Laura, shouting distance away, taking photos. No Laura with her soft hug to crawl into right now and cry.

Laura

"So how does your friend like Red Rock?" Morna asked Laura as the autobus rolled across the bumpy land. They had all gone sleepy and quiet from the heat, but in her daze Laura thought about Betsy. What was she doing right now? Shouldn't Laura be there? Were those horrible Lucks dogging her footsteps today?

"I hear the Indians talk about her sometimes," Morna said when the photographer took so long to answer. "I don't always understand, but they do seem to like her."

"With things so bad, the Indian Association isn't sending her as much money as they were. I'm always afraid her car's broken down. She's always around infectious diseases and the work is really hard. Did you know that when the patient looks like she'll die, sometimes the rest of the family leaves her to stay alone? They want her to take care of the body until they come back to burn the hogan. That's what their religion tells them to do with the dead."

"I don't understand those people. They'll walk out on their old dying mother, just leave her there," said Morna.

"I heard a funny story," said Jonnie. "Two college students were heading for Rainbow Arch. They stayed a night in an empty hogan and left one of their bedrolls behind. When the Navajos returned, they thought it was a dead body and didn't want to get close enough to check, so they deserted the hogan until the students came back on their return trip two weeks later."

"Animals avoid their dead, too," said Ruth. "It's probably the safest course of action from a hygienic point of view."

Ruth's comment felt so cold to Laura. Was that how she saw everything: scientifically, impersonally? Laura thought of the heat of Betsy's hand pressing gently on her back. Was she weighing Ruth against Betsy? How long had she been doing this? She felt even guiltier to be here and not with the woman she loved.

Morna

It had been so long since Morna had done anything outside the drudgery of the trading post. It felt like a dream to talk with white women, and even just to roll along in a car instead of a dirty truck that smelled like dead sheep. The deep cushioned leather seat felt so good. Maybe she wouldn't go back. Maybe she would have Jonnie take her to Santa Fe. If a freak like that one could get a job, surely Morna could.

She wished Jonnie would go faster. She wanted to see the strange big rocks and fields of sage and cactus rush by so fast that she could feel she was leaving the desert far behind. But she had heard too many customers at the trading post tell tales of broken axles and exploding gas tanks to urge Jonnie on. She didn't want anything to spoil this trip and send her back to Jack even a minute sooner.

Maybe one of these women could help her if she went to Santa Fe. She considered her chances with each one. What price would Jonnie ask for her help? Morna shuddered the thought away. That Laura seemed like a softer version of the same type. And Ruth? She was the strangest of them all. Hardly said a word and just stared out at the sky and the land like something secret was written there just for her. Morna tried to catch her eye and get a sense of her, but she was in another world entirely.

Jonnie

"There it is!" Jonnie called out as she turned the car abruptly around a curve that brought them into the hidden canyon where the field camp was. Cars, sheds, tents, and people in knickers and khakis were everywhere. A truck blocked their way. On its flat bed stood a little canvas structure that was more like a shed than a tent. Two men were struggling with some ropes holding it, while a group of others were watching. Jonnie stopped the autobus and stood up, waving and calling hello. June walked over, waving.

"Look who's here," she said, smiling at Jonnie. "Laura, you've come to visit again. I was afraid I'd scared you away the last time."

Laura smiled weakly.

"I've brought my friend, Ruth Weinstock," Jonnie said. She had hesitated a moment whether it would be all right to call Ruth her friend. "She's learning all about the plants."

"We were hoping to borrow a camera lens," Laura said. "To photograph a plant that Ruth found.

"You could ask Dr. Morris," said June. "Glad to have you visit, Ruth. Oh, my gosh, Morna from the trading post! What are you doing here? Who's minding the store?"

"I've told Jack to carry on without me," Morna said.

June nodded. "Good for you!"

"What is that on the truck?" asked Ruth.

June blushed. "It's a big moment here," she said. "That's the field latrine. We've sure needed one."

"I've wondered about that," said Morna. The men broke the ropes free and lifted it off the truck. The truck moved out of their way.

"How long are you here for?" June asked Laura.

"Once we get the lens, I'd like to take some photographs and Ruth wants to sketch," Laura said.

"And I was hoping to do some digging," Jonnie said, wishing June would pay her more attention. "Are you still working in that same gravesite? Have you found any more of those necklaces? "

"Necklaces?" said Morna. "I thought it was all pieces of broken dishes around here."

"Wait till you see," said June. "We've found a chief's gravesite. They buried him with everything he loved in the world. His necklace is of tiny turquoise beads, thousands of them, on a six foot string. It's so beautiful. It's the first we've ever found like this. The museums are all frothing at the mouth to get it."

"I think I'd just like to take a look around," said Morna. "I've met so many of your group, but never seen what you do. Where do you keep the things that go to the museums?"

"This way to the chief's bounty," June called out, taking Morna's hand and leading her along. Since they hadn't seen each other all winter, Jonnie was surprised that June walked off with Morna. Maybe she just liked showing new people around. Maybe she saw Jonnie as an "old-timer" now. But Jonnie had waited so long to see June again. She'd been happy driving out here, hardly thinking about Erna and her lost job, but now it all came back again.

She saw Dr. Morris at a table made of packing crates. He was holding a bone up in the sunlight and examining it through a magnifying lens. He had never paid any attention to Jonnie except an occasional grunt when she crossed his path. It was as if he didn't have a language for talking to her, since she wasn't a Navajo laborer or one of his students. Jonnie would have thought he'd show some interest in a person who didn't fit into any group, since finding where things fit into groups and putting labels on everything was what he and the rest of them were doing. There wasn't a chip of pottery or bit of ancient charcoal they hadn't written a number on and shellacked over, but no one seemed to know or care what Jonnie was.

June and Morna were out of sight and Ruth and Laura were heading over to Dr. Morris. She would join them and make him notice her. If she just went back to the hole where she had been digging, where no one ever noticed her, nothing would happen. For anything to change, Jonnie would have to do more.

Ruth

Laura slowly scanned the cliff face with its cave rooms and rock walls.

"Let's go ask Dr. Morris about the lens," Ruth said.

"The last time I was here," said Laura, "I was so distracted by the mummies that I hardly noticed the possibilities for pictures."

"Now you'll have another chance. What lens is it we need? I'll ask him."

Laura finally turned her attention to Ruth. "I'm coming. Just give me a minute. I'm getting so many ideas."

"We've got to hurry. Your landscapes won't change for centuries, but plants don't last." Ruth pictured her special plant shriveling in the dry heat, attacked by a bug, or munched by a small animal. Ease off or Laura won't want to work with you, and then where will you be? But Laura was laughing at her more than annoyed.

"You're so cute," Laura said. "Out in the field, you won't move a muscle for hours. But here you're as jumpy as if you've fallen into one of those spiny cactus you've been sketching." She smiled at Ruth in a way that made the older woman feel self-conscious, suddenly aware that Laura had been studying her the way she had been studying the plants. Whenever she saw men smile at their wives that way, it always made Ruth glad she hadn't married. Her parents had run her life for too long and thought they had known her.

"Nobody knows me and nobody owns me," Ruth spoke out loud.

"What?" Laura said. "You mumbled."

"Sorry. Let's see if he has the lens." She walked briskly towards the man at the table. Jonnie ran up and joined them.

"Welcome to our field camp, ladies" said the man in the helmet, hardly looking up, then taking another glance. "Ah, Miss Gilpin, the photographer, back again?"

Laura was about to speak when Ruth craned forward to the object Morris was examining.

"Third vertebrae?" she asked.

"That's right," he answered, looking at her. "Are you a doctor?"

Ruth giggled at the thought. "In art school we drew from a skeleton."

"How old was the skeleton?"

"I never thought about it. It looked old, but it probably was from some destitute woman who died on the streets of New York a few years earlier."

"This bone is fifteen hundred years old, if not more. Does it look the same to you?"

He handed her the piece of bone and the lens.

"It's quite worn here. See the tooth marks? Some little animal was gnawing at it," Ruth told him.

"You see more than most of my students. Have you thought of being an archaeologist?" As he said that, Jonnie's foot slipped in the slick clay slope they stood on, and everyone stared at her as she blushed and regained her footing.

"Actually, I was hoping you could lend me a special lens. You see, I've been asked by the American Museum of Natural History to send them photographs of a plant I've found. They say they've never seen one like it, and—oh, I'm sorry, my name is Ruth Weinstock. I've been sketching the wildlife near Santa Fe."

"I'm Dr. Earl Morris. I'm in charge of this field camp. Sounds like you've got a career already. But are you an artist or a naturalist?"

She couldn't answer that right away. During those endless hours of painting fruit bowls in art school, Ruth had never thought of herself as an artist, just a bored woman. And now? Could she call herself an artist or a naturalist? But she hadn't gone to school for science.

"I'm not anything. I've just been sketching the plants and animals I see. And I like to keep records. I was in the hospital and I saw how they did that. Now I just want to do it."

"If only my students would do that," said Morris. "They like to dig for buried treasure, but they don't like to record. And the folks who like to record won't spend a summer out in the sun and dust." He paused to glare at a student who had stopped to listen. "Maybe it's because most are young men. Don't have the patience of ladies like you. Maybe I should hire only ladies," he laughed.

Ruth didn't laugh with him, but turned to Laura. "Laura, can you tell Dr. Morris the kind of lens we need?" Laura named something technical and Dr. Morris chewed his lips and scratched his moustache, while Ruth impatiently pictured the plant, which wasn't that far off a trail, being crushed by the heavy hooves of a Navajo's mule.

"You'll have to ask my photographer," Dr. Morris said finally. "He's on the mesa top. I'll have to find someone who can take you up to him."

"I can do it. I know where he is," piped up Jonnie. Morris stared at her as if trying to place her.

"I've seen you," he said thoughtfully. "You're that funny—" he stopped short. "You're the driver for the tour. Say, where is that pretty tour guide?"

"She's not here today. I've borrowed the autobus so I can help with the dig, like I did last summer," Jonnie said proudly.

"Oh, too bad. My, she's a pretty sight compared to the women out here covered with dust!" Dr. Morris laughed again. "Well, why don't you take the ladies up there—" he said, pointing the way, "and tell Hooker, he's the photographer, it's okay with me if it's okay with him—if he thinks we can spare the lens for a while."

"Thank you so much," Ruth said, and Jonnie led them toward one of the big wooden ladders propped against the cliff face.

"Come back again," he called out to Ruth, "Would you like to sketch out here? I'd love to see your work." She was already scrambling up the ladder and didn't answer.

Jonnie said, "He's practically offering you a job! Don't you want it?"

"But I don't want to sketch old bones. I know just what I want to do."

"Some people have all the luck," Jonnie muttered. "Do you think I could learn to sketch like you?"

Going up a series of ladders and narrow footpaths, Jonnie led them to the top of the mesa. It was covered with broken rock walls, a few tents, and many wooden crates and makeshift tables.

"Hooker's probably down in the kiva where they've been working," Jonnie said as she headed toward the other end. Laura stopped and held out her hands to make a picture frame. She was still muttering to herself about how blind she must have been previously. When Jonnie glanced back to see if they were following, her face was sullen.

Laura almost stepped on a tiny lizard.

"I've got to look at that lizard," Ruth said. "You go ahead and talk to the photographer." Laura continued towards the man Jonnie had pointed at, while Jonnie gave a half-hearted wave and headed down the cliff.

After spending the morning crowded in the car, Ruth was relieved to be alone. She hadn't been on a high mesa top before. The immense sky was so close and the tiny trees below so far. Below, strange big rock formations broke up the view, but up here, there was nothing taller than the last few knee-high crumbling rock walls. There was scrub vegetation, but not much more. Any thing else would burn up. The people who had lived in these houses must have roasted in the sun. What vegetation might they have planted here to shade them? Fields of tall cornstalks would have helped. Would it have grown atop this rock? Did the archaeologists think about these issues? Did they have a botanist with them? So many questions to find answers to.

She spotted Laura bent over, talking to someone down a hole. Then Laura straightened up, looked for Ruth, and waved happily. Great, she had the lens.

When she walked up to Ruth with the lens, Laura chattered away about how the ancient women had carried the water and grain up the steep path from the fields. Ruth was wondering what herbs and plants they carried. Laura swung her head wildly, trying to look at everything. For a photographer, she didn't know much about seeing, and Ruth wasn't surprised when she stumbled over a wall. Laura gasped, and there was a "click click click" as the precious lens rolled down the rocks and clattered to a stop.

Jonnie

Watching the other women head off eagerly across the site, Jonnie felt deserted. She already missed being able to think of herself as the driver for Koshare Indian Detours. Every other time she had been here, it had been on the job or on her day off. It wasn't as good as being an archaeologist or a photographer, but it was something to be, and a lot better than being a cod liver barrel stirrer or a fish meal packer. She knew she would get another job again soon, but she couldn't picture anything she would like as much as driving the autobuses.

She remembered how the cans of fish used to come down the long packing table. Addie, on her left, would swipe a paintbrush of paste over it, then Jonnie would slap a label on it. Once in a while the paste would be too wet or too dry and it wouldn't hold, and Mr. Jewett, the foreman, would hold up the can screaming "We can't use this! We can't use this!" and they'd dock the pay for everyone on the line. With June running off with that Morna, and Miss Ruth and Laura trotting off all happy as if those heavy cameras weighed nothing, Jonnie felt like one of those useless cans.

"Buck up, little buckaroo," she told herself. "I've come this far from home and done all right so far, with just a few nights sleeping on hay and chewing on it too. I'll find another job, and who knows what new adventures?" Meanwhile, Miss Erna probably wasn't going to lend her the car again, so this might be her last chance out here for a long time, and she wanted to enjoy every minute of it. She had to do more than enjoy it. Maybe, somehow, there was a job here for her. If she could only make Dr. Morris notice her!

Not seeing anything else to do, Jonnie went back to the hole she had worked in last summer. The sun was high up and the heat was almost as bad as August. She didn't mind heat as much as some folks because when it got hot she just thought about how cold and wet it was working on the cod liver line in the winter. She remembered the slime and blood and smells so bad she had to wear a cloth over her mouth. "Just like the cowboys," the workers would say. But to work in the hot dusty hole at the dig, she also pulled a bandanna over her mouth. She pictured her cannery friends saying "Just like the archaeologists."

The slightly burnt smell of sage drifted past, and the sun glared off the smooth golden walls of the site, and Jonnie forgot Gloucester and the heat. She took careful tiny scoops with the little trowel. If only something really terrific would come out of this hole, something with feathers or rabbit fur, something she could give a big shout about, and one of the archaeologists would take a glance, and give a whistle, and bang on the tire rim bell, and they'd all come around to see what she had found, Jonnie the tour bus driver, the one Morris still couldn't remember.

But only sand and pottery shards came up, same as the ones that crunched underfoot everywhere here, and they did ring the bell, but for lunch, not for Jonnie. She remembered her father saying the reason folks like them never got out of the fish holds was because they ate lunch with the wrong people. Maybe the reason Dr. Morris didn't notice her was that she always ate with the Navajo workers. So this time she picked up her tin plate of beans and corn bread from the rough board table beside the cook tent and headed to the little circle under a shade tarpaulin where the students ate. They sat cross-legged on the ground, cowboy style. It was hard for her old joints to spend the morning squatting in a hole in the ground. Jonnie wanted to lean against a rock, but she painfully folded her legs and sat down with them.

The students bragged about how dirty they were. At least you don't smell like dead fish, Jonnie wanted to tell them. But they would have stared at her and she would feel odder than ever. They were sharing fantasies about taking baths in Santa Fe, when Dr. Morris joined them. Jonnie had last seen him up on the mesa watching Ruth.

"Did you all see that lady scientist up there?" Dr. Morris addressed the students. "See how slowly she moves. She's looking for rare plants. It's not much different than what we do. She doesn't have to dig, but they're hard to find just like our artifacts. When she found something, she sat for an hour drawing one little leaf. Then she pressed the plant into some plates and she told me she'll be working on it for weeks. If only you students would work so carefully!" The students had all stopped chewing and were looking at the ground.

"You like to dig for buried treasure, but you don't like to record. You should take a lesson from that lady, and you'll notice she's no spring chicken. Maybe you're all too young. Don't have the patience of maturity. Maybe I should hire more old ladies," he laughed, and they laughed too, and then he walked off.

Jonnie thought they might look at her enviously for a change, since they usually seemed to carry a silent question of why an old lady like herself would be up here crawling in the dirt, but she was as invisible to them as she was to Morris. Instead, they immediately all jumped up and shoved their lunch dishes to the Navajo cook—a grandmother, Jonnie knew, because she'd been introduced to her grandson one day when he came by with his flock. They ran back to their sites, practically falling over each other trying to impress Dr. Morris.

Back in her hole, Jonnie had to be careful not to pound her shovel against the sand. Miss Ruth had spent just one morning here and scooped up all the goodies. Back home, she had seen fist fights when the fishing fleet came in empty and then some boat no one had ever seen from Canada or New Bedford followed right after them, sailing low in the water, heavy with catch. Maybe she should climb up that mesa and haul off one on Ruth.

No, it was Morris she should go for. Nothing she was doing was working, and if he didn't notice her today, the smelly fish and the docks seemed to be moving west and coming closer all the time. At least she knew she would always have a bed back at her father's house. Mrs. Landauer was nice, but she couldn't afford to keep any deadbeats on.

The bell rang and Dr. Morris' assistant called out, "Dr. Morris needs a driver. Anyone want to go?"

Some of the students ducked down into their holes. No one liked driving for Dr. Morris. He was always seeing something off in the distance, up a hill or down some horrible ditch, and insisting on being taken there. Inevitably the car would get stuck and he'd leave the driver out there to deal with it while he went off exploring. Now that she had lost her job with Erna, this might be her last day at the dig for a long time. But if she drove, maybe, finally he'd notice her.

Morna

Morna thought the field site was even cruder than the trading post had been when she first moved there. Under a huge overhang of rocks were stacks of big wooden crates and tables made of rough boards. Ugly canvas tents made it looked like newsreel pictures of the trenches in the Great War. The white workers all wore khaki jodhpurs and helmets, even the women, so she saw why that oddball Jonnie liked it. At least she wasn't looking at the same old shelves full of cans and the same sulking Indian faces, but her sense that she was escaping to a better place soon disappeared. The field site was even more remote than the trading post.

"Dr. Morris brings the best students here from the University of Colorado, Columbia, and Harvard Universities," June said. How long had it been since Morna had talked to anyone fresh from New York City? She felt like a convict whose door had been left temporarily open, just until the guards came back. She had to make her break now or never, because by afternoon they would pile back into the autobus and Jonnie would take her back to Jack. Somewhere in all this dust and rock was the key that would set her free of her cage. Would all these people be here if there wasn't something valuable?

In his khakis and big hat and high boots, Dr. Morris, who ran the place, looked like someone on the cover of one of Jack's adventure books. He was ordering a Navajo worker to crawl down a hole with a cloud of dust hovering over it. The Navajo worker leaned on a rock, watching Dr. Morris warily but not doing what he said. Morna had seen the Navajo men do that plenty around the trading post. When they first came, Jack and Morna had thought it was insolence, but they had learned it meant not to order them so directly. Morna had sometimes wished she could stand up to Jack the same way. Finally Dr. Morris stalked off and said something to one of the students, who spoke to the Indian in a way that got him doing what Dr. Morris wanted.

"How have you been?" June asked as they walked around. "Sometimes I wonder how you are. That trading post looks like a lonely place for a woman."

Morna's heart felt like butter melting. How long had it been since she had heard anyone say they thought about her? All sorts of good things were happening for her today. Maybe the Navajos had performed one of their ceremonies for her. Sometimes one of their medicine men would offer to trade some "good medicine" for goods, but Jack would always snap out "In God we trust, all others pay cash—or blankets or wool, and that's it." Today was so strange, she wondered if she had acquired some magic power to attract the possibilities she had come West with, before she and Jack were buried under layers of sand, dirty wool, and forgotten dreams.

"I'm tired of the trading post," Morna said. "I love seeing what you're doing here."

"Watch your step and there's plenty to see," June said. As they walked up the mesa, June explained her work. She made Morna go first around a corner where a mummy sat. June seemed disappointed when Morna just giggled. "Looks like some of the old guys who sit around the stove at our store all day."

"You're certainly a better sport than some," June laughed. "Come with me." They crawled through a little door into a cave room, and then through another door into one behind it.

"Those doors were bricked over to hide them. That's how we knew where to look. See the black on the walls? That's the smoke from fires a thousand years ago. And here's the one who probably sat by the fire—"

The floor of the room was dug up, creating a rectangular trench. A skeleton lay in the trench, with its knees bent and hands neatly folded on its lap. Two big empty eye holes stared at Morna. Most of a mug stuck out of the sand by its bony fingers.

"Looks like he's thinking about taking a nice gulp of coffee from that mug, doesn't it?" asked June.

"Oh my," Morna said, "That pottery, is it—?"

But June wasn't listening. She was looking out the first door and down into the field site below.

"Oh, nuts," she called out, "Dr. Morris is leaving and he needs me to—I gotta run." She took off down the path. Morna wanted to take the mug, but she followed as quickly as she could, slipping and sliding but somehow staying on her feet, all the while searching the ground in hopes of seeing a bright gleam of jewelry or a pot.

By the time Morna was back at ground level, Dr. Morris was talking to Jonnie. June stood by impatiently. Then Jonnie got into the driver's seat and Dr. Morris, looking grouchy about it, let June climb in next to Jonnie. Morna ran around to Jonnie's window.

"Where are you going?"

"I'm driving Dr. Morris out to a new site. The Navajo workers say it's got graves, so they won't go there."

"Quiet!" Morris snapped at Jonnie. "Let's get going already." Jonnie looked puzzled, and June looked embarrassed. What didn't they want Morna to know? Maybe he was headed to one of those treasure troves she had been hoping to find. She wanted to ask if she could come, but June shot her a look that told her to shut up.

Morna waved good-bye and backed off. She scanned the area. Laura and Ruth had disappeared, Jonnie was leaving, and Morna felt alone and desperate. This site had been picked over by a lot of experts, but wherever this truck went might be a chance to go to an untouched site, one Dr. Morris wanted to keep secret.

As Morna walked away, one of the archaeologists ran up to the truck to talk to Morris. The bed of the truck was filled with blankets and crates. Without much thought, she swung as quickly and lightly as she could into the truck. She ducked under a blanket draped over a crate.

Laura

"Darn," Laura yelped. They both ran to the shrub where the lens she'd dropped had rolled. It flashed in the sun. Laura grabbed it and held it to the light. Ruth had some harsh words on her lips, but then she saw something that made her gasp. In the crevice, near where the lens had rolled, was a tiny flowering plant. Just as she bent down to see it, Laura tripped on a root and fell to her knees. Ruth pushed her right back to the ground.

"What are you doing?" Laura screamed. "Don't push me!"

"You almost stepped on it!" Ruth screamed right back.

"I'm bleeding," Laura snapped. "Stepped on what?"

"You'll be all right. It's perfect." Ruth was on her knees between Laura and the plant, painstakingly combing her fingers through the brush. The strange little plant was sheltered in a spot where two crumbling rock walls met. She could see a shallow groove where water had traveled down the wall for centuries, just enough to keep it alive, not enough to drown it. This was just what she had been wondering about. Had some of the women who carried the jugs of water up to the mesa top also put into their pockets, or maybe stuck into their baby's cradle board, a sprig of herb or flower from below, and transplanted it up here? What would it be like a thousand years later?

As she ran her fingers through the hard soil around the plant, something very sharp pierced the ball of Ruth's thumb. A bright red drop of blood burst out as she grabbed a little rock and dug out the cause—a potsherd with a sharp edge. Maybe this was the remains of the little jug in which the flower had once been planted. Perhaps the gardener had made the pot with the same loving hands and good mind that had chosen this spot to shelter the little flower through a millennium. Could this plant be like one that grew so long ago, its grandchild of a thousand summers?

"Start taking photographs," Ruth said, and then noticed that Laura was sitting on the ground, anxiously examining her wound. Laura looked up as if she expected Ruth to take care of her, and Ruth remembered that the kind nurse Betsy was Laura's special friend. Betsy would know what to do, but "Are you all right?" was the best Ruth could dredge up.

"I guess it's okay," Laura said. "It's the kind of bruise children are always getting, the skinned knee type of thing. What's that you found?"

Ruth was glad Laura wasn't angry about being pushed into the bushes. Laura got back to her feet while Ruth explained about the flower and how the photos should be taken.

"Oh my gosh, the lens!" Laura cried out. She couldn't remember where she'd put it when Ruth pushed her. They combed through the thorny brush that ripped at their skin, finding nothing. Laura stopped to catch her breath, and poked into the pocket of her skirt for her handkerchief.

"I've got it! I must have dropped it into my pocket. There it is. All in one piece. But if it's scratched—" She held it up to the light, turning it round and round, as Ruth stood by gritting her teeth.

"It's okay," Laura finally said, and then louder, "It's okay. I guess I'm okay. How are you?"

Ruth held up her thumb, ignoring the blood. "I need photos right here," she said. "I've found something maybe even better than that plant in Santa Fe."

Even as she set up the camera, Laura felt a flush on her face from the humiliation of dropping the lens. She hoped no one but Ruth had seen. What kind of professional was she? How would she ever have paid for a replacement if it had broken, let alone having to deal with Ruth's anger and disappointment? She thanked God as fervently as Betsy's nemesis

Reverend Luck would have. She looked out over the serene view and tried to calm down. The lens was fine, Ruth was beaming about some old flower she found in the wall, and maybe Laura would get a chance to take her own photos, once Ruth's requests were finished and she could put the distance lens back on.

She worried that Ruth would ask for so many pictures that she would run out of film first. Meanwhile, if she wasn't photographing what she chose, at least she was in this gorgeous place seeing all that she would love to photograph—the chalk-like cliffs in the distance, the walking rain clouds way to the north, and the patterns formed by the flattening of the path below as she looked down from her high perch. It was a challenge to take Ruth's pictures, and it would make her a better photographer, but once again she was waiting and wishing for that time when she could be making the pictures she was taking in her head into real photos on a plate of silver nitrate and gelatin. But making money always came first, and too often nothing came after that. At least she was still making some money, when so few people were now.

Maybe she could take just one photo all her own today. As she stooped and crawled and lifted and pushed and pulled the camera to do as Ruth directed, she planned her own perfect photo. Of course, the perfect photo required the perfect moment of light and shadow, and perhaps that moment was passing while she was on her knees, her cheek rubbing in dirt, trying to get the big camera low enough to photograph the root structure as Ruth directed. Ruth constantly chattered at Laura: "Be careful. Don't crush that! Oh you mustn't move that! Please, your feet, watch out!" Ruth wanted the perfect photo taken without disturbing the fragile plants. Laura held back her frustration by trying to remember what Steiglitz had said about how the goal of the photographer was to capture the image without changing the reality.

Laura was always surprised by how demanding Ruth was in the field. She normally had the calm, almost cold courtesy that Laura's wealthiest customers had when they sat for a portrait. Laura preferred the giggling and self-conscious jokes of her less polished customers. But Ruth's single-minded obsession towards her goal to the exclusion of all else was bringing her success, like the attention Dr. Morris had paid to her. Laura knew she herself was always getting sidetracked. If only she were more like Ruth.

She thought of the day when she and Betsy had visited June at this site. She had the camera, film, and time, and she could have taken so many photos. Instead she had let herself get distracted by Betsy's anger at June's callousness toward the Indians.

"Wait here," Ruth said, interrupting Laura's thoughts, "I need to look around some more."

Was this Laura's moment? It was midday and the sky was as solid and clear as a China plate. The colors were washed out in all the brightness. There was no drama, no contrast of lights and darks to be captured forever. Laura leaned back against a rock, holding firmly to the camera. When would her moment come?

There was something about this place and the thoughts she had here. Despite the placid sky, there was a storm in her head, but suddenly she was clear. What she wanted to do. How she would do it. As far as she could see, in every direction were the brushy hills, the occasional anvil-shaped buttes, and the sky that framed it all in a sphere as if she were inside a big photographic bulb. How long had it been since she had just sat and thought? Money, rent, customers, Betsy, the cameras, the bills, the Navajo people, the roads, the car: lately, her life rushed on and on with no time to think beyond the moment. But up here she was clear. At this moment, she had the perfect picture, and it was of her own life. She shouldn't have let Betsy pull her away. Betsy never let Laura's interests take her away from any of her patients, and Laura had to make sure her photography came first. She would have to be as possessed as Ruth and as dedicated as Betsy. A perfect cloud or a beautiful rock formation should capture her time as surely as a stream of blood or flash of broken bone caught Betsy's.

Jonnie

It was a good sign that Dr. Morris took her as part of the crew, even if it was for a task that the students all avoided. Just drive, Jonnie told herself. Don't try to do that thing the students are always joking about: don't try to be a Doctor Freud and figure it all out.

As they drove out of the camp, June and Morris fell into conversation. Morris spoke so softly that Jonnie could barely hear above the noise of the truck. She had the feeling that Morris didn't want her to hear.

"You haven't said anything, have you? About Deadsheep Canyon?" he asked June. "When I found that gravesite last week, I remembered seeing a similar construction up in the Canyon. At the time, I didn't think it could be a grave. But I've been thinking about it and I've got to look at it again."

Jonnie was disappointed she wasn't going to be alone with Dr. Morris. She wanted him to notice her. But he was a lot like Miss Ruth, his mind only on his own search and no one else. Jonnie imagined Miss Ruth as the leader of an operation like this, with a team of college students and dozens of Navajo laborers at her command. She probably wouldn't even turn away from her work long enough to tell them what to do. At least Dr. Morris paid enough attention to prevent complete chaos.

As they drove along, he stared intently out the window while June tried to tell him about her dissertation. The students were always talking about how hard it was to get his ear for any length of time. June probably thought she had it right now, but Jonnie didn't think he was listening.

More than once she avoided ditching the car in an arroyo, or in a spot that, looking back in the mirror, she was sure had been quicksand. When this happened, Jonnie wanted to cross herself like she had seen the Spanish ladies do in Santa Fe. She pictured how her father would roar at her if he saw that! "You're looking like a regular Portugee," he would say, "Next you'll be buying your own pew at Our Lady of Good Voyage. Viva San Pietro!" he would yell with a smirk. He thought anyone whose family didn't go back hundreds of years didn't belong in Gloucester. What would he think if an Indian treated him like the newcomer?

If June hadn't been in the truck, Jonnie would have had the nerve to speak to Dr. Morris. If Navajo laborers wouldn't go to this new site, they must know there were graves, even if Dr. Morris didn't think so. "Chindi," they'd mutter, which meant it had dead spirits in it. They had sold themselves out enough already in Canyon del Muerto, where they justified working because the archaeologists had already opened so many graves.

They reached a place so covered with bald, egg-like rocks and little towers of sandstone that the truck was barely moving. Jonnie worried about the axles with every rotation of the tires, but Dr. Morris hardly seemed to notice because he was intently saying something to June. Jonnie strained to hear the story too, but his voice was lost under the noise of the car.

As they drove along, they passed a Navajo shepherd girl and her flock. The sheep began to run, and she desperately tried to control them. Though the truck was slower than the sheep, there was a terrified look on her face, and Jonnie realized she must be from a place still so remote she rarely saw a car or truck.

After more plodding, Morris looked up and pointed some distance ahead. "When we reach that shadowy spot," he said, "the road will start to climb. Just follow it."

What road? It was just a very steep and gutted arroyo. Jonnie wanted to tell him that she had never taken a car on anything this bad, but decided he had been out in this wild country for years, knew what he was doing, and probably had never had a male driver chicken out. She decided to keep driving and keep quiet. This was her big chance. As the truck ground on, she was amazed it still hadn't blown a tire. The "road" was so steep she was glad she wasn't walking up it, especially if they had to carry the gear in the back of the truck.

Finally the way leveled off and they were on top of a small mesa. Beneath the grass and shrubs were the soft outlines of the old walls of ancient houses. Jonnie saw a bird that Miss Ruth would have loved. Dr. Morris bounded out of the car with June right behind him. He didn't tell Jonnie what to do, so she followed.

"Practically untouched," he told June. "I can't believe the pothunters haven't found it yet. I've already written the proposal to start working here next summer, but meanwhile, I just can't leave it like this. When I hiked up to here, I couldn't carry much out. Today I want to grab what I can before the pothunters find it."

So that was why he wanted the truck up here.

"We've got to work quickly," he said, "it's already well past noon."

That was the first sensible thing he'd said all day. He scraped back some shrubs and exposed a little house entrance. He had to stoop awkwardly to enter. He had June crawl inside while he held a kerosene lamp, at one point burning his fingers and almost dropping it. June was almost as tall as Dr. Morris, and Jonnie wished he'd let her be the one to do it. What would it be like to be the first into a spot like that, especially since within a few minutes June had handed him a complete pot? Jonnie had never seen one, and she gasped. Dr. Morris seem to noticed Jonnie for the first time, and he held it up smiling as smugly as if he'd been the Anasazi woman who'd made this beautiful object so long ago, her little hands so much more gifted than his big knuckled fingers.

Although the sun was no longer above, it was hot. They formed a bucket brigade, as June gave objects to her and she handed them to Dr. Morris and he put them into padded crates in the truck. As she handed over an almost perfect double spouted wedding goblet, June whispered, "Morna from the trading post would sure love to be here."

"What do you mean?"

"She was asking me all morning how to find a place like this. I told her they didn't exist anymore. Well, this is why Dr. Morris is tops. I'm so lucky to be working for him."

A little later she whispered again. "Do you think you could find this place again?"

"I don't know, Jonnie said.

"On the way back, watch really carefully, okay?"

What if June wanted Jonnie to take her here to pothunt? If she refused, Jonnie would lose her only friend—and supporter—at the site. Who was she to judge June's actions? Weren't all the archaeologists just pothunters with college degrees?

Morna

As they drove along the arroyo, Morna peaked out from under the hot, dusty blanket tent. It was hard to believe this day had started the same as every other day for the last four years. One adventure was opening into another and she wanted them all. She had known she was unhappy and that she needed more, but as the truck bumped along under the cloudless pale blue sky, she felt all that she hadn't allowed herself to feel. She remembered the young woman who had moved to Manhattan for adventure, who had gone to art school to meet interesting people, who had thrived on all the colors and changes of the city. Looking out over this drab, static land disappearing into the black smoke spewed out by the truck, she thought about how miserable that girl who wanted so much had become in this rock hard, bleached land. She wasn't going back to Jack for even one more day. Wherever this truck took her would be her springboard back to the city.

It was hot under the blankets and she pulled off the old shirt of Jack's she was wearing over her blouse. She pushed her hands deep into the pockets of her skirt. Would there be any pottery small enough to hide there? Maybe some turquoise stones could be slipped into her brassiere. Somehow she would slip away from Morris and do her own searching.

The truck bumped along for quite a while, finally heading up a steep hill and stopping suddenly. The truck rocked as they climbed out, and Morna hid deeper under the blankets. Someone reached in near her to grab some canteens, but Morna cringed back so she wasn't spotted. They called to each other as they walked off, then Morna slowly slid out of the blankets and looked around.

She was on top of a mesa covered with crumbling walls. There were more canteens so she grabbed two. Judging that they'd gone towards the center of the mesa, she turned toward the edge, keeping low and hidden behind the truck.

Soon she found pot shards and even an arrowhead. She sifted through a pile of shards for turquoise beads, remembering that Jack had told her about doing this. He said the beads were usually buried with the body, but field mice, rain, and the movement of the earth often brought them to the surface. Sometimes she heard the others calling to each other in the distance, but in the heat and excitement, she was in a trance of searching and imagining all she might find.

She only noticed that the sky was growing dark when she heard the truck engine start. Her pockets were filled with booty: beads, a feathered object, and a little clay flute. She had to get back to the truck, but when she looked around, she realized she would never make it.

Her search had brought her deep down into a pocket in the edge of the mesa. She had moved down the side of the mesa as if the petroglyphs on the rock walls were dollar signs instead of handprints and spirals. Desperately, she searched for handholds to climb back up the slick rock, amazed she had gone down so far without breaking her neck. The roots and trees broke away in her hands, and she slid further down.

Jonnie

Dr. Morris packed the crates till they were full to the very last inch. Finally, he closed the lids. Their shadows were getting long on the mesa top. They hadn't brought any food, and the water was nearly gone.

"All right," he said, "now let's hightail it back to camp. Wish I could take more. The problem with coming up here is that the Indians are sure to follow the tire tracks. Once they get here, nothing's sacred." He leaped into the front seat. "Let's go," he said, while June and Jonnie were still scrambling in.

Jonnie was turning so she could go back the way they had come in, when he suddenly cried out, "Stop!" She brought the truck to a jerking halt.

"I've got an idea," he said. "Let's go down a different way." He nodded significantly to June. "It'll leave less of a trail. Go that way," he pointed.

"I can't see any way to go."

"Just do it. We came up with no road, and we can go down without a road."

"Can I get out and take a look where we're going first?" asked Jonnie.

"Make it fast."

Jonnie didn't like what she saw and told him so. The other side was more rutted and steep than the impossible way they had driven up.

"How many years you been driving around here, little lady?" he asked.

Finally, it was her chance to impress him. "I started as a chauffeur for the—"

"How long, dammit?"

"Since last spring."

"Months! I've been in every nook and cranny and corner of the Four Corners," he guffawed. "I know what's possible, and I say drive,"

Jonnie looked at June, but she had turned away. If she stood up to Morris, she would never get another chance with him.

"Maybe I haven't been driving as long as you, but I've driven a lot. This could wreck the truck."

"Get out and I'll show you how it's done."

He shoved over on the seat so that Jonnie had to quickly jump out the driver's side and run around. When she tried to get in the other side, June shot Jonnie an angry look.

"You can sit in the middle," she said.

"Maybe I'll sit with the crates," Jonnie answered and jumped on the truck bed.

"Morris wants to show you how well he drives," June said, but Jonnie was already finding a seat on a crate. There wasn't much point in hoping she could impress Dr. Morris anymore. But still, she could count her blessings. For the first time ever, she would travel through this beautiful country as a passenger, seeing the sites from the back of the truck. The crate felt like a throne.

Starting off with a jerk that stalled the engine and almost threw Jonnie off her crate, Dr. Morris headed down the cliff, bumping all the way. Jonnie ignored it and enjoyed the view. From here, the sky was as big as it could ever be. Maybe it would look bigger than this from a fishing schooner, but with all that empty ocean, there'd be no way to tell. There were so many soft colors, of the creamy sandstone cliffs of caves off one way, the pink of the ground so far below, and the sharp buttes that stuck out here and there. Rough and smooth, brushy and slick, soft and hard, everything of life was here. As the truck lurched up and down with every little rise and fall of the land, pieces of the landscape appeared and disappeared. Jonnie sat on top of it all, like the captain on the bridge in the waves of a huge storm, only her skies were blue, clear, and sunny, and her ride a fun one.

She didn't feel worried. Any world as beautiful and bright as this one was going to take good care of her. She couldn't remember why she had been so scared, because the warm sun and the soft air holding her safe now

188 Land Beyond Maps

had been there all along. She was sure that everything was going to be all right. All this beauty was no accident, and since there was a plan, that plan included Jonnie, even so far from home. Her whole body loosened up, bobbing along with the gentler rhythm as they moved down the slope.

With a sudden bump that cracked her teeth together and sent her flying off the crate, the truck crashed. Jonnie landed in a heap on the ground, her head bouncing and eyes rolling. There was a loud blaring sound from the horn of the truck, stuck in the "on" position. Other than that it was very quiet. Her arm throbbed terribly and she screamed out "Help, stop." They wouldn't know she had fallen out. They'd just drive on without her. She would be forgotten here to die alone. So many people from Gloucester had died in a watery grave, Jonnie thought. Had she come all the way out here to end up a dried up, weightless mummy bag of bones? She screamed again and again.

Morna

Again Morna's shoes slipped on the sheer rock. She grabbed at a root, but only skinned her hands and fell back into a cactus that drove a thorn into her calf. She was trying to pull out its barbed tip when she heard a sound like a truck crashing. There was the burble of the engine stopping, and then the horn blared. It sounded like they were on the other side of the mesa. Well, she couldn't help them.

She decided that working her way down the cliff would be easier than trying to find handholds and pulling herself up. But the ground was far below and cliff face slick. She pictured herself sliding until her body pounded into the hard ground below. It was already getting dark. She still had water because she had been too excited to drink. But she had no food.

What had she been thinking to do something this impulsive? At the trading post she had heard many stories of people who died in the desert because they'd been unprepared. Jack always joked that they could advertise by displaying a skeleton with a sign that said: "I should have stopped at Lost Wash Trading Post." Now she was the one they would laugh about. Would they ever find her? Who would think to look here? They'd be searching for Morris' truck, but no one knew she had been in it. Someday, when a new expedition came to this site, they'd find her skeleton and think she was some ancient Indian woman. Instead of selling museum pieces, she was going to become one.

Jonnie

Jonnie was dreaming that the sun had swallowed her into a world of yellow, and that it had a little brown-faced brother whose black eyes were sharp teeth. An icicle dripped down her face. Then all disappeared and she was plunged under a cold, dark wet blanket of sea. Then the sun was back, her head cleared, and she saw that a Navajo shepherd girl was bathing her head with water squeezed from the corner of the blanket she wore, dipping it into her jug.

She felt the pain in her right arm and remembered hitting the ground very hard. She tried to look, but the girl gently held her head back. She pointed at Jonnie's arm and made a motion as if she were snapping sticks for kindling. It felt pretty bad, but Jonnie didn't think it was broken.

The girl gestured as if opening a pouch on her belt. Jonnie had seen the medicine men with their mysterious buckskin pouches, and she guessed it meant a Navajo healer could help her arm. She wanted to believe that, but Laura had told her that Betsy, her nurse friend, had learned that the medicine men were good with chronic sicknesses, but that even they were coming to her for injuries like broken bones.

Jonnie heard a groan. Arching her head back, she saw the black shape of the truck. She remembered hearing the drone of the horn before she passed out, but it was silent now. The girl made the sign for the white man that Jonnie had seen the Navajo workmen use to make disparaging gestures about Dr. Morris.

After a few minutes listening to the groaning and hearing a few sobs that must have been June's, she forced herself to her feet. The girl helped her. Every part of her body hurt, but she stumbled over to the cab and looked in. June was slumped against the open passenger window, her head thrown back, her face very white except for a bluish swelling bruise where she'd hit the frame of the car. Her eyes flickered and she was moaning through her swollen and bloody lips.

Dr. Morris was bent over the wheel. Jonnie leaned into the window, calling his name softly. He lifted his head slightly. His face was a mess, covered with blood and shards of glass. When he moved, his arm fell on the horn long enough to start it blaring again, but he pushed it off. His arm might be broken and just looking at his painful movements made Jonnie feel her own pain more. She looked around at the vast empty distances in every direction. The sun was getting low. She wondered if the headlights were smashed and tried to remember if there would be a full moon.

With the girl helping her hobble around, Jonnie examined the front of the truck. Dr. Morris had hit a rock low enough that he hadn't seen it, but high enough to bounce against the bumper and cause the crash. The damage was mostly to the humans, so Jonnie decided she could back the truck out of this spot and then take it down the road they had come up. But she couldn't do it with a possibly broken arm and a leg so sore she couldn't press down on the clutch. She looked at the girl and tried to pantomime holding the wheel, but with one arm it looked like she was shaking a stick. The girl moved back, understandably afraid that Jonnie was threatening to hit her.

"Chidi?" Jonnie said. She had used every chance to learn Navajo words, and now she really needed it. But why would this girl know the word for car when she may not have seen one before? The girl shook her head. Well, maybe she had never seen one before, but she was going to have to drive one. From her groggy memory, Jonnie dredged up some words. She knew left, right, up, and down from coordinating her work at the dig with that of the Navajo laborers.

The girl made the sign of the medicine bag again, offering to go for help. Would it be better to let her go so she could bring back someone who could drive? Or better to have her try driving? Jonnie wasn't used to being the one in charge, making decisions. The girl looked eager to run off across the mesa. She was probably worrying about her flock, too. Losing it could mean little food or income for her family for this year.

Dr. Morris called out. "Girl, come here," he ordered, just like he ordered the workmen around. The girl probably didn't understand his words, but his tone made her jump. She may never have been spoken to directly by a white man before. She looked at Jonnie questioningly. Leaning on the girl, Jonnie hobbled back to his window.

"I can't drive," Dr. Morris said. "You'll have to." He was talking to Jonnie. He didn't even know her name! She wanted to show him her arm, but he wasn't listening. "Get that woman into the truck bed, and then I can move over." He gestured at June, who appeared to be unconscious.

Jonnie pointed at the handle and the girl opened it. June's limp body started to slide out. The girl grabbed June and dragged her out. Fortunately this strong girl had probably been carrying sheep to shearing all her life. Jonnie could only watch as she held onto June, who was awake enough to stagger along. She didn't seem to have any broken bones, but perhaps was just suffering from the kind of knockout punch fisherman get when they don't get out of the way of a shifting sailboat boom fast enough. With the girl's help, June was able to get into the bed of the truck and lay down between the crates. If Jonnie had been sitting in the truck bed instead of on the crates, she probably wouldn't have been thrown out. Was it only minutes earlier that she had been so happy, looking at all the beauty around her?

Dr. Morris had managed to slide over in the seat, making room for a driver.

"Let's go," he grunted.

"I can't drive." Jonnie showed him her useless arm.

"Dammit!" he said. "You get in the back. The Indian girl will have to drive."

Jonnie turned to the girl, and pointed to the driver's seat. She looked shocked and shook her head, no.

"She can't drive. I don't think she's seen a truck so close before."

"Who the hell else is going to do it?"

Jonnie knew the girl wanted to help. Indians believed in helping a stranger in need. But she couldn't perform miracles by herself. Maybe they should send her to get more people. How long would it take for her to find someone who could drive? The land around looked empty, but while driving the tour bus Jonnie had often been surprised by the sudden manifestation of a Navajo horseman or even a well-camouflaged hogan.

Jonnie made the same gesture the girl had made, indicating a medicine man. She pointed at the sun, hoping the girl would understand that she wanted to know how long it would take. The girl wove her good arms up and down to show the sun going down and coming up again.

Jonnie worried that once it grew cold after sunset and the shock wore off, she and Dr. Morris were going to be in tremendous pain. He'd probably expect Jonnie to take care of him, and he probably didn't care what happened to June. Jonnie didn't want to stay here. They should leave immediately to get as much sun as possible. Her arm throbbed horribly as she climbed painfully onto the seat, slid under the driver's wheel and sat in the middle, all the while smiling encouragingly and beckoning the girl to come in. She just stood and stared.

"What do you think you're doing?" said Dr. Morris. "Get in here!" he yelled at the girl.

"Stop scaring her," Jonnie snapped. "If she leaves, we'll have nothing. She's only offering to go for help, and they won't be here until morning."

"I think I know a bit about these Indians," said Dr. Morris. "You don't have to tell me how to work them. I've been working with Indians for years. Get in here, girl." He tried to point at the driver's seat, but gasped in pain.

Before she had come west, Jonnie had seen every cowboy movie that ever came to the Gloucester Theater. When a bad cowboy caused trouble, the good cowboy punched him in the nose just to get him out of the way. Jonnie wanted to do that to Dr. Morris, but with her arm so hurt, she couldn't.

The girl burst into tears.

Jonnie had heard Navajo women say something to quiet their children, who sometimes cried when the tourists were too pushy. She wasn't sure if the words they murmured were a comfort, a threat, or a promise of candy, but she looked at the girl as reassuringly as she could and mumbled what she remembered. The girl looked up, smiling through her tears. If Jonnie had just promised her something a Navajo mother could buy from those usually almost empty shelves at the trading post, Dr. Morris would have to come up with the money. She motioned for the girl to sit down and hold the wheel. Thinking about what she would want someone to say to her if the situation were reversed, Jonnie pressed her hand to her heart to indicate that she would be right here helping her. Pointing to her left, Jonnie said the Navajo word. The girl nodded. Jonnie pointed to her right and said the Navajo word. They went through "up" and "down," the girl bobbing her head, happy with the familiarity.

Still uncertain and still with tears, the girl climbed into the driver's seat. Morris had shut up since she had cried and let Jonnie take over. After a number of jerking stalls on the clutch, the truck was slowly backed off the rock it had hit. Fortunately there was enough open flat space behind that the truck could turn in a wide circle, but when Jonnie mixed up the terms for right and left, they knocked the top layer of bricks off a low wall that had been standing a thousand years. Jonnie felt guilty until she heard June moan in the back. They had no choice. As they moved onto flatter land, she was afraid that Morris would again insist upon taking a different path, but he stayed quiet. Soon they were slowly moving along the way they had come up. The girl was driving with more confidence and Jonnie was able to relax a little, which unfortunately meant she felt the pain in her arm more. She tried not to think about how she would pay a doctor.

Morna

Morna heard the truck driving away. She was glad they were all right, but still she had a sinking feeling. She wanted to scream but she knew they would never hear her. Her throat was going to hurt enough when she ran out of water.

The sun was falling but it was still hot. She leaned against the wall of an ancient house built into the cliff, hoping to find a comfortable place to spend the night before it was too dark to explore. She crawled through the tiny waist high doorways between the rooms, sometimes halfway falling into the next room. At last she came to a bricked over doorway, and as June had explained to her at the field site, it didn't take much to push through into a small room. The floor was covered with the bricks she had knocked down, but she brushed them away, excited that what she wanted might be underneath: a burial. Her hands were bleeding but all she could think was that under all this coarse grit lay her ticket to New York City. Soon she punched through to a hollow space underneath. Tearing away at the dirt that had fallen in, she pulled out some clay objects and something wrapped in feathers.

While she dug, the sun must have set, because suddenly the room was pitch dark. She stood and ran her hands along the walls, searching for the opening. Suddenly all she wanted was to get out of the room. She tried not to step on the objects she had unearthed as she groped her way out. She left the objects where they lay.

It was dark outside. Her stomach was empty and her skin was scraped and pierced in so many places she felt that she had been turned inside out. Something flapped its wings as it flew by her. Was it a bat? There could be mountain lions up here. Would an eagle attack a human? She ran back into the front room of the little house, which the rising moon showed was empty.

No one had been in this room for a long time. She had overheard archaeologists and tourists who visited the trading post talking about their dreams of finding an untouched site. She and Jack owned a few books written by people who traveled through the area and described what they saw. One was called *Finding the Worthwhile in the Southwest*, a title which had become an ironic joke for Jack and Morna. But there hadn't been much else to read so she had read it enough to learn that the people who had lived in these cliff houses had left suddenly and mysteriously around the year 1200 A.D. The sudden move was the reason so much of their stuff had been left behind for archaeologists and pothunters. It's a lucky break, she told herself. I'll get out of here alive. I've got to believe that. But meanwhile she had the perfect chance to find her fortune. Beads, pipes, flutes, feather prayer sticks, and maybe even jewelry and ancient weavings were here for the taking. What had been in that feather-wrapped bundle? She hoped she hadn't trampled it. What would she find if she dug further? She wondered if she would be willing to proceed once she touched bones.

The risen moon lit the cliff room enough for her to see again. Its ancient builders had known what they were doing. There was a dark spot in the center of the room. It was the brittle remains of an ancient fire. She could make out dark streaks on the low round walls and ceiling from the fire's smoke. The only sounds were rustles in the brush on the hillside. She pictured huge desert rats or snakes, but told herself it was the wind. The waist-high hole that led from this room to the next was just the right height for a panther to spring at her throat. She was afraid to sleep, but staying up meant thinking about death by hunger or thirst or at an animal's teeth and claws. She was never going to get back to Greenwich Village. It was a matter of what would kill her here first.

She even missed Jack. It was growing colder and as she tried to pull her dress tighter, she felt a little box of matches in her pocket. She sometimes forgot them there after lighting the stove in the morning. The box was crushed and there were only a few matches, and she didn't want to risk one as a test. Carefully making her way on the slick steep path outside the cave room, she broke off pieces of the brittle shrubs and picked up dried hollow cactus branches. It was harder to do, but she ripped fronds off a bushy sage. It was going to burn fast and probably very smoky, but it was all she had. She placed some into the ancient fireplace, wondering if any of the half-burned charcoal might also burn after all these centuries.

Warmed by the search, she decided to wait until she was as cold as she could stand before lighting the small pile she had gathered. She sat against the cave wall, pretending the sun's warmth still held there. Every tiny rustle cracked so loud she was sure there was something walking nearby. She knew she should keep moving, but she only felt safe huddled against the smooth wall. Finally, a huge bird flew right past the doorway, wings flapping, and she imagined she saw his talons ready to pluck her bones.

Grabbing at the matches with stiff fingers, she scraped once, twice, and got a light. Bending over and blowing on the kindling, she thought smugly of the Jack London story of the freezing man which had been all the rage in the New York magazines. She would feed her fire slowly, no matter how much she wished for a comforting blaze or one that a rescuer would see. Her endless irritation at having to use a woodstove at the trading post had at least taught her this. Meanwhile the blaze quickly died to a smolder, but it wasn't going out. Soon she had a steady small fire going. She leaned over, feeling the heat on her face and rubbed her hands in the warmth. It looked like the ancient charcoals were catching fire.

In the flickering firelight, the cliff house took on a new beauty. Shadows skipped against the pink walls, with an occasional flare as the flames reflected in a bright spot of mica in the surface. Years ago, in a ceramics class, she had made a little bottle, and now she felt she was sitting in it like a genie.

It wasn't hard to imagine a family of Ancient Ones sitting here as she did, watching the fire light the faces in the circle around it. Morna had never wanted children, but she could imagine being a mother at this moment, with her family around her. There was a safety in numbers she had envied sometimes, watching the Navajo women with their toddlers grabbing onto their wide skirts and their older children nearby. In New York, she and Jack and their friends often crowded into the cramped kitchen of a railroad flat to drink wine and talk about Steiglitz' latest show or Sloan's newest scheme for getting their art shown. That had been a warm circle, too. It had been hot and close and noisy and fun and something she hadn't done since coming west.

She and Jack were so alone out here. No wonder they had created nothing but a well-constructed masterpiece of hate for each other. She needed to leave and to rebuild a life back east. It always came down to the same thing, but looking out from this high perch, the canyon below lit by the moon, she thought about her scheme to get the money to go home. Was she really willing to rob a grave? The grave of that mother of so long ago, who had warmed by this fire, too? There had to be a better way. When she talked with Schweizer, the buyer from the Harvey Company who had shown her beads and pots to watch for, all she had seen in his hands was a ticket home, not how a family lovingly buried their mother with all the wealth and tools she'd need in a land beyond death.

At that moment the fire flickered out. She was so close to sleep she had forgotten to feed it. It was very cold and looking at the few matches left, the height of the moon, and the tiny pile of twigs, she wondered how she would get through the rest of the night. The Navajos left sick people to die alone. Had other women sat cold and alone as she did now, waiting and wondering if this place was somewhere on the route to death?

Ruth

The day went by as Ruth intently probed the little patches of vegetation this hard rock soil had somehow nourished, and called Laura to take photos. Finally hungry and out of water, they carefully picked their way down, putting their feet into the smooth hollows made by bare feet a thousand years earlier. Ruth had samples of plants carefully pressed into her carrying sheath and a few pot shards in her basket, eager for Dr. Morris to tell her something about the date of the flowerpot.

They headed for the central area where Dr. Morris had been, but didn't see him. There were some pot shards laid out on his crate table and Ruth compared them to the ones she had found, while Laura went looking for Jonnie.

Laura returned looking upset.

"Jonnie's gone," she said. "Dr. Morris asked her to drive him out to some new site, and they haven't come back. The students think they probably broke down. They may have to spend the night in the truck somewhere. Someone saw Morna get on the truck, also."

"How could they leave without us!" said Ruth.

"Her husband's going to be furious. Looks like we've got to find a place to spend the night. Maybe we can sleep in the autobus."

"We could!" Ruth said. She had always wanted to spend a night out on the desert, observing the nocturnal animals and looking for phosphorescent plants. But then Laura had another idea. "It isn't that far to the Navajo village where Betsy lives. Let's go there. Even if Jonnie and Dr. Morris get back soon, it's too late to drive to the trading post and then back to town. We'll be a lot more comfortable with Betsy. We can sleep in the clinic, and she'll be so glad to see me. Plus we might see the truck, or perhaps some Navajo person who has seen it. News travels really fast with them."

"Are you sure you know the way? I don't mind staying here," said Ruth.

"We've got to leave right away, before it gets any darker, or we could get stuck out in the desert ourselves," said Laura as she grabbed her camera gear and headed toward the autobus. "Let's hope Jonnie left the keys."

I hope we do get stuck, Ruth thought as she followed.

They drove for a long time, watching the sun set and the moon rise. Ruth hadn't been this far out in the desert before. The field site had been a whole new horizon, and now Laura was taking her even farther. Laura reassured Ruth that she visited Betsy often and knew where she was going, but it wasn't necessary. Ruth was thrilled, struggling to stay awake, not wanting to miss anything, but it had been a long hot day in the sun.

She didn't wonder what kept Laura awake. Laura was always talking about Betsy. Ruth had known some girls like them at art school. They didn't care for the boys and they seemed very happy. She had envied them, because she hadn't found any boys that interested her, but she also didn't want any girlfriend around. It all reminded her too much of how her mother and father always hung over her, checking to see if she had a fever, telling her what to do, how to dress, how to stand, and even how to clap her hands like a lady. Being alone in the desert collecting plants had shown her what made her happy. She didn't want anyone chattering away at her like Laura did on this whole long drive.

"What's going on?" Laura suddenly shrieked.

Ruth woke out of her daze. For a long time there'd been no light but the moon, but some distance away she could see light coming from a group of adobe buildings.

"Something terrible must have happened," Laura said. "That's the only reason they'd all be up this late. Maybe it's Dr. Morris." She pushed so hard on the gas pedal that the autobus lurched and stalled. "I hate going so slowly! I could run there faster!"

Ruth just stared at her and gulped.

Jack

Watching the sun go down, the anger that had been bubbling within him all day surfaced.

"Where is she?" He muttered as he threw seed to the chickens, which was one of Morna's chores. If they weren't back soon, they wouldn't be coming at all that night. It was far too dangerous to drive at night on the rutted roads. He'd been caught out there many times himself. They'd probably taken shelter in one of the hogans the Navajos abandoned when someone died in them. He pictured them pulling the boards off the door and stumbling over a skeleton or even a partly decayed body in the dark. Serve them right!

Or perhaps they'd make another mistake which he remembered so ruefully he could feel his cheeks burning. He'd laid out his bedroll on the flat, cozy surface of the road. A few hours later, a cascade of freezing water burst over him, as some rain high in the mountains sent a stream of water through all the dry conduit-like paths it could find. It had been light enough to continue on home and he'd sneezed all the way, the chill in his body the coldest he'd ever been.

When he returned home, still soaking, Morna stoked up the hot red fire in the wood stove. She grabbed one of the most valuable Indian blankets they'd had on display and wrapped it around him, and when he'd protested through his numb lips and chattering teeth, she'd said, "It's a Chief's blanket, to keep the chief alive in war, and now you're the Chief and you need it," and he'd welcomed the fiery warmth it gave him. She'd taken such good care of him, even slaughtering a chicken for the first time, a task she'd always refused to do, so he could have hot soup. She had watched over him so sweetly all the days and nights until his last sniffle was gone.

That had been the last time they'd been close and loving. Even though he had been sick, it had been the best time they had since moving to this godforsaken place. They had been picking at each other since the day they got here, or even since the day they left New York in a huff because of some disagreement trying to get his easel down the five flights of tenement stairs. He still hadn't used that easel here.

With all the anger and disappointment they'd been experiencing, it was surprising that they were they still together. He was unhappy, but Morna was miserable, alone most of the time. No wonder she'd jumped at the chance to go off with the girls.

Then he remembered the letter Morna had apparently hidden from him, the one that bulldagger photographer mentioned. Maybe there'd been other letters. Maybe she'd been in touch with those queers all along. She could have made some arrangement with one of the Navajo men who went into Farmington regularly to pick up post office box mail for her. She could be slipping the Navajos a few cans of tomatoes off the shelf, which would just show up in the inventory as their own food. Maybe she and her queer friends had planned this all along to kidnap her this morning, making it look spur of the moment. Right now she was probably on the *Santa Fe Chief* heading back to New York. He ran to the safe to check the Navajo pawn silver. Just a few pieces would easily get her home. She could have taken the key from his trousers pocket while he slept.

No, everything was there. But she'd had plenty of time in the last year to cut corners here and there. Maybe she'd taken some when he was out, made up a fake pawn ticket, and never told him of it.

Now he was sure of it. This had all been a trick to sneak her away. She hadn't been able to face him with the truth that she wanted to leave. Just like a woman. If he'd wanted to leave her, he'd have told her right out and split their money and left. He would have given back her share if she'd asked. Maybe not. After all, hadn't he been the one to do all the money-making work here, the pawn and the wool and some land purchase deals, buying from the Navajos and selling to the whites? He'd give her a share of the nothing the trading post made selling cornmeal and tomatoes. But since she'd skipped out on him and probably robbed him dry, she'd get nothing more.

Maybe he could still get some of his stolen money back. Maybe the car hadn't gone right to Santa Fe. Probably went first to see that nurse at Red Rock. Couldn't keep those queers apart. Steal your women and have a chance for some sex, too. He could head out right now for Red Rock. If they were there, he'd take care of things. If they weren't, he'd get the story out of the nurse and know where to go next. It might not be too late.

He knew how to travel through the desert at night. Besides, there was a full moon now. The Navajos did it on horses all the time. Throwing the lock back on the safe, he headed out for the truck.

When he arrived at Red Rock, the little group of buildings was dark, but there was enough moonlight to see the cross on the roof that had to be the Luck's place. He knew he should stay in the car until dawn, but driving here had made him even angrier and more convinced that time was crucial to finding Morna. He parked as noisily as possible so the Lucks would be awake when he banged on the door. Besides, he told himself, they must be used to this. Hadn't they told him one time that they were ready day or night for the heathen to accept the Lord? At the time, he'd pictured how his New York artist friends would have laughed at those rubes. Hell, they'd still laugh, and he would, too. The Indians who were Christianized were much harder customers at the trading post, because when they came back from school they were thinking of opening their own stores. But right now he knew the Lucks would agree with him: a wife belonged by her husband's side, not running off with any of those uppity New Women types.

Mrs. Luck answered the door, holding her velveteen bathrobe up to her chin. She had a knitted hat pulled over her ears. Their house was as cold as the outside air.

"What brings you here, Brother?" she said, her voice sounding ragged as she looked him over suspiciously.

"It's me—Jack from the trading post. My wife is missing. I need your help."

"Come in, Brother. Father Luck!" she called to her husband. She led him in, reaching for the kerosene lamp and matches. Soon they were all sitting at the kitchen table. Jack didn't need the hot tea to warm up as he told them his troubles.

"You let your wife go off with those godless women!" Luck was almost shouting.

"Well I didn't think fast enough. So you think I'm right, then? Is she here? Have you seen her?"

"No, we were just over talking to the nurse this evening. The Lord has given us her building to be a school, and she's not happy at this blessed gift for the heathen. She wants it even though her rich, big-city friends with their radical ways have deserted her. They've all gone off to Russia, you know. They've all gone to see the godless Revolution, and now they have no money for their little Indians. You know that rich Mrs. Lujan in Taos who married the Indian from the pueblo? They buried her friend John Reed right in the Kremlin, right near that anti-Christ Lenin. That's the kind of friends that nurse has. When she leaves here, she'll probably go to Russia too, and good riddance."

"The good thing about these Hard Times," said Mrs. Luck, "is it's going to send all those artists back to the city where they have to get real jobs instead of sitting out here under a sombrero with their painting kits and their liquor. It'll leave us in peace when they're not here telling the Indians to keep up their heathen ways and painting them all naked wearing feathers and pine boughs. I think these Hard Times are just what we needed here to get the Lord's work done."

Jack, who had been to Mrs. Lujan's Manhattan salons back when she was married to his painter friend Maurice Sterne, felt a twinge of guilt listening to this. If the Indians gave up their heathen ways, they'd probably stop making the rugs and pots and silver and selling the land on which rested his only hope for getting out of the trading post business. He thought of Oliver La Farge, a writer he'd known at college, who had been raising the funds here for the nurse. What was he doing here with these Bible-thumpers? They were the reason he'd left his own small town in Pennsylvania and moved to New York City so long ago. How had he ended up here nodding in agreement with this horse manure?

"So you've had your suspicions about those women, too?" said Mrs. Luck. She and Luck looked at him eagerly. He stared back.

"I just knew it," she said. "We've felt it ourselves, but if you see it too, well, then it's for sure. We've got to do something. Oh your poor innocent wife, among those brutes."

Both men stared at her.

"They look at me funny, you know," she said.

Betsy

Betsy was used to frantic knocks in the middle of the night. Often she was already up with a sick patient. But on this quiet night she was kept awake only by anxious thoughts about losing the building. She tossed in bed and considered getting up and preparing bandages and inventorying the medicines to keep herself busy. She missed Laura and counted the days until her next visit. She wasn't half-asleep when a car pulled into the yard and crashed to a stop, the engine still roaring, and the horn blaring. She ran for her clothes as someone banged on the door.

The Navajo girl on her doorstep was frantically talking in Navajo. Grabbing Betsy's arm, she pulled her out to a truck which had hit an adobe oven in the yard. There was enough moonlight to see a white man and woman on the front seat. The man was unconscious or perhaps dead, the woman very pale and weak.

"We've had—" she whispered, and then passed out.

Betsy gasped. "I'll be right back with more help," she said. As little as she wanted to see their faces, she ran to the Lucks house. The lights were on and they were already headed her way.

Soon the clinic was lit almost as brightly as the Navajo dance had been. The Lucks rounded up all the kerosene lanterns in Red Rock, and Ethel, a Navajo woman who lived nearby, built a fire in the stove. Betsy alternated between picking pieces of glass out of Dr. Morris' face and putting a splint on Jonnie's arm. June had been in shock, but looked better after some hot soup. She had a pleased smile on her face as Mrs. Luck rubbed her back. Betsy remembered all the little tricks June used to play to get women to touch her and wondered just how much shock she was in. It probably wasn't as much as Mrs. Luck would be in if she ever found out just what kind of a woman she was practically hugging to her breasts at the moment!

The Navajo girl sat silently by the stove, her head sunk in her hands. Betsy wanted to go to her but she couldn't leave Dr. Morris. Ethel brought her soup and talked to her, then came over to Betsy.

"She never saw so many white people! She's scared. She's worried about her flock, too. You can't leave sheep all alone like that. She wants to know how she will get back."

Betsy wanted to say to tell her not to worry, but she didn't have any answers. Morris moaned. She gently turned held his head so he looked right at the girl.

"Tell her she saved your life," Betsy said. "You'll be glad to compensate her, won't you, Dr. Morris?" He nodded as he moaned, then screamed from the pain of moving.

As things quieted down, Betsy noticed a man standing back, watching. She had seen him before, but she couldn't place him.

"Where's my wife?" he said, when he saw her looking at him. "I know she's here! I know you women are hiding her!"

She recognized him then, the loudmouthed husband from the pathetic trading post where she and Laura had stopped the day they ran out of gas. She remembered his name was Jack. Why would he think his wife was here?

"She's not here," Betsy said. "Was she in the truck?"

"She wasn't with us," Jonnie said. "We left her at the field site. She and Miss Ruth and Laura are back there with the autobus. Oh, God, the autobus. It was supposed to be back by now! Well, I was already fired, what difference does it make?" She slumped back into her own worries.

"At the field site?" Jack said. He thought for a minute, then went right over to Jonnie and stared her right in the face.

"I don't believe you," he said. "She's hiding here somewhere." He turned to the rest of them. "She's stolen my Navajo pawn!" he spat out so suddenly that Betsy's arm jerked and poor Dr. Morris got a painful jab from the sliver of glass she was extracting.

"Look, she isn't here and you've got to go. Can't you see there are seriously injured people here? You're making a horrible situation much worse."

"I'm looking for my wife," he said loudly.

"Go look anywhere but get out of my clinic. You can see she's not here."

He looked from corner to corner.

"You and those other queers planned this all out," he said to Betsy with a sweep of his hands that took in Jonnie and June. "You tell me the truth and I'll leave."

When he said "queers," Betsy wanted to shrivel up. All these months of tension with the Lucks and they'd never had the nerve to say it flat out like that.

His words made Mrs. Luck jump back and drop the cloth she'd been delicately wiping June's face with. She stared at June, looking her up and down as if she'd find some mark of the devil on her.

Ruth

They had barely rolled up to the few buildings of Red Rock when Laura jumped out, leaving Ruth alone in the still coughing autobus. Stepping out, Ruth turned her back to the lighted buildings and took in the view. A bird flashed over a butte in the distance. An owl? A vulture? Maybe an eagle? If only she could walk away from the lights she could see in the moonlight, but it was probably the lights which attracted the birds.

There was a scream and then a groan from the building. It didn't sound like fear but pain, a sound she had heard so often back at Sunmount sanatorium. She didn't want to go in but knew she must. If they didn't need her help, perhaps she would be able to watch the sunrise.

As she walked into the clinic, she got a glimpse of Morris' bloody face before a large and angry man blocked her way.

"Where's my wife?" he screamed at her.

Laura stepped forward. "I told you we heard Morna was on the truck with Morris. Ruth was with me, she doesn't know any more than I do."

June groaned and every one looked at her.

"When's the last time you saw her?" June asked Jonnie, her words slurred through swollen lips.

"When Dr. Morris asked me to drive him out to that new site, and you got in, too, I remember Morna was standing there all alone, and I felt bad 'cause he didn't want her to come."

"We left right after that," June said.

"A stowaway!" Jonnie exclaimed. "It's like the sea stories I used to hear back in Gloucester."

"Huh?" said Jack.

"She could have hidden in all that junk in the back of the truck," explained June. "She might have been in the truck when we went to the new site."

"But she wasn't in it when we had the accident," Jonnie said, "because I was back there. Maybe she's back at that site."

"Where is this place?" Jack roared.

Ethel pointed at the shepherd girl. "Take her. She'll know the way and she'll be glad to get back."

Jack stormed out, pushing Ruth aside. Shaking her head at him, Betsy welcomed Ruth with the calming smile she remembered from Sunmount. Then she rushed back to poor Dr. Morris.

Ruth saw that Jonnie's arm was in a sling. Nearby, holding a bag of ice to the head of the girl archaeologist, Laura looked happier than anyone else, smiling proudly at Betsy's command of the situation.

A white woman in an unfashionably long dress was wringing out a washcloth. She and a white man both wore huge wooden cross necklaces. Missionaries! Ruth had seen plenty of their type at Mera's. The woman looked up and spoke to Ruth.

"I'm Mrs. Luck," she said. "Are you all right?"

"Yes," she said, as curtly as she could. It was always a mistake to let Bible-thumpers think you want to talk to them.

"May I be of any assistance?" Mrs. Luck said.

"I'm fine," Ruth said.

"This is my husband Reverend Luck. We're here to bring God's word to the heathen. We bring our Christian kindness to the poor in body tonight, but always to the poor in spirit. Perhaps you are poor in spirit? I'm sure it will gladden your heart to hear that the Lord is giving us this building for our work!" she said.

Ruth stared back at her. When she didn't respond, the missionary started again.

"Reverend Luck and I were about to pray for our friends here in their time of trouble. Since you are not injured, will you join us and our Lord Jesus Christ here in this desert?"

She reached out as if to pull Ruth toward her. Ruth jumped back. She hated being touched. Everyone in the room stared at her. She looked around at each face, at their hair and cheeks, deciding that she was probably the only Jew in the room. Maybe she should just pray with them and keep her mouth shut. She didn't want all this attention. It wasn't as if she were still observing all the laws and eating all the right foods, as she had in New York before she had come to the West. At Sunmount they would say a grace to Jesus over the meals and Ruth just kept her lips tight. But what if she didn't join these two now? She might end up spending the rest of the night trying to save her soul from them.

"Let us all bow our heads and ask our Lord Jesus for the healing of our friends," Mrs. Luck said before Ruth could answer. Ruth's head immediately jerked up defiantly. Jews didn't bow to other gods.

"And may we all find the fear of God within us to lead our way to our Lord Jesus Christ." Reverend Luck looked right at Betsy as he spoke, but she was pulling a shard out of Morris' cheek. He screamed so loud it made the woman archaeologist groan and Jonnie jump.

The Indian woman stood up. She murmured soothingly to the archaeologist, looked around the room without meeting anyone's eyes, and walked out with great dignity.

"Thank you Lord for putting us here to save souls like hers. I know that someday even these heathen souls shall find You," wailed Mrs. Luck.

Through the window, Ruth could see the faint apricot sky of sunrise. Without really thinking, she headed for the door.

"Sister, where are you going?" snapped Mrs. Luck.

Ruth kept walking.

"Leave her alone," said Jonnie. "She likes to be alone."

But Mrs. Luck followed Ruth. "Sister, there's more I can tell you.

We need every Christian we can get here to fight the good fight. Are you turning your back on our Lord?"

She reached out to grab Ruth's shoulder again, and Ruth jerked away. Mrs. Luck had a hurt look, like she'd offered nothing but love and Ruth had acted like she was trying to hit her. Ruth felt dizzy and faint in a way she hadn't since Sunmount. She was about to sink onto the bed near the door when suddenly something became clear to her. Her parents loved her, but this was how she felt when they told her what to do. They had grabbed her and kept her down. The asthma, the bed, and the invalid life had been the way she had fought back against their smothering, because if she couldn't have herself, they couldn't have her either. But now that was behind her. With all the strength she had built hiking, these days she felt her body to be as powerful as an eagle streaking across the sky.

Laura had been standing near the stove trying to warm up from the long drive. She looked haggard. Suddenly she came wide awake and straightened up.

"Why don't you let the nurse do her job?" Laura said to Mrs. Luck. "Why don't you get out of the way? There are injured people here who need help."

"Oh Lord, save this woman!" Mrs. Luck cried out. "Who does not know the help that comes from Jesus?"

"I think you should leave," Laura said, facing the missionaries.

"Laura, please," said Betsy.

"You've got what you wanted. You're taking away everything Betsy has worked for here. All these Indians are going to suffer very much without medical care. Is that what you want? Is that what Jesus wants for them?"

Betsy held out a hand, as if to stop Laura, but then let it drop. She was struggling not to smile.

"I can't just stand by," Laura insisted. "I can't let them hurt and bully you. I can't stand it another minute! Betsy came out here with big dreams and high hopes and she's done a lot of good. You can stop her here, now, but she's going to keep on working. And I'm going to be standing by her." She went to Betsy and put her arm around her shoulder.

Ruth wished she had told her parents off like that. How many fewer years would she have spent in bed? But then maybe she would never have been sent to New Mexico.

Mrs. Luck was the first to break the silence.

"You two are an abomination!" she shouted. Laura stared back at her defiantly. No one else spoke. Mrs. Luck turned to poor Dr. Morris, whose face was chalky white where there weren't spots of blood.

"They are an abomination!" she announced to him. "An abomination from the sinning cities of the East. We've got to rid this pure new land of this—unnaturalness."

Dr. Morris paled even more, but he struggled to keep his head up and tried to speak. He coughed instead, and Betsy held up a cup so he could sip.

"As a scientist," he barely choked out, but then his voice grew stronger. "I don't agree. My colleagues in the field of anthropology have studied the people of other lands and other ways, and they have learned that the human experience is much more varied than we here in this little part of the world might think. You would do well to learn from the Navajos, instead of teaching them to be like you."

Betsy leaned over him. "Thank you," she said. "Now please rest." She turned back to the whole room. "These people are all very injured and need to be calm. This discussion has got to stop."

Jonnie turned to June, "Is that why the archaeologists dig up the graves and take everything? Even though the Navajos don't want them to?"

"What did you think?" June said.

"They do rob graves," Betsy said. "I don't like it at all."

Ruth thought about the beautiful flowers and leaves she had uprooted and pressed flat into her specimen book.

Morna

The bright rising sun woke Morna. She could barely raise her dry eyelids, encrusted with so much grit she had to pry it off. In her sleep, she had slumped away from the wall so that her right foot rested in the cold fire pit. Getting stiffly to her feet, the morbid thoughts of the night before came back to her, and she was relieved to be still in the land of the very glaring bright sun of the living.

There was a loud sound down in the canyon. Jack had been caught in a flash flood once, and had told her the water rumbled like a train as it poured through the arroyos and swamped everything in its path. Now how was she going to get out of here?

The noise grew louder and she saw a truck making its slow way through the canyon below. Morna screamed and jumped around, waving her arms wildly. The truck stopped suddenly. In the abrupt silence, she stared, then yelled and threw some rocks down. The truck's horn sounded, the doors were thrown open, and Jack jumped out. Soon they were waving to each other, his words echoing too much to understand. He waved a coil of rope and pantomimed with his fingers that he was going to drive up the mesa. He got back in and the truck rumbled forward.

Morna felt weak and her stomach was hard from emptiness. She was about to settle down to wait when she remembered her find of the night before. The mother's grave. The archaeologists were sure to take whatever she had found. If she and Jack took it, they could split the profits and head their separate ways. She scrambled through the little rooms until she found the doorway she had busted through.

The Ancient Ones had built so that even this back room was lighted, and now she could see what she had only felt with her fingers the night before. She saw the wall she had smashed into a pile of bricks. She saw the sad little hole and beside it her pile of booty. It wasn't a ticket on the Santa Fe, but just little cooking pots. She picked up the pile of feathers, and it unrolled in a neat little woven blanket of soft fur. It was easy to picture a sleeping infant rolled happily inside it. Perhaps the mother had died in a miscarriage, buried with this empty blanket. Morna began to gag in dry heaves, her lungs jerking painfully against her ribs. The skin on her hands was shredded and scabbed from the night before. She was embarrassed to remember herself ripping open the grave and clawing out the treasures when she thought of the family she had imagined in the firelight, all warm and cozy and enjoying the beauty of this place just as she had.

"Morna! Morna!" Jack's voice called from somewhere above. Loose rocks clattered as he came down the cliff on a rope. If he saw what she had found, he'd grab it. She placed the pots and the blanket back into the hole and pushed the pile of bricks back on it, then scrambled back through the doorway just as he got to her.

"Jesus, Morna," he called as he let go of the rope and came toward her. "I thought you had been kidnapped by those goddamn bulldaggers."

"What?" Morna gasped, breathless from rushing to hide the pots.

"Did you know that the truck crashed? When you didn't come home, I went all the way out to Red Rock to see if you were with that nurse. They guessed you had stowed away. A Navajo girl showed me where you were."

"I heard the crash, but I couldn't get back up the cliff. How is everybody?"

"That archaeologist in charge and two women got hurt. One was that strange little woman who was driving you this morning. I think they're okay. Anyway, what were you doing stowing away on that truck?"

If she told him the truth, Jack would rip the site apart.

"I'm glad you found me," she said instead. They looked at each other warily. Morna knew that if they were still in love, they would be sobbing in each other's arms by now. Instead he turned and looked at the cliff.

"Well, you're okay. We've got to get back to the store before we lose a whole day of business. There's a wool buyer coming in today, too. Got to get you back behind that counter! This is no place for a woman!" The thought of being back in the store made Morna reconsider. If she could divert him long enough, she could go back to the grave, grab some valuables, and hide them in her skirt. Her ticket home was only a few feet away. She just had to tell him she had seen some artifacts off in the other direction.

Wouldn't that Indian woman who lived and died here so long ago want Morna to have an easier life? Wouldn't she have wanted the same? How hard had her life been? How demanding had her husband been? Did he make her grind corn all day, bent over heavy grinding stones, naked hungry children all around her, while he wandered the beautiful forests nearby with nothing to do but shoot arrows at deer? She'd want Morna to have better. Morna could take her possessions as a gift across the centuries.

"Say," Jack said, looking around at the crumbling walls. "This is quite a place. Looks like the archaeologists haven't been here yet. What have you been doing here? Find any pots? Baskets?" His eyes were lighting up. "You know, there might even be some grave sites here. Sometimes they have jewelry in them. Turquoise. Even silver. Maybe we should do a little searching before we leave."

Morna saw her own greed reflected in his eager eyes. She thought of her night picturing the woman who had once lived here, who had peace and riches in death. It wasn't for Morna to disturb that. Besides, it wasn't only money she would need to leave Jack.

"Jack, I'm going back to New York."

"What are you talking about?"

"I'm leaving. I don't want to live here any longer. This hasn't worked out for me."

He stared across the endless miles of desert below.

"And how do you figure to get there? It's a pretty long way. Unless you're planning to hop a train like a hobo. I hear that's what people are doing these days."

"I need money for a ticket."

"I guess if you worked another year or so in the store, you'd earn that."

"Go to hell! I've been working in that store for five years. It's my store, too. When we get home, just give me the money, and I'm leaving."

"Maybe I won't take you home. Maybe I just will go to hell. Maybe I'll just leave you here." He started over to where the end of the rope lay. She jumped and they both grabbed for it. They stood as close as they had ever stood in their years together and as angry as they had ever been.

"You can't leave me here. It was never just your store, Jack. Sure, you got to act like you were in charge. You got to be the man, and I didn't get to be anyone. I want to go back to New York and make my own life."

"You wanted to come with me. You got me to marry you."

"I hate it here. If you're so sure my work hasn't been worth anything, why do you want me to stay? It shouldn't make any difference to you."

That shut him up. He scratched behind his ear and slumped against a wall, which crumbled beneath him, the stones slipping to the ground in the dead quiet morning.

"Those bulldaggers did kidnap you. They don't need men, I guess they fixed it so you don't either, huh?"

"I don't know what you're talking about. I thought this all out last night, all alone out here. Finally got out from behind that goddam counter and took a look at the land out here and couldn't think of any reasons why I'd want to stay here. I'm dying here. We came out here to be artists, and we ended up being—" she sputtered to find the right word.

"Morna, please—"

"Nothing but wage slaves," she continued, "like the Reds used to talk about in Union Square. Not even slaves to the Bosses, just slaves to ourselves. Slaves to the Almighty Dollar."

Jack slumped back. "I guess you're right, Morna. There's nothing for you here. Nothing for me either. Now that times are hard back east, there isn't much to go home to. Maybe I can find some poor sucker to sell the trading post to, like we got suckered. Would you stick around that long?" He gave her the look that had won her over so many years ago. She hadn't seen it in a long time.

She told him she would, because she needed the rope and the ride back, but she was going to grab a ride on the next truck heading down the ruts away from the trading post and onto the highway east. She wasn't going to fall for that look again, because he was never going to give her the money for the train.

Laura

There wasn't much to pack in the car, because Betsy wanted to leave the Indians with everything she'd brought or shipped in. She'd been giving it away piece by piece, but now there was nothing left and it was time to go.

Mrs. John Billy pushed herself into Betsy's arms, tears streaming down her face. Lilly had come back to Red Rock to say good-bye, but quickly burst into tears and ran away. Even the men looked almost tearful, and the Lucks' most loyal converts were watching sadly as their car pulled out. At the last moment Mrs. Klah stumbled up, clutching her elbow painfully. Betsy reached for the door handle but Laura grabbed her arm, the car almost lurching into a ditch.

"You can't," Laura said. "You just can't. The Lucks will have to help her."

Betsy stared ahead as the car plowed along. "Maybe the Indian Association will find some more money. Maybe a letter will be there when we get home."

Laura didn't answer. Living out here, Betsy hadn't seen how much things had changed since the Hard Times hit. Even rich folks like Oliver La Farge and Mrs. Lujan were busy worrying about money just like most people always had. It was the talk of Santa Fe that up in Taos, Mrs. Lujan had opened her house to paying guests and that her Indian husband Tony was hiring himself out as a tour guide, driving one of their limos. Jonnie had been happy about it. She said she'd rather the Indians made money driving tourists than the Harvey folks.

Laura's photography business had fallen off terribly. Tourists weren't coming and local folks hadn't been in the mood to dress up in their best and have their portraits taken. She didn't know what the future would bring.

"We'll be together again," Laura said softly to Betsy. Betsy didn't answer. The car rumbled along, a vulture streaming above.

"I do want to be with you," Betsy finally said. "But I just can't feel happy now. I can't believe it's over. And I don't even know what I'm going back to."

"Me! Our home!" Laura took her hands off the wheel and her foot off the gas and let the car stall. Barely out of Red Rock, there was nothing but desert in sight. "What's bothering you? It's not just about leaving, is it?"

"You once said that you would always be at my side, no matter what," Betsy replied.

"Why are you talking like this?" Laura asked.

"Why shouldn't I? You haven't been coming out here. You've been with that Ruth."

"Ruth!" Laura snorted. "You're upset about Ruth! I'm glad you told me. I mean, it's funny."

"Not to me."

"Can't you see how funny it is? I don't think I've ever seen her eyes without looking through a camera. She's always looking in the air or way up in a tree. All she cares about is dried-up grass and birds. She hardly talks, and she acts like she never has time to be friendly. She roots around in the dirt looking for seeds like an animal." Laura paused and looked at Betsy, hoping that this awful conversation was over. But Betsy wouldn't meet her eyes.

"Laura, I never thought I'd go home feeling like such a failure," she whispered. "Leaving like this."

"It wasn't your choice. You have nothing to feel guilty about."

"There's no other way to feel. I'm walking out on my friends. They trusted me."

"You'll get back. We'll find a way."

They sat in the perfect stillness and then Betsy got out. Laura followed. Betsy leaned against the warm hood and looked all around.

"This is the place we ran out of gas last year," she said. Laura could see it all again, the way it had looked on their first trip here, the beauty and the strangeness. She remembered her desperate walk for help, the terror-filled ride back to find Betsy, and the way her heart had dropped when she saw the car surrounded by Indian men.

"It's your birthday coming up soon, isn't it?" asked Betsy.

"Forty-two," Laura replied.

"When you were a girl, did you ever think you'd be in a place like this?"

"With a girl like you?" Laura smiled. For the first time since they had left Red Rock, Betsy looked right at Laura. Laura knew her own eyes were as bright and moist as Betsy's. They went right into each other's arms then, crying and loving and laughing all at the same time, because each felt all that and more.

Laura

They all went to the train station to see Morna off. Morna had spent the last few nights at Mrs. Landauer's. Her husband had stomped around on the street below for most of the first night, but finally left when he got no response. Ruth kept Morna busy teaching her all she needed to know to deliver the specimens safely to the Museum of Natural History. Ruth considered every dried plant pressed between sheets and every delicate lichen in its little glass container to be a cherished friend she was sending off on a terrible journey into the unknown. Knowing the hot, dry hours in snake-ridden places where she'd found them, Laura understood.

"Jonnie, I still wish you were the one going. You know how hard it was to collect it all. You'd take the best care of it," Ruth said as she watched Morna's every move with the big portfolio of pressed plants and case of specimen-filled bottles. They both suspected Morna's mind was more on her own plans for when she reached New York City than on getting Miss Ruth's collection safely to the Museum of Natural History.

"She'll be fine," Jonnie said. "And I don't want to go back east. It's taken so much for me to get here and stay."

"You'll have a return ticket. You can come right back. You don't even have to visit your folks in Gloucester."

"I just don't want to," Jonnie insisted.

"Are you afraid if you see the ocean again, you'll never want to come back here?" Laura broke in. She had her camera out. With times so hard, she didn't have film to spare, but she was going to take one last picture of them all seeing Morna off.

"Not a chance. I hardly miss the ocean. I'd miss all this a lot more," Jonnie answered, waving her hand to take in the tips of the mountains that just brushed at the big blue sky.

"I'm sure Morna will take good care of your work," Betsy said. She smiled at Ruth, who appeared to take her words a lot more reassuringly than she had taken Jonnie's.

"Anyway," Morna said, "Jonnie will be busy with her new job. When do you have to be out at the field camp, Jonnie?"

"I hope Dr. Morris won't change his mind before I get back there."

"Don't worry," said Betsy. "June laid it on good and thick about how you saved his eyesight by getting him to me as fast as you did."

"Do you think he's only hiring me to pay me back? That isn't why I helped him."

"He saw for himself that you could talk to the Navajo girl. He figures he'll save plenty of money if you help him at the dig as well as drive. He knows you work harder than most anyone. He owes you, but I think you're doing him a bigger favor by working for him."

"I guess so," Jonnie said. "I guess he saw I was pretty handy. Now I just have to hope his money holds out."

They all shrugged.

"Well, for as long as it lasts, it'll be the best job I ever had," Jonnie added. "Besides digging, Dr. Morris said they'd teach me to help collect Navajo words and write the language, so they can study it."

"With Lilly's help," said Betsy. "I'm so relieved." While he was recuperating at her clinic, Betsy had arranged for Dr. Morris to meet Lilly, and he had hired her to work as an interpreter and language teacher at the dig.

"Dr. Morris promised to try to get Lilly into the university at Boulder. And June promised to tutor Lilly all summer so that she'd be ready to start in the fall."

"You listen in on the lessons, too," said Laura. "You'll need it when you go to college."

"Me? At college?" Jonnie's eyes flew wide open.

"June was pretty old when she started at Columbia. A lot of women anthropologists started college late."

"Just watch out what June teaches you," said Betsy. She grinned at Laura, who shot back a funny face.

"Let's take the photo," Laura said. "I hear the train." She had fiddled with the big camera on the tripod all that it needed. The train approached so slowly it seemed that time had stopped. They all stood stiffly, waiting to be photographed.

"This is it!" Jonnie called out as the train chugged to a halt.

As the women jumped to embrace each other, Laura thought of that moment in the desert when she had expected to have a revelation, like Thea in *Song of the Lark*. It embarrassed her to remember thinking that her life would be like a book, that if she had thought of something more spiritual than her thirst and discomfort, it would have given her the renewal and passion to achieve success like Thea. Real life wasn't like that. Real life was not getting a Guggenheim grant and her studio business collapsing just when she and Betsy most needed money.

This afternoon she was meeting with Oliver La Farge, who was working on ways to bring the arts of the Indians to the rich buyers in the East. She was going to show him how her photos of the Navajo people could help publicize the sales. She was also going to ask La Farge if there was news of more money to send Betsy back to Red Rock. She had to work fast, because one of June's archaeologist friends had found her a job on an expedition to the Yucatan. This time she would be leaving Betsy behind, but only for a month. They'd been relieved when Betsy got her old job back at Sunmount, and she was going to try for a job at the Indian School in Santa Fe.

Her life was moving along. Thanks to Betsy, she had traveled much in a land beyond maps, and had managed to find her way. No Guggenheim grant or Alfred Steiglitz would build the road for her; she would break her own trail, the people and the land waiting to be captured in the camera before her, just like now.

Laura snapped the shutter just as Morna hefted her suitcase. Immediately the platform filled with laughter and screams as travelers burst from the doors, relieved and excited. Could art ever capture an instant in time, as Thea had thought? Photography gave that illusion, but as soon as the shutter snapped, life moved along briskly.

As soon as the way was clear, Morna was up the steps and on the train. "Don't worry, Ruth," she called out, "your discoveries will be safe in that museum. I'll go over all there all the time and keep 'em dusted. Thank you so much again for the ticket."

Ruth blushed and called out, "Make sure you hold that case straight and don't let anyone sit on it!" Then Morna was gone.

"All aboard that's coming aboard," yelled the trainman as bells rang and the train began to pull out. As his car rolled slowly by, he leaned over to them and said, "Last chance to go back East, ladies?"

They all laughed and stood smiling at each other. Laura leaned against her camera as Betsy threw an arm around her.

"I've got to get going," Laura said. "I know just where."

The End

Afterword

Land Beyond Maps is an historical novel. Some characters, including Laura Gilpin and Betsy Forster, are based on actual historical people. Other characters, including Jonnie Bell, Ruth Weinstock, and Morna Brewster, are fictional composites of people typical of the times. My goal was to stay as true as possible to the facts and the spirit of the lives of the real people on whom characters are based.

The real people who appear as fictionalized characters or are mentioned in *Land Beyond Maps* are Laura Gilpin (1891-1979), Elizabeth W. Forster (1886-1972), Earl Morris, Erna Fergusson, Setah Begay, Reverend Angelo James Luck and his wife, Dr. Frank Mera, Herman Schweizer, Gertrude Ederle, Tom Killed-a-White-Man, Mrs. Hardbelly, Mrs. Francis, Yellow Mexican, Jim Ferryboat, Navajo Jim, Jim Begay, Mrs. Kellywood, John Billy, Mrs. John Billy, Mary, Timothy Kellywood, Ethel, Cecilia, and Irving Couse. Mentioned in passing are Oliver LaFarge, Clarence White, Willa Cather, Alfred Stieglitz, Ernest Blumenschein, Georgia O'Keeffe, Burt Phillips, and Joseph Sharp.

Real entities and places include Sunmount Sanatorium, Koshare Indian Detours, New Mexico Association on Indian Affairs, La Fonda, Red Rock Trading Post, Clarence White School of Photography, the Art Students League, the American Museum of Natural History, the Harvey Company, and the Southwestern Indian Detours.

Bibliography

Hundreds of books were used in the research for this book. The following were major sources:

Armitage, Susan, & Jameson, Elizabeth. (Eds.) (1987). *The Women's West.* Norman: University of Oklahoma Press.

Babcock, Barbara A., & Parezo, Nancy J. (1988). *Daughters of the desert: Women anthropologists and the native American Southwest.* Albuquerque: University of New Mexico Press.

Bonta, Marcia Myers. (1991). *Women in the field: America's pioneering women naturalists.* College Station: Texas A&M Univ. Press.

Cather, Willa. (1925. *The Professor's House.* NY: Knopf.

Cather, Willa. (1915). *The song of the lark.* Boston: Houghton Mifflin Company.

Ellis, Anne. (1984). *Sunshine preferred: The Philosophy of an ordinary woman.* Lincoln, NE: University of Nebraska Press.

Faunce, Hilda. (1928, 1981). *Desert wife.* Lincoln, NE: Univ. of Nebraska Press.

Forster, Elizabeth W. and Laura Gilpin; Sandweiss, Martha A. (Editor) (1988). *Denizens of the desert: A tale in word and picture of life among the Navajo Indians.* Albuquerque: Univ. of New Mexico Press.

Gilpin, Laura. (1968). *The enduring Navajo.* Austin, TX: Univ. of Texas Press.

Limerick, Patricia Nelson, Milner II, Clyde A., & Rankin, Charles E. (Eds.). (1991). *Trails: Toward a new western history.* Lawrence, KS: Univ. Press of Kansas.

Lister, Florence C. & Robert H. (1968). *Earl Morris & Southwestern archaeology.* Albuquerque: Univ. of New Mexico Press.

Morris, Ann Axtell. (1978). *Digging in the Southwest.* Santa Barbara and Salt Lake City: Peregrine Smith, Inc.

Norwood, Vera, & Monk, Janice. (Eds.). (1987). *The desert is no lady: Southwestern landscapes in women's writing and art.* Tucson: Univ. of Arizona Press.

Parezo, Nancy J., (Ed.) (1993). *Hidden scholars: Women anthropologists and the Native American Southwest.* Albuquerque: Univ. of New Mexico Press.

Poling-Kempes, Lesley. (1989). *The Harvey girls: Women who opened the West.* NY: Marlowe & Company.

Powell, Lawrence Clark. (1974). *Southwest classics: The creative literature of the arid lands.* Tucson, AZ: The Univ. of Arizona Press.

Ressler, Susan R. (Ed.) (2003). *Women artists of the American West.* NC: McFarland & Company.

Sandweiss, Martha M. (1986). *Laura Gilpin: An enduring grace.* Fort Worth, TX: Amon Carter Museum.

Thomas, D.H. (1978). *The Southwest Indian detours.* Phoenix, AZ: Hunter Publishing Company.

Acknowledgements

Building writing communities and supporting other people's creativity has been as important to me as my own writing, because without the many people who have been part of my formal and informal writing communities as writers, teachers, role models, cheerleaders, readers, and most of all friends, I would not have written my novel. Many generous organizations provided resources and educational presentations that built my writing skills and helped my research. "Thank you" just begins to say how much I appreciate your ideas and support.

Thanks to the Arch and Bruce Brown Foundation for awarding me the 2000 Full-Length Fiction Competition Grant for Gay-Positive Arts Projects Based on or Inspired by History, especially to Arch Brown and James Waller.

Thanks to the Astraea Foundation Emerging Lesbian Writers Fund for awarding to me their Honorable Mention, 2007.

Thanks to several organizations that provided instruction and support and a time and place to believe in myself as a writer: the Lesbian and Gay Men's Literary Circle of Bloomington, Indiana, 1976 -1980; Cambridge Center for Adult Education; Cummington Community for the Arts; Vermont Studio Center; the OutWrite Conferences of Bromfield Street Educational Foundation; *Gay Community News*; the William Joiner Center for the Study of War and Its Social Consequences Writers' Workshop; National Writers Union Boston Local; Society of the Muse of the Southwest; and the Feminist Womens Writing Workshop.

Thanks for research materials and librarian help at the Southwest Research Center in Taos; Cape Ann Historical Society; Santa Fe Public Library; Taos Public Library; Tozzer Library at Harvard University; and most of all to the Somerville Public Library and especially Wendy Mason Wood, and to the Minuteman Library System and especially Amy Hart. Thanks to all the "Friends of the Library" for the book sales at so many libraries. Thanks to all the people who write, produce, and sell books.

Thanks to so many wonderful writing groups and classes, especially the Harvard Square Scriptwriters from 1988–1993, and our facilitator, Laura Bernieri. Thanks to all the inspiring teachers: Toni Rea, Vincent Tampio, Tim O'Brien, Larry Heinemann, Jill Bloom, Erika Dreifus, Arthur Gold, Joan Larkin, Nadine Gordimer, David Farmer, Linda Sonna, Rachel Guido deVries, Leslea Newman, Lucille Clifton, Alexis DeVeaux, Summer Wood, Yani Batteau, Judah LeBlang, and so many more wonderful writers who presented at conferences and workshops. I'm sorry I've forgotten your name, but thanks to the wonderful teacher I had for college freshman English at S.U.N.Y. Stony Brook who was so enthusiastic about my writing talent. Thanks for their encouragement and for preserving lesbian history to Barbara Grier, Ann Bannon, Marie Kuda, and Tracy Baim.

Thanks to my Feminist Womens Writing Workshop online group to whom I emailed the first draft of this novel, a few pages at a time: Lynn Kanter, Robin Parks, and Rosalie Morales Kearns. Thanks for the cheerleading that kept the pages coming!

Thanks to my newest group, the Somerville Scribes: Ami Feldman, Denise Bethel-Stacke, Sharon Rogolsky, Larry Raffel, Alexander Feldman, and Annette Boothe.

Still writing, talking, eating, rubberstamping, collaging, sewing, potlucking, rummaging, and walking to the beach since 1993, there are no thanks too many to the Swampscott writing group over our many years: Ami Feldman, Anne Sears, Deborah Marshall, Deborah Muscella, Dianne Jenkins, Irene Baker, Janet Dephoure, Jennifer Wry, Lee Lewis, Mi Ok Song Bruining, Peggy Patton, Sue Anne Willis, and Laura de la Torre Bueno. Thanks to David Jenkins for being, listening, and so much more.

Thanks to Robin Cohen, Lisa Nussbaum, and Chris Guilfoy for thorough readings and copy editing. Thanks to Susan A. Miller for her invaluable feedback and encouragement.

Thanks to Susan Ressler for her online course "Women Artists of the American West" which was crucial to the research and writing of *Land Beyond Maps* and to my understanding of the history it covers. See the excellent publicly available course site on the internet at http://www.cla.purdue.edu/WAAW/, which includes the best online materials about Laura Gilpin.

Thanks to the historians who researched and wrote of the crucial roles that women, lesbians, gay men, Native Americans, Hispanics, and other previously overlooked groups performed in the building of the American West.

Thanks to the writings of Lawrence Clark Powell for inspiring me as a reader, a writer, and a library instructor.

Thanks to Ellen Larson and Thomas Hubschman for all the help to make it happen, and for their inspiring writing careers. This novel was greatly improved by the editing talents of Ellen Larson.

Thanks to the wonderful and supportive families I belong to: all the Weinstock, Rogers, White, White-Shaffer, and Asadorian families, and especially to all the Tilchens as we realize our family's American dreams.

Thanks to all my friends in Massachusetts, New Mexico, Indiana, and elsewhere for listening to my dreams and plans all these years. I can only hope to be there for you as you have been there for me. Thanks to Madge Buckley for her hospitality and stories, and to the late Kenneth Buckley for being the seed that led me to New Mexico and my "six degrees of separation" connection to Laura Gilpin. Thanks to everyone at Cambridge College for giving me the stability and income to achieve my dreams while helping others achieve theirs. Thanks to the seder women for being there for me: Myrna Greenfield, Michelle Johnson, Chris Guilfoy, Josephine Ross, and Lynn Tibbetts. Thanks to Carrie Dearborn for sharing our writing dreams. Thanks to Maida E. Solomon for sharing our name and friendship. Thanks to Laura de la Torre Bueno for the hospitality and comfort and friendship.

Thanks to Sherrard Hamilton for being, listening, and so much more.

Thanks to Marsha White for sharing my life and inspiring me to realize my dreams.

This book is dedicated to my father, George Tilchen, and to the blessed memory of my mother, Esther Weinstock Tilchen.

About the author

Maida Tilchen writes primarily to preserve and/or dramatize lesbian history. A lifetime book collector, she co-wrote the first "second wave" article on lesbian pulp novels, published in *Margins* magazine in 1975. Her writing has been published in *Gay Community News; Sojourner; Body Politic,* and books including *Nice Jewish Girls: A Lesbian Anthology; Lavender Culture; Women-Identified Women;* and *Feminist Frameworks,* and includes the foreword to the bibliography *The Lesbian in Literature.* She served as a VISTA volunteer in southern Indiana, was promotions manager for *Gay Community News (Boston),* and has had many research and writing jobs in the educational field. Currently, she is a library administrator and research skills instructor for a college serving primarily older minority women and immigrants. She and her spouse Marsha White have visited New Mexico often since 1993. After her first trip there, wanting to continue to live in the library-rich Boston area but to keep one foot in the "land of enchantment," she started writing fiction set in New Mexico.

www.ingramcontent.com/pod-product-compliance
Lightning Source LLC
Chambersburg PA
CBHW031330170626
46807CB00002B/626

* 9 7 8 1 9 3 9 1 1 3 4 5 0 *